THE ANDROMEDAN FOLD

NICK ADAMS

Elliptical
Publishing

© Nick Adams 2019

All rights reserved.

No part of this book may be reproduced, stored in a retrieval system, or transmitted by any means, electronic, mechanical, photocopying or otherwise, without the prior written permission of the author.

This is a work of fiction. While the locations in this book are a mixture of real and imagined, the characters are totally fictitious. Any resemblance to actual people living or dead is entirely coincidental.

PROLOGUE

GDA RESEARCH VESSEL VLEPON – APPROACHING SYSTEM H-91237/AK, SECTOR 97

DAY 029, YEAR 11270, 08:25FC, PCC

The GDA research vessel Vlepon had left its home planet Reez'ly four hundred and thirty-two days ago. A three hundred and fourteen metre Klaxx Class freighter, it had been recently converted for exploration to scout the far reaches of the Milky Way. After several thousand years of spacefaring and representing over a thousand races from within the galaxy, the GDA (Gerousia Dipodi Agones or Council of Bipedal Races) still had vast regions of the Milky Way relatively unexplored.

The Vlepon's eighty-nine-person crew was made up of twenty-nine ship crew and sixty scientists of multiple disciplines. Their maiden voyage involved scanning systems on the extreme far edge of the galaxy. There could be weeks of nothing of any interest, empty lifeless systems ostensibly going on forever, with the looming void of black intergalactic space stretching away on their port side. Crossing to a neighbouring galaxy had always proved an insurmountable undertaking.

That morning they'd received an unusual reading which had been emanating from a dry, almost barren, planet in a small system 5.6 light years away, designated H-91237/AK in Sector 97.

Captain D'aker ordered the navigator and pilot to jump the ship into clear space on the outskirts of the system. Once there, they proceeded to check the earlier scan results. It quickly proved to be no mistake: there were multiple returns of exotic metals that simply couldn't exist naturally. He pointed at one of the scientists, who was hunched over his array console, and raised his eyebrows.

'The planet has an acceptable atmosphere, Captain,' said the science officer. 'Well within parameters, although surface water is rare and mostly underground. No discernible intelligent life forms, only the numerous returns of unnatural alloys dotted around the surface.'

The captain nodded and turned his attention to another officer.

'Spacial report?' he asked.

'Second planet of six,' the lieutenant answered. 'Three moons that are, err—'

'Err, what?' the captain asked impatiently.

'They're all in a perfect stationary orbit,' said the

nervous officer. 'And symmetrical in a big triangle.' He glanced back at the captain, a perplexed expression on his face.

'Is that possible naturally?' the captain asked.

'No,' he said. 'Well, it's never been recorded before. They're all so equal in size too. Not identical, but close.'

He suddenly stared at the console again and scratched his head.

'Well, that's weird.'

'What now?'

'I've got a return for some of those manufactured alloys on the surface of one of them.'

'Unnatural alloys until proven otherwise,' said the captain.

'Yes, sir.'

'Navigation, plot a course over to the second planet. I want to have a closer look at those moons.'

The Vlepon accelerated and powered into the system towards the strange phenomena.

'Keep us at five thousand kilometres distant. And a full range scan please, ladies and gentlemen,' the captain asked.

The pilot brought the ship in towards the three moons and slowed, intending to stop at the agreed distance.

'I'm getting a new power reading on that same moon, sir,' said one of the array officers.

'A power reading? What? As in alien technology?'

'Yes, sir – shit. It's a weapon sys—'

'Full shields front,' shouted the captain, interrupting his junior officer. 'Flank speed now, pilot. Take us through the three moons and away.'

The laser cannon bolt took a split second to reach the ship's shields. They felt the whole ship judder as the vicious bolt dissipated around the front shields of the vessel.

'Shields at sixty-four percent,' called the helm officer.

'Keep that shield between us and that fucking cannon as we pass through,' said the captain. 'And hope it's the only one.'

The cannon fired again. This time it was a glancing blow as the targeting software hadn't quite accounted for the ship's acceleration. It was still felt all over the ship, though, and a few red warning lights illuminated on various consoles around the bridge.

'Shields at thirty-one percent,' came the call.

Then everything went haywire. The bridge lighting suddenly dimmed and every warning light on the navigation console began flashing.

'Was that another cannon?' shouted the captain, staring confused at the holonav, which seemed to be having a serious glitch.

'No, sir,' somebody called from the gloom. 'We – err – seem to have jumped.'

'Who authorised a jump?' he bellowed, staring in the direction of the helm as the lighting came back up again.

'No one. We didn't initiate the jump, sir.'

'Well, who on Reez'ly did? And where the fuck are we?'

The navigator stared at his console for what seemed like an age.

'Well, Lieutenant?'

'I don't know, sir.'

'You're the navigation officer with the latest GDA navigation array. How can you not fucking know?'

'Because – we're not in the Milky Way, sir,' he said, glancing over his shoulder at the captain, his eyes wide.

'There are three moons behind us in the same configuration as before,' said the spacial officer. 'Only they're not quite the same ones – same look, shape and size – just not the ones we flew through. The planet, on the other hand, is very different – this one's green and lush, with plenty of surface water, and shows sentient life signs.'

The captain stomped over to the navigation console with a face like thunder.

'Move over, Lieutenant,' he ordered and sat down on the warm seat. After pressing and re-pressing the 'navigate compute' icon several times, he slammed his fist down on the console, making everybody jump.

'What the fuck is up with this thing?'

'Nothing, sir,' said the navigator. 'It simply doesn't know where it is.'

'All four hundred billion star systems in our galaxy are plotted,' he replied, staring up at the standing officer. 'We might not have visited them all but they're all plotted. So, wherever we are, this machine will be able to pinpoint the location anywhere in our galaxy.'

'That's just it, sir. It can't plot our location, because we're not in our galaxy.'

'Lieutenant, the nearest galaxies to us are millions of light years away. There is absolutely no way we can—'

'Hang on, sir. I've got an idea,' he said, interrupting, and reaching over the captain's shoulder. He proceeded to press a few icons.

'What are you doing?'

'Scanning for the nearest galaxies.'

The navigation computer beeped and they both looked at the result with horror.

'That's impossible,' said the captain, his face ashen.

'No mistake, sir. That's Triangulum, about seven hundred and fifty thousand light years away from us. And that there is the Milky Way, two point three million—'

'Yes, yes, I get it, Lieutenant,' he said, scowling. 'How is that even remotely possible?'

'Sir, we've got a contact in the next system,' called one of the other officers.

The captain jumped up out of the navigator's seat and stepped up next to his raised couch and stared at the flashing anomaly on his own console. 'Is it a ship?'

'It's accelerating in this direction, sir,' said the array officer.

'Helm, turn us around. I want to see if we can get back through that gate, or whatever it is.'

'Too late, sir. He's jumped. He's here – five thousand kilometres and closing.'

'Shit,' he mumbled to himself. 'Helm, full stop. Communications, send them a polite hail.'

The huge two-kilometre-long matt black Andromedan warship didn't reply verbally; it responded with two laser cannon bolts. The first removed the Vlepon's main array and the second disabled the main drive housings.

The captain walked quickly into his private office, off the starboard side of the bridge. He called his daughter's cabin.

'Rayl, it's me. Code 10. Yes now, right now. Run.'

1

THEO ISLAND – PANEMORFI, TRELORUS SYSTEM

DAY 175, YEAR 11270, 20:46FC, PCC

Edward Virr, Linda Wisnewski, Andy Faux and Phil Theo all stood in a circle at the top of the beach, surrounding a small hole dug into the sand.

A few meters away, the light blue ocean lapped gently against the shoreline and a soft breeze struggled to move the blue-fringed palm tree leaves above. It was a gorgeous day on a beautiful island, one of many on the predominantly-ocean planet of Panemorfi.

Phil knelt down and carefully placed several charred and blackened components into the hole and swept the extracted sand back into place with his hand.

'Goodbye, old friend,' he whispered, slowly standing back up to join the other three.

The damaged components had once been part of Gabriel, the sentient computer core of their starship. The core had been irretrievably damaged during an energy weapon attack by a stolen GDA gunship a few months ago. Phil had lived and worked with Gabriel for several millennia since he was two days old. He'd also lost the other three members of his crew to a weaponised virus on the island shortly before he lost Gabriel. This was the first proper chance he'd had to say his goodbyes.

He walked near the water to a slowly disappearing circular indentation in the sand. This was where his crew mates Tony, Mike and Steve's bodies had been cremated, using an Asteri Beam from the starship while in orbit. He'd been lucky; the auto-nurse of the ship had put him into a coma until Ed, Linda and Andy had secured an antivirus from Earth, which had saved his life. Unfortunately, his colleagues hadn't been so lucky.

He squatted down again and touched the almost-covered glass circle, which had been formed by the intense heat of the beam.

'Sorry I wasn't able to help, guys. I let you down,' he muttered.

After a few moments, he stood and turned to face the other three. 'Can we drink beer, play some old Genesis songs and eat pizza?' he asked. 'It's what they would have wanted.'

'Sounds like the perfect wake to me,' answered Andy. This was followed by nods from the other two.

The four of them strolled back through the trees towards the main building in the centre of the island. Ed could see the three computer-generated girls, Marilyn, Samantha and Sandy, setting up the entertainment deck.

'Looks as though Cleo has found some computer sub-routines we all thought were lost,' he said.

'Wow, it's Samantha!' exclaimed Andy and sprinted over to meet her.

'Before you two get carried away with romantic reunions,' said Phil as they watched Andy steering Samantha swiftly off to his cottage, 'don't forget our guests will be here in four hours.'

'No problem,' said Ed. 'I can wait till later, unlike some.'

The sound of giggling and Andy's cottage door slamming could be heard in the background.

TWO DAYS AGO, they'd all been surprised by Commander Bache Loftt, the newly-promoted GDA Attaché to the Helios System. He'd turned up one evening at the Red Lion Inn, one of their favourite pubs deep in rural Kent, England.

As the GDA was still busy purging its ranks of Andromedan infiltrators, whose presence had initially been uncovered by Ed and the team in their first foray into space eight months ago, he'd asked them if they would be willing to go on an exploratory mission for them. The details of exactly where they were going was the agenda for the meeting on Panemorfi that afternoon.

Near the allotted time, a small dot appeared on the horizon and quickly grew into a decelerating GDA personal spaceplane: a sort of spacefaring executive jet, designed for the wealthy or important traveller. It swept in over the island, skimming the tops of the blue-fringed palm trees, turned and landed next to the Gabriel's shuttle in a small clearing on the east of the island.

Ed and Phil walked the short distance and met Commander Loftt as he stepped down from the plane. Ed was not expecting the second passenger, the new Earth Ambassador to the GDA, James Dewey to follow him out of the airlock.

'Ambassador Dewey!' exclaimed Ed. 'We weren't told. Welcome to Panemorfi and Theo Island. This is a pleasant surprise.'

'Good afternoon, Edward,' said Dewey. 'This seems a bit more hospitable than Mars – more hospitable indeed.'

Twenty years ago, James Dewey had made himself the most famous human on Earth. Despite being the first man to walk on Mars, he had a strange habit of repeating the ends of sentences, much to everyone's amusement.

'It certainly is, Mr Ambassador,' replied Ed.

'Call me James – please. We're not in council chambers here.'

'Thanks, James. I found Dasos looked quite pretty from orbit. They can keep their heavy gravity, though.'

'Tell me about it,' said Dewey. 'It's like permanently wading through thin porridge – porridge indeed.'

'The only thing you have to wade through here is the cocktail list,' said Ed, smiling and ushering them towards the entertainment deck.

'Fabulous,' said Loftt, eyeing up the well-stocked bar. 'I am liking new job especially much.'

His English language skills still needed a little work.

Once they were all sitting around one of the round dining tables, and Linda and Andy had joined them, Dewey started the conversation.

'The GDA has lost a couple of ships.'

'Oops a daisy,' Andy blurted out.

Everyone turned and gave Andy a glare.

'Sorry,' he mumbled and lowered his gaze.

'I take it that's not a regular occurrence?' said Ed, keeping an irritated expression aimed at Andy.

'No,' said Loftt. 'Unheard of for a thousand years.'

'Where?'

'Sector 97, on the fringes of the explored region.'

'Okay,' said Ed, looking nonplussed. 'Cleo, can you give us a holo map of the Milky Way, showing us and Sector 97, please?'

Cleopatra – or Cleo – was Gabriel's replacement on the starship, a new fully-sentient computer embryo who had been introduced to the rebuilt core shortly after Gabriel's loss. Cleo learnt fast and, within days had ingested everything left by Gabriel and more. Although they'd kept the name of the starship as the Gabriel, Cleo was very much now running the show and, over the last few months, had become an integral part of the team.

The image of the galaxy took up the space above the whole table and showed hundreds of sectors, one of which was coloured green and one, right on the fringe of the system, red.

'Thanks, Cleo.'

'You're welcome,' she said.

'I take it the green sector is where we are now and the red one is where the ship disappeared?' asked Linda.

'Correct,' said Dewey. 'The ship was the Vlepon, a mid-sized exploration ship with eighty-nine crew, two-thirds of which were scientists, with a small contingent of six marines. The ship was unarmed and without any cloaking technology.'

'How do you know it's disappeared and hasn't just broken down or something?' asked Andy.

'We don't.'

'Have you sent any help?' asked Ed.

'Yes, that's just it,' said Dewey. 'We sent a ship you're familiar with, the destroyer Vrachos – all repaired with a newly-promoted captain on his first mission.'

'Don't tell me it's disappeared too?'

'Yep – regular six-hour updates up to the final jump into the sector, then not a squeak, nothing more at all.'

'I take it the sector, being the nearest outer systems in the galaxy to Andromeda, hasn't gone unnoticed?'

'No, it hasn't, Andrew,' replied Dewey. 'If the Andromedans are setting up some sort of staging supply base there, the Gerousia needs to know – and quickly, very quickly.'

'Theo cloaking technology is better than GDA,' said Loftt. 'You can do sneaky about better.'

'I couldn't have said it better myself,' said Dewey. 'All we want you to do is go "sneaky about" and get back here with some proper intelligence so we can gauge how to deal with it. With all the Andromedan infiltration problems, the GDA is short of operational ships. But, then again, I'm told that that's a usual scenario.'

Loftt cleared his throat and gave Dewey a sideways glance.

'What's the pay like?' asked Andy, looking hopeful.

Dewey chuckled.

'I think you Brits call it "for king and country",' he said, giving Andy a wink. 'But how does a month at my ski lodge in Aspen sound?'

'In February?' said Ed.

'Deal.'

'Cool bananas,' said Andy. 'I'll order some new carvers.'

Ed glanced back at the holo map for a moment.

'You'll need to plan a route for us, Linda.'

'I think it would be best to fly into that system, instead of jumping in,' she said. 'It might take longer, but at least we would be fully cloaked and not jumping in blind.'

'Good idea,' agreed Ed. 'Sneak up on the Andromedan buggers through a side door.'

'It might not be the Andromedans at all,' said Andy.

'Whatever it is,' said Dewey, putting his hands up in a placating gesture, 'please find out for us and get back here. No rescue mission, no taking on an enemy battle fleet, just information and return. Then we can mount any rescue or attack missions with overwhelming force – overwhelming force indeed.'

Everyone at the table nodded and Ed noticed Loftt glance lovingly at the bar.

'Okay, who'd like a drink?' he asked.

'Have you got any of that England real all?' asked Loftt.

'Ale,' said Andy. 'Walk this way, Commander. I'm sure the barmaid can rustle up a flagon or two.'

Ed raised his eyebrows at Dewey, on seeing Loftt jumping up and off towards the bar as if shot out of a gun.

2

THE STARSHIP GABRIEL – ORBITING PANEMORFI, TRELORUS SYSTEM

DAY 176, YEAR 11270, 00:36FC, PCC

The Gabriel was considered small for a starship. At only four hundred and seventy metres from stem to stern, she looked more like a luxury yacht than a serious galaxy exploration vessel.

However, she carried a fearsome hidden arsenal of defence and offence capabilities, which put even some of the GDA's best naval ships to shame.

Theo-built ships were very different from other vessels, in that the hull, internal structures and bulkheads were made from semi-organic polymers and grown in the hard vacuum of space to a pre-programmed design. This made them extremely durable, damage resistant, smooth and aerodynamic in appearance, similar to an unopened flower bud, but with aerodynamic wings.

Cleo, the Gabriel's sentient computer system, never

had to sleep. She spent every moment of every day learning and working on ways to improve the ship's design and proficiency.

It was for this reason that she woke Ed early, despite the fact that Ed had only shuttled up from the island five hours ago, after a Herculean session with Commander Loftt, Ambassador Dewey and the rest of the crew. He was slightly less than overwhelmed with enthusiasm.

'Ah shit – Cleo,' said Ed as he peered at the ship's clock, which was set into the wall beside the bed. 'We're not leaving for another few hours – what's up?'

'I've got something new for you to try,' she said enthusiastically.

'Is it a hangover cure?'

'Er, no.'

'Well, can I have something? I've got a steam hammer reshaping the inside of my skull.'

A glass of clear liquid materialised on the bedside unit. He sat up and sniffed the contents warily.

'Get it down you – it's fast acting.'

Ed swigged it down in one go, discovering it tasted slightly bitter, but not unpleasant.

'Give it a couple of minutes. You'll be a new man.'

He swung his legs out onto the floor and, sure enough, the pounding in his head seemed to lessen by the second.

'Wow, Cleo. That's impressive stuff. What's in it?'

'It's Gabriel's recipe – best you don't know. And I wouldn't operate any heavy machinery for a while.'

Ed made a grimace at the glass, placing it quickly back on the table as if it were radioactive, and stood up. The reflection in the cabin's mirror that greeted him was not that of a healthy thirty-five-year-old.

'Shit, I look like I should be in the auto-nurse.'

'You look fabulous, darling,' said Cleo.

After using the bathroom, Ed sat back down on the bed. The hammering in his head had ceased, but the white walls in the cabin seemed way too bright so he reached over and dimmed the lighting slightly.

'Okay, Cleo. What have you got to show me?'

'I've been working on a new design for the POKs,' she said.

A POK was a thin helmet you wore to connect with the ship using the power of thought to either fly it or operate any of the ship's systems.

'Is it less obvious for away missions?'

'Well, that's just it,' said Cleo. 'It's not obvious at all, because it's invisible.'

'How does that work?'

'Nanos build an internal POK inside the skull.'

'An epidermal POK?'

'Yeah, kinda.'

'And you want me to be your guinea pig?' asked Ed, the scepticism obvious in his voice.

'I have to test it on someone,' she said. 'It's quite safe and painless.'

'Would it be operational all the time?'

'You can turn it off whenever you wish.'

'Okay, I trust you. Do I have to be in the auto-nurse?'

'No, just stick this small pad onto your forehead.'

A pad about the size of a small sticking plaster materialised in his hand. He stared at it for a moment, nodded to himself and stuck it firmly above his right eye.

'How long does it take?'

'You can remove the pad in two minutes, then it'll take the nanos approximately three hours to complete the fabrication and programming.'

'What are we calling this system?'

'You have a choice. In GDA speak, it's a Dermatikos Pantognostis Orama Emfytevo – or D-POE; in English it's a Dermal Omniscient Vision Implant – or DOVI.'

'I think DOVI will be the best bet,' he said, rolling his eyes. 'Can I go back to bed now?'

'Yes, I'll wake you when it's time to test the pathways.'

Ed went back to bed and slept fitfully, dreaming of insects eating his brain.

ED WAS AWAKE, suddenly aware that he could see around the outside of the ship, even though his eyes were still closed. He explored further, soon realising he had full operational control over the entire starship.

'This is cool,' he thought.

'Glad you like it,' Cleo thought back.

'Bloody hell,' thought Ed, almost jumping out of his skin. 'Do we have thought communication now?'

'Yep, good huh?'

'I take it that's controllable too?'

'Yep, just think of it being disconnected and it will be.'

'Does it have the same range as a physical POK?'

'Again, yes – so long as you're within line of sight of the ship from orbit.'

'That's great, Cleo,' thought Ed. 'Saves having to wear a hat all the time on planet visits.'

'Correct. There's one more addition to this I haven't told you about. The main memory cache – or Krypti as I've called it – is located underneath the skull at the back of your head. It's about the size of a large grain of rice and will absorb all your thoughts – past, current and future – in case you're not within contact of the ship.'

'Kinda like a back-up hard drive for my brain?'

'Yes,' she thought to him. 'There is also another

function for this.' She paused for a moment. 'If you were ever killed, the Krypti could be placed into an embryonic skeleton in a Theo birthing chamber and you could be reborn – so long as your head was retrieved, of course.'

Ed immediately sat up and opened his eyes.

'What? And have all my memories and personality back, as though nothing had happened?' he said out loud.

'Yes, your rebirth could even be pre-programmed with your same looks, height, eye colour, et cetera. Which means anything you desire could be changed and delivered in a perfect new human body.'

'What if you had a particularly violent death? That trauma can really screw you up.'

'Anything can be erased.'

Ed got out of bed and stood in front of the mirror again.

'This makes immortality almost a reality, doesn't it?'

'Yes, welcome to the club,' said Cleo. 'But you do realise you can stay just as you are now by detoxing in the auto-nurse every few months, right? That's how Phil stops his ageing process and has done so for nearly four thousand years.'

'I need to talk to the others before we take this any further. Personally, I wouldn't mind being around for longer than ninety or a hundred years, but the other two might have different feelings on the matter.'

Through the DOVI, Ed could see Linda walking through the ship. Thinking that this was a bit voyeuristic, he quickly turned it off. He dressed and made his way up to the bridge.

3

THE STARSHIP GABRIEL – DOVI TESTING IN THE TRELORUS SYSTEM

DAY 176, YEAR 11270, 08:11FC, PCC

Ed was reclining on his control couch powering the Gabriel through the Trelorus System, changing speed continuously, activating and deactivating weapon systems, cloaking and uncloaking, before flashing back into a high orbit around Panemorfi again.

'That's outstanding,' said Andy. 'Where do I sign?'

'What about you, Linda?' asked Ed, opening his eyes once he was sure the ship was in a stable orbit.

'Does this work with the shuttles and the Cartella too?' she asked.

'Yes, it does,' said Cleo. 'You won't need the POKs anymore.'

'And this rebirthing thing. Is it compulsory?'

'I've put a lot of thought into this. The default setting would be a rebirth with the last ten minutes of your life erased. If you state clearly beforehand that you do not want to be reborn after your death, then your Krypti will be put into storage on Paradeisos indefinitely.'

'Okay, I'm in,' said Linda. 'Default setting for now, although I reserve the right to change my mind in the future.'

'That's good,' said Ed. 'Phil, you cool with this?' He gave him a hopeful thumbs-up.

'Yeah, it's good with me. You have to remember, I've been through a birthing chamber before, although it was a bloody long time ago. But there's nothing to be concerned about in the process at all.'

Two minutes later, three more nano-infected pads were stuck to Andy, Linda and Phil's foreheads and three hours after that, all four of the human crew were able to operate any system on any of the ships with just the power of thought. Cleo modified the ship settings to make the private cabins secure from any voyeuristic opportunists and they all recorded a rebirth charter, listing their preferred characteristics.

At the allotted time, Linda took the Gabriel out of orbit and set a course for the jump zone, away from the Trelorus System, bemoaning the fact that flying the starship without a POK felt like riding a motorcycle without a helmet. It just felt weird.

The journey to Sector 97 would take over a week,

especially as they wanted to enter the area from another direction, cloaked, using the AVF drive.

Five days in, they finally jumped out of the GDA-controlled space. This meant that they no longer had designated jump zones and were emerging into largely unexplored systems – which also meant that they had to be extremely vigilant. Pre-scanning the next system before jumping was a must now. Although advanced civilisations out this way were rare, the thought of jumping into another ship or an uncharted asteroid field was not overly exciting.

It was now not possible to leave the flying to Cleo during sleep periods, so the crew took shifts on the bridge, scanning in all directions, but mostly ahead.

'Are you seeing this too, Cleo?' asked Andy, as the Gabriel swept through a system known only as C-29641/AT.

'Yes, I am.'

The holo map in the centre of the bridge spun round and extended out to include an incoming unidentified object, now flashing as a red icon.

'Whatever it is, it's on an intercept course at about point five light. I'll alter course slightly.'

'It's compensated and still on intercept course.'

'Who is it?'

'Still too far away. They don't appear to have cloaking or stealth tech, but they do have data blocking. I'll be able to counter that when they get a little closer.'

'Can you wake the others please, Cleo?'

'They're on their way.'

'Time to intercept?'

'Thirty-one minutes.'

Andy could detect the other crew members' DOVIs coming online.

'Are we close enough to the next system to safely jump yet?'

'No, not for forty-eight minutes.'

'Shit.'

'So long as you don't do that on my couch,' said Linda as she swept up on the tube elevator. 'Do we know who they are yet?'

'No, Cleo should be able tell before—'

'Klatt, it's a Klatt warship – Fonias Class,' said Cleo, butting in.

Ed and Phil came up through the floor together on the tube elevator.

'Did I hear it's a Fonias Class warship?' asked Phil.

'Yes, what does that stand for?' asked Linda.

'Killer,' said Phil. 'We need to be wary. The Klatt have no sense of humour – and no word in their language for friendly.'

'Weren't they the ones you saved us from last year when we were—'

'Jumping over to Uskrre at Proxima Centauri,' interrupted Phil. 'Yes, it was – and now you'll see why.'

'Receiving transmission from the Klatt ship,' said Cleo.

'Run it through the translator please, Cleo,' said Ed.

'Unidentified warship, your uninvited trespass into Klatt prepotency is an act of offence. You will immediately reverse course to avoid eradication.'

'How rude,' said Andy. 'Can I talk back with the rail gun?'

'Hang on a minute,' said Ed. 'I'm starting to feel their ship – it's getting stronger as they get closer.'

'Well, we all are,' said Linda.

'No, I mean – I'm feeling my way into their systems.'

'Good – it does work,' said Cleo.

'What does?' asked Andy.

'I made the software in Ed's DOVI invasive adaptive, which means that with ships that are near enough and don't have adaptive shielding, he may be able to infiltrate their control systems and severely ruin their day.'

'When were you planning on telling me this?'

'When I knew it worked. I couldn't test it on myself.'

'Why only Ed?' asked Linda. 'I might've liked a bit of that.'

'I reckoned it would be safer with only one of you delving about in an enemy ship's systems. If you were all in there messing about, it could get a bit confusing about who was where and control of your own ship might also get neglected.'

'Oh, wow!' exclaimed Ed. 'I just shut down their main drive.'

'They've stopped decelerating,' said Cleo.

'Hang on,' said Ed. 'I'm in their weapons suite – if I can just – there we go – have a little bit of that – see if you can eradicate anything without that, Mr Happy Klatt.'

'What the fuck?' said Andy. 'Did you just do that?'

'Do what?' asked Linda.

'One of their rail gun turrets just turned back on itself and reduced their own targeting array into scrap.'

Andy opened his eyes and looked across to find Ed staring back with a wide grin plastered across his face.

'Oops,' said Ed. 'Their rail gunner might be in a bit of strife right about now.'

'They're gonna fly right past too,' said Andy.

'Unidentified warship, you have committed an act of war by opening fire on us, you will—'

'Identified Klatt Fonias Class warship, this is Vice Admiral Virr of the GDA Exploration Ship Gabriel. Our scans indicate that it was one of your own rail gun turrets that fired on your ship. It would appear that members of your crew do not agree with your arrogant and childish bullying of peaceful, unarmed ships passing through this system which, by the way, remains unclaimed. If you wish to register a claim on system C-29641/AT, please complete the required documentation and submit to the Galaxy System Claims Office on Dasos. In the meantime, I wish you a good day as we have more pivotal business elsewhere, with more important species.'

As soon as Ed toggled the communication icon to off, he received a round of applause.

'Give 'em a wave as they go by,' said Andy. 'Oh, hang on – they've ejected something out of an airlock.'

'Ah, shit,' said Ed.

'Was that...' said Linda, stopping mid-sentence.

'Yes,' said Andy. 'They just spaced a crew member.'

It went very quiet on the bridge. Once the out-of-control Klatt ship flashed by, gradually reducing speed, seemingly using only its manoeuvring jets, the other three went quietly back to their cabins, leaving Andy to finish the remainder of his watch. He sat there wishing he could sleep too, but knowing full well he wouldn't and that the other three wouldn't be getting much rest either, after having witnessed that.

4

THE STARSHIP GABRIEL – APPROACHING SECTOR 97

DAY 183, YEAR 11270, 08:27FC, PCC

Ed had the ship fully cloaked and shielded as they approached Sector 97. All four crew were seated on the bridge couches, studying the continuous stream of data flooding in from the sector.

'I'm getting over four thousand systems in 97,' said Andy. 'We'll be getting close enough to the first few for scanning shortly.'

'I'll mark the system where the two ships disappeared in red,' said Cleo.

A flashing red icon popped up on the holo display right out on the fringe of the sector, just before the infinitesimal void of intergalactic space disappeared into nothing.

'Okay, plan us a jump into a safe system, which neighbours the trouble spot, Linda,' said Ed. 'We can scan the hell out of it from there.'

Ten minutes later, they nervously emerged into an unnamed system, only four and a half light years away from their target. Linda instantaneously cloaked the ship and made several drastic course changes before they all relaxed a little.

'Scanning,' said Andy.

They all surveyed the results, finding the system devoid of anything dangerous or untoward.

'Right,' said Ed, visibly relieved. 'Let's get over the far side of this system and concentrate everything we have on the neighbour.'

It took another three hours to reach the outer perimeter of the system and Ed found it extremely odd when he visited the blister observation lounge up at the top of the ship. In one direction was a normal sky full of stars and, in the other, just one star could be seen before the slightly daunting, complete blackness of intergalactic space.

It reminded him of a holiday, years ago during his gap year, on the east coast of Australia, snorkelling on the Great Barrier Reef. He'd scared himself when he'd moved further away from the dive boat than he thought and the beautiful, shallow blue water he'd been drifting across suddenly disappeared off a cliff face into total blackness and the unknown.

He was there again now as he tentatively peered out

from the observation blister, out from the Milky Way and into millions of light years of nothing.

The system they were in — similar to the Kuiper belt in the Helios System at home — also had an asteroid belt circling the outer reaches. Linda picked one of the largest rocks, which was sized at about five hundred kilometres across, matched its slow rotation and hid the ship close by.

'Right,' said Ed. 'Give that system the once over, Andy, and, Phil, can you prepare one of our special GDA satellite drones to jump over there and give us the what's what?'

'No problem,' came back in stereo.

Andy found nothing other than a G-type main sequence star: similar in type to, but slightly larger than, the sun, with seven orbiting globes big enough to be classed as planets. One of which — the second — was possibly in the habitable goldilocks zone: 'not too hot, not too cold'. Phil jumped the drone over, adjacent to this second planet, and hid it right next to one of its three small moons.

'I'm getting small power readings from one of the moons and two on the planet's surface,' said Phil.

'Is the drone cloaked?' asked Ed.

'Yeah.'

'Can you take it over to the moon and check out that power reading?'

'Already on its way.'

'I've analysed some of the other data from the drone,' said Cleo. 'And I think I've found ship debris orbiting the planet, although it's very small and there's not much of it.'

'Thanks, Cleo,' said Ed. 'I guess over time any large debris left in orbit would soon decay and fall into the gravity well. We'll have a look at that next.'

Phil didn't want to uncloak the drone so the journey over to one of the three moons took over an hour. They all took the opportunity to grab something to eat while they waited.

'Well, that could explain a lot,' Phil mumbled, his mouth full of shepherd's pie. He was reading the telemetry from his drone as it orbited the moon that had the faint power reading.

'What's that in English?' asked Andy as the other two looked up.

'The power reading is emanating from this beastie,' Phil said as he brought a rotating holographic image up in the centre of the bridge.

'What the hell is that?' questioned Ed, looking at a peculiar domed structure hidden inside an impact crater.

'That,' said Phil, 'looks remarkably like a ground-based laser cannon. This planet seems to have a space defence system.'

'That's a space cannon?' asked Andy. 'Shouldn't it have a barrel sticking out the top or something?'

'In a sci-fi movie, yes, but in the real world, not necessarily,' said Phil.

'That could explain why they don't have any ships in space and no satellites in orbit,' said Andy.

'Or life signs on the planet's surface,' added Cleo.

'They could be underground, like on Paradeisos,' said Linda.

'That's possible.'

'I've found three more cannons,' said Phil. 'These three aren't powered up, which is why the scanning software didn't spot them before. Now it knows what to look for – and, sure enough, there's another four over on the second moon.'

'Someone doesn't like visitors,' said Linda.

'Or, someone didn't want the natives escaping,' said Ed.

'Hell, yes. I didn't think of that,' said Andy. 'This could be someone's prison colony.'

They all opened their eyes and stared at each other for a moment.

'What's our next move?' asked Linda.

'I want to check if this cannon is still operational

and, if it is, whether it could have downed our two GDA ships,' said Ed.

'One thing I've just noticed,' said Phil, 'is that this cannon seems to power up into a more aggressive state when pointed towards the planet and powers down into a standby mode when the moon turns away from its host.'

'Does the drone carry any probes?' asked Ed.

'Yeah, six.'

'Okay, launch one out around the moon in clear sight of the cannon when it's facing out into space.'

A small one-metre-diameter scanning probe zipped away from the drone. The cannon instantly powered up and tracked the small craft, but did nothing more. As the probe passed it by, it just turned and followed it.

'Now bring the probe around and settle it into a high orbit.'

Phil did as Ed requested and, as the craft locked itself into a high sustainable orbit, the cannon blasted a huge bolt of energy at the probe, destroying it instantly. Any leftover debris fell into the atmosphere to burn up on entry.

'Well, that tells a story,' said Phil.

'Certainly does,' replied Ed. 'And explains why there are no satellites or ships in orbit.'

'Are you thinking what I'm thinking?' asked Andy.

'That we'll find wreckages of two GDA ships somewhere on the surface of the planet?'

'It'd be a good bet to make.'

'I'd like to take that cannon out of commission before we venture over there, cloak or no cloak, and can we double-check there's no more active cannons hiding on any of the three moons too?'

'I'm on it, boss,' said Phil. 'Do you want me to stick a Kataligo missile through that cannon's front door?'

'Don't tell me, GDA exploration drones are armed too?' asked Ed, opening his eyes and glancing across at Phil. All he got in reply was a wink and a wry grin.

'I thought you guys were pacifists?' asked Linda.

'We're allowed to break inanimate objects,' Phil replied, smiling now as he commanded the drone to open a panel on its underside. A rack with six Kataligo missiles dropped down and turned towards the moon.

'Permission to fire?' asked Phil.

'You may fire when ready, Mr Theo,' said Ed, closing his eyes to watch the show.

The missile streaked away from the rack and was immediately tracked by its target. The two defensive rail guns, which had been designed to defend the cannon from just such an attack, did not perform their duty. Their power supply had long since failed. Subsequently, one minute and thirty-nine seconds later, the cannon, along with its impotent rail guns, vaporised along with the crater they were housed in.

'The scans from the drone are showing no other operational cannons in the planetary system,' said Phil. 'So, I conclude we're safe to approach.'

'Thank you, Phil,' said Ed. 'Linda, jump us in when ready please. But reactivate the cloak once we're there. We don't know what other surprises this planet might yet yield.'

'Roger that,' she said as the Gabriel moved out from its hiding place.

5

THE STARSHIP GABRIEL – UNCHARTED SYSTEM, SECTOR 97

DAY 183, YEAR 11270, 16:20FC, PCC

As the system appeared relatively safe now, Linda jumped the Gabriel in behind the largest of the third planet's moons and cloaked. The drone was retrieved and so was a sample of the debris Cleo had detected earlier.

'It's not from a GDA ship,' said Cleo. 'It's an alloy of undetermined origin.'

'I imagine more than just our two ships have fallen foul to the hidden cannons trick, especially when the entire network of twelve cannons was up and running,' said Ed. 'Drop us into orbit, Linda, and keep the shields up at all times, just in case another cannon decides to go wakey wakey.'

'Okay.'

'I think it's time we had a look down below. Cleo,

can you prep the Cartella for flight and, Andy, Phil – port hangar in ten minutes.'

'Road trip,' shouted Andy, he was up out of his couch and disappeared down the tube lift like a rat down a drainpipe.

The Cartella was Ed and Andy's original jump test bed. A converted NASA mining safety shuttle, in which they'd made their first tentative jumps, many months ago. The Theos had considered it so dangerous that it had been completely rebuilt, incorporating the latest flight technology, weapons and defensive capabilities. Although it retained the same layout, it was considerably larger than before and, because of the artificial gravity system, an awful lot more comfortable.

'Cleo's given us two main areas to focus on,' said Ed. 'All emitting low energy readings. Phil, you're in charge of the drone again; that'll go down in front of us to check for nasties. I'll pilot and, Andy, can you play with defence and offence?'

'You sound like my old football coach,' said Andy. 'Do you want me to cut up some oranges for half time?'

THE CARTELLA FOLLOWED into the upper atmosphere three minutes behind the drone. The GDA drones were well-designed and had retractable heat shielding on the underside, specifically made for checking out unexplored planets. They bristled with cameras, scanning arrays, atmosphere samplers, et cetera. If there was something awry with this planet, they had three minutes to either deal with it or turn back.

'Atmosphere is thickening,' said Phil. 'Gravity at point seven six Earth and stable; ground temperature thirty-one degrees at first search area. Oxygen level is slightly higher than Earth, so no smoking.'

'I left my weed behind,' said Andy.

'You could always try some of the local flora,' said Ed.

The drone finally dropped below cloud level and communicated a dry coastline, which stretched away for thousands of kilometres in both directions. The initial scans had shown a ninety-four percent landmass. There was no evidence of sentient life, although they were coming down very near the equator where it was very dry and barren. Further north and south, it was more temperate and a little green flora was evident where the oceans had retracted to. Phil sent the drone off to where the weak power reading had been detected and Ed brought the Cartella down to a few thousand feet above the ground. The terrain was dry, rocky and reasonably flat, with a mountain range visible far away to the north.

'I'm getting a high concentrate of metals in various patches on the surface,' said Phil. 'It's weird because they're all different types and they seem to be randomly distributed.'

'Enough to be ship debris?' asked Ed.

'Not really. You'd expect a large percentage of a ship would burn up during an uncontrolled entry, but there should be larger lumps making it to the surface – more than just fragments here and there.'

'Perhaps the local scrap merchant's been busy in his old truck?' said Andy.

Phil opened his eyes and stared at Andy with a puzzled expression.

'Don't worry, Phil,' said Ed. 'He didn't take his adult pill this morning and he's having one of his plonker moments.'

Phil rolled his eyes, nodded and resumed his drone piloting.

Ed brought the Cartella to within a minute of the drone. He could see it now, ahead of them, approaching the target.

Phil swung the drone around.

The wreckage had been partly buried into the ground and there was a large chunk of it sticking up about fifty metres into the air.

'Uncloak the drone, Phil – and give it a good noisy fly by,' said Ed. 'See if we get any reaction.'

Phil buzzed the wreck for a couple of minutes, getting within a few metres on each pass. Nothing happened.

Ed brought the Cartella in and landed a hundred metres away. He handed over to Cleo and asked her to remain cloaked.

Phil remained in the ship to continue using the drone as an eye in the sky. He activated a mini rail gun that popped out the side of the drone to cover their backs.

'That drone's full of surprises,' said Ed as he and Andy waited next to the airlock as it went through its opening cycle.

They had both dressed in GDA military Krama suits, a form-fitting body armour, and carried laser rifles. As they stepped down onto the surface, Ed felt very exposed. He jogged surprisingly quickly over towards the wreck, noticing the pungent aroma of burning plastic.

'This lower gravity gives you superhero powers, doesn't it?' said Andy, bouncing by like a gazelle on steroids.

'Just don't fall over with your finger on the trigger,' replied Ed. 'I'm not particularly keen to test these suits, no matter how good Loftt says they are.'

As they reached the wreck, Ed stopped and listened. A quiet, occasional clicking could be heard from below the surface and the plastic smell was stronger.

'This wreck is recent; it's still cooling,' he said.

Andy nodded and continued to walk around the huge lump of blackened, melted metal. Two minutes was all it took to completely circumnavigate the wreck.

'How the hell are we going to identify this pile of junk?' shouted Andy as he clambered up the side of the hulk.

'Hang on a minute, I've got an idea.' Ed stood still and faced the wreck, closing his eyes. He concentrated on any ship systems that might still have some form of life. He found the ship's bridge was still partly operational, buried thirty metres down in the ground, with a few of the control surfaces still seemingly dragging juice from the power cells.

'I think I've found the power source we detected,' he said. 'The navigation console is still up, along with life support and a few ancillary systems.'

'Does it tell you the ship's name?'

'No, but it does give me an idea, though.'

Ed concentrated on the ship again. For a moment, nothing happened. Then a rattle from below and a few clunks. A hiss and the section of ship that Andy was standing on suddenly disappeared up into a bulkhead.

'Whoa, shit,' he shouted as he vanished down into the wreck with a clatter.

'Bollocks. Are you okay?' called Ed as he ran over,

clambered up and peered into the new hole in the side of the ship.

Andy was hanging in what looked to be a rather scorched wiring loom over a corridor that stretched deep down into the vessel. He looked up with a rather unimpressed glare.

'For fuck's sake, can you give me a bit of a warning next time you remove the floor?'

'Sorry, mate. I didn't know it was a door. I just asked the system to open all bulkhead emergency doors. What I didn't realise was we're already well inside the ship. Several metres of it has burnt away.'

'Whatever, a bit of help would go down better than piss poor excuses.'

'Can you climb down that corridor?'

Andy looked down for a second and then back up at Ed. 'You want me to go down there?'

'I'm coming too.'

'What if there are pissed-off aliens?'

'You have a big gun.'

'They might have a bigger one.'

'Do you really think anything could have survived this?'

Andy looked down again and when he looked back up, he appeared to have made a decision.

'I'll try and swing over to that ledge over there.'

'You be careful, guys,' said Phil, his worried voice booming in their ears. 'Broken starships are dangerous places.'

'We will,' said Ed as he clambered over the edge and disappeared down into the hulk.

It took them ten minutes to descend into the centre of the vessel. At the bottom of the corridor shaft, there was a choice of left or right down the darkened passageways. They brought their weapons up and turned left as that took them deeper into the ship and towards the bridge. Walking on the wall of the corridor made it more dangerous as the panels weren't designed to take their weight. Twenty metres along, they came to another junction. There was only one small light still working, but it showed the passageway dropping down again.

'I'm sick of the smell of burning plastic,' said Ed as he peered over the edge into the blackness.

'You can take point this time,' said Andy, patting Ed on the back as he looked downwards apprehensively.

'Okay, it's completely dark down there, so turn your gun light on to give me a clue.'

It was only ten metres down this time and there was only one choice: continuing in the same direction as before. When Ed reached the bottom, he lit his gun light too, illuminating a short passage up to a partly-closed door, which had a faint glimmering light emanating from within. Ed shone his light through the gap and peeked in.

'I can see flickering control panels and bugger all else.'

'Can't you have a chat with the computer and open this door?' asked Andy.

Ed closed his eyes again and concentrated. After a moment, he nodded and spoke.

'This is definitely the bridge. It has a secondary set of bulkhead doors that seal it in case of emergency. Stand back. I'll see if it will—'

The door dropped suddenly into the floor, or wall, with a bang.

'—open.'

'Shit, you don't want to be standing in front of that when it closes,' said Andy, stepping warily past it.

The bridge was partially crushed on the side that was buried in the ground, but the systems on the upper side were all glowing or flickering. They both shone their lights around until Andy called out.

'Hey, here you go.'

His light illuminated a section of wall on the back of the bridge where, embossed in gold lettering, were the words 'GDA Apergia Taxi Antitorpiliko, Vrachos'. They'd discovered a few months ago that the universal language of the GDA was a form of ancient Greek, thus determining where that particular Earth language had originated.

'Found you – GDA Apergia Class Destroyer, Vrachos,' said Ed.

He shone his light around the bridge a second time.

'But where the hell are the crew?'

6

THE CARTELLA – THIRD PLANET, UNCHARTED SYSTEM, SECTOR 497

DAY 184, YEAR 11270, 01:20FC, PCC

Once Ed and Andy had clambered out of the wreck and returned to the Cartella, it was getting late. It was beginning to get dark and searching for the other exploration ship would be much easier in the daylight. So, the consensus of opinion was to eat and get some rest.

Ed couldn't sleep. He kept thinking about the fate of the Vrachos crew. There'd been no bodies, no blood nor anything to suggest what fate could have become the complement of one hundred and fourteen souls. The ship's computer log was on the destroyed side of the bridge, so no answer there. There was no way of telling if the lifeboats had been launched or if the two atmospheric shuttles had escaped as the outside decks of the ship were completely burnt off.

Cleo woke him with a message, seemingly only

moments after finally dropping off.

'Are you kidding me? I've only just shut my eyes,' he moaned.

'You've been asleep for nine hours.'

'Shit, really?' He sat up with a start, blinking at the wall clock.

'I have news.'

'Okay, yes, I'm awake.'

'The debris I recovered yesterday from the planet's orbit was from the defensive cannons, not a ship – and was recent.'

'How recent?'

'Looking at the timescales, about the same time as the Vrachos went down.'

'So, you're saying the Vrachos put up a fight and took out all the remaining cannons, except one?'

'It's the only scenario that fits the residual evidence.'

'What about the crew though?'

'If the captain gave the abandon ship call in time, then the lifeboats will have been deployed; they all have planetary insertion heat shielding, as do both the shuttles.'

'The crew could be distributed across the planet then?'

'Not necessarily. A mass ejection of the lifeboats from a GDA ship is designed to initiate a swarm scenario. This means they all communicate with each other and are programmed to come down together in a safe location.'

'If that's the case, why haven't we detected— How many are there?'

'Twelve.'

'Twelve grounded lifeboats and maybe a shuttle or two, somewhere on the surface?'

'As far as the newest model lifeboats go – present GDA standing orders are to retrieve all the supplies and equipment from the lifeboat and then set to self-destruct. It stops the enemy, or lesser developed races, getting their hands on the technology. So, some of that mix of metal fragments we detected on the surface yesterday could be the remains of up to twelve lifeboats.'

'Let's hope so,' said Ed.

THE OTHER TWO were sitting talking on the bridge when Ed entered.

'I woke up thinking there was an earthquake earlier,' said Andy. 'It was just your snoring shaking the ship.'

'Says the man who can snore a ship out of orbit,' said Ed.

'You know, two minutes in the auto-nurse can cure that,' Phil interjected.

Ed jumped onto the pilot's couch, brought the Cartella up to ten thousand feet and scanned for the second faint power source. Phil, again as he'd done the day before, pushed the drone out in front and once they had a hard return, they raced across the desert landscape towards the signal and a distant mountain range. This time, when the drone reached the area, there was no lump of ship sticking up above the surface. It was hovering over a small valley in the lower reaches of the tree-covered range towering above them. The drone uncloaked and did a few drive-bys again, providing the same negative result as yesterday.

Ed put the Cartella down in the only clearing he could find that would take the ship. It was on a bit of a camber, so he adjusted the skids to level it up.

'It reminds me of an old Western,' said Andy as they cautiously walked through the boulder-strewn terrain. "Yer not from rind theyse parts, are ye?"'

Ed smiled and said, "Go ahead, punk, make my day".'

'That's not a Western.'

'What was it?'

'Dirty Harry.'

'"Right turn, Clyde".'

'That's not, either.'

They both saw it at the same time and trotted over to find a GDA military issue backpack.

'It's empty,' said Andy, after he rifled through the pockets.

'Cleo, can you pinpoint the power reading from our location?' said Ed, looking up.

'About fifty-five metres to your left. Although it's fainter than the last one, so it could be buried quite deep. The ground is softer in the lea of the mountains, so if the remains of a ship came down there, they could have ploughed in from an angle and disappeared.'

They paced out around fifty metres, dropping down into a slight depression and then up the other side. The ground was indeed softer here, with patches of long-stemmed grasses and moss eking out an existence amongst the rocky terrain. Turning and looking back the way they'd come, Ed noticed that the depression they'd walked through was unusual and contained no large rocks or boulders.

'That's a recent impact crater,' he said. 'And whatever came down there would be underneath us here.'

'Why don't you try your Jedi mind trick again, only this time I'm standing next to you,' said Andy, shuffling up close.

Ed stood still, closed his eyes and concentrated. 'Bloody hell,' he said. 'That's odd.'

'Have you found the droids we're looking for?'

'No, there aren't any ship systems below us, but

there is some sort of door, or airlock, or some sort of opening and closing control system. It's very alien, but the locking combination isn't too elaborate.'

Andy started staring around. 'There's nothing here to open, though. It's just a mountainside.'

'Guys,' said Cleo. 'I'm suddenly getting multiple power readings all around you. What the hell are you doing?'

'Got it,' said Ed and opened his eyes.

A low, bass-level rumble could be felt rather than heard and they both looked down at their feet as the ground trembled.

'What the fuck have you opened this time?'

'No idea, but I feel we need to move out the way.'

They both sprinted back the way they'd come and stopped after thirty metres once the ground beneath their feet became solid again. Turning, they saw a large twenty-metre section of hillside slowly opening upwards. What they'd earlier thought was an impact crater was in fact an excavated ramp down to the doorway. It had just weathered into a crater shape over time.

'Shit,' said Andy. 'You could get four double-decker buses through there.'

They looked at each other as the rumbling door motors went silent and left a gaping hole in the side of the hill.

Phil suddenly made them jump as the drone appeared closely behind them.

'I think I should have a look in there first, guys, don't you?'

Before they could answer, the drone whizzed over their heads and disappeared through the cavernous opening.

'I'm getting a wide tunnel, a machined circular bore, no defences and, fifty metres down, it turns ninety degrees right to a second metallic door.'

'Thanks, Phil,' said Ed as both he and Andy brought their guns up, turned the lights on and started for the opening.

'Err, gentlemen – where d'you think you're going?' said a very stern-sounding Linda from above.

'I'm following him,' said Andy, pointing at Ed and grinning.

'Bloody kiss arse,' Ed grumbled. 'We're just having a wee look in the cave, Linda. Won't be a minute.'

'Just remember what Dewey said. You're there for reconnaissance, not a rescue mission, and definitely not for blundering into unrecognised underground alien installations.'

'Yes, dear,' said Andy.

'Don't you "yes dear" me. You take that drone with you and send it in first, wherever you go – is that clear, soldier?'

'Yes, err, Linda,' he said, giving Ed a wink.

When they reached the second door, the drone was sitting on its skids, whirring away and providing a bit more light in the dark passageway. The door had an iris diaphragm design, where it opened with a circle in the middle and gradually increased in size, fashioned with interlocking, sliding plates. No obvious control or opening mechanism was apparent.

'You're going to have to use the force again, Obi-wan,' said Andy.

Ed closed his eyes again and had a sweep around.

'The control is set into the rock on the other side as before, which makes me think this is an exit, not an entrance.'

'What, like a fire escape?'

'Maybe,' said Ed as he went back to deciphering the combination.

Two minutes later the door was still stubbornly closed.

'I take it you're still working on this door and not having forty winks?' asked Andy.

Ed didn't need to answer, as the iris slid silently open and disappeared into the wall.

'About bloody time, I was beginning to— Oh, shit.'

Eight black-clad humanoid soldiers appeared from the shadows, each with laser rifles pointing at their heads.

UNDERGROUND FACILITY – THIRD PLANET, NEW SYSTEM, SECTOR 497

DAY 184, YEAR 11270, 10:41FC, PCC

They were dragged inside and the iris door closed with a clang, immediately shutting off the drone – and any immediate help – on the outside. After being disarmed and searched, they were led across an enormous cavern, big enough to lose an aircraft carrier inside.

They were ushered along deeper into the chamber by their – up to now – silent guardians. They looked around as they walked, trying to take in the scale of the place. There seemed to be a lot of concrete-based pedestals where large machines, or something similar, had once stood. The whole cavern was lit by hundreds of white glowing panels, set into the ceiling high above. Ed noticed they were being led towards a small encampment of what looked like inflatable igloos in the centre of the room. They saw several more people milling around the makeshift camp as they approached, some stopped to stare as Ed and Andy were shepherded along, into the centre of the igloos.

'Who the hell are you?' asked a short, stocky man as he stepped out of one of the inflatables.

It was the first time they had been able to test the new built-in translator Cleo had incorporated into their DOVIs.

'I'm Edward Virr and this is Andrew Faux. We have—'

'What the hell is this place and why did you destroy my ship?' he interrupted.

'Are you the crew of the Vrachos?' Andy asked.

'You're obviously not GDA, but you're carrying the latest GDA assault weapons and wearing the latest Krama suits. I think you retrieved them from the wreck of our ship. I think you're opportunist pirates.'

Ed and Andy looked at each other and nodded.

'Commander Loftt sends his regards and wondered if you required rescuing? He has a memory chip containing our introduction,' said Ed, pointing at one of the guards.

The guard in question handed over the chip, which their interrogator inserted into a handheld tablet. The two-minute miniature holographic presentation explained the mission and why the GDA had sent the Gabriel.

'It appears I owe you an apology,' he said, looking

up and giving them a weak smile. 'I'm First Officer G'ann and we are indeed some of the crew of the Vrachos.'

'Some of?' said Ed. 'Did you lose some with the ship?'

'Yes,' he replied dejectedly. 'Nine during the engagement with the planetary defences; seven, when a lifeboat failed to launch; and the captain who remained on board to try to propel the stuck lifeboat manually.'

'So, there are ninety-seven of you here.'

'Well, there were four days ago before the gateway activated.'

'The what?' said Andy.

G'ann shuffled a bit and looked hopefully over to his left. Another of his officers stared back and gave him a shrug.

'Best if I show you,' he said and walked off, indicating, with a nod, to follow.

He strode through the temporary camp and out through more of the strange base plates. At the far end of the cavern was another of the iris doors, only this one was permanently open.

He led them down another circular passage and into a much smaller cavern. In the centre of the room stood what seemed to be a huge square stone and metallic door frame. There were no doors on the five-metre frame, no markings, nothing. It just stood alone in the middle of the otherwise empty cave.

'Four days ago, when we solved the combination on that iris door –' he indicated to the door into the smaller chamber '– we entered and it looked exactly as it does now. Something then happened involving that.' He pointed at the large frame and looked down, as if struggling for the words. 'Five of the crew were in the vicinity of the gate when it emitted a loud humming. The room lit up and, for a moment, I saw trees, grass and blue sky, all within a few metres of the gateway. But as fast as it had come, it disappeared again and so did the five crew. Since then, we've tried everything to reactivate the gateway – portal, or whatever it is – to no avail.'

'It was only the crew near the gate that went?' asked Ed.

'Yes. I was standing here about twelve metres away and was unaffected. But the chief mechanic, who was two metres in front of me, vanished.'

'Does it affect both sides of the door?'

'Yes, ten metres in both directions. You can see the cleaner area of floor; it took all the dust as well.'

'Have you found any control systems anywhere?' asked Andy.

'No, nothing. It's like the iris doors; everything seems to be controlled remotely.'

Ed concentrated his DOVI to within the gate room and it immediately made him spin round and concentrate on one wall.

'What are you doing?' G'ann asked. 'Are you telepathic or something?'

'It's a long story,' said Andy. 'He has an uncanny ability to find hidden stuff,' he added, not wanting to give too much away.

Ed opened his eyes and stared at the wall.

'Sneaky buggers,' he said, stepping over to it and touched the top of a lit panel with his hand.

A clunk sounded from behind the wall and the lighting panel, the size of an ordinary door, sank back and slid to the side, revealing steps going down and around to the left. Similar panels in the small passageway lit up with a bright glow. Ed noticed the dank, musty smell of age permeating the air as the door opened.

'Well, I'll be,' said Andy. 'It's like fucking *Tomb Raider.*'

G'ann looked at Andy with a bemused expression.

'Don't worry,' said Ed to G'ann. 'It's not worth explaining.' He then started down the stairway.

The stairs led down under the gate chamber and out into another smaller room full of screens, control panels and unrecognisable electronic equipment. The three of them filed in and just stood and stared. Everything was covered in a layer of dust and it was obvious this room hadn't been in operation for a very long time. The technology was quite advanced though and, as Ed gazed around the room, he knew he'd found the control hub for the entire hidden installation.

'We need to let our friends know we're okay,' said Andy.

'Give me a second,' said Ed as he brushed the dust off what looked like the command chair, which faced the largest control desk. He sat and perused the multitude of buttons and controls, which reminded him of an old twentieth century mixing desk. Blowing the dust off and touching a big green button at the top left-hand corner seemed a good place to start. Immediately, the whole room seemed to come alive. Screens lit up, control panels illuminated and everything started buzzing, whirring, and generally sounding busy. The screens displayed a multitude of views from above, one showing the drone sitting outside the first iris door, as well as the gate room, the main cavern and a view from outside. What surprised Ed was that it could detect the Cartella: although still supposedly cloaked, the display showed a flickering outline of the ship sitting exactly where he'd landed.

'Is that the Cartella?' asked Andy, pointing at the screen in question.

'Yeah.'

'Did they have anti-cloaking—'

Ed kicked Andy's shin and, finding the right control for the screen view, changed it to show the cave entrance.

G'ann had been standing in front of a smaller panel, watching his men in the main chamber on another screen and hadn't noticed what they were talking about. He turned and wandered over.

'What's more,' said Ed, turning his seat to face G'ann and Andy, 'I believe if I spend a bit of time studying this technology, I may be able to learn how to control that gateway.' He turned his seat back again, giving Andy's boot a kick on the way round.

Andy, taking the cue from Ed, started talking to G'ann. 'Could you spare a couple of your soldiers to guard the door upstairs?' he asked and walked towards the lower door.

'I was just thinking that,' said G'ann. 'We don't want anyone coming down here randomly pressing buttons.' He turned to follow.

'I'll go back outside and let everyone know we're having fun, while he finds the controls for the gate,' Ed heard Andy say to G'ann as they ascended the stairs together.

When he was sure G'ann was out of earshot, Ed stood and surveyed the room with his DOVI. He walked over to a lit panel on the wall and, opening a small hatch about halfway down, peered inside to find six tiny black cartridge-like circuit boards, all about the size of a small book. He unclipped the one he wanted and slipped it into his pocket.

Resuming his seat at the desk, he continued to think his way round the different systems, until finally the main gate database became apparent. What he discovered when he accessed the threshold database – as he found it was called – made all the hairs on the back of his neck stand up.

'Oh, bloody hell,' he said to the empty room, his eyes wide with shock.

8

UNDERGROUND THRESHOLD FACILITY – THIRD PLANET, UNCHARTED SYSTEM, SECTOR 97

DAY 184, YEAR 11270, 18:09FC, PCC

'So, you thought you'd swan about having fun and discovering shit, while Cleo, Phil and I are out here going spare with worry, did you?' shouted Linda from up in the Gabriel.

'Sorry, pumpkin,' said Andy, cringing. 'It really wasn't like that at all. This is the first chance—'

'Bollocks. We saw you snatched at gunpoint. We were considering blowing that bloody iris door in. Next time, family comes first and alien shit second, is that clear?'

'Yep, crystal.'

'Good.'

Andy stood meekly in the control cabin of the Cartella.

'And you can wipe that grin off your face as well,' she said.

Phil suddenly sat up straight, and the grin that had lined his face disappeared.

'Shit.'

'Who were the soldiers?'

'The crew from the Vrachos – or most of them anyway.'

'Did they suffer casualties?'

'Yeah, they lost some with the ship and a few more are missing down here. We're going to try to help find them.'

'That's fine. Just keep me informed.'

'Will do,' said Andy. 'Before I go, can you move the Gabriel out of orbit and hide her somewhere on one of those moons?'

'Of course. Why?'

'The alien technology we found down here can see straight through our cloak. Power down and uncloak too; try to pretend you're one of those cannon emplacements or something.'

'Bloody hell, okay. What about the Cartella?'

'I'm going to move her right up to the open doorway to pretend to be the power source from the door system.'

'That's not going to fool anyone for long.'

'No, but it might just stall them long enough to get the hell out of Dodge. This stuff's very old, but judging from the cannon reception, whoever they are, they're not gonna turn up and invite us for a cup of tea and biscuits.'

'Just don't be long. I have a bad feeling about this place and Cleo thinks there's something funny about those three moons.'

'Okay.'

ANDY MOVED the Cartella right up to the hillside doorway and, even after adjusting the skid heights, the ship was still on a bit of a camber.

'Prepare the ship for boarders,' said Andy. 'At some point we're going to have to get up to ninety-seven crew off this rock.'

'It'll take about three trips, at a guess,' said Phil. 'But I suppose we could always tie a few to the drone.'

Andy smiled, left the ship and walked back into the installation to find Ed still sitting in the control room.

'This is a bit bigger than we thought,' he said, looking up from the control desk.

'In what way?'

'That gate upstairs – or threshold as they like to call it – it's just a staff entrance.'

'There's another one?'

'Oh, boy, is there ever,' said Ed. 'You know those three moons up there?'

'Yeah.'

'They form a triangle when you approach them from the right direction.'

'Oh, shit,' said Andy. 'I see where you're going with this. When activated, those three moons create a triangular gateway big enough for starships.'

'Yep, they like to call it a threshold, but you're right. It'd be big enough for a Katadromiko Class Cruiser to go through sideways.'

'Linda said that Cleo was a bit puzzled by those moons.'

'They're artificial. Well, when I say artificial, they're not fake or anything. But the rocks were brought here and placed very carefully.'

The panel suddenly started humming, which made them both jump.

'Did you do that?' asked Andy.

'No, I was out of the system.'

There was a shout from above and, a few moments later, G'ann flew down the stairs and into the control room.

'Did you do that?' he asked, staring at Ed.

'Oh, for fu— Do what?' said Ed, sounding decidedly pissed off.

'Reactivate the gate.'

'No, I didn't. Was anyone caught in the threshold?'

'Is that what it's called now? And, no – no one was in the disappearing zone.'

'It appears that when the system was left for the last time, it remained on a timed activation between the same co-ordinates and has been activating regularly for a very long time.'

'Every four days, by the look of it,' said Andy. 'How long has it been doing that?'

Ed looked back at the panel for a moment.

'Well, I'm not sure of their timescales and how it relates to ours, but it could be several thousand years.'

'What happened to the original owners then?' asked G'ann.

'And why did they stop coming here?' added Andy.

'Another thing you should know – is that the co-ordinates for the destination that's programmed into the system is only one of five hundred and seventy-two other destinations.'

'Oh, crap,' said Andy.

G'ann just stared, his eyes wide at the realisation.

'And, while we're on the subject of surprises, Mr G'ann,' said Ed.

He proceeded to explain the discovery of the second threshold involving the moons.

'Wow,' he said. 'A starship gate. If that activates occasionally too, it could be the reason the science ship disappeared. Does it power up at the same time as this one?'

'It could do, I suppose,' said Ed.

'Oh, shit,' said Andy suddenly, putting his hands on his head. 'What have I done?'

The other two just stared at him for a moment.

'Done what?' said Ed.

'I told Linda to hide the Gabriel up on one of the moons,' he said, his eyes meeting Ed's.

'Shit.'

'Fuck.'

They both launched past G'ann and sprinted up the stairs, through the caverns and back to the Cartella. Phil had the airlock open as they both leapt inside.

'Linda, Cleo, are you there?' shouted Ed.

No reply came.

'I think they've found somewhere really good to hide,' said Phil. 'Their communication signal dropped out a few minutes ago.'

'Shit.'

'Fuck.'

'Did you notice any strange power surges up near the moons when their signal failed?' asked Ed.

'Err, no. I had everything shut down, including the scanning array. Why, what's happened?'

Ed explained what they thought might have gone wrong.

'Shit,' said Phil and fired up the array. Much to their disappointment, he found nothing but empty space.

'What do we do?' asked Andy, looking between Phil and Ed.

'I need to construct a mobile unit to activate these gates,' said Ed. 'One for G'ann so he can safely go through and find his missing crew, and one for us so we can find the Gabriel and maybe even the missing science ship.'

'Okay, what d'you need?' asked Phil.

9

COMMAND CABIN, PCP ATTACK SHIP DAKR MON – DIVISION 2749T

EPOCH 93, SPAN 9371, JUNCTURE 86.9

Mogul Tyuk Baa grimaced as he listened to the report from his array servant. He didn't like enigmas; he liked everything cut and dried, clear and above board.

Turning his command settle to face the now very nervous-looking servant in question, he stood, approached and towered over the array desk. As a prophesied descendant from the original Dakr Caste, he stood head and shoulders above even the tallest junior servant. Having lineage supposedly linked back to the Ancients provided great privilege; from before birth, you were immediately placed on a path to a position of influence.

'Demonstrate,' he ordered.

The array servant replayed the fleeting contact, recorded as the threshold underwent a habitual revolution. It did indeed show a return that vanished as soon as it came, giving the data processor no time to analyse what, or if, anything had actually traversed the threshold.

'Initiate a jump to the threshold division and maintain drive,' the Mogul ordered.

The warship jumped to within one hundred thousand kilometres of the three small moons, which orbited the planet Hunus in Division 2750T. Hunus was the third planet in the system and had never been fully colonised; it was just a small contingent of gatekeepers who resided there. It was considered too distant and its proximity to the threshold was thought to bring unwanted attention to the facility, making it vulnerable to attack.

'Full sweep, maintain drive and circle the planet at this range.'

Tyuk Baa sat back down on his settle, not believing for a minute that there had ever been a ship at all.

Most likely a bit of debris floated in between the moons on the other side and got caught during the revolution, he thought.

He wasn't happy with this assignment at all. Never before in the history of the PCP – or Paragon Coalesce of Planets – had they needed to place a military presence anywhere near the threshold. He believed the assignment belittled his status. But since that ridiculously undefended GDA spy ship had come through a few epochs ago, he believed the Coalesce had become overly paranoid that the threshold had been discovered. After interrogating the crew, however, it seemed as though they didn't have the faintest idea where they were. They all appeared to believe they were still somewhere in their own galaxy and ostensibly had just blundered into the threshold at the exact moment of a revolution.

'Anything showing, servant?' he asked, peering across at the array officer again, already knowing the answer.

'No, my Mogul,' came the short reply.

'Helm, take us over to the fifth planet and engage a high orbit. Remain vigilant, servants. I will be in my chambers.'

The seven foot tall, dark red-skinned Mogul strode out of the command cabin and turned right down a plush, carpeted private hallway. News of his movements had travelled fast as, entering his suite, he found his most recent breeder, semi-naked and standing to attention in the centre of his reception room.

'Immediate succour,' he ordered.

'It is my honour, Mogul,' she replied, bowing, removing her underwear and positioning herself on the cradle.

10

THE STARSHIP GABRIEL – UNKNOWN SPACE

DAY 184, YEAR 11270, 18:29FC, PCC

'What the hell was that?' shouted Linda as almost every piece of the ship telemetry went haywire.

'We just jumped,' said Cleo.

'Who ordered you to do that?'

'It wasn't me. The jump drive wasn't even activated.'

'How can we jump without it?'

'We can't. It was an outside influence.'

'Where the hell are we? I'm getting bugger all from navigation.'

'We were detected on emergence – only for a split second because the auto-cloak snapped on, but someone knows we're here.'

'Shit.'

Linda moved the Gabriel two hundred and fifty thousand kilometres at maximum drive. Sure enough, a large unidentified starship jumped in system and headed straight towards the planet right where they'd just emerged.

'Those moons near the planet look very familiar,' said Cleo. 'In fact, they're identical in size and position. They also seem to have the same defence cannons that we saw last time.'

'It's a great big star gate,' said Linda. 'Battleship size and we were right down its throat when it activated. I just wish navigation would hurry up and reveal where it brought us.'

She watched as the starship moved away, still uncloaked. It seemed to be doing a wide loop around the planet.

'They don't appear to have cloaking technology and, if Andy was right, it wasn't these guys who built the star gate. But they seem to keep a presence near it.'

'I've studied their ship design and it has a similar layout and metal composition to the Andromedan ship we messed up a few months ago. I'm pushing the navigation boundaries out to include nearby galaxies.'

'You think we could have jumped to another galaxy?' asked Linda, feeling a tinge of concern.

'It's not out of the realms of possibility.'

'Bugger. Thank heavens the guys have got the Cartella and not just a shuttle.'

'Andromeda is confirmed,' said Cleo. 'We jumped

more than two point three million light years into a galaxy that's over two and a half times bigger than ours.'

'Shit the bed,' said Linda. 'I believe that makes me the first Milky Way human to travel to another galaxy.'

'Maybe.'

'What do you mean, maybe?'

'What if the Vlepon got caught by the star gate too?'

'What, the science ship?'

'Yep.'

'D'you think that's possible?'

'Well, we did.'

'Did it have a cloak?'

'No.'

'Then if it did come here, we can safely assume that that big bad Andromedan ship would have been here to welcome them. Knowing what we know about them, it wouldn't have gone well for the crew.'

'I'll scan the nearest systems for the ship.'

'Or wreckage.'

'That too.'

'We might as well make ourselves busy while we wait, cuz I'm sure the Cartella will come through that gate, looking for us at some point. It'll just take Ed a while to realise where we went and then to work out how to activate the gate.'

'There's a stationary ship in a system just over six light years away.'

'Is it the Vlepon?'

'Hard to tell. It's a long way off and it's not emitting much. It seems to be in a slowly decaying orbit around a gas giant.'

'Can we jump there without that warship detecting us?'

'Probably not, but if we jump from behind a planet and embed the co-ordinates, that would reduce the likelihood a little.'

Linda waited to see where the Andromedan ship would go and, as soon as she saw it slip into orbit around the fifth planet, she plotted an embedded jump, hid behind the third planet, uncloaked, and jumped the six light years into the new system. Quickly re-cloaking and moving swiftly away from the emergence point, Cleo was able to do a thorough scan of the system, including the inert ship, which was sitting in orbit around the eighth planet.

'It's the Vlepon, Linda.'

'Any life signs?'

'None. There's only minimal life support – the main reactors are in their stasis setting, probably because the engines are showing signs of weapon damage.'

'How long can it sustain orbit?'

'About another fifty-seven hours.'

'Can we tractor it out to a safer distance?'

'Not without uncloaking.'

'Okay, can we dock with it?'

'Normally, yes, but with the severe storms raging on that gas giant, even at the height it is now, it would be impossible to contain structural integrity with just a docking ring. We would still have to use a tractor beam to avoid a rupture.'

'So, I would need to suit up to get onto that ship?'

'Yep, but I would wait a while, just to make sure that warship doesn't appear. I want to make sure that this isn't a trap, either.'

Linda and Cleo waited over an hour before approaching the Vlepon. They had full shields up and closed on the ship from a few kilometres lower in the atmosphere of the gas giant. Initial scans had shown an airlock open on the starboard side – probably where the last of the Andromedan boarding party had left from.

Linda handed the helm over to Cleo and went to her cabin to suit up in one of the GDA's newest Keno suits. You needed to strip naked, clip a metallic collar around your neck and stand on a five-centimetre thick pad that quickly flowed up and around you, forming a completely sealed second skin.

It felt very strange as she walked down the corridor towards the weapons store. The suit flowed around her as if she were coated in thick honey. She selected a

Toufeki rifle and half a dozen mini grenades before making her way to the lower port airlock.

'Are we still clear out there, Cleo?'

'Quiet as a mouse with a secret.'

'Cool, can you open the airlock please?'

When the door disappeared up into the bulkhead, Linda took a deep breath, stepped into the airlock and touched a small recessed button on the underside of the neck ring. A helmet flowed up and around her face, which she found quite unnerving. Realising she could still breathe, even though she was totally cocooned in the liquid suit, eased her anxiety a little.

There was still the problem of stepping out the door into the cold vacuum of space and away from the relative safety of the starship. She'd naturally done her spacewalk training course a few years ago – and many refreshers since – but that was in the vicinity of Armstrong Station, with all of its nearby medical facilities and surrounded by three other astronauts.

As the airlock door sealed behind her, she now found herself alone, wearing nothing but a jar of honey, in another galaxy, about to enter a damaged starship that might contain hidden enemy soldiers, dead bodies or both.

'All set?' asked Cleo.

'As ready as I'll ever be.'

'One rule before you go: if I shout "get back here

now", you immediately run for the airlock. That'll mean there's a ship approaching at speed. Are we clear on that?'

'Very.'

The airlock was purged of atmosphere and the outer door opened. Linda could see the Vlepon's open airlock about fifty metres away. She stood with her back to the inner door and stared at the other ship.

Don't think about it, Linda, she thought to herself. *The more you think about what could go wrong, the more you lose confidence in your skills and abilities*, she remembered her instructor saying.

Lining herself up with the Vlepon's door, she sprinted across the threshold and flung herself out into the void.

The suit controlled her trajectory, using the dozens of tiny mini jets that had been designed into the suit, instead of having to control these with a small handheld device. Cleo had integrated them with the DOVI. All Linda had to do was think her way into the Vlepon's airlock.

Commander Loftt had provided them with override codes for both the Vrachos and the Vlepon, so as Linda arrived into the airlock and was pulled down by the still-operating artificial gravity, she was quickly able to close the outer door and cycle the system. Once the atmosphere had equalised in the lock, she retracted her helmet.

'What the hell is that stink?' she said to herself.

She took one step towards the inner door and wondered why her feet seemed to be slipping on the floor. She looked down and screamed.

11

UNDERGROUND FACILITY – THIRD PLANET, NEW SYSTEM, SECTOR 97

DAY 184, YEAR 11270, 03:37AC, PCC

Ed was on his hands and knees with his head stuck inside one of the many cabinets in the threshold control centre when Andy swung through the door.

'What'ya up to?' Andy asked.

'I'm rummaging around, trying to find the data node that carries the gate co-ordinates. Did you get G'ann's engineers to find me a box for the remote?'

'Yeah, Phil's taken a couple of them back to the Vrachos wreck to see what they can scavenge.'

'That's leaving us a bit exposed. Can we trust them not to commandeer the ship?'

'I thought of that. Phil's got a disabler beam set-up on voice command in the control cabin. If anyone tries anything, they'll find themselves stuck to the cabin wall.'

They finished the conversation as footsteps could be heard descending the stairs. G'ann appeared in the doorway.

'Some of the crew have asked if you could programme the drone to jump back to GDA space and call for a rescue ship.'

'That drone's our only back-up at the moment,' said Ed. 'If the owners of this facility were to turn up, it might just be handy to have around – and anyway, there's plenty of room on the Gabriel to get you all home.'

'But you've lost it.'

'Only a temporary setback,' said Andy, crossing his fingers behind his back.

'We're just worried that you'll disappear through that stargate, or whatever you call it, and never be seen again. Then we're stranded on the farthest fringe of the galaxy with a rapidly dissipating food supply and very little hope of rescue.'

'We understand your concerns, Mr G'ann,' said Ed. 'But at the moment I'm more concerned with getting your crew members back from the other side of that gate. Can we have this conversation after we've at least done that?'

'Okay, but don't you go venturing off with the only available ship without programming that drone with our whereabouts. There are a lot of very frightened people upstairs who'd like to see their families again.'

'We won't. We were sent here to find you, so we're not going to swan off and abandon you. We want to see our families too so we're going to find the rest of your crew, bring the Gabriel back and all go home and have a big party – okay?'

'I'll reassure my crew,' he said, turning and clumping his way back up the stairs.

They both looked at each other for a second.

'We need to be vigilant,' said Ed.

'And careful,' said Andy with a grin.

'Shut up, idiot – you know what I mean.'

'Yeah, I do.'

Sitting on the floor again, Ed looked back into the cabinet under the control panel. There were several hundred data nodes clipped into racks of what looked almost like Bakelite motherboards.

'The technology is hugely advanced,' he said. 'But the engineering is almost steampunk in its design. Look at all these nodes. They seem to have a separate one for every destination. If I could just work out which node was the one on the repeat activation, then we could just use it for the handheld trigger.'

'If it's been activating every four days for thousands of years, surely there must be some sort of discolouration, or something similar, to give it away?'

'It's all solid state and over-engineered to a ridiculous level.'

'Hang on, I've got an idea,' said Andy and disappeared up the stairs at a run. Three minutes later he was back with a small hand-sized unit.

'It's one of their personal scanners,' he said. 'Set to a narrow thermal detection beam. Run it down the rows of nodes and see if one of them is slightly warmer than the others.'

'It's been a while, though.'

'It only needs to be a fraction of a degree warmer.'

Ed started scanning up and down the rows of nodes, hovering the detector for about a second over each one. After scrutinising almost half of them and getting nothing at all, he handed it over to Andy, having become sore from kneeling on the hard floor at an awkward angle.

'It was your idea. You sit down here in the dust and get cramp.'

'Thanks, boss. You're a copybook employer.'

'Bollocks.'

'Is that where you got the cramp?'

'Concentrate on that,' said Ed, pointing at the scanner readout.

'It looks like I was wrong. These things don't produce much heat.'

'Or cool really quickly.'

'What was that?'

'Where?'

'Go back one.'

Andy moved the scanner back to the previous node and, sure enough, the readout changed very slightly.

'Wipe the dust off that one and continue scanning the last few,' said Ed.

After he had scanned the remaining nodes – with no reaction from any of them – he brought the scanner back to the now clean one. It registered a very slight change again.

'Two hundredth of a degree warmer,' said Andy, smiling.

'Yeah, well, don't get too cocky – we don't know it's the right one yet.'

Ed removed the node, along with what he reckoned to be a small transmitter module, and took them both upstairs. They found G'ann sitting back in one of the igloos, eating with a group of his officers.

'Ah, the officers' mess,' said Andy. 'Is the bar open?' He received six blank expressions in return.

'I believe GDA naval ships are dry, Andrew.'

'Shouldn't be allowed,' said Andy. 'I'll not be accepting the King's shilling then.'

The blank faces in the circle remained.

'Please excuse my colleague,' said Ed. 'He has humour management issues.'

'Did you find what you were looking for?' asked G'ann after an awkward pause.

'We hope so,' said Andy. 'Are the engineers back from the Vrachos yet?'

'No,' said G'ann and continued eating.

They looked at each other, nodded and went back outside the igloo.

'They're a bloody moody lot, aren't they?' said Ed as they walked towards the exit tunnel.

'Loftt's about the only one I've met with a personality and a sense of humour.'

'He's always pissed. That's why.'

'Yeah, good man, that. He's almost as bad as us.'

'To be honest,' said Ed, 'I don't know if I want the destroyer crew crammed into the Gabriel all the way back to GDA space.'

'Me neither. Perhaps we should reconsider sending the drone back for a recovery ship.'

'It would leave us vulnerable, though, when we go through that gate.'

'Only until we find the Gabriel. There's a load more in the starboard hangar.'

'You're right, of course. But I'm sure the Andromedans are watching the other end of that gate now, even if they weren't before. When it opens out of sequence for the first time in millennia, it's bound to ring alarm bells.'

'Yeah, for all we know, the whole invasion fleet could be parked up, twiddling their thumbs just waiting for some live firing drills.'

They walked down the exit tunnel in silence for a few moments, thinking.

'Shit. I hope Linda and Cleo are okay,' said Andy, finally.

'They're tough, they're smart and they've got a big ship round them,' said Ed. 'They'll have cloaked and hidden somewhere. The Andromedans won't have a clue where to look.'

'But this technology can see through the cloak.'

'The technology from an ancient civilisation does, yes. But the Andromedans don't seem to have found it. They never discovered that control room. They just used the gate as it opens every four days. That reminds me –' Ed retrieved the anti-cloak data node from his pocket '– I must hide this on the Cartella.'

'Is that the anti-cloaking software?'

'I hope so.'

'Are you going to give it to the GDA?'

'No.'

'No?'

'I think it would unbalance our region of the galaxy. It's been relatively peaceful for a long time, because everyone has the same stuff. If the GDA had this, peacekeeping might go out the window for a while and be replaced with a little empire building.'

'I hadn't thought of that. Are we going to install it?'

'Damn right. It'll be our little secret, though. No one will know – not Dewey, not the President. No one, okay?'

'Okay, at least we know we'll only use it in defence.'

Ed hid the node again as they emerged from the tunnel. It was beginning to get dark as they stood outside the entrance. The planet's sun had dropped behind the mountains, which made it quite gloomy. They noticed an increase in insect noise, and a distant howling noise made them both jump.

'Shit, there's animals here,' said Andy. 'And we're unarmed.'

'Throw a rock at it,' said Ed, smiling and giving Andy a small pebble.

'You're a real dick hea—'

The sound of the Cartella's antigravity drives stopped him mid-sentence and they watched as Phil landed as best he could on the hill slope again. The airlock opened and the two GDA engineers jumped down.

'Did you find anything useful?' asked Ed as they neared.

'Can you do anything with this?' said one of the engineers, handing over a box of various electronic parts, small box casings and a collection of hand tools.

'Yep,' said Andy, rummaging inside.

'Tell G'ann we'll give him a shout when we're ready to test the remote.'

The engineers nodded and disappeared into the tunnel. Phil stood in the airlock doorway and waved.

'Did they give you any trouble?' Ed asked.

'Not really. They wanted to know a lot about the Gabriel, though. How many crew, what security we had on board – that kind of thing.'

'Did you tell them anything?'

'No, of course not – none of their bloody business.'

'Good, well done, Phil. Okay, let's get to work.'

It took them the best part of three hours to knock together a bit of a Heath Robinson affair. The outside shell was made from an old polymer drive activator housing. It looked like a giant garage remote with just one button. Once completed, Ed programmed the Cartella's replicator to scan the contraption and add it to its database. He then pressed 'reproduce' and the system made a perfect copy.

'Don't you want to test it before you copy it?' asked Andy.

'I don't want someone disappearing through that gate, never to return, with the only one.'

'Okay, but will it operate both the gates?'

'I hope so – but I've restricted the range down to about fifty kilometres so it'll only operate the nearest gate. I don't want that big gate to keep opening and closing as we're testing the remote. That would really get the Andromedans' attention if they're watching the other side of the starship gate.'

'Good idea, Batman.'

After getting some sleep, they reproduced toasted bacon sandwiches and coffee for breakfast and went to give G'ann the good news.

There was an early morning chill in the air, even though they were near the equator. Phil had reproduced warm jackets for them and they pulled them tightly around themselves as they walked through the tunnel towards the large cavern. They found G'ann in his igloo, similarly wrapped up in an emergency blanket from one of the lifeboats, huddled around a small heater.

'Have you succeeded with the activator?' he asked as soon as he saw them.

'And good morning to you too,' said Andy sarcastically.

'I'm more interested in the fate of my crew members than social graces,' grumbled G'ann.

'Well, in answer to your question,' said Ed, 'we hope so.' And he showed G'ann the box.

'Good. I've put together a team of four to go through with you. One officer and three soldiers.'

Ed and Andy looked at each other with raised eyebrows.

'You want us to go through too?' asked Ed.

'There are mutterings amongst my crew that you're not a rescue mission and you're only here to secure this gate technology for the Theos. If you take an active part in the rescue, it would dissipate that rumour.'

'Okay, I'll go,' said Ed. 'Andy and Phil can stay here.'

Andy looked at Ed with a worried frown. 'Are you sure?'

'If we're not back by sundown today, take the Cartella through the big gate. The planet this gate goes to is most probably on the other side of that one too – you can rescue us that way.'

'But what if the remote only works one way? We'll all be stuck in Andromeda then.'

'Somewhere on that planet will be the copy of this control room – probably hidden near the gate again – so I'm sure we can rig a return activator if this one doesn't work.'

Andy didn't look altogether convinced, but nodded

anyway. 'Just make sure you're armed and have enough supplies for a few days. Just in case.'

'That's already been taken care of,' said G'ann. 'You'll have an inflatable habitat, gen-pack, heater and enough food for four days. Just in case,' he added, looking at Andy.

'Well, I suppose we'd better test this remote,' said Ed. 'It's all well and good making all these plans, but if this doesn't work –' he held up the box in his hand '– then we're royally screwed.'

They all gathered in the smaller gate cavern and stood well back from the disappearing zone.

'What are your names, by the way?' Ed asked the rescue team members.

The officer took a pace forward. 'I'm Lieutenant Zeerd, sir,' he said. 'And these are Corporals Haad'r, Jackt and Private Lendr'y.' They all stood to attention and nodded as their names were said.

'Good morning, gentlemen,' said Ed, nodding at them in return. 'Before we go anywhere, let's give this gate a test run.'

'Everybody clear.' He lifted up the remote and depressed the button. The now familiar rumble came from the gate and a vision of trees, grass and blue sky was visible for a split second before it was gone again. What they weren't expecting was the large dog-like animal standing under the gate. Everyone froze for a moment before it bared its teeth; all the hackles on the back of its neck stood up and it gave a deep growl.

'What the—' was all G'ann managed to get out before the crackle of an energy weapon silenced the growling. The smell of damp dog and singed hair filled the cavern. They all slowly approached the now prone animal.

'Did you kill it?' asked Andy, looking at Jackt who was lowering his weapon and had been the first to react.

'No, sir. Our weapons are set on medium stun; it'll be out for a couple of hours.'

The beast reminded Ed of a Tasmanian devil, only it was the size of a large bear and had bigger teeth.

'Are these loners or pack hunters?' asked Zeerd, looking around the group. 'I wouldn't want to appear amongst a large pack of them.'

'I think you'd better provide me with a weapon too,' said Ed.

The four members of the rescue party all looked at G'ann, who paused before nodding at Zeerd.

'Lendr'y, issue the captain a rifle,' ordered Zeerd.

'Yes, sir,' he said and disappeared back down to the main cavern.

Lendr'y returned a few moments later with another weapon. Ed felt a little more secure with a fully-charged rifle in his hands. He turned it over to check it was set to stun and nodded at G'ann.

The rescue party stayed in the zone, all keeping one eye on the sleeping beast, while everyone else stood back.

'See you in a few hours,' said Ed, looking at Andy.

'It's a date,' said Andy.

Ed lifted the remote again and the four soldiers all knelt in a circle, facing out with their weapons raised. Ed depressed the button again.

12

THE STARSHIP GABRIEL – ANDROMEDAN GALAXY, UNKNOWN SYSTEM

DAY 184, YEAR 11270, 23:17FC, PCC

'What the hell is that?' called Cleo. 'I can't tell from here.'

Linda stood with her back pushed against the airlock wall, trying to get her heart rate down by taking deep breaths.

'It's blood. The floor is covered in frozen trails of blood, which lead into the ship – and there's a severed arm just inside the door.'

'Make sure your weapon is on full stun with the safety off and be as quiet as possible,' said Cleo.

She sidestepped around the arm, noticing that the small hand had painted nails.

'It was one of the female crew, Cleo.'

Linda continued down the corridor, following the blood trail, trying not to walk in it. It led to what was a recreation room in the centre of the ship, directly behind the bridge. The plan of the ship Linda had studied before coming on board had shown the cabins were all on a lower deck. Just the bridge, recreation room, kitchen and dining area were on this level, along with the captain's day room, which was off the starboard side of the bridge.

She checked the kitchens and dining area first as those were nearest. There was no sign of blood or crew in either. Next, she followed the blood trail through onto the bridge. The ten crew stations were all unmanned and the control panels were alive with flashing red lights.

'Bloody hell, Cleo, the smell's worse in here.'

'Did you find any crew?'

'No, the blood trail leads into the captain's private office.'

'That's a dead end. Be careful.'

Linda tiptoed over to the starboard-side door with her rifle up. The door control had been destroyed by what looked like gunfire. She knew the captain's door code but was unable to enter it as the keypad was destroyed.

She noticed, however, that some of the wiring inside the panel had been stripped away; prodding it with the muzzle of her weapon created a spark and the door opened.

She reeled back as the air inside the room hit her. The stench made her retch several times and she paused until she regained control over her gag reflex. Standing back for a moment and letting her racing heart rate settle down a little, she poked her head round the door, one hand holding her weapon and the other held to her nose. The reason for the smell immediately became apparent. A male crew member had been trussed up against the wall of the room, his hands tied up to a ventilation duct near the ceiling. His dead eyes stared out across the room and a thick, blood-soaked coil of rope lay at his feet.

Linda stared at the body and suddenly realised exactly what she was looking at. This time there was no holding it back: she threw up and backed out of the room as fast as she could.

'Oh, shit, Cleo – they gutted him.' She staggered over and back into the recreation room again.

'It was the captain,' said Cleo. 'Facial recognition confirms it. Linda, I want you to get off this ship. The only heat signatures are from the equipment that's still running.'

'No, Cleo. I have to make sure there's no one left. I'll search the cabins and then Engineering before I come back.'

'Just be quick. I don't like it here.'

'I will.'

Linda checked to see if the elevator was still functioning. It came up from below and the door opened.

It was clean, which she found quite a relief. As the door reopened on the lower deck, she noticed a lot of personal possessions had been strewn around the corridors.

'They must have searched through everything, Cleo. I wonder what they were after?'

'Personal computers, probably – anything with GDA technology they can steal. We already know they're a bit behind us on most things, which is why they were having to infiltrate the GDA's fleet.'

She searched each cabin in turn, finding only trashed rooms and, noticeably, no electronic devices.

'I think you're right, Cleo. There's nothing down here. I'll check Engineering.'

The rear third of the ship housed all the systems involved in the running of the vessel: power supply, propulsion, navigation, life support, communications, scanning arrays, et cetera. When she arrived, she was surprised to find the bulkhead door to Engineering open. Again, she crept forward, checking each work space and corridor. The result was the same. Anything resembling a computer, or computer hardware, had been ripped out and taken. She reached the back of the ship, went across to the port-side corridor and started working her way forward again.

'Linda, a ship,' shouted Cleo. 'Get back here now. Run!'

She sprinted up the corridor, heading straight for the elevator. 'I'm on my way, Cleo. Get as close as you can.'

'Shit, it's too late, Linda. They jumped in really close. Hide somewhere near a heat source. They're already here. I'm having to move away.'

Linda stopped and turned around. She scanned her surroundings for hiding places.

'Crap,' she shouted. 'Where the hell can I go?'

'In here,' said a little voice behind her.

Linda nearly jumped out of her skin. 'Who's there? Where are you?'

A section of wall clicked open and a young girl's face appeared.

'If they find you, they'll kill you like the others. Hide in here.'

Linda didn't hesitate. She jumped over the internal frame and into a narrow gap behind the wall. The girl closed the wall panel with a *click* and beckoned Linda to follow. She dropped onto her hands and knees and wriggled though into another cavity and slid up onto the top of something solid and warm.

'It's the reactor,' she said, pointing down. 'It hides our heat signature.'

Linda looked around. The girl had made quite a comfortable nest in there: there were a few empty food containers, several bottles of water and a personal computer tablet.

The girl saw her looking at the tablet. 'I can see what they're doing on the ship's cameras,' she said.

Linda cringed, thinking what the girl must have witnessed. 'What's your name?' she asked, changing the subject.

'Rayl.'

'Is there anyone else?'

'No, just me. The others are all dead.'

'How old are you?'

'Seventeen.'

'So you're not a working member of the crew then?'

'No, my father was the captain,' she said, dropping her gaze, her voice breaking. A tear dropped into her lap.

Linda shuffled over and hugged her tight.

'Have you run out of food?' Linda asked after a moment's silence as she noticed the food containers again.

'No, there's enough in the store to last years.'

'How did you find this hiding place?'

'My father,' she said. 'He made the wall panel into a door and told me to run here if the ship ever got boarded. He was a chief engineer before becoming captain and knew the dark matter reactor would hide my thermal signature.'

'He was right about that,' said Linda.

'He was right about a lot of things, I've come to realise – sitting here all this time.'

'Did you give him a hard time – like most teenage daughters?' she asked with a wry smile.

'Yeah, I just can't tell him I'm sorry now.'

'What about your mum?'

'She was a bridge officer on the Katadromiko 37.'

'Oh, shit. I'm so sorry, Rayl.'

'That was the reason my father agreed to go on this exploration mission. It took his mind off the loss of Mum.'

'And the reason you're on the ship with him.'

'Yeah.'

There was a pause in conversation for a moment as they both felt the ship judder slightly.

'They're here,' said Rayl, grabbing hold of Linda again, the fear showing in her eyes.

'You know you're safe here. As soon as they're gone, I'll take you over to my ship.'

'We have to remain completely still. If they find us, they'll rape and kill us too.'

'Rape?'

'He raped all the women before killing them,' Rayl whispered.

'Oh, crap, no. Who's he, exactly?'

'They call him the Mogul. Even his crew are

terrified of him. He seems to think he's some sort of living god, a direct descendant of the Ancients or something like that.'

'How d'you know all this?'

She pointed at the tablet and Linda noticed her hand was shaking.

'The conversation he had with my father before he killed him. He was raping and torturing the women in front of him, trying to get the GDA cloaking technology.'

'But this ship doesn't have it.'

'No. He wouldn't believe it wasn't on a database or something.'

'What about the rest of the male crew?'

'They were taken aboard the alien ship and I've not seen them since.'

'So, they could still be alive on that ship?'

'Maybe.'

'Cleo, are you getting all this?' Linda whispered.

'Yes, I'm afraid so.'

'Who's Cleo?' asked Rayl.

'My ship's computer. She can see and hear everything I do.'

'Wow, and it's semi-sentient?'

'You'll see when you meet her.'

'Semi-sentient, my arse,' said Cleo.

'I'll tell her,' said Linda calmly.

'Tell me what?'

'Cleo says she'll make a nice cabin ready for you.'

'The ship's being pulled out to a higher orbit,' said Cleo.

'I wonder why?'

'Why, what?' asked Rayl, looking perplexed. 'What are they doing?'

'Moving the ship to a higher orbit.'

'That's the second time they've done that.'

'How do you know that?'

'My father insisted I learnt stuff while I was out here. I've been studying for my basic navigation exam so I had the ship's navigation computer reflected on my tablet.'

'Okay, but why would they keep doing that?'

'It's bait,' said Cleo. 'They're waiting for the rescue ship. Keeping this crippled vessel in a decaying orbit would attract attention.'

'Of course,' said Linda.

Rayl stared at Linda with a quizzical expression.

'They're using this ship as bait, Rayl. They're hoping a rescue ship turns up and lowers its cloak to enable the tractor beam.'

'And they jump in close with all guns blazing.'

'Yep.'

Rayl shuffled over and picked up her tablet. 'Let's have a look at what they're up to.' She switched through the camera views until she found movement. 'Oh, shit.' She held the screen up so Linda could see.

Several PCP soldiers were ripping the ship apart. Even the wall panels were being dragged off.

'If they do that down here, we're dead,' said Rayl, the fear returning to her voice.

Linda thought for a moment. 'I think I have an idea,' she said. 'We need to swap clothes, though.'

'Linda, what are you doing?' asked Cleo, sounding worried.

'Cleo, can you dig up everything the GDA knows about the PCP, especially the personnel details of Captain Fleoha Utz, aka Quixia? I know they gave us most of what they got out of her. And, Rayl, I need you to put this suit on.'

Linda touched an icon on the sleeve of the suit and felt a sharp sting on her upper arm.

'Ouch, what was that, Cleo?'

'If you're about to do what I think you're going to do, can I register my complete disapproval of this plan?'

'You can. You can disapprove all you like but I'm not leaving this young girl at the mercy of that psycho.'

'I've just injected you with something I've been holding in reserve for emergencies. You'll know what it is in a few minutes.'

The suit flowed back into a small soft pad and Linda stood naked in the tiny alcove next to the reactor. Rayl joined her, standing in her underwear. She handed over her rather smelly ship suit.

'And the rest,' said Linda.

Rayl hesitated. Linda realised she was a seventeen-year-old girl. She wasn't used to stripping naked in front of strangers.

'Okay, I'll turn my back,' she said. 'Stand on this pad when you're done.'

Linda heard the suit deploy a moment later.

'Oh, wow,' said Rayl. 'This feels really weird. It's like I'm wrapped in jelly.'

'You'll get used to it.'

Linda removed her collar and attached it around Rayl's neck, showing her the small icon on the underside to activate the helmet and seal the suit.

'As soon as I leave you, hide around the back of the reactor and engage the helmet. You'll be able to converse with Cleo then. I'm hoping she'll be able to dock with this ship now it's been dragged into a higher orbit. If she can't, throw yourself towards the Gabriel's open airlock and she'll pull you inside.'

'What, throw myself into space?' Rayl asked, looking decidedly dubious. 'I don't think I could do that.'

'You won't have a choice. Just shut your eyes and jump.'

A loud crash from nearby made them both jump.

'They're in Engineering,' whispered Linda. 'You'd better hide.'

Rayl grabbed her into a hug and held on for what seemed like way too long.

'Hide,' she said again. 'I'll see you on the Gabriel soon.'

The young girl slowly let her go and, with a look of real fear on her face, she climbed back up onto the reactor cover and disappeared amongst the plumbing at the back.

Linda quickly slipped on the soiled ship suit, wrinkling her nose at the rather ripe smell.

'Here's the GDA's file on Quixia,' said Cleo. 'Extracted from her before we left. I've also included everything they learnt about the PCP Battle Cruiser Krawth. You don't need to remember all this as I can speak their language through you, using her speech pattern.'

Reams of information dropped through Linda's near vision and she speedread it as fast as she could.

'When I'm talking to them through you, I want you to concentrate on keeping your facial muscles slack and using your body language to back up what I'm saying. The translation will be in your ears. Try not to look too wooden.'

'Okay, thanks, Cleo.'

'Are you sure you want to do this?' she asked. 'I'm

rapidly running out of crew and I don't like being on my own.'

'I don't plan on being gone for long and, anyway, you'll have Rayl with you shortly, and—'

Another loud crash nearby stopped her.

'They're getting close, Linda. If you're going to do this, it'd better be now.'

She sidestepped her way back to the wall panel door, took a deep breath and threw it open. There was a soldier trying to rip an inspection hatch open about five metres back down the corridor. To say he was surprised was an understatement. His eyes widened with shock as he watched Linda step out from the hidden passage. Dropping his crowbar and fumbling for his weapon, he tripped over a section of wall panel lying on the floor.

'When you've quite finished pissing around,' shouted Cleo through Linda. 'I am Agent 762 of the PCP Vanguard Division. You will take me to the Mogul immediately.'

13

UNKNOWN PLANET

DAY 185, YEAR 11270, 05:19FC, PCC

It was very cold, overcast and drizzling. That was the first thing Ed noticed as they appeared, wherever they were. It was a small clearing, surrounded by tall fir-like trees. They all stopped and donned their coats. The gate arch stood in the centre with a lush green grass extending to the tree line. The soldiers moved out cautiously and checked the immediate area. No more giant Tasmanian devils rushed them. As he dragged the unconscious animal off the gate's activation area, Ed hoped they were loners and this one was the only one they were going to meet.

'Over here,' shouted Corporal Jackt, pointing at the ground. Ed and Zeerd trotted over to the tree line to see what he'd found.

An arrow made from trimmed tree branches pointed to a trail leading into the forest.

'I hope they kept this up,' said Ed. 'And they haven't strayed too far.'

'They had no supplies or weapons,' said Zeerd. 'Their first priority would have been shelter, followed by water and then food.'

Two soldiers, Jackt and Lendr'y, took point, with Ed, Zeerd and Haad'r as rear guard. They cautiously followed the trail that led steadily downhill.

It was noisy inside the forest, with bird and animal calls coming from all directions. After walking a few hundred metres they could hear the sound of running water and, rounding a bend in the trail, they found a large pool fed by a tall, narrow waterfall coming from a high rock face. Ed walked over to the edge and stepped out on a couple of protruding rocks. Cupping his hands, he collected some water from the waterfall.

'Wait,' shouted Zeerd as he ran over, extracting a small device from one of several pockets in his fatigues.

'I need to test it first,' he said, dripping a little of the water onto a projecting spur then pressing a green icon.

After a second or two, the unit pinged like a microwave.

'Dinner's ready,' said Ed.

'What?' asked Zeerd, looking at Ed strangely.

'Never mind. What's the prognosis, chef?'

'It's drinkable. A little heavy in magnesium, calcium

and iron, with fourteen strains of bacteria. But nothing that'll prove harmful.'

Ed tasted it gingerly. 'A little earthy,' he said. 'But okay.' He gave everyone a thumbs-up. Again, no one recognised the Earth gesture and he received a collection of blank faces in return.

'We will continue,' said Zeerd, pointing at the path which continued through the trees.

After another fifteen minutes on the winding trail – this time going up the other side of the valley – they found themselves at the top of the waterfall and were able to look down at the pool, some hundred metres below. The view was getting better too the higher they went: a green ocean of tree tops, stretching as far as the eye could see.

'Perhaps the path is made by animals?' said Lendr'y. 'Coming for the water.'

'I don't think so,' replied Zeerd. 'Some of that trail looked as though it had been cut back to allow humans to walk through upright.'

Haad'r shrugged and Ed noticed that he ignored the sniggers from the two corporals.

'It could be animals,' said Ed confidently. 'On Earth, there are plenty of tall mammals that cut paths through forest to their regular watering holes.'

Zeerd, Jackt and Haad'r all looked at each other, shaking their heads. Lendr'y gave Ed a grin and a thumbs-up behind his back, ensuring the others didn't see.

Almost as one, they all turned away from the view to continue up the trail. As they did so, a young girl rounded the next corner, about thirty metres away, walking in their direction. Everyone froze. The soldiers reacted first and swung their weapons around, but they were too late. The girl dropped what looked like water containers to the ground and sprinted off in the direction she'd come from, disappearing back around the bend before they could subdue her with a stun shot.

'Shit,' said Zeerd. 'Follow her. Don't let her issue a warning.'

The three junior ranks thundered after her and, in a matter of seconds, they also vanished around the corner. Ed and Zeerd jogged after them, neither of them attempting to aid in the chase.

Ten minutes later, Ed could see the three soldiers up ahead, puffing heavily after their impromptu uphill sprint. They were crouching at the side of the track and, as Ed approached, he could clearly see that the trail ended here – thankfully with another stick arrow pointing to the side of the hill.

'Where is she?' asked Zeerd as he strutted up, barely out of breath.

'She's in there, sir,' said Jackt. 'Where the arrow points and the door's locked.'

'Don't be stupid, Corporal. How can you lock a cave?' said Zeerd as he rounded the corner, stopped dead and stared at the cave mouth.

'Like that, sir,' said Jackt, smirking and pointing at what looked like an old spaceship airlock door set into the hillside.

'What the...' muttered Zeerd. 'How the hell did that get here?'

Ed walked up to the door. It was obviously old, very old, and had faded lettering beside the recessed control panel. He squinted at the writing and could just make out the word, 'EPEIGON'.

'What does Epeigon mean?' he asked, looking round at Zeerd.

'Emergency,' said Zeerd, appearing quite baffled. 'It's an emergency evacuation airlock door from an old GDA ship.'

'Bloody hell. How old?'

'This design of door hasn't been used for ages – hundreds of years, I guess.'

'That's just weird,' said Ed as he secretly concentrated his DOVI on the electronic lock.

They all heard the click and whirring of the release mechanism. Ed smiled to himself and pretended to be surprised at the door opening. He grabbed the handle and pulled at the door. The soldiers behind him brought their weapons up and spread out either side of the airlock. It opened a lot easier than he expected and he staggered back, nearly falling over. The two corporals piled in, guns up, followed by Zeerd and Lendr'y. Ed decided he'd better prepare himself too, so he swung his rifle off his back and, again, checked it was set to stun before following the others.

The passageway led straight into the hillside for about thirty metres. The walls and ceiling were mostly white panelling that could have come from an old spaceship too and the lighting was electric but very dim. Small sections of the passage were tunnelled stone and the floor was bare ground.

At the end of the initial passageway was a T-junction. The left passage disappeared into darkness, but the right continued lit for seventy or eighty metres with several left turns heading deeper into the hill. They went right, meeting no one, but Ed noticed that the further they went, the smell he had detected, like pickled cabbage, became stronger.

'I have a feeling we're being herded,' said Ed, glancing at Zeerd.

'It crossed my mind too,' answered Zeerd as it became evident only one of the passages leading off to the left was lit.

'Are you thinking what I'm thinking?'

'Gentlemen,' said Zeerd. 'Lights on. We take the next unlit passage at double speed.'

'Sir,' came the reply in triplicate, followed by powerful rifle lights flickering on, illuminating the dim passage with bright, white light.

'Go,' said Zeerd and they all ran past the lit corridor and took the next left. It was only a short passage and ended with another ship door. This time it was an interior bulkhead.

Ed felt the lock mechanism with his DOVI to find it already unlocked. Lendr'y arrived first and hit the handle and slammed his shoulder into the middle of the door. Ed wasn't sure who looked more surprised: Lendr'y, who flew through the door as if it wasn't there, or the old man on the other side, who'd just pulled the door towards him. Both ended up in a heap of arms, legs and bad language, on the floor of what looked like a large communal dining hall.

There were around thirty men in the room, most sitting and eating. The soldiers spread out into a semicircle with guns at their shoulders, attempting to cover the whole room.

Ed noticed the fear on the men's faces as they stopped what they were doing and sat very still. They all seemed to be wearing old, shabby uniforms, which showed signs of multiple patches and repairs.

'Who's in charge here?' shouted Zeerd.

Nobody moved; nobody spoke. Ed walked over to the nearest table, which contained two men. They both shrank away as he approached. He shouldered his rifle and, putting his hands up in a placating manner, sat down with them. He smiled at the two men and looked over at Zeerd.

'Do we have a mobile universal translator?' he asked, realising he couldn't use his internal DOVI translator without giving away his hidden technology.

Zeerd nodded and, again, rummaged in the pockets in the front of his jacket, extracting a small device and handed it to Ed.

'You're Inspector bloody Gadget, you are,' said Ed, taking the translator and placing it on the table in front of the two men.

They both looked at it with renewed trepidation.

'My name is Edward – Edward,' he repeated, pointing at himself. He then pointed at each member of his party and said their names twice. He then made the sign of a talking mouth with his hand and pointed at the nearest of the men and then at the translator.

'Breex,' he said, nervously, pointing at himself.

'Trkors,' said the other man a bit more confidently.

Ed made the talking hand gesture again, signalling them to talk more, hoping the intuitive translator would start to do its stuff.

Trkors did most of the talking and seemed to get the idea. After a few minutes, the odd word started to be recognisable, until suddenly the translator produced a sentence.

'What clique you from? Who is Mogul?'

'GDA,' said Ed. 'In the next galaxy. What is Mogul?'

The soldiers suddenly stiffened and renewed their gun-wielding stance as a small man in a uniform three sizes too big for him rushed into the room, dragging a young girl along with him – the same girl they'd seen earlier on the trail. As soon as he saw the guns, he slowed, pushed the girl, who looked to be a young teenager, out in front and approached Ed.

'For Mogul,' he said with tears running down his face. 'Good breeder, very young – all we have.'

Ed looked horrified and glanced down at Trkors.

'He give daughter for Mogul,' he said. 'For breeder.'

A scream came from the far end of the room and a woman sprinted in. One of the men at the doorway caught her and swung her round into the wall, pinning her there as she shouted and screamed. This set the girl off, who started wailing and then urinated, creating a puddle at her feet.

Ed looked at Trkors with an expression of disbelief.

'I don't understand any of this, Trkors,' said Ed. 'We're not from this galaxy. I don't know what a Mogul is.'

Breex whispered something into Trkors's ear. Ed looked at him with a puzzled expression this time.

'He thinks it's trick,' said Trkors. 'If you're not from Mogul, then what you want?'

'We're looking for our three friends,' said Ed. 'They came this way a few days ago.'

'The engineer?'

'Yes, one of them was an engineer.'

Ed realised that the sobbing father and daughter were still waiting. He stood and the girl shrank back away from him with complete terror in her eyes. He reached out and took her hand. She was shaking with fear. He gently placed the girl's hand in her father's and pointed at the door.

'Go home. No Mogul.'

The girl's father mumbled something that the translator didn't pick up, grabbed his daughter and fled, collecting the girl's hysterical mother on their way out the door.

Ed sat back down with Trkors and Breex.

'The father said thank you,' said Trkors.

'Good,' said Ed. 'We really need to talk more.'

'Forget talking,' said Zeerd. 'We're here for the chief and his two junior engineers. Ask him where they are.'

'They're hunting,' said Trkors, smiling, and pointing

behind him. 'The engineer built electric hunting spear. He out on plains for test.'

'Does that answer your question?' said Ed, glancing up at Zeerd. 'Can you ask your men to lower their weapons now please?'

Zeerd didn't look best pleased at being told what to do, but he looked up and surveyed the room. Seemingly finding nothing awry, he turned and ordered his men to stand easy, which only meant bringing their rifles off their shoulders and holding them across their chests. It did look a lot less threatening, though, and the atmosphere in the room calmed noticeably.

'When are they due back?' asked Ed.

'Tonight.'

'What time of day is it now?'

Trkors looked at Ed with a strange expression.

'It's morning. How can you not know?' he asked.

'Because we came through the gate and I have no idea what time of day it was on this planet when we arrived.'

'Why are you lying to us?' said Breex, speaking for the first time in ages. 'We know the gate's habitual revolution isn't for another two days.'

'I operated the gate myself.'

'What with?'

'This.' Ed slipped his hand into his pocket and produced the remote to show them.

Both Trkors and Breex sat, staring, their eyes wide with the revelation of what Ed had just said. Finally, Breex slid quietly off the bench seat and whispered to the men at the next table. The level of whispering rose as the message spread around the room.

'What did you just do?' asked Zeerd, looking nervous as the whole room stood as one.

They turned to face Ed and knelt, heads bowed.

'Oh, shit,' said Ed. 'Get up, guys. It's just a box of sparks, nothing special.'

Trkors looked up at Ed. 'For nine thousand years, we've been the gatekeepers, watching over the gateway to the dry world. Not even the Moguls have the power to operate the gate at will; only a true descendant of the Ancients would have that knowledge and virtuosity.'

'We're not Ancients – so can everyone get up and finish their breakfast now?'

Trkors stood, much to the chagrin of those around him, and bowed at Ed.

'May I converse with you, my Mogul?' he asked, now averting his eyes.

'Of course,' said Ed. 'Sit with me, look me in the eye and stop this silly grovelling.'

'Thank you, my Mogul.'

'I'm not your Mogul,' said Ed. 'And, anyway, from what I've heard, Moguls aren't very nice people.'

'They're our gods,' said Breex, joining Ed at the table. 'We cannot question—'

'Direct descendants from the Ancients,' interrupted Trkors.

'These Ancients you speak of, what happened to them? I mean, they were hugely advanced, with huge starship gateways leading to over five hundred locations.'

Breex and Trkors looked puzzled.

'The gate only goes to one place,' said Trkors.

'The rocky planet with the broken spaceships,' added Breex.

Ed realised they had no idea there were more destinations. 'Is that where you collected all these bits of spacecraft?' he said, pointing at the bulkhead door they'd entered through.

They both nodded.

'We used to go through regularly,' said Breex. 'But over the millennia, there seemed to be less and less to utilise.'

'And to be honest,' said Trkors, 'there's only so many bits of spaceship that prove useful to us and we've got loads.'

'Okay, but what about my original question? What happened to the Ancients?'

'Our scriptures state that a previously unknown human race just appeared with a fleet of powerful starships and systematically wiped them out,' said Breex. 'The few survivors became the Moguls we know today.'

'What happened to the victors?'

'We have no knowledge,' said Trkors.

Ed stared at the pair of them. 'Don't you find that a little strange?' he asked.

They both squirmed in their seats and glanced at each other.

'As I mentioned before,' said Breex, 'we cannot question a Mogul or the scriptures.'

'But you must have some doubts – you don't win a war, claim half a galaxy and then bugger off. It all sounds very convenient for the Moguls. How many of them are there?'

'Six hundred and sixty-six,' said Trkors. 'They each command a region; their numbers are strictly limited to the number of regions in the PCP.'

'By whom? Surely any offspring become Moguls too.'

'Only one from each,' said Trkors.

'They mate several times a day with multiple breeders,' said Breex. 'The breeders are selected carefully from the best stock within their system. If and when a breeder becomes pregnant – which is rare – they're scanned. If the offspring is a male, they're sent to a special maternity resort on a planet called

Arus'Gan where their diet and fitness is regimentally controlled.'

'But there'd be more than one male offspring with all the mating they do?'

'No, they only very rarely conceive and only perfection is allowed to survive.'

'And if the child is a female?'

Breex and Trkors exchanged a glance again. Both seemed uncomfortable answering the question.

'Killed,' said Trkors, almost whispering, after a long pause.

'They kill the child just because it's female?' said Ed, looking shocked.

'Both,' said Breex.

'Both what?'

'Breeder and child.'

Ed felt nauseous. He looked up to find all the men in the room were standing. They bowed as he surveyed the room, not one of them making eye contact. He looked back at Trkors and Breex. 'So, why did the man immediately offer his daughter to the Mogul? She couldn't have been more than twelve. You didn't know what we wanted.'

'It's the rules,' said Breex. 'If the Mogul sends his warriors, it's only for one thing – and our Mogul likes them young.'

'She's actually eleven,' said Trkors. 'If we sent him

anyone older, he'd just kill her and her family for disrespecting him.'

'Let me get this straight,' said Ed. 'Your glorious Mogul is a psychopathic, paedophilic mass murderer. Does that about sum it up?'

They both cringed at the statement and a shocked murmur arose from the nearby tables that were within earshot.

'If you are a living god, you can do what you like,' said a nervous Breex.

'We've known no other way for thousands of years,' said Trkors. 'And to be honest, our present Mogul is one of the more affable ones.'

'Can't wait to meet him,' said Ed. He felt a chill run down his spine as he realised that, for the first time in his life, he was actually planning to kill someone.

'What do you call this planet, by the way?' asked Ed.

'Hunus,' they said together.

14

SHUTTLE BAY, PCP ATTACK SHIP DAKR MON – DIVISION 2748T

EPOCH 93, SPAN 9371, JUNCTURE 101.6

Linda's ruse appeared to be working. She'd repeated her request to the boarding party Commander – that she must be taken directly to the Mogul, as the information she had was classified. She also discovered it was her they were looking for.

Seemingly, they had left a movement detector inside the open airlock to sing out if a rescue ship came by. Thankfully, the dismantling of the ship ceased after she appeared and if Rayl stayed where she was, she would most likely remain safe.

Linda had also been reluctantly allowed to wash and gather some clean clothes after she pointed out that the Mogul wouldn't be best pleased if she assaulted him with her present odour.

She left by the same blood-soaked airlock, only this time she was able to walk straight onto a docked shuttle.

As the airlock closed behind her, she noticed that, as with the GDA ships, the gravity was higher. Nothing too overpowering, but she had to remember her hosts would be slightly more nimble than her.

She counted fourteen soldiers and crew in the shuttle. Another rather unpleasant realisation was the smell. It was evident the PCP didn't regard personal hygiene as a priority. Perhaps that's why her request to bathe before facing the Mogul was considered strange.

She found holding her nose and breathing through her mouth helped diminish the gag reflex. It certainly got her a few strange looks during the ten-minute transfer.

It was also very hot and she wondered if the environmental system was malfunctioning.

The walk from the shuttle bay to the command cabin on the PCP ship was long. No quick tube trains or turbo elevators on this vessel. It took a fifteen-minute walk and she noticed it was still very warm. They must originate from a very warm planet, she thought. She looked closely at everything and ensured her DOVI was transmitting all the data back to the Gabriel. As she continued through the large ship, she began to notice and understand what everything was around her, and what it did.

She felt her way into the systems as she would on one of the Theo ships.

'About bloody time,' said Cleo. 'Use this ability wisely – it might just save your life.'

'Oh, shit,' whispered Linda. 'This is astonishing.'

'What did you say?' asked one of the guards, glaring over at her.

'I said, the ship – it looks very polished,' replied Linda, forcing a smile.

'Yes,' said the guard, nodding. 'The Mogul is very particular, regarding his flagship.'

'Wait here,' ordered one of her other escorts when they arrived at a large bulkhead door, seemingly in the centre of the ship.

He entered the command cabin, as they referred to it. The door closed as he passed through, although this made no difference to Linda as she was already in there, via her DOVI, rummaging through the systems.

She found the helm, propulsion, offence and defence, environmental and the system controlling the artificial gravity. She considered reducing it a bit, but knew that they'd soon notice and change it back.

The guard returned.

'The Mogul demands your presence,' he said. 'You will follow me.'

The command cabin was not as big as she expected for a ship of this size. It was around ten metres square, with twelve crew members facing away from the centre down the four sides.

None of the crew turned to look. The guard pointed to a spot on the floor. 'Stand there,' he said and he stepped back by the door and stood to attention, staring at the floor.

Linda had acquired useful information regarding personal meetings with the Mogul from the soldiers on the Vlepon – the last thing she wanted was to insult him right at the beginning of the conversation.

The centre of the room was raised and the back of a large chair faced her.

'Who are you – breeder?' said a commanding voice from the raised chair.

'I am Quixia, my Mogul,' said Linda confidently. 'Agent 762, of the PCP Vanguard Division.'

'What were you doing on that ship?'

'I was trained on the Krawth and inserted into the GDA as an officer many years ago. I achieved the rank of captain last year and was awarded with one of their Katadromiko cruisers. By a quirk of luck, I stumbled on an opportunity to kill the entire crew of the battle cruiser, which left the GDA severely short of officers, thus enabling the Krawth to flood the GDA with more undercover Vanguard officers. Unfortunately, my cover was blown and I had to change my appearance and start again. The junior officer position on the Vlepon was the start of my new identity. My ultimate mission was to obtain the schematics of the GDA's cloaking technology.'

The large chair turned slowly and Linda knew to keep her eyes on the floor.

'The GDA's ridiculous obsession with breeder equality will be its downfall,' thundered Tyuk Baa. 'Voice print confirmation, servant.'

'Yes, my Mogul,' said one of the crew to Linda's right. 'Agent, you will state your name, number, planet and system of birth and parents' names.'

'Quixia, Agent 762, born on Joskoth in the Tueter system, mother's name, Iaria, father's name, Craonis.'

'Voice print confirmed, my Mogul,' said the crew member.

Linda kept her huge relief very much to herself and her eyes firmly on a spot on the floor.

'Servant, take this breeder to my chambers. Have her prepared to display allegiance to her Mogul.'

'Yes, my Mogul,' said the guard by the door. He grabbed Linda's arm, pushed her through the door and turned her down a carpeted hallway.

'I don't like the sound of that,' said Cleo in Linda's ear. 'Displaying allegiance can only mean one thing with this psycho.'

The guard walked her past a large door where the carpet ended and opened a smaller door. He led her into a side room, which contained a couple of very young teenage girls.

'Prepare her for the Mogul,' he said to the two girls and backed out of the room. Linda heard the door lock as it closed.

'She's way too old,' said one girl.

'Who chose you for him?' asked the other one.

'He did,' said Linda. 'I'm supposed to display my allegiance. How do I do that?'

They looked at each other as if she were insane.

'You're a breeder. How do you think you do it?'

'And you'd better scream nice and loud too,' said the second girl. 'He likes to think he's really hurting you.'

'Linda, you can't even be considering this,' whispered Cleo. 'This is way over the top. This just cannot happen.'

'Don't worry, I can look after myself,' said Linda to the two girls, but, in reality, sending a message to Cleo.

They took Linda into the Mogul's main chamber and demonstrated how the mounting cradle worked. Linda noticed the room was double height with a lot of plush furniture, wall hangings and artwork from several different cultures.

It was the mounting cradle that really got her attention. The girls informed her it was raised up because the Moguls were all very tall and they didn't lower themselves to anyone.

The breeder was to stand up on the foot plates, bend forward over a steel bar and grab two handles. There were electronic locks that closed over your ankles and wrists, operated by a thumb switch – but only to engage the locks. The Mogul was the only one who could disengage them.

There was an eighteen inch, slightly curved and heavily engraved sword, sitting on a stand next to the cradle.

'What's that for?' Linda asked the first girl.

The first girl pointed to a round tray underneath the cradle. It flowed quite steeply into a drain hole in the middle of the floor and disappeared.

'It's for if you don't pleasure him enough.'

Linda glanced back at the huge knife, shivered and walked out of the room.

She was horrified, but convinced she had a plan that would work. She nodded in all the right places as the two girls continued to show her where to wash and then dressed her accordingly, which wasn't with much.

While this was going on, she was concentrating on delving into the ship's electronic systems with her newly converted DOVI.

The girls, once satisfied with her, started

concentrating on preparing themselves so she wandered away from them for a few seconds.

'Cleo, be prepared to follow this ship shortly,' she whispered. 'I believe the shit will be hitting the fan in the not too distant future.'

'Okay, Linda. I hope you know what you're doing.'

'So do I.'

She spent the next half an hour sitting and watching the two younger girls go through a series of exercises. Considering they were only wearing a tiny pair of briefs each, this proved to be quite pornographic and Linda struggled to keep her mind on the job.

She'd checked and rechecked that she could quickly infiltrate the necessary systems, even re-entering the Mogul's chamber to check it wasn't shielded. She also discovered that there were no cameras permitted in the private chamber, which saved her a job.

'Linda, I have Rayl aboard the Gabriel,' said Cleo. 'I've given her one of the spare cabins and she's sleeping.'

'Thanks,' said Linda quietly.

A bell chimed suddenly. The youngest of the girls jumped up and entered the Mogul's chamber, shutting the door behind her.

'He approaches,' said the other one. 'If he summons you, remember everything we told you and you'll be okay.'

'Thanks for your help,' said Linda. 'I fully realise you didn't have to.'

'Purely selfish, I'm afraid. The more breeders there are, the less pain we have to endure.'

The door to the chamber reopened and the younger girl returned, beckoning to Linda.

'He wants you,' she said, looking a little piqued.

Linda got up out of her seat and strolled towards the door, trying to look confident.

'Quickly,' they said in stereo.

'Don't annoy him as he'll take it out on us.'

Linda quickened her step, lowered her eyes and entered the chamber. She closed the door and strode to the position in which the girls had shown her to stand, ensuring she kept her head down. She felt extremely vulnerable, standing there almost naked. It was the first time she'd been naked in front of a man since she was nine years old and this man was a whole lot more dangerous than her father.

'Well, well. How's my little breeder spy?' he growled from across the room.

'Good, my Mogul,' was all she could think of to say.

'Please me today, breeder, and I will have you transferred to my division. You will be my personal Vanguard spy. Every day you will report to me here, demonstrate your allegiance and tell me anything that goes on without my knowledge.'

'Yes, my Mogul.'

'Tell me, breeder, during your training for the Vanguard Division, did it include a torture endurance course?'

'It did, my Mogul.'

'Excellent. Shall we see if you were paying attention? Mount the cradle,' he demanded.

'It would be my honour, my Mogul,' she said as she had been instructed.

Linda took a deep breath, removed her underwear and stepped up onto the cradle. Placing her shins against the back of the locks, she bent forward and grabbed the restraining handles. Pressing the button with her thumb to engage the locks, she immediately delved into the ship's systems with her DOVI.

She knew where she was going, she'd rehearsed this at least ten times. Peering at the reflection in the glass of a picture, directly to her right, she could see him disrobing and, as he strode towards her and was in the middle of the room, away from anything to grab, she reversed the artificial gravity.

The chamber was double height and, with a shout, he shot up and smashed into the ceiling about four metres above, along with most of the furniture and everything else in the room not bolted down. She was dragged upwards quite painfully as the cradle's restraints dug into her ankles and wrists. She then set the gravity at maximum and reversed it again. Her head smashed down on the top of the cradle with the huge increase in force. She felt a searing pain in her chest and the bar she was bent over pushed into her stomach a lot harder than she expected.

Then came the sickening slap of a body slamming into the deck behind her and the unmistakable crackle of multiple bone fractures.

She set the gravity back to normal – well, normal for this ship anyway – and peered around at the Mogul. He was in a mess: obvious multiple limb fractures and a pool of blood slowly growing around his head and upper torso. His skin seemed a very strange maroon colour and, on his forehead, above two rather macabre, black staring eyes, were two protrusions, almost like stunted horns.

Linda took a deep, painful breath and started screaming at the top of her lungs.

15

HUNUS – DIVISION 2750T, ANDROMEDA

EPOCH 93, SPAN 9371, JUNCTURE 204.3

Breex and Trkors gave Ed a tour of their underground home, much to Zeerd's disgust.

The Gatekeeper colony, as they were known, was presently comprised of one hundred and seventeen families, totalling around five hundred people.

Trkors had explained that, originally, as far as they knew, during the time of the Ancients, their job was to travel through the gate and construct various pieces of engineering equipment in the cavern. At that time, they had – so the history books said – numbered several thousand with many clans populating the more temperate area around the equator.

The habitable zone was only a couple of thousand kilometres wide as the rest of the planet, both north and south, was in an almost permanent ice age.

'This is our warmer period,' explained Breex.

'During the winter epochs we can be snowed in for ages so we spend the summer hunting and filling the larders.'

They walked out on what could only be described as an observation deck. It was almost the highest point of the hill and a steep narrow path wound down the hill to the valley below. There was a cold wind, gusting strongly at times, but the view was spectacular. The outcrop extended, unsurprisingly, out of scavenged spaceship detritus, boasting a hundred-and eighty-degree panoramic vista south of their position.

'Wow,' said Ed, strolling up to the railing. 'Some people would pay a lot of money for a view like that.'

'Be even colder in the winter, though,' grumbled Zeerd as he fastened his coat right up to his neck.

'Haven't you ever considered moving somewhere a little more temperate, especially as you haven't actually been gatekeeping for quite a while?' asked Ed.

'It keeps the Mogul away,' replied Breex quietly, checking behind him to ensure he wasn't overheard.

'They don't like the cold?' said Ed.

'No, they like it a lot warmer than here.'

'I take it he doesn't visit very often.'

'He's never been here in person. He sends his thugs down to grab a girl or two every span or so.'

'You're going to need to move before long if your numbers keep going dow—' Ed stopped suddenly. He'd been scanning around with his DOVI. He turned and fronted the cliff face that loomed up above them for another twenty or thirty metres. 'What's in that room up there?' he asked.

'There isn't a room up there,' said Trkors. 'This is the highest level we have.'

Ed walked over to the base of the cliff and placed his hand on the rock face. He could sense a rectangular void above him, but due to the thickness of the rock he couldn't detect what was in it.

Situated next to the door they'd walked out of was a recess cut into the stone, almost like a sentry box.

'What's this for?' Ed asked.

'Nothing, as far as I know,' said Breex. 'A shelter for a guard, perhaps.'

Ed scanned around inside the recess. 'Do you have a knife, Zeerd?' he asked.

Zeerd grunted, pulled up a trouser leg, unsheathed a huge hunting knife and handed it to Ed.

'That's a bit ninja, isn't it?' said Ed, looking a bit surprised at the size of the thing. 'It's more like a sword than a knife.'

'Got me out of trouble more than once,' said Zeerd. 'That's my smallest one too.'

'You're the only man who could pull out a knife at a gun fight and win,' said Ed, with a grin.

He tapped around on the ceiling of the recess with the knife.

'What are you doing?' said Breex.

'Somewhere here there should be a— Ah, here it is,' he said as he dug the knife into the right-hand back corner. What appeared to be a load of dried plaster fell out of the hand-sized hole that Ed had opened. Inside, he found a handle. He jiggled it around until he discovered that the trick was to pull it down and turn it anticlockwise.

A whining noise as if from an electrical motor straining under a heavy load came from within the wall. Cracks started to run around the back of the recess. Suddenly, the whole section moved quickly to the left, showering them all in plaster and dust.

'What have you done?' exclaimed Trkors, jumping back in alarm.

The stiff breeze soon cleared the dust away, leaving a stone stairway, which led up and left.

'You seem to be making a habit of this,' said Zeerd, giving Ed a suspicious look. 'How the hell did you know?'

Ed gave him a wink. 'It's my party trick. Are you coming up, guys?' he said as he bounded up the stairs.

The gate control room was identical to the other one. Ed waited until Breex, Trkors and Zeerd were all in the room. The two locals were visibly shaking with nerves as their heads swivelled this way and that, trying to come to terms with the discovery. He brushed some of the dust off the main control panel and pressed the same power-up button as before. The main panel powered up with a hundred blinking icons, ten screens began glowing and all the hardware cabinets that lined the walls began humming softly.

'Bit of a déjà vu moment, eh, Zeerd?'

'Bit of a what?'

Trkors and Breex were still in a state of shock, standing in the centre of the room, afraid to move. Ed turned to face them. They both knelt and averted their eyes.

'Oh, for fuck's sake. We've been through this, guys. I'm not one of your Ancients or a Messiah – or anything of the sort. I'm just a physicist from Earth with a penchant for finding hidden rooms.'

He placed a hand on both of their shoulders and, as they looked up at him, he signalled to them to stand. Giving them both a hug, he could feel the tension lessening in them.

'I really don't want you bowing to me anymore. It's not acceptable, okay?'

'Yes, my Mog—'

'No, my name is Edward. You will call me Ed – is that clear?'

'Yes, my— Yes, Ed,' they both replied.

Ed noticed Zeerd disappearing back down the stairs, shaking his head.

'What does all this machinery do?' asked Breex.

'It's the control centre for the gates.'

'It's "gate",' said Trkors. 'When you say "gates", that implies more than one.'

'I did say "gates" – as there are two gates.'

'You are joking with us,' said Trkors, smiling for the first time.

Ed explained about the starship gate and that it was just for personnel to come and go while the larger one was in construction on the other side.

'So, our three little moons are another super gate?' said Breex, looking stunned.

'Yes, positioned there by your Ancients.'

'That's amazing,' said Trkors. 'And your ability to learn our language so fast – that's amazing too.'

'What?' said Ed.

'Zeerd has the translator. We've been communicating without it since he went.'

Ed looked around and, sure enough, the translator was missing, still hung around Zeerd's neck, most likely – and he was downstairs.

'Well, I'll be,' said Ed. 'How the hell does that work?'

AFTER SWITCHING the control room off again, Ed, Breex

and Trkors descended back to find Zeerd and the other three soldiers sheltering from the wind inside the door to the underground habitat. Ed closed the hidden stairs' door again.

'Don't let the Mogul know about that room,' said Ed. 'It's bad enough those nutters having access to our Galaxy; it doesn't bear thinking about if they had another five or six hundred to mess with.'

'There's more than one gate destination?' asked Breex.

'Yes, several hundred.'

'Where do they all go?'

'We don't know. It seems the Ancients were very keen to hide this fact from the invaders and the fact that the Moguls don't know about this suggests to me that they're not descendants of the Ancients at all. They're descendants of the invaders.'

Both Breex and Trkors looked horrified.

'But that cannot be,' said Trkors. 'The scriptures clearly state the Moguls have direct descendance from the Ancients.'

'And who wrote the scriptures?'

Breex and Trkors looked at each other.

'A long dead religious order on the far side of the planet,' said Trkors, the doubt starting to sound in his voice.

'And you have conclusive proof of this?'

'It was thousands of years ago.'

'I think I know who wrote them,' said Ed, feeling guilty for casting doubt on their ten-thousand-year-old religious teachings.

'I'll seal the handle back up myself,' said Trkors, suddenly changing the subject.

'It's best if we keep all this quiet from the rest of the colony as well,' said Breex. 'We've had the odd traitor before and I'm sure the Mogul has a spy or two amongst us.'

'Be careful,' said Ed. 'I don't want anything to happen to you guys just because you spoke to us.'

A loud sonic boom sounded above them and both Breex and Trkors froze.

'The Mogul. He comes,' said a now very nervous Trkors.

'We must hide you,' said Breex.

Ed looked up and caught a glimpse of a vapour trail as Breex grabbed his arm and pulled him back into the colony.

16

MOGUL'S ANTEROOM, PCP ATTACK SHIP DAKR MON – EN ROUTE TO ARUS'GAN

EPOCH 94, SPAN 9371, JUNCTURE 57.2

Linda sat in the anteroom, taking shallow breaths and feeling very sore. She'd fractured two ribs, had a massive bruise on her chin and had torn muscles in her neck.

Compared to the majority of the crew, she was barely hurt at all. Seven were dead, over a quarter had a limb fracture and some more than one. Concussions, skull fractures, broken fingers – the list went on and on. She tried to ignore the fact that this was all her doing.

The two guards that had entered the Mogul's chamber nearly had a coronary when they saw the state of him. Both obviously injured themselves, they'd still been able to organise a crash team, which quickly whisked him away to the ship's medical centre.

Finally, Linda had been released from the cradle and she really put on a show of being hurt and terrified.

She'd said no to going to the medical centre as she didn't want any blood samples taken or scans that might uncover her subterfuge. She'd remained in the anteroom to hide and see what happened.

The two girls returned from the medical centre, both covered in bruises and the youngest, whose name she found out was Gedren, had a broken wrist. The elder girl was named Chula and both had been taken from a planet called Crillon as a bestowal to keep the Mogul happy. Chula told her that the Mogul had been pronounced dead a few minutes ago and that the ship was en route to the home planet of the PCP, Arus'Gan.

'Cleo, make sure you stay close. I want to get off this ship as soon as it's possible.'

There was no answer.

'Cleo, are you there?'

Still no answer.

'Oh, shit,' she whispered.

Linda realised with horror that she was on her own. This was now a huge problem.

The ship must have embedded a jump and lost Cleo, she thought. *Oh crap, I didn't think of that.*

Gedren approached with her bandaged hand and wrist strapped across her chest. She sat opposite and smiled. Linda ignored her and closed her eyes, pretending to go to sleep. She felt guilty treating her this way, but she couldn't risk a conversation until she'd worked out what to do.

'We were wondering,' said Gedren, ignoring Linda's ploy. 'When we get back, is there a possibility you could put in a good word for us with the Vanguard Division? I – sorry – we appreciate we're still quite young but...'

Linda opened her eyes, realising she could understand what Gedren was saying.

'...we're very keen to do more for the cause. What you've been doing sounds extremely exciting and a lot more fun than being a walking sex toy.' She stared at Linda expectantly. 'Well, what do you think?'

Linda had a huge dilemma. If she spoke and English came out, she would blow her cover. What was puzzling, though, was she could see the answer in her mind and it was in Andromedan, which was weird. So, to alleviate the pause in conversation, which was becoming a little uncomfortable, she decided to go for it.

'I'll do what I can,' she said, lying, but realising, with relief, that she had replied perfectly in the local language.

How the hell am I doing that? she thought.

'Thanks, Quixia,' said a very relieved looking Gedren, giving her a slightly lopsided hug with one arm.

Linda felt dreadful for the lie and for giving these

girls false hope, but it wasn't her fault they were in this awful situation. Then again, they were the Mogul's personal breeders, which in itself was the most prestigious position possible for a breeder.

What she'd overheard from the conversations the girls had been having concluded they would achieve a very high price at auction on their return. Only industry leaders, or senior politicians, would have that kind of cash, which meant they would be living in complete luxury for the foreseeable future.

If being raped several times a day could ever be regarded as living in luxury, she thought, feeling pangs of guilt again.

She approached the girls to ask how long the flight to Arus'Gan would take and if there was somewhere for her to sleep.

'A couple of days,' said Chula. 'Take the third cabin down on the left,' she said, pointing to a narrow corridor at the back of the room.

Linda found the cabin. It was basic, small, but the little bed was comfortable, so long as she lay on her back and breathed shallowly. She had a scan around the ship's systems to find the helm. Sure enough, the course was set in for Arus'Gan, around fourteen thousand light years distant, and all the jumps were embedded.

It took her a while, but eventually she found the buoy launcher. After disconnecting the failsafes and alarms, she waited until a regular garbage packet was jettisoned and quietly ejected a small marker buoy that would activate in six hours, programmed with a simple pulsing transmission.

Finally, wondering how she was able to understand and converse in Andromedan without Cleo or a translator, she fell asleep.

17

PLANET HUNUS – DIVISION 2750T, ANDROMEDA

EPOCH 94, SPAN 9371, JUNCTURE 123.8

Trkors stood out on the upper deck and watched the small, white spacecraft circling the area. It wasn't what he was expecting at all. The Mogul's soldiers usually had ugly matt-black ships, which came straight in and landed in a clearing a few hundred metres from the base of the mountain. This ship was all sleek and looked as if it was travelling at light speed, even when it was almost stationary.

Behind him, a couple of others peered out nervously from the doorway and watched as the strange ship disappeared behind the mountain again in its continuous circling.

'Who is it?' asked Breex as he walked up and joined Trkors.

'I have no idea,' he said. 'Have you ever seen a ship like that?'

'No, but Ed might.'

THEY'D HIDDEN Ed and his party in one of the lower food stores deep inside the mountain. It took Breex ten minutes to bring him up to the deck. As soon as Ed stepped out of the door, a familiar voice sounded in his ears.

'Ed, Andy, are you there? Can you hear me?'

'I can hear you, Cleo.'

Breex and Trkors both stared at Ed as though he'd lost his mind.

'Oh, happy days, that's such a relief. I thought my systems were messing me about. I caught a faint reading from your DOVI about an hour ago while I was still in the next system. By the time I got here it had disappeared.'

'It's okay, Cleo. The rock here is particularly impermeable to all wave forms and scans. When I'm inside the mountain you can't detect me.'

'Have you found the missing crew?'

'They're out hunting. They'll be back a little later,'

'Ah, that explains the life-sign readings I picked up a few kilometres away.'

'Linda, are you there too?' Ed called.

'No, she's not,' said Cleo. 'That's why I had to find

you.'

It took Cleo five minutes to explain exactly what had happened to Linda.

'Ah, shit,' he exclaimed. 'Just when you think everything's coming together.'

'Are you okay?' said Trkors.

Ed explained the predicament, choosing not to mention that Linda had murdered the Mogul.

'So, she's endangered her own life to save the life of a young girl, a complete stranger?' said Breex, seemingly amazed by the revelation.

'Yep, it's kinda the way we roll,' replied Ed.

'It certainly wouldn't normally happen in this galaxy,' said Breex, rolling his eyes.

'For your sake, I hope she's okay. Are you going to go after her?' asked Trkors.

'Of course, but I have to finish here first. Is there any way you can recall the hunting party earlier?'

'No, and they'll have seen the ship circling, which would probably make them nervous and more likely to stay away longer,' said Breex.

'Okay, I'll have to use the shuttle. Can you get the soldiers up from down below?'

Trkors disappeared off downstairs, returning ten minutes later with Zeerd and the others.

'I understand you've found your ship,' said Zeerd, almost smiling. 'We can all go home at last.'

Ed smiled and nodded. He knew that Zeerd wouldn't agree to a rescue mission into hostile territory for just one crew member, so he kept his mouth shut.

Cleo brought the shuttle up to the deck side and hovered. The four soldiers couldn't hide their enthusiasm and leapt inside as soon as the steps appeared. Ed said his goodbyes to Trkors and Breex, promising to stop by on his way back – quietly, so Zeerd wouldn't hear.

It took them no time at all to find a very nervous hunting party – five very relieved looking Vrachos crew.

Once all ten of them were crammed into the cabin of the shuttle, Ed took over control and swept the ship back up and into space. He cloaked and headed straight for the three moons.

'Where's your mother ship?' asked Zeerd, peering out of the front screen.

'Cloaked and staying close,' Ed lied. He'd already agreed with Cleo that she would loiter on this side of the gate and await Ed's return with Andy and the Cartella.

He retrieved the remote from his pocket and, as the little ship passed in between the three moons, he uncloaked and depressed the icon. As with a standard jump, they appeared in the Milky Way almost instantaneously. The three-dimensional star map lit up as it recognised where it was and Ed re-cloaked just in case any of the cannons decided to wake up again.

After entering the planet's atmosphere, he landed carefully on the slope next to the Cartella. They all disembarked and headed straight for the tunnel entrance. They were met halfway down the tunnel by First Officer G'ann and a group of nervous soldiers, who quickly lowered their weapons when they realised who it was.

'We heard the ship land,' G'ann called as they approached. 'We certainly didn't expect it to be you.'

After all the welcome-home handshakes and back slapping was over, they all made their way back into the main chamber.

'We have a starship again,' said Zeerd, looking pleased with himself. 'We're on our way home.'

'That's good news,' said G'ann. 'We'll begin ferrying up the crew immediately.'

'Hold your horses,' said Ed. 'The Gabriel's still in Andromeda, so Andy and I will have to go retrieve it.'

G'ann stopped walking and stared at Ed.

'Why the hell did you leave the starship behind?'

'Mapping the local systems and trying to detect where they're constructing an invasion fleet,' he replied, attempting to look truthful.

'I don't think so,' said G'ann. 'One of you will go and get the starship, escorted by a security detail; the other two will stay here as security for us.'

'Still treating us as if we're the enemy,' said Ed. 'I could've been sipping cocktails on a beach, you know, instead of travelling the length of the galaxy to save your sorry arse.'

'This is a GDA military operation. You are civilians. I am the senior officer – you do as I say,' said G'ann and he marched off towards the encampment of igloos, followed by a grinning Zeerd and the rest of the group.

Andy and Phil were in one of the igloos with an armed guard standing outside. They both looked relieved to see Ed appear in the doorway.

'Unappreciative bunch of bastards, aren't they,' said Andy, shaking his head.

'Have you been under guard since I left?' asked Ed.

'Yep,' said Phil. 'Even to go to the bathroom.'

Ed just rolled his eyes, sat down with them and quietly filled them in on the situation.

'Have you still got the spare remote?' Ed asked.

'Yeah.'

'Do they know about it yet?'

'Nope.'

'Good. Cuz I might have a plan.'

Fifteen minutes later, G'ann appeared at the igloo

door.

'Okay, Captain Virr, time to get the starship,' he said. 'These men will escort you again.' He indicated to the soldiers standing outside.

When Ed emerged, he realised it was the same four men as before. Zeerd gave him a sly grin.

'Why, Lieutenant Zeerd, are we going on another holiday?' said Ed.

'There'll be no sightseeing this time, Mr Virr,' he replied.

'It's Captain Virr, Mr Zeerd,' said Ed as he walked past. 'Just remember I outrank you.'

Zeerd went red in the face and seemed to want to say something, but Ed was strolling away. The other three soldiers sniggered.

Phil patted Zeerd on the shoulder as he passed. 'Never mind, Zeerd. Some are born leaders and some aren't.' He also strode off nonchalantly, following Ed. Zeerd balled his fists and muttered something under his breath.

Andy stayed outside the igloo, seemingly uninterested. He faked a yawn and gave a slight nod as Ed glanced back.

Once outside, Ed opened up the Cartella airlock and pointed to the other shuttle.

'You're going in that one,' he said to Zeerd. 'There's more seats in it.'

Phil leant casually against the other shuttle, watching, with his hands in his pockets. Ed used his DOVI to open the other shuttle's airlock door. Phil threw himself backwards up into the airlock, which quickly closed behind him. He jumped in the pilot's couch and, ignoring the shouting and banging outside, he powered up and took off, following along behind the Cartella.

Andy, meanwhile, had wandered over to the bathroom tent, which was luckily situated near the iris door through to the gate room. His bored guard who'd followed in tow loitered outside instead of using the facilities.

Andy cut a tall slit in the tent material at the back. A quick check out front to confirm the guard was facing the other way and then he slid out through the cut and bolted through the iris door, down towards the gate.

The guard caught the movement as Andy went through the door and set off in pursuit, struggling to get his rifle out of its shoulder as he ran. The soldier was, as Andy had hoped, too slow, as he had the spare remote out of his pocket, the button hit and stood within a grassy clearing in another galaxy before the guard had even taken the safety off.

18

MOGUL'S ANTEROOM, PCP ATTACK SHIP DAKR MON – EN ROUTE TO ARUS'GAN

EPOCH 94, SPAN 9371, JUNCTURE 180.7

Linda awoke to the sound of raised voices coming from out in the corridor. She quickly dressed and opened her cabin door to find two soldiers searching the other girls' cabins.

'What's going on?' she asked as one of the soldiers pushed past her and started rummaging around in her cabin.

'The Mogul was murdered by someone on the ship,' said the soldier.

'Well, it can't have been me,' she said. 'I was kinda tied up at the time.'

'We know that,' he said. 'It doesn't mean they didn't hide a remote control or something in your cabin.'

A few moments later, seemingly satisfied there was nothing suspicious in the cabins or the anteroom, they departed.

'They're searching the entire ship so it's not just us,' said Chula as Linda emerged from the cabin corridor.

'I don't see how he could have been murdered, though,' said Gedren. 'I thought it was a system malfunction.'

'That's what I thought,' said Linda.

'They must have found out something to suggest it was manipulated then,' said Chula. 'I also heard from a friend in the kitchen that the ship's quartermaster is in the cells.'

'What's he done?' asked Linda.

'Lost a marker buoy,' she said. 'Could've compromised the ship, they're saying.'

Linda felt the pangs of guilt again, but soon shrugged it off.

'We're going to be at Arus'Gan in a few hours too,' said Gedren.

'I thought you said it'd be a couple of days,'

'I did, but they've undertaken emergency jumps which are much longer, which means we could be at the station for today's auction.'

'What's the station?'

'Locy'fer Station,' said Chula, looking at Linda strangely.

'I'm sorry,' she said. 'I've been away in another galaxy for more than half my life. I was so young when I left, I've forgotten so much about my home.'

'You must have been through that station before,' said Gedren. 'I mean, everything and everyone goes through there.'

'Yes, you're right of course. I'm sure I'll remember it when we get there.'

FOUR HOURS LATER, a chime sounded throughout the ship and the background hum changed pitch. Linda had retired back to her cabin with a tablet screen to secretly learn more about the Andromedans. She walked back along to the anteroom to find the other two girls sitting patiently with their bags packed.

It transpired that Arus'Gan, the planet, was off-limits to everyone but the Moguls, their families, invited guests and the army of staff.

Locy'fer Station, however, wasn't. It was enormous: home to over twenty million people and the size of a small moon. It orbited Arus'Gan at a height of twelve hundred and forty kilometres and up to two thousand ships could be docked at any one time, utilising the seventy-two docking facilities, which could each hold up to thirty ships.

It was a gargantuan floating city and the centre of PCP-ruled space, but pretty, it was not.

Built gradually over several millennia in countless

styles and in what seemed like completely random directions, it permanently appeared half finished, with hundreds of small craft flying, seemingly haphazardly, through and around the station.

The continuous flash of a thousand welding torches, indicating people mostly making repairs rather than building new habitats, made it look as if the paparazzi was having a field day with hundreds of celebrities.

LINDA WAS SITTING with the girls in the anteroom, her eyes shut, pretending to have a snooze. In reality, she had connected her DOVI up to one of the outside camera pods and was in absolute awe at the scale of this thing. She'd seen some big space stations in GDA space, but this monster made them all seem very mediocre. She was sure they were going to collide with several smaller ships as they approached, but every time the inferior-sized ships came close, they would veer away at the last minute and disappear around the ship or into the labyrinth of station voids.

Finally, after much prolonged shuffling, with dozens of manoeuvring jets, the battle cruiser docked with a slight shudder. Linda opened her eyes to witness the two girls exchange a worried glance.

'Do you think you'll be bought together?' she asked them.

'Doubtful,' said Chula. 'With the Mogul dead, we become the property of the First Officer and he'll want to maximise his profit. Selling us separately will achieve a much higher return.'

'What about me? Do I go with you?' Linda asked.

'Technically, he owns you too,' said Gedren.

'But considering your history, he might have to hand you over to the station's Vanguard office,' said Chula.

They didn't have to wait long. A bridge officer entered the anteroom with two soldiers.

'Come with us,' he said, looking at the girls.

'And me?' said Linda.

'Yes, you too.'

The escort took them away from the bridge and back down the length of the ship, which confused Linda as she'd seen the docking ring umbilical attach on the opposite side of the bridge. Now they were being led in the other direction, although the girls didn't seem to find this unusual.

After a fifteen-minute walk through the ship, they arrived at a hangar bay and boarded a tiny shuttle. It sat up to eight people, so the six of them all had a seat.

The First Officer piloted the small craft and powered them out through an invisible force field and around the bulk of the cruiser. Linda watched as he engaged the autopilot and sat back. The tiny craft swung around and through the station for about five minutes before he retook control and entered a small hangar, settling next to another newer looking, almost identical ship.

'Follow me,' he said, powering the airlock sideways into the bulkhead.

This time there wasn't a long walk, as just through the back door of the hangar, he indicated that they should enter an elegantly decorated small suite of rooms.

'There are fresh clothes for you all in that room there and you may use the bathroom to freshen up before you meet your new owner,' he said, nodding and exiting the room through the same door.

'A private sale then,' said Chula. 'I was wrong.'

'Someone has some serious cash to afford the three of us,' said Gedren.

'So, I've been sold then?' said Linda, not knowing whether to be intrigued or horrified.

'A private sale avoids the exorbitant auction house fees,' said Chula. 'It's also illegal as you circumvent the government taxes.'

'These clothes are beautiful,' said Gedren, peering into the dressing room.

'Yes, they are, Gedren,' said an elegantly dressed teenager, who entered suddenly through a side door, flanked by two huge, heavily-armed bodyguards 'My name is Erebus. The three of you have recently become my property. You will refer to me as Mr Erebus. You will bathe, dress and be ready to shuttle out of here in thirty minutes.'

He turned and exited through the same door. The bodyguards glared at the three of them as they slowly turned and exited to follow their charge.

'Who's he?' asked Linda once the door was closed.

The two girls looked at each other with raised eyebrows.

'If he's who I think he is, then we're the property of an old Plecoran family,' said Chula. 'This is not good.'

'They're one of the wealthiest non-Mogul families,' said Gedren. 'A dynasty formed out of arms supply. They have quite a reputation amongst the breeders.'

'In what way?'

The girls both paused and exchanged an anxious look.

'They say his father threw a girl out an airlock once for making him orgasm too quickly,' said Chula.

'What is it with men in this galaxy?' said Linda, but then shut up before she accidentally blew her cover.

'Are they different in other galaxies then?' asked Chula.

'I can only answer for the Daxxal galaxy. It's the only other one I've been to and the answer is, yes, they generally are. On most worlds – or civilisations – that I've visited, they have gender equality.'

'You're kidding. That's sick, that is,' said Chula, screwing her face up in disgust.

'What, breeders running stuff?' said Gedren, her eyes wide with astonishment.

'Yep, shocking as it is,' said Linda. 'It seems to work for them.'

Again, the girls exchanged a look and both shook their heads.

'We know you're joking,' said Chula. 'Just the thought of it makes me feel sick.'

'Everyone knows we're only made for pleasure and breeding,' said Gedren. 'Anything else would be simply disgusting.'

They quickly showered and chose an outfit each. The dresses were all the same pure white, stitched with gold thread and toga-like. But short – very, very short.

'You do look good for your age,' said Gedren, eying up Linda's legs as they waited for their new boss to return.

'Well, thank you, Gedren. I'll take that as a compliment.'

She glanced at herself in a large wall-mounted mirror.

'This thing's so short, you can see what I had for

breakfast,' she said. 'But then again, the temperature here kinda warrants a summery wardrobe.'

The door opened and one of the bodyguards beckoned them to follow. He took them over to the other small shuttle that had been there when they arrived. It took off as soon as they were seated.

Looking around, Linda was surprised to find they were the only passengers, apart from the bodyguard and a skinny, but smartly dressed pilot. She also noted that the furnishings on this craft were in another league compared to the spartan, military model the First Officer had flown. The seats were soft and plush, in a light blue fabric, which seemed to emit a faint glow and was warm to the touch. The walls and bulkheads were soft and in the same light blue colour, with gold edges and matching filigree. She thought it looked quite nice, but could just imagine Ed or Andy's face if she decorated the Gabriel in a similar fashion.

The pilot, who'd up to that point been completely silent, suddenly emitted a yelp.

'The helm – it's not responding' he said, desperately hammering away at icons on the control panel, seemingly to no effect. 'We're suddenly going backwards.'

'Tractor beam,' said Linda. 'Can you spin the ship around with the manoeuvring jets?'

The sudden hiss of the port-side nose jets meant he

could at least try. It seemed to take an age to turn the ship as the tractor beam was exceedingly powerful. What finally came into view sent shivers down Linda's spine: a battleship similar to the one they'd destroyed several months ago in orbit above Paradeisos.

'What's going on?' cried Gedren, hanging on to her seat as the tiny shuttle shook.

'They've jammed our transmissions too,' cried the pilot, looking at them over his shoulder.

The bodyguard was busy checking his weapons and swearing under his breath.

'I don't think those will be any match against that,' said Linda, pointing at the opening hangar on the starboard side of the ugly, black monster.

The bodyguard looked up, following Linda's finger, and then turned to meet her gaze.

'You talk a lot for a breeder,' he hissed.

'Well, that's the crux of it, you see,' she said. 'I'm not a breeder. I'm a Vanguard Division officer.'

'Ah, fuck, they never told us that,' he said. 'The boss paid fourteen million for you.'

'Fourteen million,' shouted Chula, glaring at the bodyguard 'How much did I go for?'

'Eight.'

'Eight?' she spat. 'What d'you mean, eight? She's fucking ancient. I should be worth twice as much as her.'

'The young boss likes experienced breeders,' he said. 'Now shut up.'

Chula opened her mouth, closed it again and sat back in her seat with a face like thunder, glaring at Linda.

It suddenly got very bright as they were dragged into the hangar bay and they all shielded their eyes from the glare.

'Everyone belt up,' said Linda. 'I have an idea.'

'What the fuck can you do?' said the bodyguard. 'Vanguard Division or not, you're still a breeder.'

'O, ye of little faith,' said Linda under her breath as they all secured their turbulence belts.

The tiny ship clunked down on the decking and was instantly surrounded by heavily armed soldiers.

'Open the airlock or we'll blow it open,' said a loud, booming voice from outside.

As the pilot looked at the bodyguard for instructions, Linda closed her eyes and searched around with her DOVI. She soon found what she was looking for and tripped all the fuses for the tractor beam. She wormed her way into the helm, set up a manoeuvring sequence and left it ready to initiate. Finally, she came back to the nearby control room and waited.

The airlock powered sideways into the bulkhead and, immediately two soldiers appeared, guns up onto their shoulders, sweeping around the cabin.

'Which one of you is Quixia?' the leading soldier shouted.

They all looked over at Linda.

'That would be me,' she said.

'You're under arrest for the murder of—'

Linda closed her eyes and returned to the hangar control room. She gave the initiate command and the hangar door force field failed. The explosive decompression was like a cannon going off. Boom, and everything and everyone vanished. The screams of the soldiers lasted a millisecond as they all flashed out into space, along with everything not screwed down. Tools, vehicles, storage containers, the window of the control room, along with the two engineers inside.

The leading soldier had somehow grabbed a handle in the doorway and was hanging half out the door. Linda turned her head and looked across the cabin. She met the gaze of the rather shocked bodyguard, who was desperately trying to hang on to his laser rifle, and gave him a nod. He got the idea, raised the rifle and took a moment, attempting to aim, which was difficult against the gale of escaping air.

The soldier saw what he was doing and shouted, 'No, don't do—'

The laser rifle flashed, the soldier's upper arm vaporised and he was gone, leaving just his hand and forearm flapping about, but the fingers soon released their grip and that vanished too.

The ship was being slowly dragged across the hangar floor and the pilot, realising the airlock was now clear, forced his arm up to the control panel and hit 'airlock close'.

'Release the magnets,' shouted Linda. 'Let us tumble out with all the other stuff.'

As soon as he released the magnetic struts, they flew out the door, spinning uncontrollably.

She thought her way back into the helm of the battleship before they were out of range, initiated the pre-set action she'd memorised and engaged a system lockout.

All the manoeuvring thrusters on the starboard side of the battleship flared, pushing it towards the station. What also happened – something she hadn't envisaged – was, without any stabilising jets, the huge ship started to roll. Their pilot, meanwhile, had regained control of the tumbling shuttle, avoided hitting anything substantial and was heading as fast as he could in the opposite direction.

'What the fuck just happened?' shouted the bodyguard, which sounded very loud as the cabin was suddenly very quiet. Linda realised that both the girls had been screaming the whole time and had only now shut up.

'Don't have a clue,' said Linda, lying. 'That wasn't my plan. Did someone fire on that battleship?'

There was complete silence. Everyone stared at Linda. Even the pilot kept glancing nervously over his shoulder at her. He turned the shuttle and pointed it at a group of ships sitting stationary a few hundred kilometres away. They were shocked to see what was happening to the battleship. Now they'd turned, it was visible out the port-side cabin window. It was still in an uncontrolled roll, only now it was digging its way into the side of the space station. Lumps of ship and station were being chewed off and flying in all directions, setting in motion an almost continuous cascade of explosions, some small, others large. Fire began to envelop the huge ship as it dug in. Its tumbling roll finally ceased, with its bulk almost completely buried into the space station. One final monumental detonation blew the battleship in two and severed a large chunk of station.

When her eyes had recovered from the flash, Linda looked on with horror at the unintended carnage. She could see an entire section of the space station had separated. It slowly began to drop into the planet's gravity well, the remainder of the wound glowing and exploding outwards as compartments depressurised. It was difficult to differentiate what was ship from station now.

Shrapnel from the last big explosion rattled against the hull of the shuttle. The pilot spun the ship quickly, so they were flying backwards, and peered out nervously, swerving the ship around to dodge any larger chunks. Once he was satisfied the worst had passed, he turned the ship back to face their destination.

Moments later, a beautiful white starship swung into view. Linda thought it looked like one of the massive mega yachts she'd seen as a kid on childhood holidays, moored in St. Petersburg, Florida. The pilot dipped underneath the large ship and rose up through a force field into a hangar, which was situated in its lower decks. Once they were inside, the mega ship moved quickly away.

Two minutes later it vanished out of the system.

19

PLANET HUNUS – DIVISION 2750T, ANDROMEDA

EPOCH 94, SPAN 9371, JUNCTURE 237.2

Ed dropped the Cartella into Hunus's gravity well as fast as was safe. He knew Andy would be relatively unarmed and he didn't want him coming face to face with one of those dog-bear beasties.

He'd sent Phil straight back to the Gabriel to prepare the ship for its search and rescue mission. Phil would also programme a drone to re-enter the Milky Way on the next rotation and jump back to GDA space. It would carry all the information regarding the whereabouts and the unwarranted behaviour of the Vrachos's crew. It would also give the details about the ancient civilisation's multi-galaxy gateway and the immediate need to secure the system and gate.

Ed detected Andy's DOVI signature as soon as he exited the gateway so he knew exactly where to re-enter the planet's atmosphere.

Sure enough, he saw Andy, who was leaning against the stone gateway, waving. He landed in the clearing and opened the airlocks. Andy stuck his head inside the door.

'Good morning, driver. Is this the 15.34 to Marylebone?'

'No, it's the 15.34 to get the fuck in.'

'That'll do,' said Andy, jumping up through the airlock, so he could recline in a couch. 'I'll have to change at Peckham, though.'

'Did you remember the jellied eels?' asked Ed as he launched the ship skywards.

'No, a giant Tasmanian devil bear ate 'em.'

'If you two have quite finished talking bollocks,' called Cleo. 'You'd better cloak as we've got company up here.'

'Oh, crap,' said Ed, touching the cloak icon. 'Who is it?'

'Four – no five – Andromedan navy ships have just jumped in system. Hang on – make that six.'

'Bloody hell,' said Andy.

'Have you been detected, Cleo?' said Ed.

'Don't think so.'

'Is Phil back with you?'

'Yes, I'm here, Ed. I docked about two minutes ago.'

'Okay, cool. Bring the Gabriel into a low orbit and

be ready to open the airlock facing the planet.'

Ed slowed a little to avoid leaving any vapour trails or sonic booms. This, of course, made the ascent a lot longer, but greatly reduced the chances of detection. Just over an hour later, they zipped into the port hangar and immediately made their way up to the bridge.

'What're they up to?' asked Ed as he and Andy appeared on the tube lift.

'As you can see, they've spread themselves around the planet,' said Phil, indicating to the holo display, which was floating in the centre of the room.

Five of the six Andromedan ships were circling the planet; the sixth one was sitting a couple of kilometres outside the gate zone and seemed to be laying eggs.

'Are those mines?' asked Andy.

'Yep,' said Cleo. 'Anyone coming through the gate with any forward momentum will be on them before they know it.'

'How did they find out we're here?' asked Andy.

'I hope it's not Linda,' said Ed.

The silence in the room was confirmation that everyone was of the same supposition.

They gave the six Andromedan ships a wide berth and powered out to hide behind the fifth planet, where it was reasonably safe to uncloak and jump into the next system. As they approached the unnamed planet that the

Vlepon was orbiting, the tube lift arrived out of the floor again.

'Hello,' said a young girl, nervously looking around at the three people in the room.

'Hi,' said Ed, jumping up from his couch. 'You must be Rayl. My name's Ed,' he added before giving her a hug and introducing the others.

'Is Linda back?' she asked, a hopeful look in her eyes.

'Not yet,' Ed replied. 'That's our next priority.'

'Do you know where the Mogul's ship went?'

'Not as yet, but Cleo got close to it, so we know its signature intimately, which enables us to detect it from a long way off.'

'But they embedded their jumps.'

'Don't worry. We'll find her.'

'Promise me you will. She saved my life.' A tear ran down her cheek.

Cleo appeared and enveloped her in a hug and led her back to the tube lift. 'Have you seen the view from the blister?' she asked Rayl, giving Ed a wink as they stood on the lift circle.

'I promise we'll find her,' said Ed as the lift disappeared down into the floor.

'After what that girl's witnessed, I'm amazed she's as chirpy as she is,' said Andy, shaking his head. 'It really doesn't bear thinking about.'

The mood on the bridge was very business-like after that. Cleo took the ship out to where the battle cruiser had jumped and they spent a while scanning as far out as they could.

'Have we got any busy planets within scanning range?' asked Ed.

'Nope,' replied Phil.

'Okay, let's jump five hundred light years straight into the galaxy. We're right on the edge here so set the emergence in a system directly away from the edge.'

After quickly re-cloaking after the jump, Phil scanned around, again finding nothing of particular interest. They went another five hundred light years in. Cleo formed a holo grid, which sat in front of them all, so they never covered the same area of space twice. On the twenty-third jump, Phil suddenly shouted out.

'Hey, I've got something here.'

'The ship?' said Andy, hopefully.

'No, but it's a buoy in a system eighty-seven light years from here and it's singing like a canary.'

'Andy, jump the—'

'Already plotting the emergence, Captain, sir,' he said, beginning to sound a bit more Andy-like.

As the ship emerged and cloaked, Phil looked puzzled.

'What's up?' asked Ed.

'Erm, well, it's definitely a buoy from Linda's ship – but I don't understand the transmission.'

'Play it,' said Andy.

A series of beeps sounded around the bridge in what Phil thought was a completely random pattern.

'It's Morse!' exclaimed Andy. 'Hang on, I used to know this. Cleo, can you bring up the letters I say?'

'No problem.'

'INTOFLAGERARUSGANTWO-DAYSMINESANICEP'

'Ah, it keeps repeating the same sentence,' said Andy. 'Hang on, I'll just sort it into words.'

'ARUSGAN TWO DAYS MINES A NICE PINT OF LAGER.'

'Good girl,' said Ed.

'What's that about then?' asked Phil.

'Well, Arusgan must be the destination and it takes two days to get there,' said Ed. 'And the mention of a nice lager means she's okay. If she had talked about a nice pint of bitter, I'd know she was in distress.'

'Because she hates bitter?'

'Correct.'

'Cool,' said Andy. 'Now we just need to find this planet called Arusgan.'

'Cleo, can you draw a line between our start point and this point and continue it on into the galaxy?' asked Ed.

'Done.'

The line appeared through their search grid and disappeared out the far side.

'Follow the yellow brick road,' said Andy, pointing in the direction the line went.

'Ah,' said Phil. 'Elton John, 1973.'

'Don't tell me – you went to the gigs?' said Ed, smiling for the first time in hours.

Phil just grinned and plotted the next jump as Andy destroyed the buoy with the Asteri Beam.

They decided to take turns commanding the ship so they could all get some sleep and food. It was on Andy's shift, many hours and multiple jumps later, that Cleo woke him from his daydreaming.

'If Ed was correct, Arusgan should be in this busy system four hundred light years out,' she said, indicating a system flashing red on the holo map.

They'd passed many populated worlds and systems during the last few hours, but after listening in on the local ship chatter, they could quickly discount them.

On the last shift, Ed used his DOVI to infiltrate a couple of the passing Andromedan ships' navigation systems. He tried to transfer their star maps across to the Gabriel but found that to be an impossible task because of the size. What he did, however, was check out the location of the planet called Arusgan. He discovered that it was, in fact Arus'Gan, and it appeared to be a major hub within PCP space. It was still many thousands of light years distant, so he'd handed the helm over to Andy, annihilated a large supreme pizza and got his head down.

'Okay, Cleo,' said Andy. 'Can you wake the others?'

He jumped the Gabriel in behind a large gas giant in an adjacent system to Arus'Gan, cloaked and began to run a systematic sweep of its neighbour.

'Bloody hell,' he said, staring at the holo image as it began to materialise in the centre of the bridge.

Ed and Phil emerged, both yawning, on the tube lift.

'Did I hear you exclaim a degree of stupefaction?' asked Ed as he strolled over to a spare couch.

'Oh, yes – big lumps of stupefaction,' said Andy. 'Look at this mess.'

As the holo map gradually produced more detail, the three of them stared in disbelief.

Arus'Gan was what could only be described as a war zone. Vast amounts of debris circled the planet, causing mayhem amongst the multitude of ship traffic. A space station the size of Manhattan had a gaping fiery hole in one side with what looked suspiciously like the remains of a battleship hanging out of it. Ships of all shapes and sizes were flooding out of the station's every pore, which only made things worse as they were colliding with each other in the panic. The ship avoidance system seemed to have failed and, of course, the more collisions, the more debris, and so it went on. Down on the planet, plumes of smoke could be seen rising up into the stratosphere, caused by larger lumps of burning debris hitting the surface at many times the speed of sound.

'Linda's ship,' shouted Phil, pointing to a huge battle cruiser still attached to the space station.

'Andy, get over there,' said Ed.

'Won't they detect us before we re-cloak?'

'I believe they have bigger problems than that at this precise moment.'

'Okay, I'll put us in between them and the star.'

As they emerged in system, Andy took the Gabriel, as close as he dared, to the station. At forty-six thousand kilometres out, they still had lumps of debris bouncing off the shields.

'I have no readings from her DOVI on the ship, station or planet,' said Cleo.

'Which means one of two things,' said Ed, glaring at the holo images.

No one wanted to voice what one of those things were. The silence around the bridge was total.

Eventually, Cleo broke the hush. 'Ed, can you check

the station's video records since her ship arrived and for any ships jumping out of system since then?'

'Err, yeah – sorry, I should've thought of that,' he replied, glancing apologetically at the other two before closing his eyes and concentrating.

A few moments later, images taken from the station's video logs appeared adjacent to the holo map. It showed Linda's ship docking with the station.

'Who was the pilot?' Andy asked. 'He made a right pig's ear of that. This was only three hours ago too,' he added, looking at the time code.

They watched as, twenty minutes after docking, a tiny shuttle left the rear of the battleship, flew a circuitous route around the station and finally entered a small hangar on the outer fringe a few minutes later.

'Would that be the captain's shuttle or something?' asked Phil.

'Well, technically the captain's dead,' said Andy. 'And anyway, who would want to walk all that way through the ship when there's an airlock adjacent to the bridge with only a five-minute walk to that hangar?'

'Good point,' said Phil.

'And why would someone wait twenty minutes before flying that shuttle, quickly mingle in with lots of traffic, go in the wrong direction for a couple of minutes before circling back to that hangar?'

'Someone who doesn't want to be noticed or followed,' said Ed.

'Let's watch that hangar,' said Andy. 'There's something fishy going on.'

'Ah, you idiot,' said Ed, slapping himself on the forehead. 'Why don't I check the video images from Linda's ship?'

'I'd hurry up if I were you,' said Phil. 'They've got several fires on that ship now and they seem to be getting worse.'

Ed concentrated and worked his way through the ship's systems.

'Don't worry,' said Cleo. 'I've got them and transferred them all over here.'

The holo image changed from the hangar door to inside the battle cruiser. Cleo flicked through the various feeds quickly before halting at a view of a corridor somewhere on the ship. The facial recognition subroutine she'd used caught Linda, with two other girls, being escorted through the ship.

'Got her,' cried Andy. 'What the hell's she wearing, though?'

'Is that a toga?' said Ed.

'Now you know where your Romans got their dress sense from,' said Cleo as she followed the small party through the ship to the hangar with the small shuttle.

'Right, we now know she was on that little ship,'

said Ed. 'Cleo, have you got the rest of the feed from the station?'

'Yep,' she said. 'You might want to see this.'

It was a close-up of the hangar door as the shuttle entered, clearly showing another identical ship sitting inside.

'So, there's two of them in there,' said Phil.

As they watched, the same shuttle left about three minutes later and underwent the same strange circuitous route back to the battle cruiser. They went back to the battle cruiser's footage from the hangar and watched as three males disembarked.

Cleo took them back to the view of the space station hangar again and fast-forwarded until there was movement about thirty minutes later. The second tiny shuttle zipped out of the hangar and headed straight out, away from the station. Before it had got five kilometres, it suddenly stopped and began going backwards and up.

'What the hell?' said Andy.

'Tractor beam,' said Phil.

Cleo flicked around through the images she'd stolen before stopping at a wide shot of the little shuttle going backwards and slowly turning around to face one of the PCP's menacing black battleships.

'That's the same ship that's now buried in the side of the station,' said Cleo.

'The next few minutes are going to get loud then,' said Andy, his eyes transfixed by the holo image.

They all watched as the small shuttle got dragged into the hangar – and then nothing happened.

'Are you sure it's the same ship?' asked Phil.

The airlock force field then seemed to fail, as everything loose in the hangar suddenly streamed uncontrollably out of the door and into space.

'Quite sure,' said Cleo.

Next, the shuttle came tumbling out and the battleship began moving strangely sideways and began to roll.

'Fuck me,' exclaimed Andy. 'What is it with these shit pilots?'

'The pilot isn't doing that,' said Cleo. 'Linda is.'

'Linda?' he said. 'How the fu—'

'Did you give Linda the same experimental DOVI upgrade as me?' asked Ed.

'Yeah, just before she gave herself up to save Rayl.'

They all looked back at the image to see the battleship roll straight into the station and trigger the catastrophic chain reaction they were now witnessing. But, more importantly, they watched the tiny shuttle dodge around several large lumps of flying shrapnel and safely disappear inside a private starship. It quickly moved away from its allocated buoy and jumped out of the system.

'We need the full details of that private yacht, Cleo,' said Phil.

'Busy,' replied Cleo.

Moments later, a stream of information appeared:

Starship Erebus IV
    Registered Home Planet – Erdonious
    Owner – Erebus Corporation
    Principal Cabins – 8
    Crew – 45
    Range – 419 LYPJ
    Speed – .79 L

'Cleo, can you find out where Erdonious is?' asked Ed.

'Busy.'

'Are you getting slower, Cleo?'

'No, all done now. I was downloading a large file, but was restricted by the slow computing speed of the PCP's systems.'

'What the hell have you got?'

'The classified data shielding failed on that battle cruiser a few minutes ago, so I accidentally helped myself to the entire memory core.'

'Oh, you bad girl,' said Ed, wagging his finger. 'You must give it back and apologise this instant.'

'What did you get?' said Andy.

'This.'

A holo map of the entire PCP-controlled region of space lit up.

'Oh, you beauty,' said Andy, promptly entering a search for Erdonious.

The three waited as the Gabriel's helm familiarised itself with the enormous quantity of information available. The star map was four times the size of the GDA's and seemed to contain data on every single rock bigger than a football.

The familiar chime sounded and, as they watched, a planet, just over one hundred thousand light years away, gradually grew in size within the hologram. The helm set a course, the Gabriel turned, moved well away from the catastrophe unfolding above Arus'Gan and winked out of the system.

20

STARSHIP EREBUS IV – EN ROUTE TO ERDONIOUS

EPOCH 95, SPAN 9371, JUNCTURE 136.1

Cort Erebus knew it was the obvious destination and when the investigation gained traction, this ship would very swiftly be sought out. For this reason, he had instructed the captain to run the vessel at the ragged edge of its capability. Military ships were certainly faster, but they had – he hoped – a large enough head start.

His father had been quite explicit in his instructions: two fresh breeders had to be delivered to him by Epoch 96 at the latest and Cort knew only too well that disrespecting his father's orders had serious consequences.

His learning of the Mogul's death had been quite shocking – not something that happened every day. But, on hearing that his old school friend Jeehgan, the First Officer on the Dakr Mon, had the Mogul's personal breeders available for the next Locy'fer auction, Cort had promptly contacted him and secured a private deal.

He had been especially keen to secure the Mogul's only long-term breeder – perhaps a little too keen – as he believed Jeehgan had read his enthusiasm and adjusted the price accordingly. But, overly expensive or not, with his family's copious wealth, it was mere pocket change.

Cort's father was Sachem Zeht Erebus XII, of one of the oldest Plecoran families. The Erebus linage could be traced back to the time of the Ancients.

The texts told of the Plecoran region of space, which totalled eight systems and had been at war with each other for over five hundred years. Finally, when peace had prevailed many thousands of spans ago, the Erebus family on Erdonious had risen to power and had ruled the region from that day forward.

Legend says that this was because, during the wars, the Erebus family had been the largest weapons supplier in the region and no one dared stand against them.

Whatever the truth was, they were certainly a weapons supplier now. They had, for as long as anyone could remember, been the principal arms designer, manufacturer and supplier to the PCP. Everything from the smallest hand weapon to the new Hercules Class Battle Cruisers were designed and constructed by the Erebus Corporation here in the Plecoran Region.

Cort stared at the large screen on his suite's wall. It displayed a view from the crew's dining area, showing the three breeders were sitting, eating in the corner of the room. He watched how Quixia's eyes were constantly on the move, surveying everything around her, while his father's girls just stuffed themselves and barely looked up from the table.

'So, you believe they want her for murdering the Mogul?' Cort asked.

'The soldier tried to arrest her for murdering someone,' said Dahkyn, the bodyguard from the shuttle.

'He didn't say who?'

'He was about to when the hangar force field blew out.'

'That was very well-timed.'

'I thought the same, but she was sitting right in front of me with her empty hands in her lap.'

'Have you checked out the pilot?'

'He's worked for your father for thirty-two spans and I checked the video logs from the shuttle. He did nothing, either.'

'We built those battleships. What happened is absolutely impossible. There are layers of redundancy systems and failsafes that ensure those airlock fields can't possibly fail like that and, as for the manoeuvring thrusters, the odds on those failing in that fashion are zero – they just can't.'

'I can only tell you what I saw, Mr Erebus.'

'I know,' said Cort, walking over to the bar to pour himself a drink. 'Keep an eye on her and send her to me here at Juncture 95.'

Dahkyn nodded and left the principal suite.

Cort continued to watch Quixia, undecided if she really could be a useful asset to the Macchia.

Linda still hadn't been summoned by her new employer. She sat in the crew galley, eating what seemed to be a – bold – attempt at a cottage pie. It tasted okay, so she decided against inquiring about its origins.

She kept a sharp eye on everything that went on, knowing there were probably cameras everywhere. She didn't spark up her DOVI to have a look around either just in case it was detected.

The girls were still trying to quiz her about why the PCP suddenly wanted to arrest her for murder, so she continued to play the innocent and kept sparking conjecture about who had fired on the battleship.

This starship, however, was quite luxurious, although the crew quarters, which were almost adjacent to the hangar on the lower decks, were a little more austere – but still more spacious and comfortable than the navy ship.

The girls had discovered they had been bought for Mr Erebus senior, which they were a little disappointed about, as they thought his seventeen-year-old son was quite handsome, or in their crude slang, 'a bit of a pump'.

Chula was still in a fit of pique over her price, but Linda tried to keep her active in conversation, thus making it hard for her to sulk.

The fixation with the blue colour scheme continued into the starship: everything, including her cabin, bathroom, bed linen and even the lighting, was a shade of blue.

The thermostat was set up high again; she was glad the uniform was only a mini toga.

Later, while she was sitting and talking to Gedren in the crew lounge, the bodyguard – whose name she'd discovered was Dahkyn – approached.

'Mr Erebus has requested your presence,' he said to Linda, pointing at the door.

'You lucky bitch,' said Gedren. 'You get to fuck one of the richest boys in the galaxy.'

'I'll put in a good word for you, I promise,' said Linda.

Chula ignored them and continued reading.

Dahkyn led Linda through the ship and up to the principal cabins. Once they were off the crew deck, she found it hard work to drag her feet through the deep pile carpets – the level of opulence here went through the roof. They passed several numbered cabins and their journey ended at a blank lift door.

'This ascends straight into the principal owner's suite,' said Dahkyn, handing her a bracelet. 'Put that on – if Mr Erebus feels he's in any danger, he can activate it and it will render you unconscious.'

She clipped on the bracelet, realising it was impossible to remove. He nodded and pressed the unsurprisingly blue icon, recessed into the blue wall. She saw it scan his finger and, within a couple of seconds, the door opened and she stepped in.

When it reopened, she was faced with the biggest suite she'd ever seen. It covered the entire top deck of the ship and sported a wraparound floor-to-ceiling glass wall, which revealed an amazing panoramic view of the galaxy.

Walking into the centre of the room, she slowly turned to take in the amazing spectacle.

'Pretty view, isn't it?' said Cort as he entered up a stairway, which ascended from underneath the bar.

Linda jumped and spun around at the sound of his voice.

'Bloody hell,' she said. 'Are you sure you're not Vanguard Division, creeping around like that?'

Cort stopped at the top of the stairs and stared at her.

A wry smile slowly overtook his initial shocked expression.

'Now I see what Dahkyn meant when he said you weren't the orthodox breeder.'

'Really? And what else did he say about me?'

Cort shook his head. 'Well, where do I start,' he said, strolling over to the bar and pouring himself a drink from a crystal decanter. 'You claim to be a vanguard officer, just back from an undercover operation in the Daxxal galaxy. You meet a Mogul and, two minutes later, he's dead, his ship allegedly experiencing a critical malfunction. The PCP military tries to arrest you for murder and, immediately, a brand new state-of-the-art battleship experiences another critical malfunction, parking itself into the most strategically important space station in the galaxy. So, perhaps you can tell me if my ship is going to reach its destination or is it suddenly going to fly into a black hole or a star?'

'All just coincidence, Mr Erebus,' said Linda. 'None of those occurrences had any input from me and, anyway, Dahkyn was sitting right opposite me. So, if your crew are competent, then you and your ship are quite safe. Although the obsession with blue is a bit lethal.'

Cort burst out laughing and almost spilled his drink. 'My father's taste,' he said, continuing to chuckle.

'It's your father's ship?' she asked.

'*Was* – he gave it to me on my sixteenth span. He has a much bigger one now.'

'More blue?'

'Yes, even more blue,' he said, nodding and grimacing.

There was a pause. Linda noticed a thoughtful expression take shape on Cort's face.

'You're very different to any breeder I've ever met, you know,' he said. 'They're normally, "Yes, Mr Erebus. No, Mr Erebus. What can I do for you, Mr Erebus?"' He paused. 'I quite like it. Don't talk to anyone else like this, though, especially my father. He'll—'

'Chuck me out an airlock?'

'Ah, you've heard that rumour already.'

'It's not true then?'

'Well, partly,' he said. 'She did pull a knife on him and he lost half a finger in the ensuing struggle.'

'Hence the bracelet?' she said, holding her arm up.

'Yes, it's been family policy ever since.'

'I can understand that.'

His expression changed again and he looked out at the moving starscape.

'Can I ask you a question?' he said. 'And, please, sit down, Quixia – although, if any member of the crew approaches, you must stand, avert your eyes and keep calling me "Mr Erebus". Is that clear?'

'Yes, quite clear. What was your question?'

'I've never met a Mogul,' he said, looking at her intently. 'And you have. My father deals with them all the time, but he never permits me to go near them.' He paused, seeming to be searching for the right words. 'Truthfully, what was it like to actually meet a Mogul?'

'The same as meeting any overly tall, bright red, uneducated, oversexed, child-molesting, murdering, psychopathic, half-brained rapist – I suppose.'

The awkward silence that followed was palpable. Cort's expression changed from a smile to a look of absolute horror, his eyes as large as dinner plates.

'F–fucking hell,' he stammered. 'I don't think there was a word in that sentence that wasn't treasonable. I would keep that opinion very much to yourself.'

'You did say "truthfully".'

'Just lie, like the rest of us.'

'You all think the same as me then?'

'No, not all, but some do. The Moguls have made a lot of people very wealthy, my father included. I think he'd airlock me if he knew my real feelings.'

'Or perhaps he does. That's why he hasn't let you near one.'

'Possible, but I'm sure he doesn't know everything.'

'How d'you know he hasn't bugged the ship?' she said, peering around the huge room.

'First thing I had checked.'

'Can I ask you a question now?'

'Fire away.'

'Did you buy me for sex?'

Cort winced and looked away, his face flushing.

'I'll take that as a yes.'

He nodded.

'What's stopping you then?' she asked. 'You can render me unconscious with just a word.' She waved the bracelet in the air.

'I kinda like you. You're different from the girl my father provided.'

'Am I the first girl you've ever bought?'

'Yes.'

'That explains why you paid so much.'

'Did I get scammed?'

'I don't think you got scammed, so much – just a little overenthusiastic. They would have picked up on that.'

'He was an old school friend too.'

'There are no such thing as friends in business; I'm sure your father taught you that.'

'You wait till I see him again.'

'That would be the wrong play. Next time you see him, pat him on the back and say, "Thank you, she was absolutely fantastic and I sold her on for three times as much".'

Cort stood up and strolled over to the glass wall. He

stared out at the vista for a few moments. 'Is it true – the breeders in Daxxal have equal status to the males?'

Linda had realised earlier that the Andromedan name for the Milky Way was Daxxal.

'In most societies, yes,' she answered.

'I take it that's where you became so confident and outspoken?' he said as he turned to look back at her.

'Do you think that's a bad thing?' she asked, looking up at him.

Their eyes met and he slowly shook his head.

'I have some friends I'd like you to meet.'

'Should I be concerned or happy about that?'

'I think you'll find they're kindred spirits, Quixia.'

21

STARSHIP EREBUS IV – EN ROUTE TO ERDONIOUS

EPOCH 96, SPAN 9371, JUNCTURE 121.8

Linda woke with a start. She gazed around her cabin, trying to determine what had woken her. Something had changed. It took her a moment to realise the background hum of the ship was lower and then she felt a slight bump and a shudder.

She closed her eyes and opened up her DOVI. The outside camera view of the ship showed a huge, black warship of some kind. They appeared to have just docked with it.

'Shit,' she said, jumping up and throwing on her toga dress. She scanned through the outside camera images again until she found one from right at the top of the starship. She discovered a planet close by and another warship and another. When she panned the image right out, it showed not only a row of warships, but many rows going on for tens of kilometres, most still in various stages of construction. She could see dozens of small craft milling around the huge ships and the continuous flashes from welding torches. The design was new to her, as was the size. These were behemoths, much larger than any Andromedan ship she'd seen before.

'Oh, shit,' she whispered to herself. 'Could this be the invasion fleet?'

She made her way to the crew lounge, finding Gedren and Chula about to leave. Dahkyn was hovering, waiting for the instruction to transfer the breeders across to the docked warship.

LINDA GAVE both the girls a hug. Gedren seemed quite emotional when she realised Quixia wouldn't be leaving with them and clung on a bit longer than was comfortable. Linda recognised she was still very young and clearly without a mother figure for a long time. She let her cling on for as long as she wanted, reassuring her she'd be okay.

After the girls had left, she grabbed some breakfast and went back to her cabin. On her bed was a smart new crew uniform. This was like a two-piece pant suit, in black – with the inevitable light-blue trimmings. Linda didn't care as it was a lot less revealing than the toga. It even came with shoes and a cap. Once dressed, she looked at herself in the mirror and laughed.

I look like a junior pilot, fresh out of flight school, she thought.

The ship juddered slightly again as they released from the warship and slowly moved away.

CORT BREATHED A SIGH OF RELIEF. His father had seemed quite enamoured of his new breeders, especially when he learned they belonged to the late Tyuk Baa. He'd given his son, after a little gentle coercion, the codes to one of the family holiday resorts on Kqett as a reward. The planet was in a system only one jump away from Erdonious and, more importantly, close to the Macchia base on Reeme Station.

Unbeknownst to his father, for the last two years Cort had been a confidential benefactor to the Macchia by squirrelling away some of his substantial allowance. The self-effaced principal of the Macchia was Huwlen Senn, Cort's professor of politics, during his education on Erdonious.

Huwlen had once been a staunch supporter of the

PCP up until the death of his mother. His mother had been a commercial caterer and, through Huwlen, had secured the catering contract at a prestigious university presentation evening.

The event had been held on a Mogul's personal starship while in orbit around Erdonious. It was unusual for a breeder to run any kind of business and at the event she stood out, dressed in her immaculate white uniform rather than the typical breeders' attire.

The Mogul, Tyuk Hass, had been unimpressed and summoned her to his chamber to force her to show allegiance.

Two hours later, the crew unclamped her unconscious, naked body from the mounting cradle and took her straight to the medical centre. She died a few hours later from massive internal injuries, never regaining consciousness. The verdict – as was usual in these events – was misadventure.

Huwlen was crestfallen and, from that day forward, swore to avenge his mother's death. He wasn't suicidal, though. He'd spent many years searching out others of the same perspective and building a secret militia named the Macchia, based on an old mining planetoid in the Kqett system called Reeme Station.

Reeme Station – or in its heyday, Reeme Mining Station – was part of the Kqett Belt, one of millions of assorted rocks orbiting far out in the Kqett System. It had long since ceased to operate as a mining operation and, as far as the PCP were concerned, it was a backwater home for the region's undesirables. If you wanted to live on that cold, dark, distant lump of rock, then by all means, help yourself. It never caused any problems, nobody really cared; it just got forgotten about.

But for Huwlen Senn and his growing band of agnostic miscreants, it was the perfect foxhole.

'Now that looks a little more professional,' said Cort as Quixia exited the lift into his apartment.

'Thank you, Mr Erebus.'

'Can I make a rule for when you and I are alone in this cabin that you call me Cort?'

Quixia appeared a little taken aback.

'Okay, if you're sure? Cort it is,' she said, looking at him suspiciously.

'Don't look at me like that, I'm not trying to seduce you,' he said. 'I'm just sick of being Mr Erebus all the time and having no friends. I suppose I'm asking if you'll be my friend.'

'Of course I will.'

'But as far as the crew are concerned, you're my breeder and only here for sex.'

'Don't you like sex?' she asked.

He quickly looked away and felt his face redden.

'Erm, yes, of course I do,' he said, finding it hard to meet her gaze again. 'But I have Kisten for that.'

'Kisten?' she asked, giving him a quizzical look.

'She's the breeder my father provided,' he said with a shrug.

'Is she nice?'

'She's lovely – pretty and everything, but…'

'But, what?'

'Err – a bit too young.'

'How young is too young?'

'Thirteen.'

'Shit, that is young.'

'And I don't want to end up like my father.'

'You don't paint a very good picture of him.'

'He's a disgusting pervert who sucks up to the Moguls.'

'It's his money that provides all this, though,' she said, sweeping her hand around the room. 'And getting back to the original dilemma, why don't you send Kisten back and ask for someone older?'

'Because she's really sweet and, if I do, he'll just abuse her before dumping her back in an auction to be bought by some other sexual deviant.' He sat down again and inspected his fingernails closely. 'So, I look after her and keep her safe.'

'You mean you haven't touched her?'

'No. Only Dahkyn knows,' he said, glancing up nervously. 'He organises an older breeder for me when I need one.'

A soft chime sounded that made them both look up.

'We've arrived at Kqett,' he said, standing up and walking towards the lift door. 'Follow me. We're going for a little trip.'

He took her down to the hangar along with Dahkyn, where they boarded another larger shuttle, one capable of planet insertion. Cort sat down in the pilot's seat, quickly prepped the ship, and took them out into space.

'No pilot this time?' asked Quixia.

'The fewer people that know where we're going the better,' Cort replied, glancing over his shoulder and grinning. He took the shuttle around the planet in the opposite direction of the starship's orbit. When they were on opposing sides of Kqett, instead of dropping into the atmosphere, he pointed the little ship out away from the planet and hit the gas. Dahkyn opened a panel on the wall of the cockpit and unclipped a small unit.

'Have we just gone dark?' asked Quixia.

'Does it make you feel at home?' said Cort, taking the ship up to its maximum speed of .7 light.

'It is rather intriguing. Are we going anywhere nice?'

'A nice romantic holiday spot I know,' said Cort, smiling again. Even Dahkyn sat back down chuckling.

Quixia sat, staring out the front screen into complete blackness. 'It looks nice and sunny,' she said, raising her eyebrows.

A few minutes later Dahkyn disappeared into the back of the shuttle, reappearing with three large coats and woolly hats. A loud beeping sounded in the cockpit, followed by a stern voice.

'Unidentified shuttle, this is Reeme security. Please announce your intentions.'

'Reeme, this is Cort. Please tell Mr Senn I have supplies for his mining operation.'

A short pause ensued before Reeme came back to them.

'Cort, this is Reeme. You have permission to dock in hangar 117b. Here is your flight trajectory.'

The helm beeped and showed a green flight path. Cort hit the lock icon, the helm beeped twice and the autopilot system lit up. He stood up and passed Quixia a coat and woolly hat.

'You'll certainly need these until we reach the living area,' he said while donning the same.

The three of them watched as the stars all slowly disappeared from the front screen, replaced by a growing dark rock face. As they approached, the immensity of the planetoid became clearer. It gave the impression that you could crash into it at any moment, but in actual fact, the ship was still several kilometres out.

What seemed like a small mark on the surface grew and grew into an opening hundreds of metres wide. As the small ship passed through the entrance, Linda noticed three huge laser cannons hiding in the shadows.

'Looks like Huwlen's been investing my donations back into the family coffers,' said Cort, indicating to the cannons.

The shuttle went to the back of the cavern, turned left down a side tunnel, stopped, spun on its own axis and reversed through an opaque force field into a small hangar. Cort shut down the ship and opened the airlock. Immediately, a small drone entered the ship, hovered in the middle of the cockpit for a moment and disappeared back out again.

'Don't worry,' said Cort. 'Just a—'

'Security and bio check,' said Quixia. 'Don't want to bring in any surprises, do we?'

Cort looked at Quixia with a renewed respect.

'How did you know that? They're brand new. The first ones only came off the production line a few epochs ago.'

'They've had them in Daxxal for decades.'

'So that's where the blueprints came from. It took our engineers a few days to translate them.'

'Have you had any others like that?' she asked.

'A few little bits,' said Cort. 'My father's been gearing up a new factory on Erdonious ready for the GDA cloaking technology. He's planning on fitting it into all the new Hercules Cruisers that are being constructed around the planet. He's been waiting a couple of spans now. Allegedly one of our warships – the Kwarth I think it is – will be in possession of the blueprints when it returns in a few months.'

'How many Hercules Cruisers are we building?' she asked, quickly changing the subject as they descended the steps.

'That's classified, you know.'

'So's knowledge of my existence,' she countered.

'Fair point,' he said. 'Six hundred and sixty-six.'

'That's a strange number.'

'Each region and Mogul is financing and providing a crew for their Hercules. It spreads the cost; they're over seven hundred billion each.'

'Shit,' she said. 'No wonder your family's got a dollar or two.'

'What's a dollar or two?'

'Ah, Daxxal slang for lots of cash – sorry. It's hard to get out of the habit.'

The hangar exit door they were approaching

opened and a skinny, unkempt-haired man of indeterminate age trotted through. He wore what could only be described as a very second-hand, blue boiler suit, which was covered in oil and grease stains. 'Cort,' he called. 'How's my favourite adopted son?'

They embraced.

'You needn't have dressed up for my sake,' said Cort, grinning.

'Ah,' he said. 'All the rage in downtown Reeme, you know. The girls go crazy for a bit of rough.'

'All lubed up and ready to go,' said Quixia, immediately getting Huwlen's attention. 'I'm Quixia by the way,' she added, giving him a sly grin.

'Indeed you are,' said Huwlen, looking her up and down and raising his eyebrows at Cort. 'Well, I could do with a drink. How about you, Quixia?' he asked, leading them through the hangar door.

'Got any lager?'

'What's lager?' asked Huwlen, striding off down the corridor at such a rate, everyone else had to trot to keep up.

'It's all the rage in downtown Daxxal,' she said, giving him a sideways glance.

'Ha – why, have you been there then?' he asked, sarcastically.

'She's just got back,' said Cort.

Huwlen stopped dead, and stared at her. 'You've been to the Daxxal galaxy?'

'I have – for many spans.'

'She was an undercover vanguard officer,' said Cort.

Huwlen took a step back and shifted his gaze to Cort. 'You've brought a Vanguard spy onto my fucking station?' he shouted. 'Are you insane?'

'You haven't heard the best part yet.'

'You mean there's more?'

'You've heard about Tyuk Baa?'

'Who hasn't? It's all anyone's talking about.'

Cort nodded at Quixia. 'It was her.'

'Now hang on a minute, I never said it was me,' said Quixia, glancing between the two of them.

'And now the PCP is trying to arrest her,' Cort continued, giving Huwlen a smirk.

Huwlen continued to glare at Quixia.

'Did you have anything to do with that battleship accidentally bumping into Locy'fer station yesterday?'

'No, no, that was just an accident,' she said, starting to sound a little riled.

'Bloody convenient accident,' said Cort. 'The fact it happened at the precise moment the soldiers arrived to arrest you – and, as I said before, it was an impossibility for all those simultaneous failures to occur on one of our ships.'

'So, let me get this straight,' said Huwlen. 'In the

last few days, you've murdered a Mogul, along with a few members of his crew, destroyed a Xenon Class Battleship, rendered about half of Locy'fer station uninhabitable, along with damaging or destroying another seventy-nine smaller PCP vessels, and caused the worst environmental disaster in Arus'Gan's history. Did I miss anything?'

Before Quixia could say anything, another man came barrelling down the corridor towards them. Dahkyn jumped in front of him and pinned him to the wall.

'It's okay, Dahkyn. He's my communications officer,' said Huwlen.

Dahkyn released the man, who gave him a very unfriendly glare as he waved Huwlen away from the group. He began talking to him quite animatedly, but in hushed tones so they couldn't hear. Huwlen looked suddenly shocked and glanced over towards Cort. He nodded a few more times and Cort heard him say, 'Okay, leave it with me. I'll let him know.'

Huwlen walked slowly back, staring at the floor, obviously in deep thought. As he reached them, he looked straight at Cort. 'A PCP battleship jumped into the Kqett system a few minutes ago and attacked a starship in orbit around Kqett.'

Cort's face went ashen. 'The–the Erebus IV?' he stammered.

Huwlen nodded.

'Oh, shit, how bad is it?'

Huwlen shook his head slowly and lowered his gaze. 'They laser-cannoned it into pieces,' he said.

'What about lifeboats?' said Quixia.

Huwlen looked over at her. He was visibly shaking. 'They vaporised them with a beam weapon as they launched.'

'So, no one made it down to the surface?' said Cort, already knowing the answer.

The following silence confirmed it.

Cort stood, staring at the floor and clenching his fists over and over. 'Poor Kisten,' he said, his bottom lip trembling. 'I hope she didn't suffer.'

Huwlen turned and called one of his colleagues over. 'The shuttle in hangar 117b,' he said. 'Move it deep, somewhere it can't be found.'

'Yes, sir.'

'And make sure the airlock's sealed. We don't want any rock rats setting up residence.'

'No, sir.'

'Rock rats?' quizzed Quixia. 'What, like animals?'

'No, stubborn descendants of the miners from eons ago. They refused to leave when the mining ceased. There's an increasing number of them skulking in the deeps. They'll steal anything they can get their hands on.'

Cort glanced behind him at Dahkyn, who was standing a few feet away, just to reassure himself he was still there. He was the only survivor of his crew of forty-five. He didn't need to ask if he'd heard; the murderous expression on Dahkyn's face as their eyes met answered that. He turned back to Huwlen.

'It seems you have three fugitives requiring asylum.'

22

THE STARSHIP GABRIEL – EN ROUTE TO ERDONIOUS, ANDROMEDA

EPOCH 96, SPAN 9371, JUNCTURE 161.6

'We're an hour away, Ed,' called Cleo.

'Huh – what? Sorry.'

'From Erdonious – an hour away. You asked me to wake you.'

'Ah, yes. Thanks, Cleo. Can you wake Andrew please?'

'He's already up.'

'What? Did he shit the bed or something?'

'No, he's in the gym.'

'Now I know you're taking the piss.'

Ed showered and made his way up to the bridge.

'You're not going to believe this,' said Phil as Ed appeared out of the floor on the tube lift.

'What, Andy in the gym?'

'No,' he said, giving Ed a strange look. 'The amount of activity around Erdonious.'

The holo map display showed a hive of activity around the planet, with around a thousand ships in the vicinity.

'Bloody hell, look at that lot!' exclaimed Ed. 'Are they military?'

'I think so. The majority are huge ships – not a design we've seen before: stationary, line after line of them and still under construction. We'll know more as we get closer.'

'Mornin' all,' said Andy, grinning as he stepped off the tube lift.

'Gym?' questioned Ed, giving him a sideways look.

'No, it's Andy,' he said, pointing at himself.

Ed just gave him a glare, so Andy decided to continue. 'D'you realise, I've put on over fifteen pounds since we came into space?'

'Well, stop the beer and pizza diet and jump in the auto-nurse every few days for a detox.'

'I feel like that's cheating a bit and I like the endorphins after a good workout.'

'Who are you and what have you done with our Andy?' asked Phil with a smirk.

Andy was about to answer when he noticed the holo map display. 'Fuck me, look at that lot.'

On closer inspection, he noticed that most of them were of a similar design, in rows and under construction.

'Have we found the invasion fleet?' he asked.

Ed and Phil exchanged a glance.

'Hadn't thought of that,' said Phil.

'The Erebus Corporation is based here and they're registered as an armaments design and construction company,' said Andy. 'I was just reading up on it in the gym.'

THE GABRIEL WAS at .9 light and entering the system fast. Phil had jumped into non-system space so there was less chance of being detected on emergence. They were now cloaked and zipping by the first of the outermost planets.

As they got closer to Erdonious, Andy's question was answered. These were indeed military ships: huge battle cruisers, although not as large as the GDA's Katadromiko class, but all had planet-busting capabilities.

'Linda's ship isn't in the system,' said Cleo, sounding disappointed.

'This region is made up of eight systems,' said Andy. 'Check the others, Cleo.'

'Found it.'

'That was quick. Are you sure?'

'Yep, it's in the nearest system, just one jump away. The Kqett system and…'

Cleo paused for a moment, which was unusual.

'And what?' asked Andy.

'I got a faint reading from Linda's DOVI and now it's gone.'

'On the ship?'

'Well, that's the strange thing. It came from an asteroid belt on the outer fringe of the system. I only just caught it and, when I concentrated the scan on that area, it disappeared.'

'We need to go there. Phil, can you get us to the Kqett system asap?'

'On the way,' said Phil. 'It'll take a while as I can't jump until we're away from detection from all this traffic.'

'Bloody hell,' shouted Cleo. That made everyone look up from their stations.

'What is it?' said Ed

'A PCP battleship just jumped into the Kqett system almost on top of the Erebus IV and opened fire without any warning.'

'But that's an unarmed civilian ship,' said Phil. 'It only has navigational bow shielding.'

'They must be trying to stop it running,' said Ed. 'What part of the ship have they targeted?'

The silence that followed was unusual for Cleo, so Ed tried again. 'Cleo, are you there?'

'Yes.'

'Did you hear my question?'

'Yes, I heard the question. It's just they haven't targeted any particular part of the ship – they're cutting it to pieces.'

'What?'

'Oh, no,' said Cleo.

'Now what?'

'They're vaporising any lifeboats that launch with a beam weapon.'

'You're kidding?'

'Murdering fuckers,' said Andy. 'Can't we get there any quicker and target that bastard?'

'No,' said Ed. 'If they knew we were here, the entire fleet would converge on us. We need to concentrate on getting Linda first and then inflict as much damage as we can on the way out.'

'We'll have to be careful with that too,' said Phil. 'All they need to do is blockade the gate and we can't get home.'

'That's a very good point, Phil,' said Ed. 'They wouldn't need to hunt us at all. They'd know there was one place we would have to be, sooner or later.'

'Okay,' said Andy. 'If we do have to target one of their ships in the future, targeting their transmission arrays is a first priority.'

'I can be of help here too,' said Cleo. 'When I downloaded the data core from that damaged PCP ship,

I obtained all their recognition codes and, with a bit of holographic manipulation, I can make this ship appear to be the PCP Attack Ship Dakr Mon.'

'That may prove invaluable, Cleo. Well done,' said Ed. 'And now we've got all that organised, can we get over to that faint DOVI signal you received?'

'We'll be there within the hour,' said Cleo. 'Ah, shit – what now?'

'What's happening, Cleo?' asked Andy.

'The battleship is firing on the planet with a beam weapon.'

'At what?'

'Too far away to tell. Do you want to go there first?'

'No, following Linda's trail is the priority,' said Ed.

Andy brought up the holo map of the Kqett system. 'There's an old mining station on one of the larger rocks in that belt. It ceased production some time ago but there's no information about it being uninhabitable.'

'Perhaps she knew about the pursuing battleship and went there to hide,' said Phil.

'Let's hope so,' said Ed.

'The PCP battleship has left orbit and is heading in the direction of the mining station,' said Cleo.

'Shit,' said Andy. 'Pedal to the metal please, Phil.'

'Thirty-four minutes to jump point,' he said.

'She'll be well hidden,' said Ed, crossing his fingers.

23

REEME MINING STATION – KQETT SYSTEM, ANDROMEDA

EPOCH 96, SPAN 9371, JUNCTURE 166.4

When it became apparent the battleship was heading their way, Huwlen put Quixia, Cort and Dahkyn on a small train carriage – with a one-way ticket into the deeps – and completely wiped any audio and video footage that involved them from the data logs.

'What the hell is that stink?' asked Cort as they disembarked the carriage several kilometres below the surface.

'Phosphines,' said Linda. 'From mining metallic ores.'

'How the hell would you know that?' asked Huwlen.

'Flying ore freighters in Daxxal,' she said. 'You never forget that smell.'

'You seem to have many skills for just a breeder,' said Dahkyn, giving her a contemptuous glare.

Huwlen led them through a huge steel doorway into

a massive cavern, of which Linda was unable to see the far side. It must have been at least five hundred metres high too.

As they entered, the door sealed behind them. They all looked at Huwlen, when a loud rumbling sounded from outside.

'It's a rock door to disguise the opening,' he said, smiling.

A sprawling metropolis stretched out before them, full of people and traffic and noise. A vehicle pulled up – what Linda thought looked just like an electric tuk tuk – and Huwlen beckoned them to board. It set off into the streets as soon as they sat down, weaving through the narrow lanes, past homes and shops and businesses. But what really shocked Cort and Dahkyn, she noticed, were the people: men and women walking together, arm in arm, equals.

'Welcome to Macchia Town,' called Huwlen, shouting above the hubbub.

'You never brought me here before,' shouted Cort.

'No,' he said. 'You have to have a reason to really hate the PCP before you're invited to join us here.'

The tuk tuk pulled into a small doorway and stopped. Huwlen patted the driver on the back and waved the three of them inside through a partially hidden door. He closed the door, punched a code into a keypad on the wall and the whole floor of the small room descended several floors until another doorway appeared. As he ushered them inside a seemingly small airlock, they heard a series of clicks, whirring sounds and a hiss before the door at the other end opened. They emerged into what looked like a starship bridge.

The room was circular, had video displays around the walls and crew couches set in a circle similar to the Gabriel.

'How close is that battleship?' Huwlen asked.

'Ten minutes out,' said one of the crew. 'And they're not sparing fuel.'

'Okay, everyone. Usual drills – give them every courtesy and, if they want to board, give them hangar 90a to play with. Do not power up any of the Mark Thirteens, but ensure you have their transmission and targeting arrays locked in for the first salvo, just in case.'

Huwlen waved his guests towards some seating at the far side of the control room and settled himself onto a spare control couch.

Linda sat with the others and watched the monitors. It wasn't long before the recognisable silhouette of a PCP battleship swept into view and slowed quickly.

'PCP battleship, this is Reeme Station. Are you in need of berthing protocols?' asked Huwlen.

'You will deliver Vanguard Officer Quixia and the

Erebus child to this ship immediately. Failure to comply will result in your destruction,' came the stern reply.

'PCP battleship, we have no knowledge of these people. I have made hangar 90a available for you to search the station.'

The six laser cannons on the starboard side of the battleship all fired as one; five just blew lumps of rock off the surface of the station, but the sixth destroyed hangar 90a.

'Shit,' shouted Cort. 'There goes one of your biggest hangars.'

'It's a hangar we never use,' said Huwlen, winking. 'That's why I gave them the co-ordinates. It hasn't been operational for spans and was due for a refit.'

'Perhaps you misunderstood the word, "immediately",' boomed out around the control room.

'Are they all as arrogant as this idiot?' asked Cort. 'I've never had any dealings with the PCP once the ships are handed over.'

'Sir,' said one of the control room operators. 'I've just had a message stating that after destroying the Erebus IV, the battleship fired on the Erebus resort on Kqett.'

Cort's eyes widened.

'That's not all,' he continued, staring at the floor. 'A major news agency on Erdonious is reporting the PCP just arrested Cort's father and is taking him to Arus'Gan.'

'What?' shouted Cort. 'They can't do that.' He stood up and pointed at the monitor that showed the battleship still blasting lumps off the station. 'Give that fucker a taste of our Mark Thirteens and let's go get my father back.'

'What in—' said Huwlen, turning to face Cort. 'You have an unarmed, unshielded shuttle. Are you going to hang out the airlock with a laser pistol and take on a PCP warship?'

Cort opened his mouth, closed it again and sat down with his head in his hands. 'Shit, shit and shitty shit,' he shouted at the floor.

'Well – while you're being seventeen, I have work to do,' said Huwlen and turned to face the monitors again as a now familiar voice boomed around the room:

'Reeme Station, prepare to be boarded. Any resistance will be met with lethal force.'

'So, you've been using blanks up to now, have you?'

There was a short pause, but they all noticed a hangar door slowly opening on the side of the battleship.

'Your execution will be our first priority,' came the cold reply.

Huwlen turned towards his station defence officer. 'I'm getting a little pissed off with this arsehole,' said

Huwlen, clenching his fists. 'How many thirteens can we bring to bear?'

'Five, sir,' came the immediate reply.

'Okay, target the arrays first, then propulsion and finally one straight into that hangar.'

'Charging.'

'Fire when ready.'

Huwlen, unbeknownst to the PCP, had mounted twenty-six hidden Mark Thirteen planetary laser cannons around the station.

Everybody in the control room had their eyes fixed on the monitors.

'Weapons charged and targeted – firing now,' said the defence officer.

A huge flash caused the monitors to white out. It made them all blink and shield their eyes for a moment.

'Someone make a note to issue eye protection next time we do that,' said Huwlen, squinting and rubbing his eyes.

The white out on the monitors gradually faded.

'Where's the battleship?' said Linda, looking around at all the monitors.

'I have three ships in the vicinity, sir,' said a second officer. 'All spinning and moving away in an erratic fashion.'

'Three?' questioned Cort.

'He didn't have any shields up,' said Huwlen,

realising the battleship had been blown into three pieces. 'The stupid arrogant halfwit – he's just murdered his crew as well.'

'What about any remainder, sir?' asked the second officer, glancing up from his controls.

'Tractor the pieces into the ore processing hangar, cut them up and reprocess them. Lock up any survivors and make sure you vaporise any remaining debris before it floats too far away. We don't want evidence of that ship having ever been here.'

'Can you really get rid of it that quickly?' asked Cort.

'There's a smelter in that hangar that'll do the job in a few hours, then I can sell the metals back to your father.' Huwlen had said it before he could stop himself.

Cort glared at him.

'Shit, sorry, son,' he said. 'They won't harm him. He's far too valuable to them.'

Cort nodded slowly and looked up at a monitor. They all watched as the last section of battleship disappeared through an enormous doorway into the blackness within, then the sudden brightness of several industrial laser cutters as they chewed into the wreckage. The huge hangar doors gently closed and the Tasmin Class Battleship was gone.

Huwlen glanced down from the monitor to find everyone looking at him.

'Well,' he said. 'I hope that idiot captain was as lazy with his reporting as he was with everything else.'

'It must be standing orders to report your movements,' said Linda.

'It's standing orders to have your shields up in potential combat situations too,' replied Cort. 'Or so I was led to believe.'

'Okay,' said Huwlen. 'Enough with the hypotheticals. We need to provide you three with some new identities and some clothing so you blend in.'

'Sounds good to me,' said Linda, thinking anything would be better than a light blue fringed ship's uniform.

24

THE STARSHIP GABRIEL – EN ROUTE TO REEME STATION, ANDROMEDA

EPOCH 96, SPAN 9371, JUNCTURE 191.6

Phil brought the Gabriel out from behind the Kqett system's star and set course for Reeme Station at .9 light. He calculated that jumping in behind the star was the safest and quickest way to get to the asteroid belt.

Ed and Andy had gone below to get breakfast and reappeared just as the ship emerged from behind the star.

'Got ya a bacon sandwich with barbecue sauce, Phil,' said Andy, handing it over.

'Thanks. Well, that's weird.'

Andy looked back at him with a puzzled expression. 'You liked it with barbecue sauce last time.'

'No, not the sandwich. The battleship. It's disintegrated.'

The holo image appeared in the centre of the room, showing the station and a battleship in three pieces.

'That must have happened while we were behind the star,' said Ed.

'The information I have regarding that mining station was that it's supposed to be non-operational and undefended,' said Andy.

'It must have been something substantial to dismantle one of their battleships,' said Phil, looking concerned. 'We need to be cautious.'

Phil slowed the ship to .5 light and scanned the area around the station thoroughly.

'Nothing,' he said. 'I can't see inside the station at all. The rock's too dense—oh, hang on.'

As they watched, a huge section of what looked like rock wall slowly opened on the side of the station. The sections of battleship ceased spinning and gradually reversed their outward trajectory to inward towards the station.

'Non-operational, my arse,' said Andy. 'That's one powerful tractor beam set-up they've got. What are the odds they've got a few heavy cannons as well?'

Almost on cue, two large-capacity laser cannons vaporised any remaining evidence of the battleship ever being there.

'Well, how about that?' he said, grinning at everyone.

'Smart arse,' said Ed.

'It seems we've found some buddies,' said Phil.

'They may not be in bed with the PCP, but it doesn't mean they'll welcome us,' Ed reminded Phil. 'Those planet-sized cannons could damage us through our shields – I think we'll stay incognito.'

'Can you detect if Linda's here, Cleo?' asked Andy.

'No, I can't penetrate the station at all. Most of it's solid rock.'

'Okay, can you find somewhere we can safely get inside the station undetected?' asked Ed.

'You're going to go in there?' said Phil, nervously.

'Can you think of a better way?' said Ed.

'Send in a nano cloud, like we did to find you last time.'

'The PCP ships have nano infiltration detectors. I can't imagine, with the level of defensive hardware they have here, they'd have neglected to put a few of those in.'

'Ah, bugger.'

The tube lift appeared out of the floor. Rayl stepped off and smiled at everyone.

'Have we found Linda yet?' she asked, sounding hopeful.

'We think she's on this station,' said Ed, pointing at the holo image. 'Andy and I are about to go take a sneaky peek.'

'Why don't you just ask them?' she said.

'Cuz they're not very welcoming to visiting ships,'

said Andy. 'And she's probably still undercover as Quixia.'

'Can I stay and watch? I'm bored with sitting around on my own.'

'Sure,' said Ed. 'You can have my couch here and keep Phil company while we're gone.'

Phil gave Ed a withering look.

'Give her a POK and play some of the gigs you and the boys went to,' he said with a wink.

'What's a gig?' she asked.

'There you are, Uncle Phil. The girl needs an introduction into the wonders of seventies progressive rock.'

'Poor girl,' said Cleo. 'Wouldn't thirties trojan beat be more up her street?'

'Judging by her hairstyle, perhaps eighties new romance would float her boat,' said Andy, giving her the thumbs-up.

Rayl looked at everyone, seemingly bemused, not understanding a word.

'Is this music?' she asked.

'Some of it is,' said Ed, getting a disapproving look from Andy.

'We have movement,' said Cleo, suddenly.

Two small ships emerged from a crevice in the rock and began inspecting the outside of the station, occasionally firing small laser weapons at debris on the surface.

'They're cleaning up evidence the big guns can't get,' said Andy.

'Cleo,' said Ed, 'can you scan those ships and see what the crews are wearing? And make us something similar.'

'I'm on it,' said Cleo. 'And, Andrew, do you want to have the same DOVI manipulation abilities as Ed and Linda?'

Andy made a big show of putting his finger against his lips and pretending to be in deep thought.

'Could I use it to change channels on the telly? And start my motorbike?'

'Yes, Andrew, but careful you don't strain yourself,' said Cleo, sarcastically.

'Well, that's using the latest technology to its full capacity, isn't it?' said Ed, shaking his head.

A glass of what looked like water appeared in front of Andy.

'Are you sure we should all have this? I thought it could get confusing if we all had the ability?' asked Andy.

'Just drink it,' she said. 'In your case you're normally confused anyway.'

'You could've put it in beer or something,' he said, drinking the water and wrinkling his nose.

'I'm about to issue you with a weapon, so no beer.'
'Yeah, but fish shit in water.'

Phil brought the Gabriel to within a few thousand kilometres of the station and parked just inside the asteroid belt. Ed and Andy donned the clothing that Cleo produced and pocketed stun guns that looked like torches.

'Are you sure this's what they're wearing?' moaned Andy, looking down at the scruffy shirt and trousers he'd been provided. 'The coat looks like it came out of a dumpster.'

'Perhaps sir would like to find a local gentleman's outfitters when you get inside,' said Cleo.

'Or a nice country pub with good ale and pretty barmaids,' Andy countered.

'Shut up, you two,' said Ed as they made their way over to the tube lift.

Ed chose one of the shuttles as it was smaller than the Cartella and would be easier to hide in a corner.

Exiting the Gabriel took a bit of extra concentration as the asteroid belt was constantly in a state of flux. Even with the shields on full, they were still nudged around by some of the larger rocks before entering clear space.

Cleo had instructed them to investigate the cavern where the two smaller ships had appeared from earlier. It took eleven minutes to reach the entrance and Andy watched the proximity scans closely as they were unable to see inside until they were right in the mouth of the opening.

Ed edged the shuttle inside, close to one side, just in case someone came steaming out of the dark, thinking it was clear.

The cavern opened up around them and, as their eyes adjusted to the gloom, it became evident this was not a fully operational station anymore. Three huge planet-sized laser cannons hung from the ceiling, obscuring rows of abandoned hangars, which stretched away in all directions. Ed reached out with his DOVI, trying to find an unmanned but operational hangar. Most he found were dark and dead but, just as he thought all was lost, he found a small side tunnel with three operational hangars. The first was small and only contained a tiny sleek-looking ship; the next hangar was much larger, lit and probably was where the two cleaning up ships came from; but the third was, again, big enough for several ships – it was in darkness, empty and had '117b' stencilled on the back wall. Ed turned the ship, backed it into the far corner and killed the drives as quickly as he could.

They waited five minutes; no alarms sounded, no

soldiers came running, just silence. Ed investigated the hangar controls. Ignoring the lighting, he initiated the entrance force field and pressurised the hangar. Again, they waited and, again, nothing happened.

Sealing the ship, they quickly made their way over to the airlock. Ed had already opened the outer door so they could jog straight in. He cycled the airlock as soon as they were in and, with a clunk, the outer door closed. A slight hiss followed and the inner door opened.

'Fuck me, it's cold. And what's that stink?' said Andy, reeling back.

'I don't know, but get used to it quick.'

The corridor they found themselves in ran in two directions: left went to the other hangars and right went deeper into the asteroid, which was the way they chose.

'Walk casually,' said Ed, slowing Andy down by grabbing his shoulder. 'Act like you know where you're going and put your torch away.'

They began to see others, seemingly all lost in their own thoughts, going about their business without giving them a second look.

'I think Cleo got the clothing right,' said Andy.

'Make sure you tell her that – after all your whinging. You'd have looked a right tool here in shorts and a Thompson Twins T-shirt.'

They continued walking and talking, looking as if they belonged. Ed put out a call to Linda on his DOVI every so often but, so far, had no reply. After a few minutes of random wandering, they came across a large dining room. They stood, leaning against a wall outside for a few moments, monitoring the routine inside and pretending to have a conversation. It didn't seem as if anyone was taking money for anything or being scanned for payment. Deciding to risk it, they walked in and helped themselves to a couple of what looked remarkably like doughnuts and a drink that the majority seemed to favour.

Secreting themselves away at a table in a corner of the room, they continued with their fake conversation, watching what went on around them.

'Oh! Shit, erm, this isn't very—' said Andy, grimacing and trying to talk through a large mouthful of doughnut.

Ed peered down suspiciously at his own plate. 'Isn't very what?'

Andy chewed for a moment with an anguished expression, swallowed and immediately took a sizeable swig from his drink.

'It's filled with meat of some kind,' he said, dropping the remainder back on his plate and frowning at it.

'Chicken?' asked Ed. 'Beef? Pork? Lamb?'

'Sloth,' Andy replied. 'Stewed in diesel and underpants.' He pushed his plate away, wiping his mouth on his sleeve and sporting a look of sallow disdain.

A shadow loomed over their table, which caused them to freeze.

'New faces,' said a tall, skinny guy in a rather grease-stained coat, what looked like swimming goggles and a fur hat, who suddenly sat down with them, completely uninvited. 'Did you come in on the Erebus shuttle?'

Ed and Andy's eyes met in a look of panic.

'Er, yeah,' said Ed.

'Thought so,' he said, removing the goggles and polishing them with an oily old rag from his pocket. 'I'm Sticky, by the way – and don't ask. Everybody here calls me that.' He glanced around the room. 'Not sure why, though.'

'I'm Ed and this is Andy,' said Ed, pointing at himself and Andy.

'You had to be very new here,' he said. 'No one tries those a second time.' He pointed at the doughnuts. 'Kqett Shaggie pies – only the locals can stomach them.'

'What's a Shaggie?' asked Ed.

'Some sort of hairy rodent, breeds like fuck down in the mines. My hat's made from the pelt.' He snatched said hat off and waved it under their noses. 'Stinks a bit, but keeps the Keeters away.' He looked at them for a moment with a quizzical expression. 'So, what have the Putrid Cowardly Plague done to force you to visit this luxury resort?'

'The who?' asked Andy.

'The PCP,' he said, giving them a peculiar look. 'What galaxy are you from?'

'One far, far away,' said Andy and received a kick in the shin from Ed.

'We're from Hunus,' said Ed, quickly. 'And do we need a reason to be here?'

'Ah, fringers,' he said with a faraway look. 'You're a long way from home. And, yes, nobody joins the Macchia without a tale of woe, goaded by the horned, red fuckers.'

'He took our sister,' said Andy, giving Ed the smallest of nods.

'Did you ever see her again?'

They both shook their heads slowly.

'Isn't that the bastard who was killed recently?'

They both nodded.

'Yeah – system malfunction? Not a chance. System manipulation, more like. That's why that battleship turned up here. It's all got something to do with that Erebus kid.'

'You think he murdered the Mogul?' asked Ed.

'And caused the Arus'Gan incident, so I'm told.'

'What about the female with him?'

'Don't know who she is. I hoped you might know from being on the same shuttle. There's a rumour going around that she's Vanguard, but I can't imagine Senn allowing her anywhere near the station if that was true.'

'What's Vanguard?' asked Andy.

'Fuck, you really are from the fringe of society. They're the Moguls' secret police. Don't you ever get them on Hunus?'

Ed and Andy looked at each other and then stared back at Sticky.

'If they're secret, how would we know?' said Ed.

Sticky looked at his hands and wiped what looked like grease onto his trousers.

'That's a very good point,' he said, grimacing slightly. 'Have they issued you with bunks yet?'

They both shook their heads again.

'We don't even have any of the local currency,' said Andy.

'Well, that's easy to solve,' he said. 'Because there isn't any. Everyone here is issued with somewhere to sleep and a job. All the basics are taken care of; you can even get a beer at the bar in town.'

'A free bar?' said Andy, suddenly brightening up.

'Don't get too excited. You only get four a day maximum – and Reeme ale wouldn't win any awards.'

'Perhaps I could get a job at the brewery,' said Andy, with a wry grin.

'You mentioned the town,' said Ed, ignoring Andy. 'Is that near here?' he asked, pointing at the door.

'You get the train to the last stop, but don't worry, you'll get all this information at your induction when you're issued your bunks,' he said, standing up.

'Okay, Sticky,' said Ed. 'Thanks for your advice.'

'See you soon, boys. It'll be your round with the beers,' he said, smiling widely and pointing at them both.

They watched him cross the room and exchange greetings with a couple of other diners before disappearing out the door.

'Fancy a trip into town, Mr Faux?'

'It's where the only bar on the station is – what do *you* think?'

'Let's go catch a train then,' said Ed and they both stood and dropped their doughnuts into a bin.

25

REEME MINING STATION – KQETT SYSTEM, ANDROMEDA

EPOCH 96, SPAN 9371, JUNCTURE 213.9

Huwlen had walked the three of them out of the control room and into the town. He'd taken Linda to one side and told her that Cort probably needed some recreation time to take his mind off what had just happened. He'd taken them over to a bar near the edge of town where Linda was surprised to find the local brew was not only reasonably drinkable, but free.

'Whose round is it?' asked Linda, standing and giving the barman a nod.

'We've had four. That's all we're allowed each day,' said Cort, pointing at the sign on the wall.

Linda turned her gaze to Huwlen and raised her eyebrows. He smiled and gave the barman a nod. Four more beers were promptly pulled.

'Privileges of rank,' said Huwlen, nodding his

thanks as Linda placed another jar of Reeme ale in front of him and sat opposite.

'What's the plan now?' asked Linda, taking a sip of her beer.

'You think I have a plan?' said Huwlen. 'I was kinda hoping you did,' he added and laughed. 'This all started as a bit of fun – a secret safe haven for waifs and strays. For people who wanted to get away from the tyranny of the horned scourge. It's now gotten a bit more serious, especially after today.'

Huwlen's expression changed and Linda saw that, in actual fact, he was quite scared.

'You feel responsible for all these people, don't you?' she said.

He nodded. 'Yeah, it's becoming a bit big now.'

'Do you want some help?'

He looked at her, seemingly perplexed. 'Who are you really?' he asked. 'You're not Vanguard at all, are you? I've known a few vanguard officers in my time and they were all complete bastards.'

She shook her head. 'No, my name's Linda.'

'And who do you work for exactly?'

They paused as they noticed that the conversation between Cort and Dahkyn had ceased and were both sitting stock still, staring wide-eyed at Linda.

'I'm so sorry, Huwlen. I had no idea she wasn't—'

Linda held her hand up to quieten him. 'You're all

quite safe and I am genuinely here to help you with the PCP problem.'

'What can a breeder do to help us against *them*?' Dahkyn sneered and leaned back, folding his arms across his chest.

Linda looked up at the ceiling. 'You know it's a bit bright in here for my taste.'

She clicked her fingers and the lights dimmed.

They all jumped.

'You've got the dimmer switch,' said Cort. 'It's in your other hand. That's an easy trick.'

She raised her left hand to show it was empty, along with the right one. She clicked her fingers and the lights came up again.

Linda watched Dahkyn glance over at the barman, but, like them, he was looking up at the lights and appeared just as baffled.

'Okay, so you can dim lights,' said Huwlen. 'You still haven't answered my question.'

'I'm sort of self-employed,' she said. 'I'm from a planet called Earth—'

'Never heard of it,' said Cort, butting in. 'And I would have done, because the Erebus Corporation has dealings with every populated planet within PCP space.'

'That's because it's not in PCP space,' she said. 'It's in Daxxal.'

'But that makes you our enemy,' said Huwlen,

sitting back, seemingly distancing himself from her. 'The PCP is building a huge fleet of cruisers to defend us from you.'

'What exactly have the Moguls told you about us?'

Huwlen looked at Cort.

'You'd better answer that one. You're building the defensive fleet.'

'Erm, we've been told that you're a galaxy full of genocidal races. That you wipe out whole planets for sport and you're massing an invasion fleet of huge, invisible ships on the other side of the gate.'

Linda looked around the table to be met with two nervous faces and Dahkyn, who just glowered menacingly.

'Can I start by stating that not one word of that is true? Well, actually, there is an advance party of an invasion fleet in Daxxal – but it's yours, not ours. The remainder of the invasion fleet is under construction above Erdonious.'

'That's not true,' shouted Cort. 'My father would never have agreed to that.'

'He might not know, Cort. The PCP has had battleships infiltrating Daxxal for many years, training and distributing sleeper agents as a vanguard to the now imminent invasion. The only thing holding you back was obtaining the blueprints of the cloaking technology,' she said, pointing at Cort.

'I thought it was just one ship – the Kwarth?' he said.

'Actually, don't expect the Kwarth to return with that cloaking tech any time soon.'

'Why, doesn't the technology really exist?' asked Cort.

'Oh, yes, the tech exists, but the ship doesn't anymore – sorry,' she said.

Huwlen and Cort looked at each other again.

'So, you're saying there never was any threat of an invasion from Daxxal?' said Huwlen.

'None whatsoever,' she replied.

'Shit,' said Dahkyn. 'For years, the Moguls have been feeding us that bullshit so we all tighten our belts and contribute to the defence of the region, when all along it was to feed their own imperialistic greed.'

'Oh, fuck,' said Cort. 'My father will go apoplectic when he finds out.'

Huwlen sat, looking into space. 'Cort, are any of those new cruisers operational yet?'

'Err, yeah. The first should be beginning field testing right about now.'

'Will it be fully armed?'

'Well, it wouldn't have its inventory of mines or missiles, but all the laser cannons and beam weapons should be operational.'

'Hmmm,' said Huwlen with a faraway look again.

'I see where you're going with this,' said Linda. 'But if they're anything like the Katadromiko cruisers in Daxxal, they have a crew of forty-seven thousand. I don't think you have even ten percent of that here.'

'What the fuck are you two on about?' asked Cort, gawking at them in turn.

'Cort,' said Huwlen. 'Do you still have computer access into Erebus?'

'Err, probably. I don't know – why?'

Huwlen looked at Linda and grinned. 'We wouldn't need a full contingent, Linda,' he said and turned his gaze to Cort. 'How many officers make up a bridge crew on one of those?'

'About thirty, I think,' he said, looking horrified. 'You're not thinking what I think you're thinking, are you?'

'I'd need a good pilot and—'

'Hello,' said Linda, putting her hand up and grinning.

'Don't tell me,' said Huwlen, 'you can pilot a starship as well.'

'That is actually my current profession.'

'It would certainly shorten our military coup timetable, wouldn't it, Cort?' said Huwlen.

'Fucking hell, you really are thinking of stealing a Hercules Cruiser, aren't you?' said Cort, shaking his head in bewilderment.

'But what about the other ones?' said Dahkyn. 'They could soon come after you with two or three of them. There must be several that are verging on ready.'

Cort nodded.

'Destroy them,' said Huwlen.

'What, all of them?' said Cort.

'Yep, all of 'em.'

Cort abruptly sat back in his chair. 'But–but, that's destroying trillions' worth of ships,' he stammered. 'The corporation hasn't been fully paid yet.'

'Think of the trillions of humans they're designed to kill, Cort. If what Quixia, sorry, Linda – says is true.'

Cort raised his hand to continue the argument, then noticed the other three shaking their heads.

'Ah, fuck it,' he said. 'I'm being seventeen again, aren't I?'

'No, you're just wearing the wrong hat,' said Linda. 'Take the Erebus hat off and put the Macchia one on.'

'She's right, boss,' said Dahkyn, suddenly.

Surprised, Linda turned to look at him, getting what could almost be construed as a smile in return, but was really only Dahkyn not grimacing for a second.

'Cort, you remember a while ago when you told me you had a back door into all the corporation software?' said Huwlen.

'Yeah.'

'Is that still the case?'

'I would imagine so.'

Huwlen thought for a moment.

'Okay,' he said. 'I say we have one more beer, we organise some bunks for you three and, first thing tomorrow, we start planning the biggest heist in PCP history.'

Linda raised her glass and downed the remainder of her beer.

'Sounds like a plan,' she said, wiping her mouth with the back of her hand. 'And can I say, this beer's really quite nice.'

26

REEME MINING STATION – KQETT SYSTEM, ANDROMEDA

EPOCH 96, SPAN 9371, JUNCTURE 248.2

'Can I say, this beer's really quite revolting,' said Andy, gritting his teeth and staring at his glass. 'It has a bouquet similar to three-week-old hamster cage newspaper.'

Ed sipped at his tentatively, a look of deep concentration on his face. 'No, you're wrong,' he said, sucking it through his teeth as though he was wine tasting. 'Gerbil cage – they urinate more.'

It had taken them a while after leaving the dining room to find the train; it was well hidden down a side tunnel. They followed Sticky's instructions and alighted at the third and final stop, deep inside the station.

Both had been taken aback at the amazing vista of the underground cavern as they emerged into the vast town. On Reeme, it was getting quite late in the evening so the illumination had been reduced and the streets were now almost deserted. A bored driver with an electric tuk tuk had picked them up and delivered them to the pub, moaning all the way about having to do late shifts.

THE BARMAN FINISHED POLISHING the last tray of glasses. There were only a handful of drinkers left now. Ed noticed him look in their direction and sidle over. He was probably in his sixties, short, stocky, with a trimmed greyish beard and glasses. They were the only ones left at the bar, so he must have decided they were fair game for a conversation.

'Newcomers?' he asked with raised eyebrows.

'Yeah,' said Andy.

'You'll get the taste for it, eventually,' he said, indicating to their glasses.

'You sure?' said Ed, pensively.

'No, not really. Did you come in on the Erebus shuttle earlier?'

'Yeah,' said Andy again.

'The Erebus kid was here with Huwlen only a few minutes ago. You've only just missed them.'

'Was a girl with them?' asked Ed.

'Yes, a girl and the kid's bodyguard. I overheard her saying her name was Linda. She actually liked the beer,' he said, boasting.'

Ed and Andy exchanged a glance.

'She's got no bloody taste, that girl,' said Andy.

'D'you know where they went?' said Ed.

'To bed, I think. They're having some sort of serious pow wow in the morning and went to get some sleep.'

'Then we'd better do the same,' said Ed, standing up. 'What's your name by the way?'

'Robin.'

'See you tomorrow, Robin.'

'And order some Spitfire from Faversham,' called Andy as they walked towards the door.

'Some what?' was all they heard before hitting the pavement.

'She must have revealed her true identity,' said Andy as they walked back to the station.

'She must have come to the conclusion it was safe to do so,' Ed replied.

'Well, it does seem like we've stumbled on the secret rebel base, doesn't it?'

'Except this time there's no death star – just several hundred death ships under construction above Erdonious,' said Ed. 'These guys are going to need our help.'

'Death ships – destroy – we must,' said Andy, in a squeaky, croaky voice.

'Yeah, but we don't have the force.'

'I find your lack of faith disturbing.'

'Feel free to shut up anytime you like, Andrew.'

The walk and subsequent train journey continued in silence. They retraced their route all the way back to hangar 117b, only making a wrong turn a couple of times. The hangar was still in darkness and was deserted.

Andy operated the airlock and opened the ship, practising his new abilities with his DOVI. The tiny cabins on the shuttle were very welcoming. Ed set an alarm for six hours' time and they both fell asleep within minutes.

THE CANTEEN WAS busy the following morning. Ed had called out for Linda, using his DOVI as soon as they arrived with no reaction. They'd hoped that Huwlen didn't have his own dining arrangements and they'd all use the same facilities and that Linda would appear at some point for a meal.

They both sat with their backs to the wall, overlooking the room, which was tactically correct in any circumstances, but useful for them here as they could observe everyone entering. The doughnuts had been given a wide berth. This time, they'd chosen something that resembled toast. After watching others smearing what appeared to be jam on theirs, they did the same. It was indeed some kind of conserve, but neither of them could pinpoint the exact flavour.

'Loganberry, with hints of penetrating oil,' said Andy.

'Blackcurrant and ear wax,' said Ed.

The general hum in the room suddenly changed, which made them both look up. A tall man with wild hair and a grungy boiler suit had entered, which had seemed to create a bit of a stir. He was followed by a young boy who didn't look a day over fourteen and was dressed in something resembling a purple Hawaiian shirt and obscenely baggy trousers.

'Hammer time,' said Andy, which made Ed suddenly choke on his toast.

'Can you warn me before you do that again?' said Ed, coughing, laughing and trying to breathe at the same time.

MC Hammer was followed by a huge, armed, scowling man who dwarfed everyone around him. He scanned the room menacingly and, seemingly finding nothing awry, turned back to follow his charge.

Then Linda walked in and the sun came out. Andy gasped and went to stand, but was held back by Ed.

'Wait until she gives us the go-ahead,' said Ed, pulling Andy back into his seat. 'We don't know if we'll be welcome yet.'

Ed called out with his DOVI.

'Hi, Linda, it's good to find you safe.'

She suddenly stiffened and stared straight ahead.

'Ed, is that you?'

'Yes, I'm here with Andy.'

'Are you near Reeme Station?'

'Er, yes. We're very near. We need to know it's safe to reveal ourselves.'

'Call the station and ask for Huwlen Senn and me. That way, you'll get permission to approach without activating the station's defences.'

'We don't need to do that.'

'Why not?'

'Look to your five o'clock.'

She turned her head and stared out across the dining room. They both stood up. Her reaction was instantaneous: her eyes opened wide and she sprinted across the room, dodging people, tables, trays of food, getting surprised looks from all directions. The three men she'd entered with turned and stared in complete consternation at what the hell had got into her.

She flew into Ed's arms and hugged him to within an inch of his life. Then she did exactly the same thing to Andy. By the time she let him surface, Andy noticed that the tall man had made it across the room and was standing patiently behind her.

'Unless these two have an aftershave that I really need to know about, you've met them before,' he said.

Linda turned and wiped tears from her eyes. 'Ah, yes, Huwlen. This is Edward and Andrew, my closest friends. They're also here to help.'

'Well, that's fantastic. It really is,' said Huwlen, visibly bristling. 'But what's concerning me the most at this precise moment is how the fuck they got onto my station without detection.'

'I think that's best explained in private,' said Ed.

TEN MINUTES LATER, in his private suite of offices, Huwlen had calmed down, following the initial shock of believing his fiefdom was not as secure as he thought it was.

'So, you have full cloaking technology on your vessel, here, right now?' he said, his eyes wide with anticipation.

Cort was grinning from ear to ear.

'That's just fucking outrageous,' he said. 'With a couple of Hercs with cloaks, we could wipe out the PCP's navy in a matter of weeks.'

'What's a Herc?' asked Andy.

'You might have seen them under construction above Erdonious,' said Linda.

'Ah, the death ships,' said Ed. 'I take it you want to borrow some of those?'

'Yes,' said Cort. 'Only a couple. Use them to destroy all the others and then hunt down and destroy the Moguls and their power base.'

'It seems we have a bit of planning to do,' said Ed. 'Let's go back and complete breakfast first. Empty stomachs won't make planning a galactic coup easy.'

'I agree,' said Huwlen. 'Most of this galaxy has waited millennia for an opportunity like this. We need to get it right first time. If something were to go wrong, the retribution would be swift and brutal.'

27

SACHEM MOGUL'S PRECINCT, CORE BUREAU – ARUS'GAN, ANDROMEDA

EPOCH 97, SPAN 9371, JUNCTURE 171.0

The Sachem Mogul, Dakk Reeph, scowled as the two senior Moguls strode into his precinct and bowed before the pedestal. The last two days had severely embarrassed his court and called into question his leadership. Never in the last nine thousand spans had a Sachem's authority been questioned.

The murder of a Mogul was highly unlikely, but the subsequent deaths of four others during the aftermath of the Locy'fer Station disaster was unheard of.

Reeph was, of course, blamed – 'incompetent leadership', they said. The decisions he made during the next epoch would either save or destroy his Sachem.

'You first, Adjudicator,' he roared. 'And you better know something substantial today. I want facts, not rumours.'

The Adjudicator, Hassik Triyl, oversaw the

intelligence arm of the PCP. This included the Vanguard Division. He wasn't as tall as some of the Moguls, but to believe his lack of stature paralleled a lack of resolve was extremely dangerous.

His oppressive ambition had surprised many rivals along the way. Knowing that the Mogul in front of him – who was held high on a pedestal by all – was appearing weak, made him double his efforts, not to aid the Sachem, but to ensure it looked as bad as possible without any blame being placed at his door. He had been deliberately drip-feeding information to the Sachem in such a way that made his decisions appear slow and careless.

'Yes, Dakk Reeph,' he said, using the Sachem's name instead of his rank, which was slightly disrespectful. 'I can now confirm that Mogul Tyuk Baa was, in fact, murdered by a Daxxal spy masquerading as a Vanguard officer named Quixia. This denotes that the real Quixia has been compromised and, most probably, the GDA has knowledge of our future enterprise.'

'Do we have the designs for the cloaking technology in our possession now?' Reeph asked, turning his glare upon Tyann Kky.

Commander Tyann Kky was the overseer of all the armed forces within the PCP, as had his father before him. A relatively young Mogul, excessively cruel with a very short temper, he had reportedly spaced an entire ship's crew merely for coming last in a war game scenario.

'We've had no contact with either of our ships in the Daxxal System for a considerable time, Sachem Mogul,' he said, bowing his head. 'I would like your permission to send a cruiser into Daxxal to determine our position and attack one of their small ships to obtain the cloaking technology.'

'Do you?' roared Reeph. 'Do you really? You lose two battleships and your answer to that is to send a bigger ship to lose? Well, my answer is no, Kky – absolutely not. I'll tell you what you can have.' Reeph stood up and pointed at him. 'A fucking corvette – which you will travel on yourself.'

'Me?' said Kky, his jaw almost clanking to the deck. 'Captain a corvette?'

'No, Kky. The captain will captain the corvette. You will oversee the operation to Daxxal, as your title suggests. Now, get out of my sight and don't you dare come back without that cloak.'

Kky's face went even redder than normal. He turned and exited the chamber, deliberately slamming the doors on the way out.

'Do you want me to have someone keep an eye on him?' asked Triyl, realising he needed to calm Reeph down and prevent him from getting too involved – his aspirations would be unattainable if he was also sent to Daxxal, or dead.

'Put a trusted man on that corvette and give him my full authority to step in if he deems it necessary.'

'I understand exactly, my Sachem.'

Reeph nodded and sat down again, much to Triyl's relief.

'Tell me about Locy'fer – facts not bullshit hearsay this time.'

'The Erebus child bought three breeders from Tyuk Baa's cruiser on its arrival from Hunus. They were the Mogul's personal breeders, one of which was the breeder claiming to be Quixia, who'd been found hiding on the Daxxal science vessel. The two youngest were for his father and, according to a trusted source, Quixia was for the Erebus kid – he, unlike his father, likes them older.'

'Did he know she was a spy?'

'We don't believe so. I've had an officer on his crew since his father gave him the ship and have had full tracking on him since he was born. He's never even met a Mogul, let alone anyone from Daxxal.'

'Do we have any evidence the Quixia spy caused the Locy'fer disaster?'

'If I did, it's gone now because of Kky's usual heavy-handedness.'

'Explain.'

'Kky sent a battleship after the Erebus kid's ship. It caught them up in the Kqett System and just blew the yacht into gas. No warning, no questions, no prisoners – and an experienced Vanguard officer dead. It then turned its guns on a holiday resort on Kqett, reducing it to slag and killing the forty-three resident staff.'

'Have that ship returned here and the captain sent to me.'

'Well, that's difficult,' said Triyl, wincing slightly. 'Kky seemed to have lost contact with the battleship shortly afterwards.'

'Are you telling me he's lost another battleship?'

Triyl shrugged. 'It might be just a systems failure, but going on his present record, who knows?'

'That's four, Triyl – four fucking battleships.' Reeph stood up again, waving his arms about in anger. 'We're not even at war and he's losing a major fucking warship almost daily.'

Triyl averted his eyes and stared at the floor. He knew when to shut up.

'I want you to sort this shit out for me, Triyl,' he said. 'Send a couple of cruisers to Kqett to find that battleship and, as soon as Erebus senior arrives, find out what he knows about his brainless offspring.'

'He's the Sachem of one of the oldest families,' said Triyl. 'How far can I go?'

'To the desired result, Triyl. No limits. I never did like that imperious native anyway.'

'What of the Hercules project? He was overseeing that personally.'

'After you've finished with Erebus, get over there and crack the whip. I want to see at least two of those operational and in orbit here within ten days.'

'As you wish, Sachem Mogul,' said Triyl, using the Sachem's full title this time. He bowed and then turned to leave the precinct, chuckling to himself, looking forward to his trip to Erdonious.

It was most certainly better than a suicide mission into Daxxal with a corvette.

28

REEME MINING STATION – KQETT SYSTEM, ANDROMEDA

EPOCH 98, SPAN 9371, JUNCTURE 122.9

The mission planning was now well into the second epoch. Huwlen had turned his offices into a multi-area think tank. They needed three teams: one to take each of the Hercules cruisers and Cort's computer team to oversee and open doors for them.

The cruiser teams were divided into two: bridge crew and ship security. They'd decided that along with the thirty bridge officers, a contingent of twenty armed personnel would shut the bridge off from the rest of the ship.

It had been apparent very early on that searching the ship and evicting everyone on it would take days. According to Cort, a small contingent of up to nine security officers were stationed in the entry hangar, but they didn't stray far as they had a habit of getting lost.

Huwlen was in charge of team selection as he knew

everyone on the station and, with his knowledge of everybody's strengths and weaknesses, he was able to build two reasonably competent bridge crews. Cort had provided them with holographic mock-ups of their individual stations and they were all busy learning about their particular control stations and responsibilities.

'Have you sorted out the work passes?' asked Ed, noticing that Cort was leaving his work station for a break.

'I'm getting through them,' he said. 'I just can't put through too many at once. Someone might notice a hundred new personnel files suddenly appearing on the system.'

'Are we going to be able to take our shuttles straight into the cruiser's hangar?'

'No, I can make the electronic signature look like one of ours but, as soon as they approach the ships, they'll be noticeably alien. I'm planning on dispatching the teams to a transport hub down on Erdonious. You'll be able to get the normal land train into the orbital construction transit hub from there.'

'Has there been any change to the first operational trial?'

'No, it's still due on Epoch 100.'

'What about the second ship? Is that going to be potentially operational too?'

'Absolutely. In actual fact, the first five are pretty

much ready to go. They're using the first for trials already.'

'We need to make sure the other operational three are disabled as a priority.'

'The weapons operators have a strict order of business. They know where to hit to maximise damage, minimise casualties and, with luck, put the project back several years.'

'Are you sure this will give you time to eradicate the Moguls?'

'Destroying their ability to strike back is our first goal. Once the PCP navy is gone, they'll have no power base and we can concentrate on hunting them down. Of course, we'll get some of them in their command cruisers, but they're no match for a Hercules with cloaking.'

'You do realise they'll throw everything they have at you?'

'That's what we're counting on,' said Cort as he wandered off in the direction of the mess hall.

Ed walked through to Huwlen's office and found him grimacing at a tablet. 'What's up?' he asked, noticing the frown.

'Two cruisers are on their way to Erdonious from Arus'Gan.'

'When do they get there?'

'Tomorrow.'

'Shit.'

'And that's not all,' said Huwlen. 'Hassik Triyl is on one of 'em.'

'Who's he?'

'They call him the Adjudicator. He's the security chief – and one of the most vicious Moguls of all. This changes everything. Those two medium cruisers will be on an operational footing with shields up at all times and with alert weapons officers.'

'Do you think they know what we're planning?'

'No, I think they're looking for the missing battleship.'

'Well, they're bound to come here then – apart from Kqett, this is the only other populated satellite in the system. They'll know very quickly it disappeared somewhere around here.'

'We have the Mark Thirteens, though.'

'One battleship with its shields down was easy. Against two medium cruisers on a full battle footing – not so easy. It would only take a couple of missiles into that hangar area and we're in the shit. My shuttle might be cloaked, but it's not impermeable to damage and, if what you say is true about this Hassik Triyl, when he finds out the battleship was destroyed, he's going to be seriously pissed and not handing out kittens.'

'That's true,' said Huwlen, staring intently at his monitor.

'I think we need to get the mission teams aboard the Gabriel and wipe the computer systems here as soon as possible.'

Huwlen was silent for a moment and continued to gaze at the monitor, even though the screen was blank.

'I know you don't want to abandon this place—'

'It's more the people, Ed,' he said. 'They trust me, they're my friends and came here to escape all that shit.'

'They're going to offer no resistance. There'll be no evidence of the battleship, or Cort or any of us being here. And, anyway, if they do start something, our second job – after wiping out the remainder of the Hercules fleet – is to come here and give them the good news.'

'Okay, you're right of course—'

'Don't tell him that. We'll never hear the end of it,' said Andy as he strolled in, looking from one to the other with raised eyebrows.

'Change of plan,' said Ed, recognising Andy's questioning look.

'We're going to the pub?'

'No, Andrew,' he said, giving Huwlen an apologetic glance. 'We're taking the teams to the Gabriel asap.'

'Ah, trouble brewing?'

'Two medium cruisers en route.'

'Ah, shit.'

'Precisely – and the pun was crap.'

'No, it wasn't.'

'Yes, it was.'

'It was pure punificence.'

'Bollocks, was it.'

Huwlen stared at them both with an expression of complete bewilderment. 'Gentlemen, I'm becoming slightly dubious regarding your suitability for this job,' he said. 'May I see your resumes again?'

'If you look closely, you'll find "saving galaxies" under the transferable skills section,' said Andy.

'No, you won't,' said Linda, sticking her head around the door. 'It actually says, "saving breweries from bankruptcy".'

They all turned as she entered the room.

'We need to get out of here,' she said.

'We know,' said Ed. 'We've just come to the same conclusion.'

'How long have we got?' she asked.

'About sixteen hours if they're running the cruisers at max,' said Huwlen.

THEY BROUGHT the two teams together in the canteen and sealed the doors. The planning of the operation had been kept from the general populace to protect the operation itself and to protect the remaining station dwellers. The two crews involved had no idea where they were going or even which ship's controls they were rehearsing.

They were instructed to report back to hangar 117b in one hour with just the clothing they were in and a sleeping roll. One of the Gabriel's hangars would become a dormitory for the night, so something to sleep on was a certain requirement.

Ed flew the first group out to the starship. As soon as he was clear of the station, he contacted Phil to bring the Gabriel out of the belt and close to the station, but to remain cloaked. It took three hours to ferry everyone across.

As soon as Linda stepped off the shuttle, a very excited Rayl ran into her arms. They retired up to the blister and had a long conversation, mostly about what Rayl had learnt from Cleo during her absence. Though Rayl's excitement was curtailed somewhat when she learnt that Linda was off on another mission in the morning.

Last to arrive were Huwlen and Cort. They'd wiped the station's data files of anything involving the arrival of the Erebus shuttle, the battleship and the operation. Cort's shuttle was also retrieved from its hideaway and parked in a corner of the Gabriel's starboard hangar, just in case the PCP participated in a thorough search of the station.

The Gabriel's port hangar on the other side was a flurry of activity. Over a hundred people milled about, mostly trying on uniforms, which Cleo had produced from designs Cort had retrieved from the database of clothing suppliers on Erdonious. Some had already discovered the Theo food replicators and were enjoying a multitude of gourmet foods not available on Reeme.

Once everyone was in and settled, Phil jumped the starship over to the fringe of the Erdonious system, cloaked and powered in to sit in the shadow of one of Erdonious's two moons. There they sat watching and waiting for the two PCP cruisers to arrive.

29

THE STARSHIP GABRIEL – ERDONIOUS SYSTEM, ANDROMEDA

EPOCH 99, SPAN 9371, JUNCTURE 039.5

'They're here,' whispered Marilyn.

'Eh, what,' mumbled Ed as he stirred from a deep sleep.

'Cleo says the cruisers have arrived,' she said, kissing him on the forehead then promptly disappearing.

He looked up at the ceiling of his cabin, trying to make sense of what he'd just been told.

'Shit, the cruisers,' he shouted as it all came back to him. Three minutes later, he stumbled out of the tube lift, onto the bridge, yawned and plonked himself down on his regular couch.

'Marilyn keep you up did she?' said Andy, grinning widely at his little joke.

'Bollocks, it's too early for puns,' he replied, yawning again. 'Where's Phil, by the way?'

'Catching up on some shuteye,' said Andy. 'He was on duty here all the time we were away.'

'He should get a mention in dispatches for that, at least,' said Ed.

'He is a worrier, isn't he?'

'After what happened to his last crew, I'm not surprised.'

They watched the holo display as the two cruisers approached, then parked in a high orbit above Erdonious.

'Where did Cort set up in the end?' asked Ed.

'Up in the blister. He said the view reminded him of his ship.'

'Poor bugger,' said Ed. 'He's led a sheltered life because of who he is and just about everyone he knew was on that ship.'

'Yeah, from what I understand, his father's a right cold kettle of fish.'

'Well, he's certainly cold now,' said Linda, getting off the tube lift. 'He died of a heart attack while under interrogation at Arus'Gan.'

'Shit. Does Cort know?' asked Ed.

'Yes, he's tapped into the communications from those two cruisers. He heard them organising the transfer of the body down to the planet.'

'How is he?'

'In a state of shock.'

'Does he want to abort?'

'No, that's what I came down here to tell you. He's even more resolute now. He doesn't want sympathy, just your help in ridding the galaxy of the Moguls.'

'Guys,' said Cleo, 'one of the cruisers is moving.'

They turned back to watch the holo map. One of the cruisers was moving quickly away from the planet, then it disappeared.

'Where'd it jump to?' asked Ed.

'The Kqett system,' said Cleo.

'The planet?'

'No, Reeme.'

'Shit, I was hoping they'd both go to Kqett,' said Ed. 'Ah, well, the plans don't change just because there's a cruiser still here sniffing around.'

'Is Huwlen about?' asked Andy. 'I've just got a message from Cort.'

'He's down in the hangar getting the teams prepared,' said Linda.

'That's good, because—'

They all looked across at Andy to see what had stopped him. As he listened to the communications in his ear, his face changed.

'Fuck, wow. That's going to screw up everything. The cruiser has just given orders for the first two Hercules cruisers to depart for Arus'Gan.'

'When?' said Ed, his eyes wide.

'Asap.'

'Have they got a crew?'

'Er, no – that's what's being discussed now.'

'Cleo, can you tap in on the conversation?' asked Ed.

'Sure.'

'…could have two full thirty-man bridge crews on board first thing in the morning.'

'That's not acceptable. You will have two full bridge crews ready to fly in four hours. Just one second longer and their first order will be weapons testing on their own homes, including yours. Is that quite clear?'

'Yes, my Mogul. They're on their way. Please instruct the security details on both ships to evacuate all personnel and await our crew shuttle's arrival – Chief Engineer out.'

'Shit,' said Ed. 'We're too far away to stop them. If they get two of those monsters crewed up and away, we've already lost.'

Everybody stared at each other, desperately trying to think of a way out. They all turned to see Cort, popping up on the tube lift.

'Hi, everyone,' he said with a little wave. 'We'd better get a move on. Hassik Triyl never makes idol threats.'

'How can we beat them from here, Cort?' asked Andy.

'Beat who?'

'Their crew. We overheard the conversation.'

Cort looked around the room with a puzzled expression and suddenly realised the problem. 'There is no "their crew",' he said, grinning. 'That was me. I used one of my back doors to breach the cruiser's communications. Triyl was talking to me.'

'That didn't sound anything like you,' said Ed.

'Ah, yes. I changed my voice electronically to sound like my father's Chief Engineer,' he said, waving a small headset with a microphone.

'Bloody brilliant,' shouted Andy as he began moving the Gabriel in towards Erdonious.

Ed and Linda ran down to the port hangar, picking up a sleepy Phil on the way. After giving everyone the news, they lined them all up next to the two shuttles. It was going to be a real squeeze getting one hundred and two people into two Theo shuttles, but not impossible.

Andy ignored all the safety protocols and literally threw the starship into a low stationary orbit around Erdonious on the opposite side to all the action. The two crews crammed themselves in and, with Ed piloting one and Phil the second, they cloaked, exited the hangar and dropped into the upper atmosphere.

They both followed the flight plan, which Cort had provided them, to the Erebus Construction shuttle port on the far side of the planet. They'd scrapped getting a land train into the port as time was of the essence, so an area of waste ground behind a deserted industrial warehouse was chosen for the landing.

Cort, meanwhile, had contacted the shuttle port, using his Chief Engineer ruse and organised two Erebus shuttles to be available to take them straight back up again.

A quick scan to check the area was clear of unwanted witnesses and the two shuttles dropped down, one in front of the other. Less than thirty seconds later they lifted off again. Ed felt pangs of guilt as he watched Linda leap out into the light drizzle without a second thought, exposing herself to untold dangers again. 'Please be careful,' he said out loud to an empty ship as he powered up through the low rain cloud.

LINDA FELT guilty for not giving Ed a hug before she exited the shuttle. She'd been so focussed on leading her team out quickly, she'd completely forgotten. She looked up as the whine of the shuttles dissipated above in the rainy mist. 'Fly safe, Edward,' she said out loud before turning and checking whether her team were all accounted for.

It was only a few hundred metres over to the

construction port but the two groups took slightly different routes. Evidently they needn't have bothered to split up as no one was out and about in the inclement weather anyway and, fifteen minutes later, they were all drying off inside the terminal.

Linda – or 'Lynda' as Cort's counterfeit identification spelt it – was nervous. She stood first in line as she was the pilot and technically the captain, with her team behind her. Huwlen's team had thankfully gone first and she was extremely relieved to see them filing through the security checks without a problem. Sure enough, her team did the same and they joined the others at the departure gate.

'Can you talk?' asked Ed through her DOVI.

Linda thought her way back along the signal and replied: 'We're all through security and awaiting our ride.'

'Okay. Cort says all the regular shuttles are busy evacuating the work teams from our two ships. They're bringing down a couple from one of the other cruisers to grab you guys.'

'How long?'

'They've just passed us and are dropping into the upper atmosphere now.'

'I don't like this sitting about bit. It's cold and wet and we're just asking to get discovered.'

'You're doing fine. Get yourself something to read. There's bound to be a bookshop in one of the departure lounges.'

'Ha, bloody ha.'

TWENTY MINUTES LATER, a loud roaring outside woke Linda from her daydreaming. She watched through the rain-streaked windows as two ugly, bulbous looking shuttles landed in a cloud of water vapour. The flight crew hastened into the building and began ushering the two teams towards the ships. They looked nervous and stressed. Linda hoped it was on account of Hassik Triyl's reputation and not because they were leading them into a trap.

The two rotund shuttles screamed their way upwards as soon as all the passengers were seated – no safety demonstration on this flight. There were no windows in the passenger area either, and the cockpit seemed to be on an upper deck, so Linda closed her eyes and delved around with her DOVI. By the time she'd discovered a cockpit view camera, they were exiting the upper atmosphere and arriving in clear space.

She watched as the ship turned and headed across the top of the planet's ice cap towards what looked like a bunch of stars, which had all been condensed into one area of space. Gradually, the stars grew and appeared to be lined up in perfect rows. She soon recognised them as the giant cruisers, which were under construction and which she had first seen from the Erebus IV a couple of days before. There were over six hundred of them parked in rows of fifty.

The nearest ones seemed complete, in contrast to the half-built ones at the far end of the rows. They reminded her of dinosaur skeletons she'd seen in New York some fifteen years ago on a school visit to the American Museum of Natural History.

They passed by the first ship that Huwlen's team would be taking and slowed before dropping down between the monster ships. A huge lit hangar came into view and the pilot paused their approach as two other shuttles of similar design, carrying the last of the construction teams, made their way out through the hangar's force field. Getting clearance to enter was almost immediate and she heard a familiar buzz as they passed through. The pilot turned the ship on its axis and banged it down on the deck in a corner of the hangar.

Linda watched as her team of twenty security officers exited the shuttle and engaged in conversation with the few remaining guards. Their body language seemed relaxed and, from what she could see through the back door of the shuttle, the guards had their backpacks on and seemed very keen to get off the ship as soon as possible.

Perhaps the surprise arrival of Hassik Triyl was an unexpected bonus, she thought.

Nine PCP guards lined up at the back of the shuttle and paid Linda's team scant attention as she led them onto the hangar floor. She knew which direction to go as Cort had given her a road map to the bridge. The shuttle lifted straight off as soon as the outgoing guards had filed on. It lunged forward, buzzed out through the force field and was gone within seconds.

'Bloody hell, they weren't hanging around,' said Ed in Linda's ear. 'They nearly took the paint off the doorframe.'

'I think we should be a little careful regarding this Hassik Triyl character,' she replied. 'He seems to have a lot of people rattled.'

'His ship has just been promoted to the top of the playlist – oh, hang on.'

Linda was loading half her team onto a small monorail carriage and paused, waiting for Ed to explain the meaning of his interjection.

'Has something happened?' she asked.

'The cruiser just moved closer.'

She sent the first carriage off and called for a second. 'Do we know why?'

'No.'

'Shit, we need to get a move on. How long till you get here?'

'About fifteen minutes.'

'Okay. I'll get this monster warmed up while you're en route. Those power connectors better fit or we're going to be a very big target.'

'That's what held me up slightly. Cort wanted to check Cleo's fabricated connectors, just to make sure.'

The second carriage arrived and Linda and the remainder of her team piled on. It took five minutes to reach the bridge deck and a further five to get along the stupidly narrow corridors. The bridge, however, was quite spacious; a lot of the work stations were already fired up and glowing a dull blue. Linda quickly jumped into the captain's seat. It reclined, almost horizontally, as the holo map appeared above her.

'Entering the hangar now,' said Ed.

'Be careful,' she said. 'Don't scratch the fenders.'

'Wings.'

'Whatever – are you sure it'll fit?'

'Phil says it will if Cort's dimensions are correct.'

Linda felt around with her DOVI and, finding a camera in the main hangar, she watched as the hangar force field seemed to disappear before reappearing again. Then, in the blink of an eye, the hangar was filled with starship as the Gabriel uncloaked.

'Bloody hell!' she exclaimed. 'That's a tight fit.'

'I'll refrain from the obvious joke.'

'You'd better. Now get out and connect up.'

'Yes, ma'am.'

'Andy, are you inside cruiser one yet?' she asked.

'Just landing now.'

'Okay. You do the same.'

'Anything for you, dreamboat. Would you like the windshield wiped and the oil checked?'

'The only dipstick around here is you,' she countered. 'And somebody turn the fucking heating down on this ship.' She glared over at the environmental control operator.

'I'M ALL HOOKED UP,' said Ed. 'How about you, Andy?'

'Still single, sadly. But I'm quietly confident.'

'Andy, get a move on,' Linda shouted.

'I know, I know. I had to move the ship; my cable was too short.'

'Your reverse parking always was dodgy,' said Ed.

'Linda, can I exchange these two for adults?' called Huwlen from the bridge of cruiser one.

'Be my guest,' she said. 'I've had to put up with this shit for months.'

'Okay,' called Andy. 'Cleo, can you power up the

interface and see if you can detect the surface area of the cruisers?'

'Done – and yes I can,' replied Cleo.

'All yours, Linda,' he said.

'Right,' she said, looking around the bridge from her raised seat. 'Do we have propulsion?' A row of green lights in her overhead display confirmed this. 'Shields?' Again: all green. 'Weapons?' Same again. 'Huwlen, are you ready to rock?'

'All green over here too.'

'You're the senior captain,' she said. 'It's also your operation. You really should give the command to start this thing.'

There was a momentary pause, but a split second before she asked if he was okay, his voice boomed out.

'Cruiser 1, cruiser 2 – release from the construction gantry; helm, hold steady; weapons, stand by.'

Linda felt a slight shudder as the docking clamps released.

'Cruiser 1, cruiser 2 – proceed to predetermined attack positions and initiate cloak.'

The helm officers on both of the huge ships hit the initiate icon almost together, but instead of the ships' sub-light engines moving them into their attack positions, they experienced a complete power shutdown and the bridge went dark.

'What the fuck,' shouted Linda as emergency lighting flickered on, turning the bridge a dark red.

'Full ship-wide power outage,' called one of her team from somewhere in the gloom. This was followed by the sound of small-arms fire in the corridor outside the bridge.

Linda's worst nightmare had eventuated. They'd walked into a trap.

30

HANGAR 26X, NO 1 HERCULES CRUISER – ORBITING ERDONIOUS, ANDROMEDA

EPOCH 99, SPAN 9371, JUNCTURE 087.0

Andy peered out the front screen of the Cartella. He could make out the stars through the main hangar door: the lights going out and being replaced by a low red glow, he thought, was probably standard battle procedure. But the fact that it was eerily quiet and the stars outside were stationary worried him.

'Linda,' he called on his DOVI. 'Why aren't we moving?'

'Andy, Ed,' replied Linda. 'It's a trap. Cloak and run.'

He didn't need to be told twice. Cloaking and putting on full shields, Andy lifted the Cartella up from its corner of the hangar. But before he could command the ship to exit out the main door, a large PCP troop ship entered and turned to settle on the hangar floor. The rear door began powering down as soon as it was inside the force field, revealing dozens of heavily armed soldiers lining up to disembark.

'Shit, if they get into the ship...' he shouted to himself.

He armed the cannons and fired.

He would never know exactly what he hit, but the troop carrier exploded in a huge fireball. Even though the hangar was a considerable size, the explosion was so violent it blew the Cartella into the side wall, flipping it over and onto its roof.

Andy was thrown out of the pilot's couch. He clouted the navigation board hard, rendering him unconscious.

WHEN ANDY OPENED HIS EYES, he wasn't sure how long he'd been out. He was puzzled as to how he could see across the hangar while lying on the floor. On further inspection, he discovered he wasn't on the floor at all; he was lying on the ceiling, looking out of a cracked side-window. The next thing that struck him was the lack of debris. A ship of considerable size had exploded inside an enclosed space. There should be flaming detritus everywhere. Only a small percentage would have found the outer door.

'The outer door,' he said out loud. Crawling closer

to the window, he peered around to the left and noticed he could no longer see the force field shimmering across the main hangar door.

Thank fuck I closed the airlock, he thought, now realising why there was nothing left in the hangar. It had all been sucked out when the force field had been destroyed by the blast.

Then, why am I and the Cartella still here?

His mind was a bit foggy. He also realised his left foot hurt and there was a lump on the side of his head you could hang your coat on.

'The power lead,' he said suddenly, out loud again. 'It was the power lead that stopped the Cartella getting sucked out.'

Pleased with himself that he'd worked out why he wasn't a little white meteorite, he tried to decide what to do next.

'Ed, can you hear me?' he called out through his DOVI.

'Yes. Are you in one piece? Cleo said there was a massive explosion in your hangar.'

'Yeah, it was a troop carrier trying to land.'

'Ah, so that's what it was that hit us then.'

'Did yours explode?'

'Yes, we were cloaked and completely filling the hangar. He must have just flown into us.'

'Is the Gabriel okay?'

'We think so. We used a soft shielding to hold us centrally in the hangar as the ship doesn't have landing struts. Cleo says we've got a few dents but, otherwise, we're good. She's trying to find how they shut the power off.'

'So that's what happened.'

'We think they only got wind of the plan right at the last minute. The nine security guards swapped clothes with nine of the workers and hid on the ship close to the bridge. We saw nine in security uniforms leave the ship and presumed that was everybody.'

'Yeah, same here.'

'They weren't expected to retake the ship, just to keep everyone busy until the troop carriers full of real soldiers arrived and stormed the bridge.'

'We need to get the power on again, Ed. They'll have more troops on the way.'

'Or they'll just destroy these two ships with us in 'em. We're defenceless without shields.'

'Well, let's hope that's their last resort.'

'I forgot to ask,' said Ed. 'How's the Cartella?'

'Do you know a good panel shop?'

'Oh, dear.'

'Hi, guys,' said Cort. 'Cleo just patched me into your little private network. They've left someone down in Main Engineering to disconnect the major power conduits. It's the only way to do what they've done.

They'll feel quite safe down there as they'll think everyone is contained on the bridge, so you could sneak up on them.'

'How do we get there?' asked Ed, just as Andy opened his mouth to ask the same question.

'I'm sending a route plan to your GOFIs. Please use a stun setting. They're company engineers, not soldiers, remember.'

'We'll do what we can, Cort,' said Ed. 'Andy, are you going to be able to get out of the Cartella?'

'I'll have to suit up and hope one of the airlocks is operational. I'll keep you posted.'

'I'll watch out for any more troop carriers,' said Cort. 'Then you can mess about with them using your GOFIs.'

'It's DOVIs,' said Andy.

'Yeah, yeah – whatever.'

There was a slight pause before Andy whispered, 'Teenagers, eh! Different galaxy, same bullshit.'

'I can still hear you, you know,' said Cort in a small, whiny voice.

ANDY CLAMBERED around in the Cartella, limping and treading carefully as the ceiling wasn't designed to take a lot of weight. He tiptoed through to the back of the ship to one of the storage lockers, activated one of the liquid Theo suits and pressed the helmet activation icon on the neck ring. The helmet sealed up around his head – he winced as it pressed in on his bruise – and waited for a row of green lights in his peripheral vision to indicate that all was rosy.

The next potential problem was the airlock. If it was damaged, he'd have to find a way to force it. A quick check proved the interior was still pressurised and, after slowly opening the inner door, he went to enter – but then stopped, thought for a moment and went back into the rear compartment. Returning with a laser rifle, he checked it was set to stun and re-entered the airlock. As the inner door swept shut behind him, he vented the atmosphere and checked whether his suit was functioning correctly.

The outer door was a different story. It opened a few inches, juddered and stopped.

'Bugger.' He sighed and kicked the door with his good foot. It shot open and disappeared into its housing.

'Nothing like a bit of technical knowhow,' he muttered to himself with a wry grin.

He scanned the nearby airlocks with his DOVI, reasoning that the ones furthest away from the blast would be his best bet. The third one he tried to activate opened. It was on a mezzanine level above the main hangar floor. The stairs up to it hadn't fared quite as well. They were leaning at an angle, away from the explosion, but still looked reasonably well attached.

He gave them a shake and, finding nothing moved, carefully inched his way up, leaning over to match the angle of the stairs. He eyed the open hangar door warily, expecting another troop carrier full of bad news to swing in at any moment.

Entering the open airlock, he activated the cycle and waited as the outer door closed and air hissed in. He brought the rifle up as the inner door disappeared into the ceiling. No one was waiting for him on the other side: no soldiers, no armed security, just an empty corridor stretching away north and south along the length of the ship, bathed in the eerie red lighting.

He deactivated the helmet of his suit and checked the rifle was still operational and on stun.

The route Cort had sent him flashed up in his vision, showing that he needed to go right – or south – towards the aft of the ship.

He grimaced as he started to limp as fast as he could along the passageway, keeping one eye on his surroundings and the other on the route map.

They could've turned the artificial gravity off as well, he thought. *I'd be able to fly myself along the two kilometres of this.* He noticed the hand holds everywhere.

The map showed he had to go down two levels at

some point and then deeper into the ship to reach the entrance to Main Engineering. After he had walked for about fifteen minutes, a stairwell on the left came up and he took it, plunging two levels down. He then followed an eastbound corridor for three hundred meters.

As he turned into the final passage that would lead him to his destination, he ran straight into one of the miniature drones. Ducking and firing at the same time, he heard a panic-stricken voice loud in his ear.

'Don't shoot the drone,' shouted Cort. 'It's waiting to guide and assist.'

'You could have warned me,' said Andy, dragging himself back to his feet, realising he'd just tried to shoot an armoured drone with a stun setting.

'Sorry, I was assisting Ed. He's already there and ready to go.'

'Oh, right,' he said. 'No pressure then.'

'Yeah, tick tock,' called Ed. 'Galaxies to invade and all that.'

Andy shook his head and started off down the corridor again.

'Fuck me, it's all go in this job,' he mumbled, continuing south towards a large bulkhead door. He sniffed the air and wondered why he could smell food.

'Was it just one guy on your ship?' he asked.

'Yep, he certainly wasn't expecting us and gave up

without a fight. Don't let your guard down, though. It might be different over there.'

'I doubt it,' he said, moments before the bulkhead door opened and several bolts of laser fire zipped down the passage, narrowly missing his head.

'Bastard,' he shouted as he dived onto the floor. 'Well, mine isn't fucking giving up.'

The drone above him returned fire and flashed away. Peering up from the floor, he watched as it neared the door. As it scanned inside with a green, flat laser light, another bunch of laser bolts hit it square on and it dropped onto the floor with a loud clunk. It tried to return fire, but its stabiliser was damaged and all it managed to do was spin around firing in all directions.

Andy ducked again as some came in his direction.

'I've lost control,' called Cort. 'Get out of there.'

More laser bolts flew over Andy's head, some from the malfunctioning drone and some from inside the door.

'That's easier said than done,' he shouted. 'Can you close the door?'

'No, but you might be able to with your overactive imagination thingy.'

'Shit, I'd forgotten about that in all the excitement,' he said, thinking his way into the local electrical systems.

The drone finally stopped firing and went quiet, except, as soon as it did, a new noise started up.

Rattle, clunk ... rattle, clunk ... rattle, clunk.

A huge eight-foot-tall metallic robot man loomed into view just beyond the door, carrying a large laser cannon.

'Well, that's just perfect,' said Andy to the empty corridor. 'Ed gets a complete coward and I get the fucking Terminator.'

'It's the reactor suit,' said Cort. 'It's what they use to do repairs inside the reactor core. It's heavily shielded, as you would imagine.'

'It gets better all the time,' Andy moaned as he retreated around the corner.

'Andy,' shouted Ed. 'The PCP cruiser is on the move. We've cloaked and will be engaging it shortly. You'll have to—'

An enormous explosion nearby drowned out the end of his sentence. It was so severe it knocked him over. Not only that, to his horror, he began sliding back out into and down the main corridor towards Engineering. Alarms began blaring, blue lights were flashing and, pushing with his arms, he managed to turn himself over so he could see where he was going.

'Shit, hull breach,' he shouted, fumbling for the helmet icon.

He sealed the suit as he began picking up speed. The

Terminator-suited man gradually fell backwards, in graceful slow motion, dropping his weapon, which disappeared through the door. It was almost like a comedy show as he windmilled the suit's arms as he went down.

He fell in the doorway. The bulkhead door attempted to automatically close, trapping him there.

Andy watched this with a smile as he used the soles of his suit boots to slow his progress, initially relieved to see Arnie fall over. His elation was temporary, though, as it quickly became evident that the door would be unable to close and the decompression was going to continue unchecked. His soles squealed on the flooring as his speed increased and he saw the Terminator reaching out an arm for him. Guessing this wasn't for charitable reasons, Andy jumped up, wrenching his bad ankle as he pushed off the ground, and sailed over the top. The Terminator made a lunge for him but he managed to kick the arm away. He closed his eyes and braced himself for impact, in the engineering department.

Nothing happened.

As he opened his eyes he saw stars spinning around madly. Realising, with a shock, that he was in open space, he quickly activated his suit thrusters to arrest the spin. Once he'd sorted himself out, he glanced back at the ship. A whole lump was missing from the starboard side and there were sparks and fluids jetting out from hundreds of severed cables and pipes. It almost looked as if a giant animal had taken a bite out of the rear of the ship.

Realising there had been a voice in his ear calling for the last few moments, he turned his attention to it.

'Andy, please come in. Can you hear me?' called Linda, sounding exceedingly worried.

'Er – yeah, I can.'

'Oh, thank fuck. Where are you?'

'Out for a walk.'

'What?'

'I seem to have found myself devoid of a spaceship.'

'This is no time to piss about, Andrew,' she shouted. 'Things are getting serious.'

'I kinda guessed that when I was sucked out into space.'

'You really are outside?'

'I have a great view of a hole where an engineering department used to be.'

'The PCP cruiser fired at us as soon as the other Hercules cloaked.'

Andy saw a couple of large flashes in his peripheral vision. He turned his head in that direction.

'What was that?' he asked.

'I'm hoping we just managed to disable their ship,'

she said. 'Their shields are quite tough but luckily no match for these laser cannons.'

'I've just pinpointed your position,' said Cleo. 'Can you get back to the Cartella?'

'I suppose I could have a stroll in that direction,' he said, adjusting his trajectory back towards the side of the damaged super cruiser.

'That's an irresponsible attitude,' she said. 'Get indoors now or there'll be no dinner.'

'Yes, Mum.'

31

THE BRIDGE, NO 2 HERCULES CRUISER – ERDONIOUS SYSTEM, ANDROMEDA

EPOCH 99, SPAN 9371, JUNCTURE 143.5

Linda, along with the rest of the bridge crew, watched as a continuous stream of lifeboats poured out of the stricken PCP cruiser. They'd completely disabled all major functions of the ship and, finally, the captain must have given the order to abandon the wreck before it dropped into the atmosphere of Erdonious.

'Do you want us to target the lifeboats, Captain?' came the call from the head of weapons systems.

'No, let them go,' said Linda. 'Where I come from that's considered a war crime.'

'Not even if there's one with a Mogul aboard?'

'No, from what I've seen, you're wanting a change of regime to get rid of that murderous attitude.' She glared across at the man. 'The Moguls will be hunted down and dealt with individually. I'm not going to kill twenty other innocent people just to get one of them.'

The man nodded and turned back to his panel. She glanced around the bridge and, after seemingly getting nods of approval from the majority, she instructed them to be vigilant – the second cruiser was bound to return from Reeme at any moment.

The resistance from outside the bridge had died down once the ship had become fully operational and the attackers realised the promised back-up wasn't going to arrive. Eventually, they surrendered, were disarmed and locked in the brig.

They finally managed to contact Huwlen on the damaged Hercules and he was able to squeeze everyone into two bridge lifeboats. Linda had them tractored aboard her ship soon after launch.

ANDY MANAGED to get back to the Cartella through the open hangar door. The artificial gravity on the Hercules had failed soon after the attack on the engineering department and the little ship was floating free above the hangar floor, only attached by the umbilical power lead. He disconnected it and entered the airlock. The damaged outer door refused to close again, so he had to override the system to open the inner door. Once inside, he eyed the cracked window warily and decided to keep his suit on and sealed.

He turned himself upside down and strapped himself onto the pilot's couch. A sea of red lights faced him as soon as he tried to power up the main systems; this earned the control panel a couple of slaps and a stream of bad language directed at it.

He went through a full systems reboot, only to find that the main drive was offline. About to give up and call for help, he discovered a few of the manoeuvring jets could be worked independently. It was slow, but he was able to right the vessel and then crab the Cartella sideways across the hangar and out the main door. He moved away a few kilometres into clear space, called Linda and waited.

Linda brought her Hercules gently down beside him so the Cartella was adjacent to the hangar with the Gabriel. Cleo used the tractor beam to pull the Cartella through the huge hangar door and inside the Gabriel's port hangar. Once inside, the Hercules re-cloaked and moved away.

Andy discovered only two of the Cartella's landing struts would extend, so Cleo provided invisible beams of energy to hold the ship in place while he exited and made for an airlock. All construction or repairs of semi-organic hulls would have to be carried out in zero gravity and zero atmosphere, so the port hangar would be out of bounds for a while.

'Do you realise you broke a world record?' said Ed,

giving Andy a hug as he exited the Gabriel's hangar airlock.

'What, most times shitting yourself in a spacesuit?'

'No,' he said, unable to stop himself giving Andy a little sniff as his helmet retracted. 'A five-kilometre untethered space-walk.'

'Really, was it that far? I've only got three percent left in my suit jets, so I'm glad it wasn't any further. I wasn't worried about the distance at all, really. It was getting hit by a piece of debris that scared me the most. There was shit flying all over the place.'

'I'm surprised it missed you after all the pizza you've been eating.'

Ed dodged the arm that swung in his direction and turned towards the tube lift, closely followed by a cursing, limping Andy.

THE MEETING on the Hercules bridge had been running a while when Ed and Andy joined in, holographically, from the bridge of the Gabriel.

'Ah,' said Huwlen, noticing them on the image. 'It seems we owe you our lives, young Andrew.'

A spontaneous round of applause rippled around the Hercules's bridge.

'I thought I'd screwed up,' he said, looking a little surprised.

'I know we didn't get the ship,' said Huwlen. 'But if that troop carrier had unloaded its cargo, we'd all be dead and there was no way anyone would have got past the metal man with just a laser rifle.'

'We all thought the worst after they targeted the engineering section with a missile,' said Linda. 'When we couldn't get any response from you it was the worst ten minutes of my life.'

'Anyway,' said Huwlen. 'We have one ship away and secure—'

'What about the other three flight-ready Hercules?' asked Andy. 'Can't we grab one of those?'

'They landed a troop carrier on those three too,' said Linda. 'Which meant we had to disable them before they could power up.'

'So, they're all out of commission?'

'Just slightly,' said Huwlen. 'We cut them into three with our big particle beam weapon.'

'And the other six hundred and sixty-odd?' asked Ed. 'What are we doing with them?'

'Exactly the same,' he replied. 'But we're sitting here cloaked, waiting for the other cruiser first. We detected it jumping away from Reeme a while ago, but it didn't emerge here.'

'Did it embed the jump?' asked Andy.

'Yes, but it'll be close, though. If we start waving the beam weapon around, it gives our location away. So, we're going to wait.'

'What about other PCP ships?' said Ed. 'Surely they'll have been called?'

'I'm sure they have,' said Huwlen. 'And I'm sure they'll be on their way at flank speed as soon as they can. But remember, it takes hours for the message to get there and even the closest ships are at least two days away.'

'Do we know where Hassik Triyl is?' asked Andy.

'We believe he's on the missing cruiser. All the more reason to wait for it. I'd like to jump over to Reeme and load a more substantial crew and supplies, but again it gives our presence away.'

'Have we heard from Reeme?'

'The cruiser attacked without warning, sending twelve troop carriers into the station. Only four made it past the Mark Thirteens…'

'You're welcome,' said Cort in the background.

Huwlen smiled and continued.

'The cruiser's shields were taking such a pounding, it was forced to retreat out of range. The soldiers that made it into the station are now becoming acquainted with all our booby traps. The troop carriers have been disabled, their numbers are severely depleted and their cruiser has finally pissed off. Let's just say, they've had better days.'

There was suddenly a shout from one of the bridge crew, who was manning the array suite.

'Oh, fuck,' said Linda, staring at her display, her eyes wide.

Everyone turned to look at her as she changed the holographic display to show an overview of the Erdonious System.

Four, then five, six, seven and finally eight PCP cruisers emerged in system, followed by four Moguls' attack ships, over twenty battleships and a plethora of smaller warships.

'How the shit did they organise this?' shouted Cort. 'Get us out of here.'

'In what direction?' said Linda, holding her hands up. 'They're everywhere.'

Huwlen smiled and reclined onto one of the empty control couches.

'No, wait,' he said. 'Let's hang around for a while.'

Everyone on the bridge turned to stare at him as if he'd gone insane.

32

THE BRIDGE, PCP CRUISER TYRAAN III – ERDONIOUS SYSTEM, ANDROMEDA

EPOCH 99, SPAN 9371, JUNCTURE 182.2

Hassik Triyl paced around the bridge impatiently, stopping every so often to glare at Gan Ruuger, the Captain of the PCP Cruiser Tyraan III.

'Explain to me again, Captain – why? With seventy-two ships in one small system, we don't know where one ship, the size of a small planet, is located?'

Ruuger, a locally born Erdonion, had been a senior officer in the PCP for several decades and a captain for two. He was educated, intelligent and probably one of the most experienced officers in the PCP. If he had a weakness, it was an extreme intolerance of blatant ineptitude and the Mogul, strutting around his bridge at that exact moment, was the worst example.

'Until they try to jump, use their weapons or one of our fleet runs into them, we won't know,' he replied through gritted teeth.

'Our operative on Reeme said the aliens had only been here a couple of days,' said Triyl. 'How were they able to install their cloaking technology on two Hercules without being detected?'

'They didn't,' replied Ruuger petulantly. 'They parked their ship in the hangar and slaved the systems.'

'How would you know that?' Triyl fired back, glaring at the captain, partly because of his disrespectful tone and partly because Ruuger knew something he didn't. 'I thought they only had one ship?'

Ruuger received a sideways glance from his First Officer, Drel'ik Xhin, also an Erdonion. They both exchanged an almost imperceptible nod.

Two things happened very quickly. Ruuger walked across the room towards the exit, where two of Triyl's four-man protection detail were standing either side of the bridge door. Before they could move, the captain pulled his sidearm and shot them both in the head from point blank range.

Triyl's eyes bulged, not quite believing what he'd just witnessed.

'Captain Ruuger, have you lost your—'

His outraged reaction was cut short by Xhin's sidearm, which was set to stun. He collapsed to the floor, a look of astonishment frozen on his face. The remaining ten bridge officers let out a cheer and a round of applause filled the room.

'Communications,' called Ruuger, above the noise. 'Signal the four attack ships with the agreed code and order the rest of the fleet to stop and hold their present positions. We don't want any collisions with invisible ships.'

Ruuger opened the bridge door and met a security detail, who was standing over the bodies of Triyl's other two protection officers. He ordered all four to be ejected out of the nearest airlock. Triyl's unconscious body was dragged through the ship and also placed inside airlock C226d. The inner door was sealed and they waited for him to regain consciousness.

A few minutes later, Triyl opened his eyes and glanced around the airlock. For a moment, he didn't seem to recognise where he was, but he jerked upright when the truth dawned on him.

He stood and glared through the glass-panelled inner airlock door at the small group of officers and security, who were watching him with impassive expressions. He fixed his gaze on Ruuger.

'You do realise, Captain Ruuger –' spitting his name as if it were toxic '– that if you go ahead with this, your entire planet will be exterminated.' He glanced over his shoulder at the beautiful, blue planet, which was visible through the outer door. 'Murdering a descendant of the Ancients is a galactic offence and that goes for all of you,' he growled, forcing eye contact out of everyone.

'You're quite correct, Mogul,' said Ruuger. 'The murder of any descendant of the Ancients is indeed a serious offence, which is why you are in the predicament you find yourself.'

'Open this airlock door, Ruuger,' he shouted. 'Now.'

'Oh, I intend to open it,' he replied as he accepted a data screen from Xhin. 'You see, these files were recently discovered by our counter espionage technicians and downloaded from a database hidden deep beneath the assembly building on Arus'Gan.'

Triyl's eyes opened wide.

'Is there no end to your treachery?' Triyl spat, his nose almost touching the armoured glass.

'Well, actually, that's what I was going to ask you,' said Ruuger with just a slight smirk. 'It seems for nine thousand, three hundred and seventy-one spans, you and your descendants have been living a lie.'

'That's rubbish,' shouted Triyl. 'The scriptures are quite clear in their representation of our—'

'I think the word "fabrication" is more apt, Mr Triyl,' said Ruuger, interrupting and pushing his face close to the glass.

Triyl took a step back, a shocked look on his face.

'What did you call me?'

Ruuger ignored the question and continued. 'It seems you are not the descendants of the Ancients at all. You're the invaders who all but wiped them out over nine millennia ago. It also explains why you've never had any understanding of how the Daxxal gate works. It was never your technology in the first place. The true home planet of the Ancients was Erdonious, not Arus'Gan. You only picked Arus'Gan because the climate was warm enough. Erdonious was too cold.'

'You seem to think you have everything worked out,' said Triyl.

'Not worked out,' said Ruuger. 'Just downloaded from your database. Your obsession with record keeping has finally been your downfall.'

Triyl looked at Ruuger's dispassionate expression and at all the other similar faces on the other side of the airlock. His demeanour seemed to change from its earlier aggression.

'Let's talk a deal then,' he said after a pause.

'I think it's nine thousand years too late for that.'

Ruuger looked left and right at his colleagues. They all nodded at him and he faced Triyl once more.

'Hassik Triyl, you and your murderous race are guilty of multiple counts of genocide and cruelty, stretching over more than nine millennia. It is the decision of the new interim ruling body of the Ancients' Order of Planets that you are given the same privilege as many of your victims.'

Ruuger nodded at Xhin, who pressed a code into a

recessed keypad on the right-hand side of the airlock door.

'No – no, you can't do this!' screamed Triyl, suddenly pounding on the inner door.

They watched, stony-faced, as the outer door opened. Triyl grabbed one of the weightless handles as the air began to suck out. He clawed at the window as he emitted a pitiful squeak like a wounded animal, his face seemed to swell slightly and then, in a blink, the suction of the evacuating atmosphere overwhelmed his strength and he was gone.

Xhin closed the outer door and, in silence, they all walked back to the bridge.

33

THE BRIDGE, NO 2 HERCULES CRUISER – ERDONIOUS SYSTEM, ANDROMEDA

EPOCH 99, SPAN 9371, JUNCTURE 182.3

The array officer suddenly sat up straight in his seat, called over to the captain and expanded the view of one of the seventy-two ships within the system hologram. It showed a close-up of the cruiser that had emerged back from Reeme. Four items had flown out from the side of the vessel.

'Are they bodies?' asked Linda, squinting at the display.

'Yes,' he said, expanding the view further.

'They're black guards,' said Linda, recognising them as the image panned in. 'Same as the ones that took me to see the Mogul.'

'They must be Triyl's personal bodyguards,' said Cort, looking over with a perplexed expression. 'What's happening on that ship?'

It went very quiet on the bridge as everyone watched the PCP cruiser closely. For a few minutes nothing happened, but, just as Linda was beginning to lose interest, another tall body was ejected out of the same airlock.

The array officer again concentrated his scanner on, this time, a *very alive* body.

'That's a Mogul,' said Cort as the view homed in on the wriggling body, which then became still after a few seconds. 'Shit, did someone just murder Hassik Triyl?'

Before anyone could answer, another ship – one of the attack ships – expanded into view, also having ejected a very tall, live body. Then one of the other attack ships did the same, and another one and, finally, the last Mogul ship did the same.

'Fucking hell, Linda,' called Andy from the Gabriel. 'Are you seeing this?'

'We are,' she said.

Huwlen stood up, smiling, and walked across to Linda.

'Can you put a narrow beam transmission through to that cruiser?' he asked, pointing at what was Hassik Triyl's ship.

'That'll give our location away to them, though,' she said, eyeing him suspiciously.

'Don't worry, I think you'll find they're friendly.'

Linda nodded at the communications officer, who

pressed a few icons and nodded back. The bridge of the cruiser appeared in the centre of the room

'Good evening, Gan. Are you doing a little housework?' said Huwlen, staring at the image in the centre of the room.

'I'm very glad it's you in that invisible Hercules, brother,' said Ruuger. 'Otherwise we'd all be fucked.'

'We would have had two Hercules if it wasn't for your trigger-happy colleague.'

'Yeah, sorry about him. Triyl brought him along at the last minute so I couldn't organise it to be one of ours.'

'Hang on a minute,' said Linda. 'What's all this "brother" stuff and "one of ours"?'

'Ah, yes, sorry,' said Huwlen. 'Can I introduce my half-brother Gan Ruuger and the inaugural fleet of the AOP.'

'AOP?' asked Linda.

'All obviously pissed,' said Andy, following the conversation from the Gabriel.

'I heard that,' Ruuger said sternly.

'Sorry about him,' said Linda, cringing. 'We believe he had a bit of oxygen deprivation on a space-walk recently.'

'Make sure he's reprimanded and sent to the medical centre,' said Ruuger.

'Actually, he saved my life,' said Huwlen, 'and all my crew.'

'Best give him a medal then – cheeky bastard,' said Ruuger.

'You never answered my question,' said Linda.

'Ah, yes. The Ancients' Order of Planets.'

'Well, that rolls off the tongue better than Paragon Coalesce of Planets,' she said.

'It certainly does,' said Ruuger. 'Tell me, are you the alien female who killed Tyuk Baa on the Dakr Mon?'

Linda looked at Huwlen with a questioning expression.

'Yes, she is,' said Huwlen. 'Although she doesn't talk about it much.'

'She should,' said Ruuger. 'Stuff of legends, that.'

Linda rolled her eyes and Cort laughed in the background.

'Is that the young Erebus I can see hiding in the background?'

'It is.'

'I'm sorry about your father,' said Ruuger. 'Once Triyl got his hands on him, there wasn't anything I could do.'

'Thank you. I understand,' said Cort. 'Although, watching Triyl learning the airlock tango was somewhat therapeutic.'

'It was for all of us. I must admit, it's not something I relish doing, but you just have to keep reminding yourself what those monsters did to innocent people over many millennia.'

There was a slight pause as everyone considered that statement.

'Actually,' said Cort, breaking the silence. 'Regarding the other Hercules, I reckon I could get one of the others flight-ready in a couple of weeks if we put all the company resources to work in just one place.'

'What do you reckon, Gan?' asked Huwlen.

'It'd certainly shorten the timescale if we had another one of those,' he said. 'We just need to keep the hot horns away.'

'Did Triyl call for back-up?' said Linda.

'Not from my ship, he didn't.'

'What about the one we messed up?'

'Well, if they did, we didn't receive it.'

'We need to work on the assumption they did,' said Huwlen. 'Put twelve ships out a few systems in every direction and have them scan for incoming PCP vessels.'

'Does that mean the second ship is on then?' said Cort. 'Because I can project manage it from my father's yacht. It's berthed over there on the fourth string.'

'Fine by me,' said Ruuger.

'You get over there and do your stuff,' said Huwlen. 'We'll keep the dogs off.'

OVER THE NEXT FEW DAYS, the new fleet consolidated its position. All but one of the part-constructed Hercules ships were demolished. They reasoned there'd be too much debris to let it all drop into the atmosphere. The part-built ships were tractored out on a one-way trajectory towards the local star to burn up.

Linda ensured her Hercules – renamed Ancients' Retribution – had full supplies from Erdonious and took it over to Reeme for a larger contingent of crew.

The PCP agent on Reeme, who had informed Triyl about the Hercules plan, was sent a message using codes taken from one of the last surviving and surrendered PCP soldiers on Reeme. The message sent was in regard to a fictitious pick-up location for his exfiltration and they waited to see who would show.

It was Sticky who turned up. He was, at first, sentenced to be executed until they confirmed Triyl had imprisoned his two sons, with a threat of torture and death if he didn't comply. He was instead given a job in the kitchens on the Retribution and made to wear a security collar.

Cort ran triple shifts on the second Hercules – now

named Ancients' Reparation. He struggled at first to get crews up to the ship, but as news filtered down that it was safe now, and good money was on offer, by the fourth day he was having to turn people away. Big as the ship was, there was simply not enough space to get them all in and to work safely.

Only certain areas of the ship were to be finished; a skeleton crew of a few hundred wouldn't need several thousand cabins. Cort concentrated on getting the ship flight-ready first, then moved on to defences and armaments and, finally, after thirteen days, he began to bring on final fixings and supplies.

Cleo had concentrated her time on repairs to the Cartella. Although the rebuild was mostly automated, she was able to speed things up a little and, on the fourteenth day, Andy was able to fly the little ship over to the main hangar on the Reparation.

'Déjà vu comes to mind,' he said to Phil, who'd come along for the ride and a change of scenery.

'Just don't want any exploding troop carriers this time,' Phil replied.

'Or Arnies with fuck-off laser cannons,' he said, spinning the Cartella around and settling her down near the power terminal.

They exited the ship and connected it up to one of the Reparation's power nodes in the corner of the hangar.

'Phil, can I ask you a question?' said Andy as they walked back to the Cartella's airlock.

'Of course.'

Andy paused at the bottom of the steps. 'When you were watching over Earth – it would probably have been two or three thousand years ago – did you witness any other aliens visiting the planet?'

Phil smiled and put his hands in his pockets.

'You want to know if we saw a Mogul visit earth, don't you?'

Andy nodded. 'Ed, Linda and I were discussing it the other night.'

'You think the Moguls are what you know as devils.'

'Well, don't you?'

'Yes,' said Phil. 'It would explain the depiction of them being red-skinned, horned and liking a hot environment.'

'And inherently evil,' added Andy.

'Six hundred and sixty-six of them … a space station called Locy'fer…' continued Phil.

'The evidence is pretty compelling, isn't it?'

'It is,' said Phil. 'And in answer to your question: yes. We did witness other visitors over time. But none of them resembled the Moguls. You have to realise we weren't there twenty-four-seven, so if they didn't trigger the jump detector, we wouldn't necessarily have known.'

Andy nodded again.

'I'm certainly glad they didn't stay,' he said before jumping up into the airlock.

'You and me both,' replied Phil, following along.

34

HANGAR 23K, ANCIENTS' REPARATION – EN ROUTE TO KQETT, ANDROMEDA

EPOCH 115, SPAN 9371, JUNCTURE 076.1

'Are we moving?' asked Phil as he peered through the Cartella's front screen.

Andy looked up from his tablet and followed Phil's gaze out across the hangar deck. The stars visible through the massive doorway were definitely shifting around and, they watched a huge, gleaming, sleek, black ship, almost as big as the Gabriel, entered the hangar, turned and settled on six huge retractable legs. Andy quickly powered up his console and activated the cannons.

'Hold your fire,' said Phil. 'I don't think it's a PCP ship this time.'

'Morning, guys,' said Cort over the comms. 'Like my new runabout?'

'You dick for brains,' said Andy. 'I nearly ventilated it with tungsten.'

'It's okay. It's got shields,' he said. 'Unlike my last one.'

'Where the hell did you get that monstrosity? I need fucking sunglasses, it's so shiny.'

'It was my father's new yacht. It's kinda mine now. Cool, eh?'

'Cort, is the Reparation moving somewhere?' asked Phil, completely ignoring his enthusiasm.

'Yes, we're going over to Reeme to pick up the remainder of the crew, the same as the other one did last week.'

'There won't be many left on Reeme at this rate,' said Andy. 'We must make sure we finish all the beer before we leave.'

'I'll help you with that,' said Cort, sounding hopeful.

THE MASSIVE SHIP negotiated its first jump successfully, along with its twenty-vessel support fleet, emerging one hundred thousand kilometres distant from Reeme. They all cruised in to around five hundred kilometres and waited for the crew shuttles to commence the transfers.

Huwlen had joined to captain the ship and was on the bridge of the Reparation, talking to a colleague on Reeme who'd agreed to stay and run the station in his absence.

'…and finally, can you have my private shuttle brought over to the Reparation?' he asked. 'It's in hangar 117a.'

'Yes, Mr Senn. I believe it's leaving as we speak.'

'How can that be? I've only just asked you to move it.'

'The pilot said you'd already asked him to take it over.'

'What pilot? I don't have a pilot. I always fly it myself.'

Huwlen glanced across at the holo map, which was suspended in the middle of the bridge and showed the immediate area of space around Reeme and the AOP fleet. His Arrow Class Shuttle materialised out of the gloom of the station's hangar cavern and turned towards the Reparation.

'Arrow 114, this is the Reparation. Please confirm pilot identification.' Huwlen transmitted on an open frequency.

There was silence from the little ship as it continued to accelerate.

'Could someone scan that ship please?' asked Huwlen.

'One life sign,' came the reply.

'Anything unusual on board?'

'No, sir.'

'Okay, have it tractored aboard and the pilot questioned.'

'Yes, sir.'

The arrow shuttle jumped before he could press a single icon.

'Track it,' shouted Huwlen.

'Sorry, sir. The jump was embedded.'

Huwlen stood for a second, staring at the now-empty spot on the holo map.

'Who the hell was in my shuttle?' he transmitted, looking puzzled.

'The pilot was the same guy you had installing the new fission generator at the back of the nuclear engineering cavern,' replied Reeme.

'Reeme, I did not authorise a new fission generator,' said Huwlen, a note of concern in his voice. 'You'd better check out exactly what he was doing.'

There was a slight pause before Reeme came back online.

'I've instructed a security detail to search the engineering department. I'll let you know when— What the fuck was—'

Everyone on the bridge looked up at Huwlen, the conversation suddenly cut short. Movement on the holo map caught their attention and they all gasped in horror as Reeme Station seemed to swell and explode outwards.

'Full shields – emergency jump now,' screamed Huwlen.

But, as quick as the bridge officers were, the shock wave was quicker. Even at five hundred kilometres, it was on them in a blink of an eye.

The nuclear annihilation of Reeme was of an epic scale. Shields on modern starships can sequester huge amounts of energy, but this was on another order of magnitude. Twelve of the twenty-one vessels were hit side-on and broke apart with that first shock wave. The remaining nine were either facing away or caught it head on, the Reparation included.

They survived the initial onslaught, with some hull buckling and a few decompressed compartments, but this was followed up with the first wave of shrapnel. Lumps of Reeme, some the size of mountains, some just pebbles and everything in between, peppered the doomed fleet.

The Reparation, having been swung around by the shock wave, was hit side-on by a mass of jagged rock, which severed the bow like a knife through butter. The newest ship in the fleet was in two pieces and already as good as scrap.

Over two hundred lifeboats were launched from the flailing vessels, but with the sheer volume of Reeme matter and the addition of starship detritus ricocheting around in all directions, very few survived.

Cort, in his new starship, and Andy and Phil in the Cartella were lucky in the fact they had a huge ship around them. That, and the fact they had had their shields up anyway to hold themselves centrally in the bigger ship's hangar.

The rear section of the Reparation took multiple hits as it slowly spun away from where Reeme had once been, protecting the two ships inside. Several lumps of rock had found the open hangar door, along with ship debris, but had either buried themselves in one of the bulkhead walls or been repelled by the two smaller ships' shields.

'I think we're through the worst of it,' said Phil after it had been reasonably quiet for ten minutes or so. 'D'you want me to go out and uncouple that cable?'

'Only if you put a suit on and remain tethered to the ship,' said Andy as he peered out across the hangar. 'The main power could fail at any time, along with that force field.'

'Andy, are you there?' called Cort, with a nervous edge to his voice.

'Yep, we're here.'

'Is the Reparation okay?'

'I don't know. There's no reply from the bridge.'

'I can't get a reply from anyone.'

'If you give us a moment, we'll uncouple and have a

quick peek outside. Our scanning array doesn't work inside here.'

'No, nor does mine,' Cort replied, pausing, then asking, 'Was that the station?'

'What, the explosion?'

'Yeah.'

'I don't know what else it could have been. Are your crew okay?'

'Apart from a couple of broken bones, yes.'

After Phil had suited up and quickly disconnected the power cable, Andy cautiously tiptoed the Cartella through the hangar force field. The stars were spinning madly and he wanted to remain with the spin of the bigger ship while he inspected it. The reason neither of them could contact the bridge immediately became obvious. Only two-thirds of the Reparation remained. The front section was completely missing.

He moved away from the wreck and scanned about and, finding no immediate danger from debris, he contacted Cort.

'Are you sure there's no one left in that rear section, Cort?'

'Yes, they were all on the bridge.'

'You'd better get your shiny ship out here then.'

'Really, why?'

'In about twenty minutes you'll be meeting the asteroid belt.'

'Oh, shit. Right.'

The Erebus V slowly emerged from the hangar, addressed the spin and joined the Cartella.

'Shit, where's the bridge section?' asked Cort, sounding shocked. 'All that bloody work for nothing.'

'Story of my early career,' said Andy.

'We must try and find it; they could still be alive too.'

'Absolutely,' said Andy. 'We'll transmit an open hail on all frequencies and scan for life forms. I would imagine any surviving lifeboats would make a beeline for Kqett – it's the only habitable place left in this system now.'

'Our lifeboats are designed to keep you alive for at least thirty days in space and drop you down on a dry, flat landing area if there's a habitable planet within range.'

'Right, so we should concentrate on finding any bigger lumps of ships first – anyone who survived in a lifeboat will be reasonably secure for now.'

'Your array is more powerful than mine, so you find them and we'll pick 'em up.'

'Sounds like a plan,' said Andy, giving Phil a nod to take over the piloting. He sat on the navigation couch and began the search.

There was so much crap flying around in this section now, he found he had to keep the scans relatively local to avoid missing anything. After an hour, they'd picked up only four survivors, found spinning uncontrollably in a damaged lifeboat – it wasn't much to show for over two thousand missing crew.

Andy nearly jumped out of his skin when four starships jumped in close by. He was very relieved to see one of them was the Retribution.

'About bloody time,' he called.

'Sorry, Andy,' replied Linda. 'We couldn't jump in until the debris had subsided. Are your ships okay?'

'I think so. The Reparation protected us from the blast wave and the following rock storm.'

'Is Huwlen with you?'

'No, the front section of the Reparation was completely severed. We've been trying to find it. There's just so many lumps of ship and station out here, it's all spreading out fast and if it went into the asteroid field, the same as the rear section, then we're screwed.'

'Shit, okay. Let's spread out. How far had you spun when you exited?'

'About seventeen thousand kilometres and at a slight angle in towards the belt.'

'So, if the lump that cut the ship in half spun you slightly inwards. It's fair to think the front section would be spinning the other way and possibly at an angle slightly away from the belt.'

'You're not just a pretty face, eh?'

'Do I get a medal?'

'No, this is a British operation. You don't get a medal for putting your boots on the right feet. You have to have been in actual combat.'

'I was. I messed up that PCP cruiser pretty good a couple of weeks ago.'

'I stand corrected. You can have a Blue Peter badge.'

'Cool, is that good?'

'Absolutely,' said Ed, butting in to the conversation. 'Only one step down from a Victoria Cross.'

'Can we get on with finding Huwlen?' moaned Cort.

'Sorry,' said Linda. 'Do you want to park your gin palace in one of my hangars just in case the PCP pays us a surprise visit?'

'Okay, light me a route. Have we checked Huwlen's bridge crew aren't on any of the surviving lifeboats?'

'There are seventeen of them, heading towards Kqett. We've contacted all of them. There's a cruiser picking them up one by one. They're not amongst them.'

'Where the hell are they then? The front section of a Hercules is huge. It can't just disappear.'

'I'll try extending the range to two hundred thousand.'

'Narrow the scan parameter down to high

concentrations of Corthenium alloy. We use a lot of that in the external structures and hull.'

'Nothing still. I'll extend the range out again.'

Linda spent the next five minutes pushing the array further out into the system.

'We're coming up on the first lumps of station now. They can't possibly be— Ah, now that's strange.'

'What have you got?'

'I'm getting intermittent returns for— Oh, hang on.'

'The suspense is killing me,' said Cort as he flew onto the bridge astride an electric motorcycle.

'Where did you get that thing? Whatever it is and whatever you do, don't show it to Andy.'

'It was one of my dad's toys. It beats walking. More importantly, what have you found?' he said as he stopped circling the bridge, braked the bike to a stop and looked up at the holo map.

'There's a huge fragment of station spinning away that has a high concentration of your Corthenium alloy on one side of it. That's why the reading is intermittent.'

'How big is the fragment of rock?'

'Three kilometres in diameter.'

'That's got to be it. It must have taken the front section of the ship with it.'

It took fifteen minutes to reach the outer limit of the explosion and, after a visual inspection, they were very pleased to see the front of the Hercules hanging off one side. It was apparent that several decks on the starboard side had been crushed in the impact, but the bridge was deep in the interior so they were reasonably confident it would have survived the collision.

'Let's hope the emergency life support system has remained operational for this long,' said Cort.

'Do they have suits on the bridge?' said Linda.

'Yes, there would have been more than enough for the small crew, but they're only good for around two hours.'

'There's no response from them on any frequency,' said the communications officer.

'Can we slow it down with our tractor beam?' said Linda, glancing over at Cort. 'It would make a rescue attempt a lot safer.'

'Maybe,' he said. 'That's a big rock carrying a lot of inertia. But we have six of the latest, most powerful Dicouran tractors down each side of the ship. If we used all six together, we may be able to slow it down.'

'It's only travelling at sixty-six kilometres per second so we don't need to actually slow its speed down, just arrest the spin to make docking with one of the airlocks easier.'

'Ah, I see what you mean now. If we had three pulling and three pushing on the top and the bottom of the rock, that could make a difference.'

'I'll organise that while you go and spark up one of

your shuttles. Our ships won't have compatible airlocks – and make sure you wear a suit; there might not be an atmosphere on the inside.'

'I'm on it,' he said as he jumped back on the bike and zipped away, disappearing off down the main corridor.

ED HAD DECIDED to get some exercise and visit Linda on the Retribution's bridge, leaving Phil and Rayl on the bridge of the Gabriel.

He'd only got a few hundred metres up the corridor, away from the hangar, when he detected a strange humming noise coming from up front. What started as a small dot in the distance rapidly became some sort of two-wheeled vehicle travelling at speed towards him. He jumped to one side as Cort, on the electric motorbike, hit the brakes, slid past him and stopped.

'Where the hell did you get that?' asked Ed, admiring the sleek machine.

Cort ignored the question. 'I'm going over to dock with what's left of the Reparation. D'you want to give me a hand?'

'Absolutely,' he said as he threw his leg over the bike behind Cort. Patting him on the shoulder, he leant forward and spoke in Cort's ear as the bike accelerated away: 'Don't, whatever you do, show this thing to Andy.'

Cort chuckled the short distance back to the hangar.

They quickly fired up one of the Retribution's shuttles and donned zero-atmosphere suits.

'Is that you as well, Ed?' called Linda.

'Yes, I'll give Cort a hand in case there's any casualties that need carrying across.'

'Okay, you just make sure that suit's sealed up properly and any if problems arise, you get back here straight away.'

'Yes, Mum.'

The tractor beams had slowed the rock's spin a little, but they soon realised stopping it completely would take too much time – time any potential survivors didn't have.

Cort expertly matched the spin of the rock with the shuttle and slowly closed in on the wreck. He chose the airlock that appeared to have the least damage. Unfortunately it was the furthest from where the bridge was, but beggars couldn't be choosers.

The automated docking sequence locked on and they waited while it did its thing. The reassuring clunk, followed by the whining of the locking mechanism and a green light on the airlock panel, was very welcoming.

They were also pleased to see a pressure reading on the other side of the door. It was a little lower than theirs, so they activated their helmets and lowered the pressure on their side to enable the airlock doors to release.

It was dark inside the remains of the Reparation and the suit telemetry told them it was cold and the oxygen level was approaching critical. There hadn't been explosive decompression, but there was most definitely a leak. They lost gravity as soon as they left the sanctuary of their own ship and activated the gas jets, which were incorporated into the suits.

Ed found it quite eerie, even with the aid of his helmet-mounted lights, as he followed Cort through the maze of silent, dark corridors. He found it strange being on a ship in total silence; you got used to the permanent hum of a plethora of systems working to keep a ship alive. It was with you all the time – everywhere you went – and every ship had a slightly different tone.

'How you doing, guys?' said Linda suddenly.

'Ah, shit,' said Ed. 'You nearly gave me a stroke.'

'I almost crapped a kidney,' said Cort.

'Can you give us some warning before you call, Linda? It's like floating through a scene from *Alien*, here.'

'Sorry, I'll incorporate some white noise into the signal. Any sign of life yet?'

'Nothing yet. We'll keep you posted. Cort reckons we're about three hundred metres from the bridge.'

'Roger that.'

Rounding the next corner, Cort pointed to the far end of the corridor.

'Those are the bridge's main entrance doors.'

'Will we be able to open them without power?'

'Hopefully.'

Ed thought this was a bit daft, coming all this way with no tools or anything and being thwarted by one door.

They reached the end of the corridor and Cort opened a panel on the wall beside the door. He proceeded to enter a code into the keypad and stood back.

Nothing happened.

'That's odd,' he said. 'Oh, well. Plan B.' And he began tapping at the keys again.

'No, wait,' said Ed. 'Have you checked—'

The doors slammed open and they were both sucked into the bridge. Ed flew across the room and slammed into the far wall.

'Ow, shit.'

'Ah, crap,' shouted Cort as he clipped a couch on the way across, spun and hit the wall upside down.

'I'm glad I wasn't standing in the middle of the room,' said Huwlen as he floated over with his arms crossed and watched the two newcomers checking their suits.

'You're alive,' said Ed, a wide smile displaying inside his helmet.

'Yeah, we're all okay,' he said as the other members of the bridge crew materialised out of the captain's study.

'I thought these suits were only good for two hours,' said Cort, righting himself and flexing his left arm as it had taken the brunt of the impact against the bulkhead wall.

'They are,' said Huwlen. 'We collected all the suits and the oxygen bottles from the medical centre in the front section of the ship before the levels leaked away, then shut ourselves in the captain's study as it was small and seemed airtight. We then turned everything off on the suits, including the communications, to conserve power. We finally sat breathing as shallowly as possible and waited.'

'Didn't you need the communications to stay on so you could call us?'

'Without the boosted power from the ship, the suit comm's range is only about four hundred metres. It flattens the power pack very quickly and renders the whole suit useless.'

'Are all your suits good for about twenty minutes' journey back to the shuttle?' asked Cort.

A few went back into the office for a fresh suit, after having checked their readouts.

'How many suits did you find?' said Ed.

'Enough for four each,' said Huwlen. 'With the oxygen bottles, it gives us about ten hours. How many ships did we lose, by the way?'

'All of them.'

Huwlen's head dropped. 'How many crew survived?'

'About ten percent.'

'Did you catch whoever it was in my shuttle?'

'What shuttle?'

'Shit.'

They formed a buddy chain back through the remains of the ship to ensure no one got lost. On the way, Huwlen explained to Ed and Cort that the stranger must have smuggled in a nuclear device and placed it next to the station's main nuclear power supply in the centre of the rock. The stranger must have escaped on his private shuttle.

'We need to rethink some of our battle plan now. We've lost a third of the fleet already,' said Cort.

'I've been doing some thinking while I was waiting,' said Huwlen. 'I have a new plan.'

35

THE OFFICERS' MESS, ANCIENTS' RETRIBUTION – ERDONIOUS SYSTEM, ANDROMEDA

EPOCH 116, SPAN 9371, JUNCTURE 125.5

Huwlen had gathered the remainder of the fleets' captains in the officers' mess aboard the Retribution.

Fifty grim-faced men and women quietened as he strode into the large room and stepped up onto a chair. He glanced around at them all with a sombre expression and waited until the room was completely silent.

'Twenty-one ships, one thousand seven hundred and twenty-four colleagues and friends. To say yesterday wasn't a disaster would be kidding ourselves,' he said. He nodded and gestured to some empty chairs as Ed, Andy and Linda appeared in the doorway.

'We're still fifty-one ships, though. One of those is the only remaining Hercules and two have the ability to cloak, thanks to our allies here from Daxxal.' He pointed to the three of them.

'Actually, that's what we're here to talk about,' said

Ed, standing and walking towards the front. He stepped up onto another chair next to Huwlen.

'Are you leaving us?' said Huwlen.

'No, nothing like that,' said Ed, putting his hand on Huwlen's shoulder to alleviate the worried tone in his voice. 'After yesterday, we believe you need a break. Something to give you the upper hand against the PCP. We know that a considerable number of their ships will join you in the AOP once they know the truth. In the meantime, you're fifty-one ships against potentially a couple of thousand.'

'We won't be meeting them all together, though,' said someone in the front row. 'At least half the fleet is several months away and will have no knowledge of this.'

'This is what we're gambling on,' said Huwlen. 'Initially confronting each major battle group with superior numbers, giving them the option of joining the new order or being disabled or destroyed. With luck, we can gradually whittle down their strength until we have greater numbers and are finally in a position to confront the Moguls' nest at Arus'Gan.'

'This is where we believe your main problem lies,' said Ed. 'You just said, "gambling" and "with luck". In our experience, even the best laid plans go to shit as soon as the first shot is fired. What's almost always proved to be the best opening gambit is to cut the head off the snake with that first shot.'

'What, attack Arus'Gan first?' asked Huwlen, aghast. 'There's always in excess of one hundred navy ships loitering around the planet, not to mention the space-based defences. We'd be wiped out before even half their ships—'

'What if your entire fleet was cloaked?' said Ed, interrupting.

The room fell suddenly silent as if he'd fired a gun.

'But you've already pointed out the risk of the PCP taking one of our ships with your cloaking technology installed,' said Huwlen. 'It would be all over for us and your galaxy too.'

'Not necessarily. Our sentient computer has designed a sealed cloaking unit that can be plugged straight into your ship's engineering console. It's tamper-proof so it can't be reverse-engineered and they all have individual or group self-destruct codes.'

The room fell silent again as everyone took in the implications of Ed's last statement.

'When can these be ready?' asked Huwlen.

'Right now,' said Ed. 'Okay, Cort. Wheel them in.'

Everybody turned to face the door as a trolley laden with small six-inch cubes rolled through into the mess. Cort steered it over to Huwlen and Ed.

'Is that all they are?' said Huwlen, stepping down

from the table, picking up one of the cubes and examining it.

'It's all they need to be,' said Cort. 'The alloys we use in our hulls are compatible with the Theo cloaking technology.'

The captains were issued a cube each, each one having a serial number registered to their particular ship. Then they returned to their ships and the fleet began the journey to Arus'Gan.

The plan was to split up and reconvene in the Dahroine system, which was adjacent to Arus'Gan. The final mission planning would occur after a full assessment of the enemy's strength.

Huwlen took over command of the Retribution from Linda, which permitted her to return to the Gabriel.

Ed had decided to take the Gabriel to Arus'Gan, as fast as possible, to initiate the scans. Theirs was the fastest ship and it meant the fleet would have the full picture as soon as it arrived.

Cort agreed to remain on the Retribution and help train the Reeme survivors for jobs aboard the big ship. He kept his yacht parked in the giant hangar for safety, but insisted on a manned bridge at all times, with the drives warmed up, just in case.

'Did you tell them?' asked Cleo.

'No,' said Ed.

'Tell them what?' said Linda.

'That the cloaking units also self-destruct if they ever travel to Daxxal.'

'It's a secondary safety feature,' said Cleo. 'I don't imagine Huwlen would double-cross us, but if the PCP did somehow get hold of the units, it would render them useless if they continued with their invasion plans.'

'We need to start planning our primary mission,' said Ed.

'Which is?' said Linda.

'The rescue of the Vlepon's crew. And if their ship's still in orbit around that gas giant we'll tow that back too,' said Ed.

'Do you think there'll be any of them left alive?' said Andy.

'Well, they were certainly feeding them well enough on the Dakr Mon,' said Linda.

'I'm hoping they're still on the space station,' said Ed. 'But if they've been split up and sold on as slaves—'

'Like I was,' said Linda.

'—then they don't have much of a hope, unless sometime in the future AOP liberates them.'

'How are we going to find them?' said Andy.

'I was thinking about using our DOVIs to search the station,' said Ed.

'That would take forever,' said Cleo. 'I should be able to do it a lot quicker with the information I gained from the Dakr Mon's memory core.'

'Where were they at that time?' asked Ed.

'In a detention facility on level twenty-eight of the cruiser.'

'How many of them?'

'Twenty-seven.'

'Okay, guys,' said Ed. 'That's our mission before we head back. Getting those twenty-seven crew home is the objective. Helping Huwlen gain Arus'Gan for the AOP will also be an excellent outcome.'

36

SACHEM MOGUL'S PRECINCT, CORE BUREAU – ARUS'GAN, ANDROMEDA

EPOCH 118. SPAN 9371, JUNCTURE 126.8

Haken Garre strode nervously through the Core Bureau towards the precinct of the Sachem Mogul.

As one of the newest and youngest Moguls, he'd only been in the Bureau once before, a single span ago, for his enthronement. Although a sombre occasion, at least it had been planned; he'd been expecting and planning for it for many epochs. Today wasn't exactly expected, the summoning only having arrived a juncture ago. Although after the shocking news that had reached his department that morning he guessed that, as the most junior officer, he'd be lumbered with informing the Sachem, hence his trepidation.

He'd been very excited when given a position within the intelligence arm of the administration under the Adjudicator, Hassik Triyl. But right now he wished it'd been with Sanitation.

The two precinct guards were expecting him. They opened the double doors to the Sachem's inner sanctum as he approached and he jumped as the doors crashed shut behind him.

He stopped and stood stiffly in front of the Sachem Mogul's raised desk, staring at the floor.

'You have news of Triyl?' Reeph growled, breaking the silence and glaring down at the junior Mogul.

'Y–yes, Sachem Mogul,' said Garre, annoyed that he sounded so weak. 'We have reliable intelligence that indicates Hassik Triyl's fleet was ambushed at Erdonious by Huwlen Senn and the Daxxal invaders.'

'Did he survive?'

'Er, we believe not, Sachem Mogul.'

'Good, saves me a job. Incompetent idiot. Why did they send you to inform me of this?'

'I–I believe I was the only one available, my Sachem.'

'Crap,' Reeph thundered, slamming his fist down on his oversized desk, which caused Garre to reel back in alarm. 'They sent you because they're a bunch of cowards. Now get out and send in Kky. He's supposed to be in fucking Daxxal.'

Garre turned and almost ran to exit the chamber, the doors strangely opening before him without any input. He found the outer hall considerably busier than a few moments before.

'YOU,' thundered a voice from his left.

'COME HERE,' shouted Tyann Kky, pointing in his direction. Garre turned and reluctantly moved towards him, a gap opening before him through Kky's entourage.

'What mood's he in?' Kky spat, looking down his nose at him.

'A bit pissed,' he said before he could stop himself and then waited for the reprimand.

'What?' said Kky, seemingly surprised by Garre's lack of respect. Kky stared at him, a sly smile appearing on his lips. 'You used to work for Triyl didn't you?'

Garre nodded.

'Good, you work for me now. Follow.' He slapped Garre on the back, almost knocking him over, and strode back towards the Sachem Mogul's chamber.

'Oh, shit,' mumbled Garre to himself, as he slowly fell into step behind the small group.

The huge doors reopened and Garre hung back, hoping he wouldn't have to face Reeph again.

'Garre, with me,' came the shout as the group parted once more and he knew then he would regret this day for a long time.

Kky strode confidently into the Sachem Mogul's chamber, having first stopped to converse with the two chamber guards. This time they entered the chamber too, closely followed by four black guards. Garre nervously crept in behind them and, when everyone stopped in front of Reeph's raised desk, he purposely hung back nearest the door.

'Sachem Mogul,' said Kky, his gaze remaining on his leader.

There was an awkward pause before the Sachem looked up from his screens. His eyes bored into Kky's. 'I believe it is customary for the Sachem to speak first and your gaze to be averted, young Kky,' said the Sachem in a quiet but chilling voice. 'Why is it you're here and not in Daxxal where I believe I sent you?'

'In normal circumstances I would have been, Sachem Mogul,' he replied confidently. 'But in this case, no.'

'And what case is that?'

'I have declared a state of exigency, Sachem Mogul. It seems a fleet of warships, overseen by Huwlen Senn, could well be on the way here. It is my duty to ensure the safety of the Sachem and the ruling council.'

'Do you not think you might be overestimating this Senn character?'

'No, Sachem Mogul. He has, it seems, defeated Triyl's cruiser fleet. He has at least one of our new Hercules cruisers and, we are led to believe, the Daxxal cloaking technology too.'

'And you think he's on his way here?'

'Yes, it's what I would do.'

Reeph looked over Kky's head and noticed Garre by the door.

'What are you doing back here, emergent Garre? I thought I dismissed you?'

'He's working for me now,' said Kky. 'He will be my representative, staying with you and the council.'

Garre opened his eyes wide and swallowed hard as the new responsibility dawned on him.

'So, your plan is to run away and hide?' said Reeph, moving his gaze from Garre back to Kky. 'And I'm to be babysat by an emergent?'

'After you and the council are in a place of safety, I will be putting together a large battle fleet, Sachem Mogul,' said Kky, 'to ambush Senn and his band of traitors and to watch over the Daxxal gateway. Our Daxxal guests will be wanting to return home at some point and I would very much like to give them a special send-off.'

'You do realise this is the first time in our history, even since the invasion, that a state of exigency has been declared?'

Garre noticed two of the guards exchange a glance at the mention of the word 'invasion'.

'It's not a decision I thought I'd ever have to make, Sachem Mogul,' said Kky, shaking his head and averting his eyes to the floor. 'But a necessary one, I believe.'

'For your sake, you'd better be right, Kky,' said Reeph, standing and raising his gaze to the rear of the chamber again. 'Come on then, Garre. It's no use trying to hide at the back. I believe we have a shuttle to catch.'

Garre followed the Sachem and his two chamber guards towards a small door to the left-hand side of the raised desk, glancing at Kky as he passed.

'Report the Sachem and council's status to me twice an epoch,' Kky said, staring and pointing at him menacingly.

Haken Garre nodded and left the Sachem's chamber once more, enveloped in an overwhelming feeling of dread.

37

THE STARSHIP GABRIEL – EN ROUTE TO ARUS'GAN, ANDROMEDA

EPOCH 118, SPAN 9371, JUNCTURE 177.0

'Andy, be alert. We're about to jump into the Genrox'Ba system,' called Linda.

'I don't want to be a "lert" – I want to be rich and loved,' he replied sleepily from his cabin.

'Just shut up and get up here, you idiot.'

Five minutes later, the entire ship's crew were sitting on the bridge, watching the holo display. Even Rayl had dragged herself out of bed and had sat on one of the side couches.

'Were you out late gigging again, Rayl?' asked Ed, noticing her yawning. 'Who was it this time?'

'The Foo Fighters in California,' she said. 'I think I'm a bit deaf this morning.'

'Oh, wow,' said Andy. 'My dad went to see them a couple of times when I was young. Wasn't it Dave Growl in that band?'

'Grohl.'

'That's him. Used to be the drummer in Nirvana.'

'Yeah, he's super cool,' she said. 'I saw Nirvana the other night. I really would like to come back and see Earth with you guys. It looks an amazing place.'

'No problem,' said Andy. 'I'll personally give you a—'

'That will have to be decided by the GDA,' said Linda, giving Andy a withering stare. 'Until then, we have work to do,' she said, putting emphasis into the word 'work'.

'Okay, sorry.'

'Right,' said Ed, quickly gaining everybody's attention. 'I know you've all been dying to know what Huwlen and I cooked up in our secret planning meeting. I can – now I've seen what's here – let you all in on the state of the game.'

Ed paused as he glanced over the results from the neighbouring system.

'We seem to have four hundred and twelve ships within the Arus'Gan system, of which one hundred and seven are armed PCP navy vessels. There's quite a lot of activity around the damaged side of Locy'fer station.'

He brought a view of the station and planet into view on the holo map. The damaged side was still prominent, with the flashes from dozens of welding torches lighting up the nearside of the station, where the majority of the battleship was still wedged firmly.

'Shit, it looks even worse now. Did you really do all that?' said Andy, glancing across at Linda.

'You wouldn't like me when I'm angry,' she said with a straight face.

'Bloody oath.'

Ed spun the view around and zoomed in on one of the planetary defence platforms.

'There are eight of these,' he said.

'What do they carry?' asked Linda.

'Four Mark Thirteen cannons, two big beams and seventy-two nuclear missiles.'

'What, on each one?' said Andy.

'That's what Cort told me was installed on commissioning, yes. Although they could have added more since then.'

'Then we need to shut them down right at the start. Do they have a central control room somewhere? Or are they independently manned?'

'Remote – from somewhere on Locy'fer.'

'We'll need to find and assume control of that command centre.'

'Can I leave that to you?'

'Sure,' said Andy. 'We'll need to get in reasonably close to enable our DOVIs to do their job.'

'I was thinking of sitting next to that nearest defence

platform,' said Ed, pointing to the platform that was adjacent to the space station. 'Understandably, no one flies too near those things, so there's less chance of any accidental collisions while we're cloaked.'

'That's all well and good, so long as the platform doesn't detect us,' said Phil. 'But knowing we're sitting point blank to seventy-two nuclear warheads makes me a little jittery.'

'I understand your concerns, Phil,' said Ed. 'That's why I want you to take over from Linda as pilot and if that station as much as blinks in our direction, you use your superhuman reactions to hit the jump icon. Just make sure you've programmed a nice embedded jump to somewhere out here into the nav computer.'

'Okay, that makes me a little happier,' said Phil. 'Couldn't we disable the platforms with our own weaponry though?'

'Too dangerous. I'm trying to avoid damaging the planet's defence grid. Huwlen will need it further down the track to discourage retaliatory strikes from returning PCP ships and, anyway, just a slight miscalculation with a shot could set off all those nuclear warheads at once. The result would be similar to the Reeme Station detonation.'

Phil grimaced and glanced over at Linda.

'What am I doing then?' she said.

'Your favourite: interfering with battleships,' said

Ed. 'Once the defence platforms are offline, we start transmitting Huwlen's "Truth About the Moguls" presentation. Cleo reckons she can get it to appear on every holo emitter, screen, advertising medium, personal tablet and communication device on both the planet and Locy'fer station. On continuous repeat. Your job is to mess with any PCP ships that react unfavourably.'

'How do you mean "unfavourably"?'

'Anyone who starts firing on communication satellites or media outlets and so forth. Anything that reduces the impact of the message getting to the masses.'

'Right,' she said. 'Any rules of engagement?'

'Try to disable rather than destroy this time. There may be a percentage of the crew on those ships that would be sympathetic to the AOP. The Moguls haven't gone out of their way to make a lot of friends over the years. Huwlen has proved that, once most people know these freaks aren't descendants of their ancestors and were actually the invaders that wiped them out, they don't have any qualms about bundling them out an airlock.'

'Do we know how many of them are on the planet?' asked Linda.

'No,' replied Ed. 'That's my job – to help detect and pinpoint the Moguls on the surface so Huwlen, with the aid of the Retribution's armaments, can take them out from space.'

'Will your DOVI have that range?' asked Andy.

'Cleo reckons she can boost the range by using the planet's own communications network. But that's just theory – we won't know until we get over there. I may have to go down to the surface to initiate the search.'

'You're fucking kidding?' said Linda. 'You're actually considering flying down there into the dragon's lair on your own in the middle of the mother of all space battles?'

'I'll be cloaked in the Cartella. Cleo will be with me and I don't even need to land – only get close enough to—'

'No, Edward, no. Absolutely not. We're risking enough as it is without you risking suicide. If it can't be done from the relative safety of the Gabriel then Huwlen's going to have to live with it,' she said, giving Ed a glare.

'I'll go then,' said Andy, but then wished he hadn't as Linda slowly swivelled her head and glared at him just as menacingly. 'On second thoughts, I think I'll stay here,' he said quickly and busied himself with smoothing a crease in his trousers.

'Erm, is it just me or does anyone else think it seems a little quiet?' said Phil.

'How do you mean?' said Ed.

'Well, I'm not sure. I may be wrong, but, after what's just happened here and with their fleet of new super cruisers, you'd think there'd be a bit more urgency around the home planet.'

'But there's hundreds of ships milling around in that system. What more d'you think should be happening?' asked Linda.

'That's just it – I don't know. I mean, Huwlen's private shuttle with the Reeme bomber must have run back here and spilled the beans about what went on. I just feel we're missing something. It all seems a little pedestrian.'

'Perhaps it's just arrogance,' said Ed.

'Or a trap,' said Andy.

'Well, if it's a trap,' said Cleo, 'they'll be the ones to get a surprise, with the entire AOP fleet cloaked. The shuttle bomber won't have been able to tell them that.'

'If it's any consolation, I've scanned all the outlying systems and there's no sign of a PCP ambush fleet,' said Linda.

'According to Cort and Huwlen, although the PCP has a lot of ships, their territory is so large and the fact that they keep everyone in line by fear, the majority of their ships are always weeks or months away, showing a presence and keeping the natives in line,' said Ed.

'So it might be that they're so unaccustomed to

being challenged and their navy assets are spread too thin,' said Linda.

'The shuttle bomber might have thought he destroyed our entire fleet,' said Andy.

'Whatever the reality is,' said Ed, 'we need to keep our eyes wide open, plan for the worst and hope for the best. We can ask Huwlen what he thinks tomorrow when the AOP fleet arrives. In the meantime, we watch and wait.'

'Is Huwlen's AOP transmission ready to go, Cleo?' asked Linda.

'Yes. I've recognised over two thousand communication sources in the system.'

'And they won't be able to trace the transmission?'

'No, it'll bounce around the satellites and ground stations so fast, on continuous repeat, they'll never be able to discover the origin.'

'Right, I think we're ready,' said Ed. 'Is everybody happy with what they're supposed to be doing?'

'I don't have a job,' moaned Rayl, sticking out her bottom lip and drawing circles on the floor with her toe, seriously overacting.

The other three all glanced over at Ed who thought for a moment, theatrically rubbing his chin.

'Hmm,' he said. 'How about Mission Array Specialist?'

'Sounds cool,' she said, a grin appearing on her once-sulky face. 'What do I have to do?'

'Cleo, can I have a fifth couch please? Furnished with an array suite.'

It materialised between Linda and Andy's couches.

'Your job, Rayl, is to watch over the whole scene, looking for anything unusual that others may have missed. Are you familiar with an array suite?'

'Yep, my father trained me on all the bridge stations.'

'Good, I can't give you an exact job description, but just watch everything that's going on and report anything you consider out of the ordinary, okay?'

'Okay, brilliant, thanks, Ed.'

He sat back down and winked at Linda, who smirked back.

'Right everyone,' he said. 'We have the best part of twelve hours before Huwlen arrives. That's three hours each at the helm, so get fed and get some rest.'

38

THE STARSHIP GABRIEL – GENROX'BA SYSTEM, ANDROMEDA

EPOCH 119, SPAN 9371, JUNCTURE 087.4

It took just over an hour for the AOP fleet to join the Gabriel in the Genrox'Ba system. A large jump zone was designated to avoid the obvious hazard of over fifty ships jumping into the same area. They did it a few at a time, taking wide berths. The zone was behind a particularly large gas giant known as Genrox Tore to avoid the chances of detection before the ships could re-cloak.

As each group arrived, they spread out across the system, along with full shields and an embedded emergency jump plotted and ready. This was now a standing order after the Reeme disaster.

The Retribution was in the last group to emerge. Huwlen immediately hailed the Gabriel as the huge ship made its way out from the shadow of Genrox Tore and over to the far edge of the system.

Andy was in command of the Gabriel when Huwlen's signal arrived.

'It's about time you turned up,' Andy said. 'Did you stop at the pub?'

There was a slight pause before Huwlen answered. 'What's a pub?'

'Just ignore him,' said Linda as she appeared out of the floor on the tube lift. 'He's being an idiot as usual.'

'Is a pub a bar to us?'

'Yes, it is.'

'Ah, "did I stop at the bar". I get it now – that's quite funny.'

'Oh, please don't encourage him. I have to live with him every day.'

'It's that Daxxal sense of humour, Linda. It's a breath of fresh air to us. We haven't had much to laugh about here for a very long time.'

Andy smiled at Linda, who rolled her eyes in return.

'Well, let's hope we can begin to change that today,' she said.

ED AND PHIL entered the bridge together a few minutes later.

'Have we sent Huwlen the updated data from Arus'Gan?' Ed asked.

'Yeah, about five minutes ago,' said Andy. 'It'll take them some time to ingest the information and nominate specific targets to each vessel.'

'Okay, is there much change since yesterday?'

'Not really. A few civilian ships have left, replaced by other incoming vessels, just the normal trade comings and goings. There hasn't been any change in the navy presence at all. I sent a cloaked drone in a couple of hours ago to scan the station and try to get me a head start as to where the command centre is for the defence platforms.'

'Good idea. I'd forgotten about the drones. They're armed as well, aren't they?'

'Yeah.'

'Can you instruct it to give the planet a once over too?'

'I'm way ahead of you. I programmed it with the frequency of the Moguls' dermal implants that Huwlen gave us. So, in a few minutes, I'll know how many of the horned bastards there are on the planet and the station.'

'Love your work. We'll have to be quick, though. Apparently they have the ability to deactivate them.'

Rayl appeared on the tube lift and immediately adopted a modelling pose. 'Array Specialist Rayl is in the room,' she said and swayed suggestively over to her couch, giving Andy a wink on the way.

The slightly scruffy, unkempt teenager look was gone. The borrowed, baggy ship suit was no more and had been replaced by skin-tight black jeans and a white T-shirt under a dark blue leather biker jacket, with matching blue canvas boots and accessorised with long blue nails. Her blonde hair had been cut and styled into a long, slightly curly affair and she wore striking makeup, highlighting her eyes.

'Holy bloody moly,' said Andy. The clunk as his jaw dropped open was almost audible.

Linda stretched across from her couch and covered Andy's eyes with her hand.

'Get on with your work,' she said. 'Nothing to see here.'

Everyone sat and stared for a moment before Ed broke the silence. 'Erm, who are you and what have you done with our Rayl?'

She grinned and swept her hair back theatrically. 'Teenager Rayl is gone,' she said. 'Cleo helped me with a little update.'

'No kidding,' said Andy, his mouth still hanging open.

'It's like that scene from the end of *Grease*,' said Phil.

'She's the one that I want, doo doo doo,' sang Andy.

'We'll have none of that,' said Ed, shaking his head and rolling his eyes.

'She's electrifying,' said Cleo.

'And don't you start.'

'Start what?' said Huwlen, appearing on the large wall monitor.

'Sorry, Huwlen,' said Ed. 'Just a little pre-battle banter.'

'Well, let's hope you're all as cheerful post-battle,' he said, without any humour in his tone. 'Are you ready to transmit my message?'

'Absolutely.'

'Okay, on my command, we all jump in behind the star, re-cloak and proceed at flank speed to these pre-planned zones.'

The holo map updated as he spoke, showing the standby positions for all the AOP ships, including their particular operating zones to ensure no cloaked blue-on-blue collisions.

'You have the fastest ship so you can begin transmission as soon as you're there. Full shields at all times and these are your emergency jump co-ordinates. Just make sure they're embedded, ladies and gentlemen.'

Thirty minutes later, the stationary fleet jumped as one, using the star to shield their emergence. Phil, now piloting the Gabriel, cloaked the ship and accelerated at maximum drive out from behind the star and towards Arus'Gan.

'He didn't seem very chipper this morning, did he?' said Andy.

'Who, Huwlen?' said Linda.

'Yeah, no "hey ho, here we go" today.'

'I think the loss of Reeme affected him more than he wants to admit. After all, he did lose a lot of friends, coupled with the stress of today—'

'Five minutes to transmission point,' interrupted Cleo.

'Okay, game faces, everyone,' said Ed. 'Let's make this quick and clean and, Cleo, make sure the Palto is ready to go, just in case.'

'*Está bien.*'

Andy glanced across at Ed with a puzzled expression.

'It means "okay" in Spanish,' said Ed, noticing Andy's bewilderment.

'How did you know that?'

'I spent a month at the University of Valencia during the third year of my bachelor degree.'

'I didn't know you spoke Spanish, though.'

'I don't. I can order a beer – that's about it.'

'That's where I went wrong, wasn't it? I collected motorbikes and you collected degrees.'

'There's plenty of things you're good at that I'm not.'

'Like what?'

'Stripping a Kawasaki.'

'She was pretty, wasn't she?' A nostalgic expression appearing on Andy's face.

Rayl looked up from her station and glared at Andy. 'Who was she?' she asked.

'A 1988 Kawasaki GPZ 1000RX.'

'A what?'

'It's a motorbike,' said Ed.

The angry look on Rayl's face turned to one of bewilderment. 'A what?' she said again.

A rotating holographic image of the motorcycle materialised in the middle of the holo map.

'That's her,' said Andy. 'It's red too – same as mine.

'That's an ancient ground-transportation device,' said Rayl, seemingly surprised. 'Is that powered by a fossil fuel drive too?'

'Yeah, isn't she beautiful? Should never have sold her.'

'I'll buy you another when we get back,' said Linda.

'They're hard to find these days.'

'I'll construct you a brand new one,' said Cleo.

'It wouldn't be an original though and—'

'Transmission commencing in thirty seconds,' said Cleo as the Kawasaki disappeared from view.

The Gabriel's bridge was silent as Huwlen's 'Truth About the Moguls' transmission initiated. Cleo had written something similar to a virus to act as a carrier for the message. It infiltrated the inferior PCP computer networks with ease and indelibly cemented itself on continuous repeat into the data hardware of every satellite, media station and device on both the planet and space station.

At first nothing happened. But as the AOP fleet took up their hidden positions around the planet, some of the PCP navy vessels suddenly powered up and moved out into defensive positions.

But what was heartening was the fact that at least half of their fleet didn't move. It might have been because the majority of the crews were off ship or because they were just sitting waiting to see what happened but it didn't concern them.

Because it meant the discrepancy in numbers was reduced dramatically.

ANDY WAS SITTING, his eyes closed and, activating his DOVI, he delved into the space station's systems. The drone had provided him with a few clues as to where the defence platform's control centre was. Several areas were heavily shielded and protected by serious firewalls. On the third try he hit pay dirt, but the system detected the infiltration and abruptly took itself into a higher level of invulnerability.

'Ah, shit,' he said. 'Don't do that.'

'I had a feeling this might happen,' said Cleo. 'Give me a few minutes.'

'What are you planning?'

'I'd already considered this scenario so the drone, which is presently sitting next to the station, has released a nano cloud.'

'You consider a lot of scenarios.'

'Just a few million.'

The cloud had penetrated into the station and was, at present, moving through the ventilation ducts, percolating its way towards the control centre. Andy could tell the moment when it arrived as the system shut down and instigated a reboot.

'Can you sneak in now?' asked Cleo.

He could and, with the aid of the nanos, they rewrote the command pathways for the entire network of platforms.

'I've found access to the planet-based defences too,' said Cleo.

'Get in there, girl.'

'I can provide a pathway for you, but remember I can't operate anything that resembles a weapon.'

'That's cool. Just shut them out, get me in and I'll take over— Oh, shit.'

As Andy spoke the huge planet-based cannons came

to life and began systematically vaporising the planet's network of transmission satellites.

'Almost there,' said Cleo.

'Quickly.'

'Almost there.'

The cannons suddenly went quiet.

'I've arrived.'

'I love it when you talk dirty.'

'Don't tease. Just get in there.'

'You're doing it again.'

'Go and play with your cannon.'

LINDA HAD WATCHED the PCP warships moving out to form some sort of wide protective ring around the planet. This, she thought, was a good sign as they obviously didn't realise the threat was behind them and, so long as their weapon systems were all trained away out into an empty system, she wouldn't interfere with them.

She concentrated on the stationary ships. Infiltrating one ship at a time, she could watch what was happening on the bridge. It seemed there was a lot of conjecture over Huwlen's message.

On some ships, the bridge crew just sat and stared at the monitors; on others, there was obvious disagreement, with considerable arm-waving, pointing and shrugging.

She switched to the bridge of one of the larger battleships where a full-blown gun battle was taking place. The bridge crew had barricaded themselves into the captain's office and were attempting to fight off a seemingly superior force, which was attacking them from the main bridge entrance. She couldn't tell from the footage which side was which, so she was loath to interfere.

'I've got a large ship powering its weapons systems over here,' said Rayl, pointing at the holomap, to a lone PCP cruiser, moving in towards the space station.

Linda recognised it as a sister ship to the Dakr Mon, the vessel she had been taken on after surrendering on the Vlepon.

She penetrated the bridge cameras and, sure enough, there was a Mogul waving his arms about. He had four members of his black guard personal security standing around the bridge, pointing hand weapons at the crew.

She thought for a moment before deciding on a course of action. After being busy with her DOVI for a few minutes, she sat back, disabled the ship's main engines and, remembering what Ed had done to the Klatt ship a few weeks ago, infiltrated a cannon turret and blasted its own targeting array into scrap. Then she waited to see what would happen.

As expected, the Mogul seemed to have a fit, launching himself across the bridge, grabbing someone who was probably the weapons officer and throwing him across the floor. He gesticulated at one of his personal guards. The guard nodded, approached the cowering officer and pointed his weapon at him. But the guard's body language suddenly changed. He looked at his weapon, shrugged and indicated for one of his colleagues to take over as he stepped away. Linda wished she had audio to go with the video.

The second guard strode over and, again, pointed his weapon. Again, nothing happened. It was the same with the third and the fourth.

In the background, Linda could see a couple of the bridge officers conversing while the Mogul had his back to them. They suddenly stood as one and launched themselves at the Mogul's back. The impact threw all three into the navigator's console, the Mogul catching his head on the corner of the unit. He was unconscious before he hit the floor.

The guards flew at them from across the bridge. Two were intercepted by other crew, who had realised the Mogul was down, giving them a good opportunity to save their colleagues and take the bridge. The third was felled by a shot from a newcomer on the bridge, who was holding a weapon that Linda quickly disabled, and the fourth reluctantly surrendered.

She returned control of the ship to the pilot and watched again to see what they would do.

The huge vessel stopped, powered down its weapon systems and transmitted a signal on all channels:

'This is a message for Huwlen Senn and the AOP. I am the First Officer of the Attack Ship Dakr Hal. We wish to surrender our vessel. Please respond.'

Almost as he finished the last word of the message, five bodies were ejected from an airlock, adjacent to the bridge, four of which were dressed in black; one was very tall and red.

'Three PCP ships are converging on him,' said Rayl, glancing over at Linda, who closed her eyes again and concentrated on the biggest one.

Three of the PCP ships that had formed the outer defensive cordon suddenly headed for the Dakr Hal: two destroyers and a battleship. The destroyers opened up their cannons as soon as they were in range, but the battleship remained silent – Linda had already disabled its heavy weapons.

The Dakr Hal's shields flashed a brilliant white, where the cannon bolts impacted, and streaks of white lightening stretched away around the ship, dispersing the energy.

Four Mark Thirteen cannons on the nearest defence platform fired in succession at the nearest destroyer. Its shields absorbed the first bolt, the second overloaded the shields and the third and fourth removed huge chunks of ship. The destroyer was irreparably damaged and spun away, throwing out fountains of debris and gasses. The second destroyer quickly veered away too and retreated out of range as fast as possible.

Linda opened one eye and glanced across at Andy, who had his eyes closed but a malevolent grin on his face.

She reclosed her eye and went back to the toothless battleship. It had slowed significantly and had changed trajectory away from the Dakr Hal and the defence platform.

Having a peek inside the bridge, she saw another crew in the throes of a mutiny. There was a lot of pushing and gesticulating going on in the middle of the room and an armed group was outside the bridge, attempting to break in.

She established control of the helm, moved the vessel in close to Andy's closest defence platform and instigated a full stop, dropping the shields. The arguing on the bridge soon ceased and they all stared across the room at the defence suite as the weapon-lock siren caught their attention.

Linda found the battleship's communications suite and burrowed in to find the ship-wide public address system. She took a deep breath and made an announcement.

'PCP battleship crew, this is Commander Wisnowski of the AOP. Your vessel has made aggressive manoeuvres towards a neutral vessel and has been disengaged. You have no drive, no weapons and no shields. The bridge crew will stop squabbling amongst themselves and return to their stations. The armed posse outside the bridge doors will replace the weapons in the armoury and return to their places of work or cabins. Failure to comply will result in the immediate decommissioning of the vessel. Please await further instructions. Resistance is futile.'

A snort from Andy caused her to open an eye again. He was staring at her, chuckling away.

'What's got you all sparked up, chuckle head?' she said.

'Resistance is futile – classic.'

'Don't tell me? Twentieth century sci-fi?'

'Make it so.'

'Oh, for fuck's sake.'

ED WAS HAVING A REASONABLY easy time of it with his Mogul-spotting. He couldn't believe a race that had been overseeing such a large proportion of a galaxy for nine millennia could be so cowardly. But, then again, they hadn't had any real opposition since they'd originally invaded, which brought up another question: how had such an advanced race, one that had designed and built such a magnificent multi-galaxy gateway system, been so completely decimated by so few of these ignorant bullies?

He found another Mogul signal from within Locy'fer station and passed the location on to Huwlen. So far, he'd pinpointed twenty-seven of the monsters: nine on the station and eighteen on the surface of Arus'Gan.

Huwlen was able to target the planet-side Moguls with narrow beam weapons from his ships that were encircling Arus'Gan. The weapon, similar to the Asteri Beam used by the GDA, had been narrowed down to just over two metres in diameter, thus reducing collateral damage and innocent civilian casualties.

Targeting the Moguls on Locy'fer, however, was a different matter. Drilling two-metre holes through a space station would decompress huge areas and kill hundreds. It would be too much devastation just to target one Mogul.

To avoid this, Huwlen had put together twelve four-man Mogul hunter teams and inserted them at different entry points across the station.

Eleven teams were still operational – unfortunately one had been mistakenly targeted by an anti-PCP vigilante group, which had been roaming the station and mistook the AOP team for PCP black guards.

Apart from that isolated incident, resistance on the station had proved surprisingly light. Huwlen's transmission had worked and the general population had taken heed and remained in their accommodation units.

Even the majority of station security, especially the civilian officers, were remaining impartial. They'd disarmed themselves and were ensuring that the civilian population and any private property were secure and safe.

'Are you able to detect anything at the precinct in the Core Bureau?' asked Huwlen.

'It's strange,' said Ed. 'The one place you'd think to find them, and core members at that, but nothing – not a peep. Either they all very quickly went dark or there really aren't any there.'

'Yes, I agree. All the Moguls we've eliminated so far have been relatively junior. I'll dispatch a cadre of elite soldiers down to the precinct, backed up by narrow beam weapons from orbit.'

'The ships that rushed out to form that defensive ring have gone very quiet.'

'They haven't moved a muscle since Andy gave that destroyer the good news,' said Linda. 'There seems to be a lot of debate on most of the PCP ships. A few threw in the towel and swore allegiance to the AOP relatively quickly, but the majority have put their shields up, kept their weapons offline and are sitting it out.'

'Unusually, there were very few attack ships here when we arrived,' said Huwlen. 'And the members of the Core Bureau are conspicuous by their absence. In my book, this can only mean one thing: they had prior knowledge of our plans.'

'You reckon they've initiated a tactical retreat in the big ships,' said Ed, 'then they can muster in the majority of their fleet and wallop you with a counter attack?'

'Precisely – it's what I would have done.'

'I reckon they found out from the Reeme saboteur.'

'So do I.'

'They can't be gone long then?'

'No, my shuttle wasn't that fast – couple of days at the most.'

'D'you want us to see if we can track them?'

'No, let them go. They'll be several embedded jumps away by now and you'll never find them. The one thing they have no idea about is our ability to cloak, so when they come back all tooled up, they'll get a big surprise.'

COUNCIL PRECINCT, AOP BUREAU – ARUS'GAN, ANDROMEDA

EPOCH 120, SPAN 9371, JUNCTURE 203.9

Ed waited patiently outside the precinct chamber. Huwlen, along with twenty-eight of his most senior captains, had arranged the inaugural meeting of the fledgling government for the AOP.

Although, at this time, very few of the many outlying worlds were represented, there were a lot of fires to put out regarding the new governing of the region. Representatives from most of Arus'Gan's continents were present, including four planetary presidents who just happened to be visiting Arus'Gan at the time.

The outer hall he sat in was huge. He marvelled at the solid stone construction that had hundreds of huge pillars, reaching up over thirty metres. It reminded him of the Maison Carrée in Nîmes, France, only this was ten times the size.

It was extremely humid, which he found surprisingly uncomfortable. His body had become accustomed to the temperature-controlled environments of starships. He decided he ought to have a holiday somewhere warm soon, but not as hot and sticky as this.

He wondered whether the constant heat might have been what attracted the Moguls here in the first place ten millennia ago.

Glancing up at the sound of footsteps, he saw Andy marching back towards him across the wide cloister with a face as red as a smacked arse.

'Who designed this stupid place? It's a fuck of a walk to the toilets,' he said, as he sat down next to Ed, huffing and puffing.

'Only you could knock an architectural masterpiece like this because of the lack of a handy urinal.'

'Don't these buggers drink any beer?'

'They probably sweat it out.'

The huge metal doors to their left cracked open and a tiny face – compared against the size of the doors – peered through.

'The council commands your presence,' the usher said, beckoning them to enter.

'Bloody hell, it's like being in court,' said Andy as they stood and followed him.

Ed glanced at Andy, wondering how he would know that.

The government – or council – chamber they entered was large and circular. It had the capacity for many hundreds of representatives from around the galaxy in tiers that ascended over fifty metres. The massive domed roof was constructed of thousands of triangular smoked glass panes, held up by countless stone pillars that completely circumnavigated the chamber.

Ed looked up in awe at the magnificence and sheer scale of the building, noticing that even Andy was rubbernecking, his eyes wide.

Today there were fewer than two hundred in the chamber, all on the lower levels. But as Ed and Andy emerged into view, the entire congregation stood and broke into applause.

They both froze on the spot and gazed around the chamber, nodding and trying to look casual. Ed noticed Huwlen on the third level and smiled.

The usher who had walked on, unaware they'd stopped, rushed back and quite vigorously encouraged them to continue. After taking them up a couple of rows, he signalled to them to take two allocated seats on the fourth level. Ed glanced at the designation label on the desk in front of the seats, which read, 'Ambassadors of Daxxal'.

'After you, Mr Ambassador,' he said, allowing Andy to take the first seat.

'Thank you, Mr Ambassador,' Andy replied with a smirk.

The applause died down and everyone retook their seats as Huwlen raised a hand and called for quiet.

'Presidents, ambassadors, ladies and gentlemen, may I introduce two good friends and important allies to the Ancients' Order of Planets: the Ambassadors of the Daxxal Galaxy, Edward Virr and Andrew Faux.'

Another round of applause, quickly checked by Huwlen raising his hand again.

'May I also bring to your attention Ambassadors Linda Wisnewski and Philip Theo who are at present manning an advanced Daxxal starship in stationary orbit above us, ensuring our safety.'

After further applause, he continued:

'As many of you are aware, without the help of these brave visitors, the forming of the AOP would not be possible at this time. Their friendship, skills and – let's not deny it – technology have brought about a scenario that, without them, would have been decades away. We all appreciate we're not out of the woods yet. I've recently confirmed that the Sachem Mogul and the majority of the Core Members left Arus'Gan only hours before we arrived. They have adopted a tactical withdrawal, reinforced by a fleet of sixty-three vessels, twenty-nine of which are attack ships. Bearing in mind there are still several hundred vessels out amongst the settled planets, that are, and will, remain to be a considerable threat for some time to come.'

He looked down, the expression on his face changing to a more sombre one.

'We must remember, however, a large majority of the crews on these vessels are completely innocent, under duress and most likely have no knowledge of the AOP. I therefore submit to the chamber an edict of engagement, wherefore all military exchanges with any remaining PCP vessels are conducted, in the first instance, to disable the vessel. Shoot to kill is only authorised as a last resort or if you have an individual Mogul in your sights. Please indicate your determination for this edict on the screen in front of you.'

Both Ed and Andy pressed the green 'for' icons.

Huwlen glanced over at the Government Preceptor, who was waiting for the final few responses to the vote.

He finally stood and announced the result: 'Those in favour – one hundred and seventy-seven. Those against – six; and three abstentions. I therefore asseverate the edict as carried.'

Ed looked around the chamber, wondering who the six were that didn't care about the lives of so many crew.

THREE HOURS LATER, several more edicts had been passed by the initial AOP council meeting, including the setting of a date for the first galaxy-wide presidential elections. Supporting, aiding or hiding a Mogul became an interplanetary crime and they had completely banned the possession of, and use of the term, 'breeder'.

Huwlen had to rush away afterwards as he had to address Arus'Gan's military commanders at a meeting on the Retribution.

Cort, on the other hand, came bounding up to Ed and Andy as they waited in the outer cloister, a grin from ear to ear.

'Did you hear the news?' he said, unable to conceal his excitement. 'I can't believe it's true.'

'Crystal Palace won the premiership?' said Andy,

'The what – who?'

'Ignore him,' said Ed, pushing Andy away. 'He lives in a dream world.'

Cort looked confused for a moment and then continued with his news.

'It's Kisten. She's alive. A signal came through from Kqett a few minutes ago. She was picked up from a remote mountainous area with the captain from the Erebus IV a couple of days ago.'

'Wow,' said Ed. 'They survived the battleship attack.'

'Yes, it seems everyone on the bridge dived into the

two bridge lifeboats as soon as the attack happened. The captain grabbed Kisten and shoved her into his. He watched to make sure the others ejected safely before he did the same. Only, he witnessed the other lifeboat deliberately targeted after it ejected, so he didn't release and stayed with the wreckage until it reached the upper atmosphere of Kqett, then ejected. By that time, the battleship had probably moved on. He didn't turn on the lifeboat's transponder either, just in case. It was only by chance they were found by local police flyers, who'd been checking sparsely populated areas after lumps of Reeme had caused havoc, dropping around the globe.'

'Is she coming here?' asked Andy.

'Yeah, I authorised for them both to get passage on the next commercial vessel coming in this direction.'

'Cool,' said Andy. 'Does this mean we have to drink beer and celebrate?'

'It's compulsory.'

'Oh dear,' said Ed. 'Auntie Linda won't be happy.'

'Auntie Linda won't know,' said Andy.

'What? She won't notice we're both pissed and stink of beer? I beg to differ.'

'Come on, you two,' said Cort, steering them both towards the far doors. 'I know a little place near here that my father used to frequent. They do cracking Gan ale and their Undul pies are legendary.'

'Better than those fucking rat pasties on Reeme, I

hope?' said Andy, shading his eyes as they exited into Arus'Gan's bright sunshine.

The bar was only two blocks away from the main parliament buildings. It was in a basement under one of the city's police hubs. Cort led them down a few steps, opened a plain, unmarked door and ushered them inside.

They noticed it was surprisingly cool inside and the low lighting reminded Ed of a blues bar he used to visit in Cambridge.

'My dad said they keep it colder down here to discourage the Moguls from visiting,' said Cort as they made their way over to the bar.

'Mr Erebus,' said the barman as soon as he saw them. 'A pleasure to see you again and I'm sorry to hear about your father.'

'Thanks. I'm surprised you recognised me. I only came here once with him.'

'Ah, yes,' he said. 'But not many lads throw up over their father's bodyguard after two Erdonion Pinn Fizzs. You're an urban legend.'

'Oh, shit.'

'Awesome,' said Andy, grinning widely. 'I'm glad I'm not the only one present that gets embarrassed in bars.' He nodded in Ed's direction.

'Oh, do tell,' said Cort, glancing at Ed.

'Where do I start?' said Andy

'Let's start with a beer,' said Ed, realising he really didn't want Andy going down that particular rat hole.

The barman stared at Ed for a second. 'Are you the guys from Daxxal?' he asked.

'Guilty as charged,' said Andy.

'Well, that changes things,' said the barman, standing up to his full height, a distinct revision to his demeanour, and heading for the bar hatch.

Ed and Andy both took a step back as he rounded the corner and approached them. Before he could react, Ed was enveloped in a bear hug, before the barman moved on to Andy and Cort.

'You guys are welcome here anytime you wish and the drinks are on the house,' he said. 'You've bloodied the nose of those red fuckers and got them on the back foot. I never thought I'd see that in my lifetime.' He walked back behind the bar. 'My name is Starl and anything you need while you're on Arus'Gan, you just ask.'

Ed noticed Cort looked puzzled.

'Do you have a problem with the way things have turned out?' he asked, giving Cort a questioning look.

'Well, it seems to me they've capitulated way too easily,' said Cort. 'I know there were only six hundred-odd of them, but they ruled over this region of the galaxy for ten millennia, with fanatical support, huge financial backing, the Vanguard division, their own personal security and the black guard. Where the hell has all that suddenly disappeared to?'

'It hasn't,' said Starl. 'You need to be vigilant. They made many of the old families very wealthy, present company excepted.'

'My father hated them, though.'

'That may well be, but they still had considerable sectarian support from the private sector. So, don't expect the present empathetic mood to continue unabated. There's a significant number of all the things you just mentioned waiting in the wings, ready to retaliate and cause dysfunction.'

'How do you know all this?' asked Andy.

Starl gave Andy an exasperated glance. 'I'm a barman underneath the biggest police station in the galaxy, almost next door to the parliament. How do you think I know?'

They all turned to look at Andy.

'Sorry,' he said. 'Just being particularly dense for a moment.'

'It's okay,' said Starl. 'Unless you've done the job, you have no idea how much information a bar owner acquires.'

'We ought to let Huwlen know,' said Ed.

'He already does,' said Huwlen, moving up behind them.

They all jumped and turned as one.

'I thought you were having a military meeting on the Retribution,' said Ed.

'I'm learning to delegate,' he said as he gave Starl a hug. 'How've you been, Star man?'

'Makin' a crust. They may be murdering arseholes but their credit's good,' said Starl, grinning at his friend.

'Your information has proved invaluable.'

'Then accept some more – they're still here.'

'What subterfuge do I have to look forward to?'

'We're not entirely sure, but we know there are factions of Vanguard and the black guard who didn't leave with the fleet.'

'Do you know where they are?'

'They've gone dark. We used to know where most of them lurk, but all the regular offices and safe houses seem to have been abandoned.'

'Facial recognition?'

'Nothing.'

'Hmm, we need to be extra vigilant.' Huwlen signalled to a member of his security detail near the door. When he approached, he spent a moment whispering to him, which was followed by the guard nodding and disappearing outside.

'Is it normally this quiet?' Cort asked Starl, glancing around the bar.

'No, since the truth transmissions began, trade has dropped considerably. They'll come back once the furore has died down. People are just afraid that the parliament and police stations will be targeted by an invading force.'

'There's an awful lot of disinformation being touted,' said Huwlen. 'Classic rear-guard action.'

'Is there anything more we can do?' asked Ed.

'Actually, there is,' said Huwlen. 'That's why I'm here. We've found some survivors from the Vlepon.'

'Really?' said Andy. 'How many are there?'

'And where were they?' said Ed.

'We found nineteen of them being used as forced labour, repairing the space station of the damage they were being blamed for.'

'Only nineteen?' said Ed.

'There may be more,' said Huwlen, putting his hand up in a placatory manner. 'They've told us they were split into two groups. They're not sure where the others were sent, except it had something to do with mines.'

'We'll need a list of all the nearest mining colonies then,' said Andy.

'No, not that kind of mines,' said Huwlen.

'The variety you lay?' questioned Ed.

Huwlen nodded slowly.

'Oh, shit. That could be anywhere,' said Andy.

'No, not necessarily,' said Ed. 'I think I know exactly where they are. Huwlen, can I borrow a couple of destroyers?'

40

THE STARSHIP GABRIEL – EN ROUTE TO HUNUS, ANDROMEDA

EPOCH 122, SPAN 9371, JUNCTURE 091.2

Nineteen very anguished, undernourished men were given makeshift beds in a corner of the Gabriel's starboard hangar.

They were glad to have been rescued and to still be alive. But although recovering from their lack of physical condition would only take a few weeks, it would take much longer, if ever, to recover from losing their wives, girlfriends and colleagues in such a disgustingly brutal fashion.

They were, of course, overjoyed to discover Rayl was alive and well, which eventuated in an awful lot of tears at the reunion.

Ed remembered witnessing the PCP laying mines to cover the exit of the gateway at Hunus. He reckoned the remaining Vlepon crew were being used as human shields to protect the minefield from being demolished and that was where they should go.

Huwlen had insisted on a farewell banquet for the departing heroes. This had to be held on the Retribution so everyone could attend. Cleo, for the first time, was watching over the Gabriel on her own, even though the ship was secured inside the Retribution's largest hangar.

A mountain of food was demolished along with an ocean of local beer and wine, with speeches of gratitude made to the visiting allies, as well as promises of regular visits. A preliminary alliance with the GDA back in Daxxal would also be firmed up and made official once the AOP was in full control.

It was with heavy hearts and hangovers that they all – with the exception of Andy – sat in a circle on their regular couches.

The previous evening, Andy had decided to introduce some of the senior council members to the wonders of the Gabriel's replicator with pizza and margaritas, which went down very well, until one particular president, who acquired an inordinately enthusiastic taste for the tequila-based cocktail, managed to throw up on a neighbouring president's shoes, very nearly causing a serious diplomatic incident.

So, the following morning, no one seemed surprised that Andy had not yet surfaced.

HUWLEN HAD ORGANISED two destroyers to provide escort back to Hunus and the gate. It was early the next morning that the three ships began the trip.

Linda peeked at the empty couch next to her through one squinty eye and said, 'Has anyone checked in on Cactus?'

Andy had been awarded the astronaut nickname after a heroic tequila session the night before his first flight into space.

'I think he's plugged himself into the auto-nurse,' said Ed, his eyes obscured by sunglasses and a very furrowed brow. 'Although, in his defence, I think he's the most sensible one amongst us.'

'I feel okay,' said Phil cheerfully.

'Ah, but did you have any of the Cargenion red wine?'

'No.'

'Well, there's your reason,' said Ed, grimacing from talking too much.

'Drink this,' said Cleo as a glass of a grey-coloured liquid materialised next to Ed and Linda.

'Are you sure?' said Linda, wrinkling her nose. 'It looks like liquidised clay.'

'Doesn't smell too enchanting, either,' said Ed, sniffing it tentatively.

'Just get it down you,' said Cleo. 'If you drink it straight down, you can have a doughnut.'

'With chocolate sprinkles?' asked Linda.

'Oh, for fuck's sake – yes, with chocolate sprinkles.'

Everyone suddenly turned towards the tube lift, their attention caught by the sound of singing. Andy arose out of the floor, standing bolt upright with his hands behind his back and sporting a beard.

'Mornin', crew mates,' he said, glancing from face to face. 'What'ya think?'

'About the singing or the fungus?' asked Linda.

'You look like a twenties porn star,' said Ed. 'How'd you grow that overnight?'

'It's another feature of the auto-nurse. You can do loads of stuff to change your appearance.'

'We used it when we wanted to blend in during certain periods of history,' said Phil. 'I made a particularly dashing Edwardian.'

'You mean, you were down visiting England even at that early stage?' asked Ed.

'Yep, at that time we naturally assumed it would be the British Empire that would eventually venture into space first, then two world wars put paid to that.'

'Couldn't you have helped in some way to lessen the impact of those wars?'

'Believe me, we tried. I'd hate to think what you would have done to yourselves without any of our influence. Didn't you ever wonder why the Nazis suddenly stopped at the English Channel and didn't invade England?'

'Because their resources were running thin after advancing so far so quickly?' said Andy.

'Well, that was the official line, yes,' said Phil. 'We managed to convince Berlin that the Americans wouldn't intervene and it would be easier to build defences along the coast and wait for Britain to collapse.'

'But the Americans did get involved. Was that you too?'

'No, that genuinely was the Japanese. We were as surprised by the Pearl Harbour attack as anyone.'

'Bloody hell,' said Ed. 'I covered all this in history at school. To think that a lot of it was manipulated by little green men in a flying saucer...'

'You're confusing us with the Megala Matia – or large eyes – in their strange gyrizo ships.'

'So, they're real then?' said Andy.

'Yes, but they aren't green. They're small flesh-coloured humanoids with large eyes.'

'This conversation's getting a bit weird,' said Linda.

'Where are they from?' asked Ed, ignoring Linda's comment.

'Nobody knows,' said Phil. 'They're pretty harmless. Their gyrizo ships – or saucers, as you call them – have no weapons or shields and they always jump away when approached. We've caught them abducting humans from Earth before, but they always return them without being prompted, so we and everyone else leave them alone. Silly buggers crashed a gyrizo in the Arizonian desert a hundred years ago. Luckily, it was still sealed and the Americans were unable to open it. We used the Gabriel's tractor beam to drag it back into orbit one night. It was the only time we've taken the Gabriel into the Earth's atmosphere.'

'What did you discover inside?' asked Andy.

'They must have damaged the standard drive but not the jump drive, because as soon as we got it back into space, it vanished.'

'Hence the old Area 51 rumours,' said Linda, rolling her eyes.

'Yeah,' said Andy, smiling and giving Linda a wink. 'They've never been able to admit it being there because then they'd have to admit to losing it.'

'And, of course, the British government never fucked anything up, did they?' said Linda, sticking her tongue out.

'Absolutely not, old chap. A model of dependability and honesty,' said Andy, trying to keep a straight face.

'Linda, can you ask the captain of the destroyer on our port side why his targeting array has just lit us up?' asked Ed.

'The other destroyer's captain has just asked him the same question,' said Linda. 'He's not responded.'

'I'm getting a strange power build up on that ship too,' said Phil. 'It's almost as if his reactor is about to—'

The jump took them all by surprise. They winked back into existence five hundred thousand kilometres away from the explosion.

'Sorry to override the helm,' said Cleo. 'I didn't have time to ask your permission.'

'It seems we owe you our lives,' said Ed as they all watched the ball of fire expanding on the holo map.

'Did the other destroyer escape?' asked Linda.

'I don't believe so,' said Cleo. 'No jumps detected within one hundred light years.'

Ed sat in silence for a few moments, watching the explosion gradually dissipate and thinking of the pointless loss of life triggered by that suicidal act.

'Prepare a drone to return to Arus'Gan,' he said eventually. 'We need to let Huwlen know to be extra vigilant. Include the footage of the incident and tell him he is not to send any replacement ships.'

'Do we continue to Hunus?' asked Linda.

'Yes – full shields and cloaked at all times. We need to find those remaining Vlepon crew and head home. We've been away for far too long.'

41

THE STARSHIP GABRIEL – ON ROUTE TO HUNUS, ANDROMEDA

EPOCH 127, SPAN 9371, JUNCTURE 132.6

Linda had jumped the Gabriel in behind one of the moons of a particularly large gas giant in a system fourteen light years away from the Hunus system.

Now cloaked, the ship was at maximum drive, flashing across the system with the arrays stabbing out in all directions. She'd taken a random route after the suicidal destroyer which meant it had lengthened the trip by a day, but reduced the risk of an ambush.

The surviving Vlepon crew were in reasonable spirits and hadn't been told about the near miss. Some of them had asked for tours of the ship so Linda and Phil had occasional visitors on the bridge, which broke up the boredom.

One of them was on the bridge as the holo map updated and they saw the winking icon of a ship in orbit around a large planet in a nearby system.

'What's that?' he asked Linda, unfamiliar with the Theo technology and icons.

'That's your ship,' she said. 'The Vlepon.'

'Really, are you sure?' he said, staring incredulously at the flashing icon. 'We were under the impression it had been destroyed.'

'It was left by the PCP as a lure for any rescue ships.'

'We must take it back with us. You have a tractor beam that could tow it.'

'If we went near that ship, I'm sure the PCP would be on us within minutes. I was almost killed boarding it last time, saving Rayl and, anyway, it doesn't have a cloak.'

'I'm going to have to announce this to the others,' he said, glowering at Linda and disappeared down on the tube lift.

Linda contacted Ed and warned him that there might be some disquiet regarding the Vlepon being abandoned. He decided to nip the problem in the bud and took the tube lift straight down to the hangar-cum-dormitory.

As soon as he entered, it was obvious the mood amongst the survivors had changed. They were all sitting in a group, listening to a man who was standing, acting as spokesman. He stopped mid-sentence as Ed approached.

'Is it true the Vlepon is still in one piece?' he shouted and they all turned to face him.

'It's still in space, if that's what you mean,' said Ed.

'Then it must be retrieved. There are many months of research in that ship's data core. We cannot express how important it is to safeguard our commissions. Most of us won't get paid without that information.'

Ed stared at the group as if they were deranged and felt an unfamiliar rage building inside him.

'You're lucky to be alive, for fuck's sake,' he said. 'Over half your partners and colleagues have been horribly slaughtered or are presently being used as human shields. Both myself and my crew have risked our lives to save your sorry arses – and you're whining about money.'

He noticed many heads dropping. The spokesman couldn't sit back down quick enough and began inspecting his fingernails.

'I have never heard anything so selfish,' he said, clenching his fists, taking a breath and stopping himself from saying any more. He looked up.

'Cleo, are you there?'

'Yep.'

'Would you be able to remotely download the data cores from the Vlepon?'

'Yep, so long as I'm close enough.'

'How close?'

'A few kilometres.'

'While we're cloaked?'

'Yep.'

'Thank you.'

He glanced back at the seated group again, none of whom were making eye contact.

'Ship tours are hereby cancelled. You will remain here until we hand you over to a GDA vessel. If you require anything, ask Cleo. Good day, gentlemen. I hope you enjoy your money.'

His footsteps echoed as he walked off the now silent hangar deck. He went straight to the bridge and instructed Linda to approach the Vlepon very carefully.

She jumped into the system on the outer fringes, adjacent to a large asteroid field, cloaked and accelerated to .95 light in towards the fifth planet.

The Vlepon had remained in its higher orbit after being tractored there by the PCP, shortly before Linda was captured. The orbit was still decaying but at a much reduced pace. Cleo calculated the ship would remain out of the planet's grasp for another nine hundred and twelve days.

'I don't want to go too close, Cleo,' said Linda. 'How far away can you do the data transfer?'

'Fifty kilometres should be manageable.'

The download, once Linda had positioned the Gabriel close enough, took longer than expected.

'Some of the data appears to be a bit corrupted,' said Linda, looking at the files as they streamed across.

'No, not corrupted – manipulated,' said Cleo. 'There's been a clumsy attempt to bury a virus within the data, which must have been designed to disable the ship's systems. I'm having to strip it out as I go. That's what's leaving the gaps in the coding.'

'Sneaky bastards.'

'Oh no, that's not the half of it,' said Cleo.

'Mornin', campers,' said Andy as he zipped up out of the floor on the tube lift. 'Ah, is that the Vlepon?'

He dropped down onto his couch, closed his eyes and activated his DOVI.

'No, don't do—'

The sudden flash on the holo map nearly blinded Linda and, as she blinked away the effects, she realised the Gabriel was already at full drive away from the Vlepon.

A huge shudder rattled the ship. She struggled to regain her senses and immediately went for the shielding controls. She found them already activated, covering the rear of the ship in a large cone-like designation to deflect the blast wave away from the ship.

'What the fuck just happened?' said a now wide-eyed Andy as the shaking subsided.

'That's what I was about to tell you,' said Cleo.

'They also booby-trapped the ship. Any activation of the vessel's physical systems would cause—'

'What the fuck just happened?' shouted Ed, just as Andy had, as he appeared on the bridge.

'He happened,' said Linda, stabbing a finger at Andy.

'What the fuck just—'

'Don't say it,' said Linda as Phil appeared too. Her finger was still pointing at Andy.

They all looked across at him.

'Oops,' he said.

'I'll give you fucking "oops",' said Ed. 'Cleo, how much of the core data did we get before Mr Hobnail Boots blundered in?'

'Eighty-seven point nine percent.'

'Well, at least we got most of it. But now everyone within a thousand light years knows where we are.'

'Sorry,' said Andy. 'I had no idea.'

'No, your brain must've spent all its energy growing that fuzz out your face,' said Ed. 'Linda, take the Gabriel somewhere quiet and wait a while. See if anyone turns up.'

'Roger that.'

42

THE STARSHIP GABRIEL – APPROACHING HUNUS, ANDROMEDA

EPOCH 128, SPAN 9371, JUNCTURE 101.3

Linda, after catching some sleep, took over command of the ship again.

They'd waited, hidden in the neighbouring system, for the best part of a day, seemingly in vain, for the PCP reaction to the detonation of the Vlepon.

She finally gave up and moved the Gabriel at full drive towards the Hunus system, asking Cleo to wake everyone and request their attendance on the bridge.

Unusually, Andy was first to arrive.

'Did you shit the bed?' she asked, glancing at her watch as he yawned and slid into, rather than sat on, his couch.

'I had an early morning appointment with my barber.'

She looked over again and realised something was missing.

'You shaved the beard off.'

'It was proving a liability and Samantha didn't like it much.'

'You shaved it off because your computer-generated girlfriend didn't like it?'

Andy reclined back and stared blankly at the holo map.

'Sounds a bit weird when you put it that way, doesn't it?'

'Just a bit.'

'Did we all get some rest?' said Ed as he, followed by Phil and Rayl, made an appearance via the tube lift.

'I did,' said Linda. 'But I think someone else was up plucking his face so his girlfriend didn't get a rash.'

Linda noticed Rayl blush and glance at Andy with raised eyebrows.

'I didn't say that,' he said, rubbing his chin and meeting Rayl's gaze. 'A lot of girls like a bearded man. I just found it annoying.'

Linda smiled to herself and, realising she was the only one who had recognised their subtle interaction, deciding to file that one away for future machinations.

'What's the latest?' asked Ed, shaking Linda out of her preoccupation.

'Absolutely bugger all,' she said. 'Not a peep from anywhere within a thousand light years.'

'Have we been scanning out into intergalactic space?' he said.

'Visibility indistinct into intergalactic districts,' said Cleo.

Ed sighed and looked up at the ceiling.

'Cleo, can you put the tongue twister subroutine back in its box please?'

'The sixth sick sheik's sixth sick sheep.'

'Oh, for fuck's sake.'

'How many ducks could a duck duct-tape, if a duck could duct-tape ducks?'

'Cleo.'

'Hello.'

'Have you quite finished?'

'Yeah, I think so.'

'Thank you.'

'You're welcome, Eddie.'

'Cleo.'

'What?'

'It's Ed, not Eddie.'

'Got it.'

Ed glanced up, pausing, waiting to check that Cleo had actually shut up.

'Right,' he said finally. 'Today, we're going to need our mature heads on.' He gave everyone firm eye contact to ensure they understood. 'Our first priority is the missing crew members from the Vlepon. Also, I would like to go back down to the gate control room on Hunus and remove all the destination data units from this side of the gate.'

'Do you think they'll let you?' asked Linda.

'I wasn't planning on giving them a choice. But I was kinda hoping they wouldn't know what I was doing.'

'Well, let's hope they haven't gone back in there and started fiddling with it,' said Andy.

'Even if they have, I've still got the remote switch to take us back to Daxxal.'

'Milky Way,' said Linda, waggling her finger.

'Yeah, sorry, Milky Way,' said Ed, raising his eyebrows. 'I seem to be picking up the local lingo. That in itself shows we've been here too long.'

'I'm not getting any life signs anywhere near the gate minefield,' said Linda, staring at the array screen.

'How many mines are there between the three moons?' asked Ed.

'Just over five hundred.'

'Nothing near, or even inside, any of the mines?'

'No.'

'Nothing on the moons?'

'No.'

'Shit, I would've bet money they'd have brought them here.'

'There's a damaged PCP shuttle on Hunus,' said

Phil, glancing across from his display. 'I don't remember that being there before.'

'Where is it?' asked Ed.

'In a clearing adjacent to the underground colony.'

Phil brought it into close-up on the holo map.

'That's the landing zone they said the PCP uses when they visit the colony,' said Andy.

'It seems to have had a hard landing – the struts seem crushed into the ground,' said Phil. 'Although, I can't work out how it got the damage to the top of the fuselage.'

'Did it roll?' said Andy.

'I don't think so. There'd be damage to at least one side of the vessel and marks on the ground. Oh, and there's two bodies near the wreck.'

'Life signs around it?' asked Ed again.

'None – our scans can't penetrate through this particular rock though, so we've no way of telling how many are inside or where.'

'Linda, take us over there as safely as possible. We need to be closer.'

She jumped the Gabriel as close to the star as she dared on the opposite side to Hunus, re-cloaked and powered around the star, towards the planet with its three artificial moons.

As they approached, all eyes were on the holomap

as a more detailed image of the crash site became apparent.

'Doesn't really give us much more, does it?' said Andy.

'Still just the two bodies next to the wreck,' said Phil.

'Okay?' said Ed. 'Can you make out who they might be?'

'In a few minutes when we're in orbit above I might be able to.'

Linda had the Gabriel's Alma drive at the stops so, nineteen minutes later, she inserted the ship into a stationary orbit above the crashed shuttle and gate colony on Hunus.

Everyone turned to stare at Phil who was busy touching icons on his display and grimacing at the results.

'Well?' said Ed, getting fed up with the wait.

'Not good,' he said. 'The bodies are, without a doubt, crew from the Vlepon.'

'Oh no,' said Rayl, her face dropping.

'Well, that's pants, that is,' said Andy, saying exactly what Ed was thinking.

'I need to get down there,' said Ed.

'That's probably what they're hoping,' said Linda.

'Who though?' said Ed. 'There are no PCP ships anywhere near here and whether there are or not is immaterial. We can't just abandon these people until we know one way or the other and, to do that, someone has to go down there.'

'Why does it have to be you? Can't we just send down a drone?'

'That would work until we need to go inside the colony, but our—'

'Array can't penetrate that rock strata, yes I know that,' said Linda. 'But at least we could recce the area from here first.'

'All right, we'll do that. Phil, can you organise one of our GDA drones?'

'Sure.'

'Ed,' said Cleo.

'Yes?'

'Would you like me to programme a nano cloud to infiltrate the colony?'

'What, like Gabriel did for Andy on Paradeisos that time?'

'Worked a treat,' said Andy, nodding.

'Shit, should've thought of that.'

'That's what I'm here for, boys and girls,' said Cleo cheerfully.

'You are in a strange mood today,' said Ed.

'Upbeat and proficient,' said Cleo, 'with a sprinkling of auspiciousness.'

'She's been eating alphabet soup again,' said Andy, shaking his head.

Ten minutes later, the drone flashed away from the Gabriel, its heat shield quickly beginning to glow as it dropped into the planet's upper atmosphere.

There was complete silence on the bridge. They all watched as Phil expertly piloted the drone towards the northern hemisphere. He inverted the machine, ejected the spent heat shield and extended the various scanning array appendages.

Initially, he took the machine in a loop over the colony at five hundred metres, scanning studiously. Finding nothing new and seemingly attracting no attention, he descended and released the nano cloud twenty metres above the colony entrance.

The invisible cloud provided a three-dimensional image of the inside of the colony. Phil projected it beside the holo map in the centre of the bridge.

As they watched, images of the colony's corridors and chambers came and went with absolutely no sign of life.

'It's like the Mary Celeste,' said Ed. 'Everything is just as it was when we were here a few weeks ago.'

'Only, no people,' said Andy.

Ed glanced at Andy, wondering if he was joking and then shook his head when he realised he wasn't.

'How many lived here?' asked Rayl.

'If I remember rightly, it was about five hundred,' said Andy.

'Then where are they?' she said.

The silence on the bridge returned as they watched the feedback from the nanos delving deeper into the outpost, finally reaching the back door that Ed and the soldiers had originally entered through.

'Well, that's about it,' said Phil, looking around at everyone. 'We've covered the entire complex now.'

'Time I went down there then,' said Ed.

'Ah, shit,' said Linda. 'Do you really think you have to?'

'I'll come with you,' said Rayl before Ed could answer.

'No, you bloody won't,' said Andy. 'If anyone's going with him, it'll be me.'

'Tell you what,' said Phil. 'To stop all the arguing, I'll go with Ed. It's about time I had a change of scenery.'

'Okay,' said Linda. 'That works a little better. Rayl, you go and look after our guests in the hangar and, Andy, you can man the arrays and weapons while I pilot.'

'Sounds like a plan,' said Ed. 'Let's do it.'

43

THE CARTELLA – HUNUS GATE COLONY, ANDROMEDA

EPOCH 128, SPAN 9371, JUNCTURE 177.1

Phil was piloting the Cartella for a change. He programmed it with the same route as the drone and brought the small ship to a complete stop, hovering five hundred metres above the colony.

Another full scan of the area proved fruitless and he descended and landed, still cloaked, near the crashed PCP shuttle.

Ed grabbed a laser rifle and offered one to Phil.

Phil looked at the weapon and shook his head.

'You know I can't use that.'

'Well, at least take an Exo stun gun for some protection.'

'Okay, and you have one of these.' Phil held out a small black box with a red stripe on one side.

'What is it?'

'It's like that individual force field unit you and

Andy had on Krix'ir. Cleo improved it so they activate automatically if you're targeted by any nearby handheld weapons and they're magnetic so you can stick it to the side of your weapon.'

'Oh, cool. That's a much better design,' said Ed as he clicked it onto the underside of the rifle.

'She's working on one that's a permanent dermal implant.'

'Now that really would be something.'

'Lastly,' said Phil, 'bung one of these in your backpack.'

He handed Ed what looked like a small cylindrical grenade.

'What does this do?'

'It provides a bit of back-up when the proverbial hits the fan. Andy used one while rescuing you on Paradeisos. Just open the safety cover, depress the plunger and toss it towards whoever you don't want to play with anymore. It'll keep them busy for a while.'

'Anything else?'

'No, we can go now.'

Ed grabbed a storage bag with 'NASA' printed on the side from one of the galley lockers. Phil looked at it with a quizzical expression.

'It's to put all the data units in,' said Ed. 'There's over five hundred of them.'

'Ah, okay. You're not planning on robbing the colony then?' said Phil with a smirk.

'Well, technically we probably are.'

Phil did a quick, last scan to ensure there wasn't anyone lurking outside and gave a thumbs-up. Ed opened the inner airlock and they stepped inside.

'Cleo, can you take the Cartella up to five hundred metres and wait? Give us a shout if anything moves and I do mean anything.'

'Righty-ho, Mr Ed.'

Phil rolled his eyes.

'Just Ed is fine,' said Ed. 'I'm not a horse.'

With the inner door sliding closed, he opened the outer door.

They stood at the foot of the steps for a moment, shivering and waiting for something to happen. It was early morning on this side of the planet and there was a nip to the air, but Ed knew if you remained in the sunlight it wouldn't be as chilly.

'Didn't think to bring a coat,' he said, pleased that no gunfire was forthcoming from within the tree line that surrounded them.

'We could get Cleo to manufacture some.'

'Don't worry, we're not going to be here long enough.'

They walked across the clearing, scanning the tree line for movement, slowing as they passed the crashed

PCP shuttle and peering cautiously at the two bodies nearby.

'Laser weapons,' said Phil, pointing to the wounds. 'And that shuttle is the type normally found servicing a PCP cruiser.'

'Well, that rules out being killed in the crash then,' said Ed, giving the inside of the shuttle a quick look.

'This was no crash, either,' said Phil. 'The undercarriage is intact and in holes that were dug beforehand. This has clearly been staged.' He turned and nervously watched the tree line again.

'Cleo, is there anything around here that wasn't here last time?' asked Ed.

'Apart from the shuttle and bodies, no.'

'Then, why go to the trouble of setting up this charade and not staying to initiate the ambush?'

'Perhaps they were attacked themselves?' said Cleo.

'By who? And with what?' said Ed. 'The locals didn't have any weaponry capable of overcoming armed PCP military and they certainly didn't have anything able to see off a warship that this shuttle came from.'

'I don't like this, Ed. I vote we abort,' said Phil, giving Ed a worried glance.

'I don't like this, either. But we can't leave that gate control room fully operational. There are over five hundred destinations programmed into it. They could all be galaxies. I really wouldn't want the Moguls to get their hands on that. They could disappear off to hell knows where and then return at any time with a rebuilt fleet.'

Phil turned and stared back into the trees for a moment before speaking.

'You're right, of course. We need to contain them to this galaxy or we could all be doomed.'

'I know it's a risk, Phil, but we're the only ones here and it needs doing right now before we go back.'

'Come on then,' said Phil, striding off towards the colony. 'Let's get this done.'

'Good man,' said Ed, running to catch up. 'And when we get back, we'll have pepperoni pizza and a nice bottle of Sancerre.'

ONE HUNDRED KILOMETRES ABOVE, Linda watched as Ed and Phil left the clearing and strode towards the steep path, which led up to the control room and the entrance to the colony.

Andy was sitting opposite her. He had the Asteri Beam activated, set on its narrowest setting, and was also watching the situation with avid concentration.

'I have some strange readings from a planet in a nearby system,' said Cleo.

'"Strange" isn't very specific, Cleo,' said Linda. 'Can you be a bit more defined?'

'Well, there's an exceptionally large gas giant in the Flaxx system, seventeen light years away. It seems to have something large moving around in its upper atmosphere that I haven't detected before.'

'Could it be a ship?'

'Too large.'

'Could it be a fleet of ships?'

'Hard to tell. The interference on all wavelengths inside the atmosphere of some of the gas giants is absolute. A fleet of ships would be under enormous risk of collision unless they had some way of detecting each other's whereabouts.'

'Keep an eye on—'

Linda didn't have time to finish the sentence as three PCP attack ships emerged only a few hundred kilometres away from them; then four … six … nine… They just kept coming.

'Oh, fuck,' shouted Andy, quickly activating all the Gabriel's weapon systems.

'Don't fire, Andy,' called Linda. 'They don't know where we are.'

'But they know we're here somewhere and directly above the colony is the most obvious place.'

'Ed, Phil, get out of there,' she called, a tone of desperation in her voice.

She got no reply.

'The PCP ships are producing some kind of jamming signal,' said Cleo. 'I can't penetrate it.'

'What about the Cartella? Can't you send that down to them?'

'No, the signal to that is severed too.'

'Shit.'

'What happens to the Cartella when the controlling contact is lost?' asked Andy.

'It will stay where it is.'

'Will it remain cloaked?'

'Yes, for as long as it has the energy to remain where it is, it will.'

'And how long is that?'

'It's expending a lot of energy to remain in its present location.'

'How long, Cleo?' said Andy, sounding exasperated.

'About seven hours.'

'Good, we've got a bit of time then.'

'We need to move away,' said Linda. 'We're much less likely to be detected if we're not where they think we are.'

They both glanced back at the holo map as more and more PCP attack ships and cruisers emerged into the Hunus system.

'I'll take a shuttle down to get them,' said Andy.

'No, you bloody won't. You're staying right here.

They'll have to look after themselves for a while until we can sort out this shitstorm up here.'

Linda quietly extricated the Gabriel from orbit and threaded her way through the proliferating enemy fleet. Once they were clear, she put the ship into an ever-changing holding pattern and they both watched as the number of emerging battleships slowly reduced until it stopped.

'Ninety-seven,' said Andy. 'We might have stood a chance against seven – but ninety-seven? Not a fucking hope.'

'We need some suggestions. Cleo?' said Linda.

'Working on it.'

The gateway opened suddenly. Something small appeared, travelling fast, but was immediately targeted by a beam weapon from one of the mines, causing it to disintegrate in a fireball.

'What was it that came through?' asked Linda.

'Don't know,' said Andy, peering at the array screen. 'The jamming is affecting all our systems and I didn't know those mines were multi-platforms, either. We're going to need to do something about those at some point.'

ED AND PHIL, completely oblivious to what was

occurring above, continued to make their way up the steep path towards the colony entrance.

'I really should use the gym more on the Gabriel,' huffed Ed after a couple of minutes, stopping to suck in some oxygen, leaning forward and putting his hands on his knees.

'Just use the auto-nurse,' said Phil, apparently not out of breath at all.

'The auto-nurse?' said Ed. 'How does that work?'

'Dial in the level of fitness you require and, five minutes, later you're an Olympic athlete.'

'I know you've been able to rejuvenate yourself for several millennia, but what about us? Are we able to use it and live indefinitely too?'

'Yeah, as whatever and whoever you want to be.'

'Are you saying I could use it to live forever?'

'Yep. Level of fitness, body shape, anything you want.'

Their eyes met and Ed raised his eyebrows.

'Yep, even that. As big as you like.'

'I could be a legend,' said Ed, smirking, as he continued up the path. 'Best not tell Andy about that feature.'

'He knows.'

As they reached the top of the climb, Ed noticed the door to the colony was still open and swaying gently in the breeze, causing it to bump against the inner wall every so often. Stopping to catch his breath, he looked out over the treetops and down to the clearing. He could clearly see the shuttle sitting nose-down on its belly, but he quickly realised something was wrong.

'Phil,' he said, continuing to stare down at the shuttle. 'Where are the bodies?'

Phil followed his gaze down the hill and turned back, looking puzzled.

'They were only a few feet from the airlock,' he said.

'Cleo, have you detected any movement around the PCP shuttle since we left a few minutes ago?'

He received no answer.

'Cleo, are you there?' he said, checking the icons in his peripheral vision to make sure he was transmitting.

Again, no answer. They both peered up at the sky.

'Something's happened,' said Ed.

'Is the Cartella still there?' asked Phil. 'Can you get it down here with your DOVI?'

Ed closed his eyes and concentrated on finding the Cartella. His brow furrowed with the effort.

'I can't detect a thing. It's just a load of foggy, white noise.'

He turned his attention to something more local. The door lock clicked twice.

'I have control over electronics nearby, but it seems anything more than a few metres away is hidden in fog.'

Phil glanced back down the hill.

'I have a bad feeling about this,' he said. 'Those bodies didn't get up and walk away by themselves. They had holes in them.'

'We need to find some food, water and somewhere to hide for a while,' said Ed as he made his way over to the colony doorway and tentatively peeked inside.

They slowly crept through the old airlock door, down the corridor and began searching each room. Without Cleo, they were unable to communicate with the nano cloud. The place seemed deserted.

'How can a colony of this many people just vanish?' said Phil as they collected a few supplies.

'It's the Mary Celeste again,' said Ed.

'You mentioned her before. Who is she?'

'She was a perfectly seaworthy, abandoned ship found in the Atlantic in the late 1800s. Just the crew and one lifeboat were missing.'

'Was it solved?'

'No, to this day, no one knows why the ship was deserted.'

'The crew and lifeboat were not found?'

'No.'

Ed found the main dining room he'd been in before. The last embers of a fire were still hot in the grate and plates of uneaten food were still on some of the tables.

They collected some water bottles from a pantry and

a few pies – or at least what looked like pies – from some sort of food chiller.

'Where do you want to wait?' said Phil.

'The gate control room,' said Ed. 'We can keep an eye out with the camera screens and it's near the path down to the landing zone.'

They hurried back through to the entrance. Ed checked there was no one lurking outside and walked over to the railing to ensure nothing had changed in the clearing.

'Where's the control room then?' asked Phil, glancing around the raised patio.

'Here,' said Ed as he walked over to the recess in the rock face and reached up to the small hidden hole at the top.

The door slid open and they both climbed the stairs into the hidden chamber, the door closing silently behind them. Ed touched an icon on the main control panel and the room lit up. Everything whirred to life, including the screens, which showed views from around the complex.

'Ah,' said Phil. 'That's quite a comprehensive view.'

Ed knelt down and opened the fascia under the main panel. Retrieving the NASA bag from his belt, he began removing the five hundred and seventeen destination data units.

'What's in there?' said Phil, pointing to the door at the far side of the room.

Ed looked over his shoulder to see where Phil was pointing.

'It's like a small crew rest room,' he said. 'A couple of beds, table and chairs – that sort of thing.'

Ed heard him walk over and open the door. There was a low thud, a scraping noise and a squeaking of his boots on the shiny floor.

'What have you found?' said Ed, not bothering to turn around.

'Me,' said a deep guttural voice.

Ed jumped up and banged his head on the underside of the control panel. Slowly turning his head, he was faced with a seven-foot monster of a man with unusually reddish skin and what looked like stunted horns on his forehead.

'Sorry to disturb your little act of sabotage, Mr Virr,' he boomed. 'But we've been waiting for you.'

44

THE STARSHIP GABRIEL – HUNUS SYSTEM, ANDROMEDA

EPOCH 128, SPAN 9371, JUNCTURE 191.9

Linda was getting annoyed with Andy. All he'd done for the last couple of hours was whinge and swear a lot.

Rayl had joined them on the bridge. She was on her couch with a face like a wet weekend, staring at the roaming shapes of PCP ships on the holo map.

'For fuck's sake,' said Andy after a short but rare moment of silence. 'Can't we just engage the Palto and fly around randomly for a bit? We'd be bound to get a few of 'em.'

'That'd be a great idea,' said Linda. 'Have you ever stuck a stick into a wasps' nest? That always calms things down, doesn't it?'

'Well, it'd make me feel better.'

'Until you got stung,' said Rayl. 'I'm the only one here with first-hand experience of what these monsters can do if they got hold of us.'

Andy sat back on his couch, grinding his teeth and stared at nothing in particular.

'Give Cleo some time to work on the jamming problem,' said Linda.

'Has she got anywhere with it?' said Andy.

'I have,' said Cleo. 'The jamming signal is emanating from just one ship.'

One of the indistinct lumps started flashing red on the holo map.

'This leads me to believe it's something new. They haven't perfected it yet and, judging by the way their fleet is positioned and the amount of shuttle traffic between them, I think it affects them too.'

'So, you're saying their arrays are also like an English foggy morning?' said Andy, perking up from his fractious funk.

'Yes, they're communicating with messages in shuttles.'

'So if we disabled just that one ship, we could contact Ed and Phil again?'

'Yes, but remember, the PCP gets their shit back too.'

'Cleo,' said Linda, 'since when did you start swearing?'

'Significant combat intonation.'

'What is it you Brits say?' Linda asked, looking at across at Andy. 'That's a right load of bollocks, that is.'

Andy smirked and nodded.

'That's better,' said Rayl. 'I like you better when you smile.'

'I like you better when you're nake—'

'Andrew,' shouted Rayl, interrupting, her face going crimson. She glanced nervously at Linda.

'It's okay, you two. I'm quite au fait with your little secret. Just make sure you don't fall out while you're on the ship and tell Ed and Phil when they get back. It's a small ship and secrets are against the rules.'

'You can't pull the wool over Auntie Linda's eyes,' said Andy, smiling at Rayl.

'Apparently not,' said Rayl. 'Thanks, Linda.'

'You're welcome.'

Andy looked back at the holomap and thought for a moment.

'Cleo, do you know where on that ship the jamming equipment is?'

The image of the PCP cruiser in question increased in size until it was a couple of metres long and resembled a long fuzzy cigar. An area within what was probably the engineering department flashed red.

'Hmm,' said Andy.

'What are you thinking?' asked Linda.

'I have a cunning plan,' said Andy, interlacing his fingers and cracking his knuckles.

LATER, after a visit to the hangar which contained the GDA drones, Andy returned to the bridge and retook his seat.

'Are we game on?' said Linda.

'Yeah, I believe we are,' said Andy. 'So long as they don't notice the first jump and that cruiser doesn't move, we're good.'

'Their arrays are at least as foggy as ours, so I doubt they can see shit or dare move without bumping into each other,' said Linda.

He activated one of the drones in the hangar, cloaked it and sent it out towards the system's sun. They had to wait over an hour for it to get there and swing around the back of the star before jumping.

'Any time now,' he said, crossing his fingers and holding his breath, realising that Linda and Rayl appeared to be doing the same thing. The PCP fleet didn't react in any way – no movement, nothing.

'They didn't see it jump,' said Rayl.

'Well, let's hope they have enough data to work out where it jumps from in a few minutes,' said Linda.

'They'd better,' said Andy. 'I've programmed the jump to be about as noisy as Led Zeppelin.'

'What's a Led Zeppelin?' said Rayl.

'Ah, now that's going to have to be a lesson for another day.'

'Take ear plugs,' said Linda.

The drone suddenly jumped back into the system inside the defensive shields of the cruiser, initiating the jamming signal.

The cruiser's nearest laser turret quickly swung around to engage the infiltrator, firing as soon as it had a lock. The drone's destruction was immediate, owing to its close proximity to the ship, but it was still too slow. It had already unleashed its programmed salvo of missiles at the rear section of the huge ship.

Andy had set a slight delay into the main warhead of the weapons, allowing them to penetrate through several bulkheads before detonating. The effect was calamitous.

At first, all the rear airlocks blew out, which caused the ship to twist and slew sideways; secondary explosions blew out huge sections of the superstructure until a third massive detonation blew the whole back off the ship. This launched the two halves of the cruiser off in opposite directions, spinning, twisting and throwing out an ever-expanding debris field.

In the ensuing chaos, three other ships were seriously damaged: one attack ship whose pilot must have been asleep was hit by the remains of the tail section and two other cruisers collided in their attempts to avoid the front section.

'Would you look at that? These idiots can't fucking drive, can they?' said Andy, watching the pandemonium on the holomap.

Rayl giggled and looked at Linda.

'I don't believe they've had any serious opposition for quite a while,' said Linda. 'If the shit hits the fan, they all run around like headless chickens.'

The array screens and holomap lost their fogginess and cleared again.

'Ed, Phil, do you copy?' said Linda.

They waited, but no reply came.

'They must be in the colony,' said Andy.

'Or the control room,' said Linda. 'We've got movement in the fleet, though.'

Ships began disappearing from the holomap.

'They're taking the bait,' said Andy. 'They think we're in the system I jumped the drone back from.'

Linda moved the Gabriel in towards the planet again and Cleo was able to regain control of the Cartella.

'What do you want me to do with it?' she asked.

'How much longer can it wait there?' said Andy.

'Another five hours.'

'Keep it there for now.'

As they got closer, images from the colony entrance and landing site came into view.

'The bodies have gone,' said Linda.

'Cleo, would the Cartella have kept a video log while it was waiting?' asked Andy.

'Yep, here you go.'

They watched a speeded-up version of Ed and Phil exiting the ship. The Cartella ascended to five hundred metres and then they could see the pair walking slowly up the path to the colony entrance.

'This is where we watched up to earlier,' said Rayl.

They all laughed, watching Ed huffing and puffing his way up the steep incline.

'Stop,' said Linda. 'There,' she said, pointing.

Four hooded figures swept out from the tree line, checked their surroundings, picked up the bodies and, as quickly as they appeared, they disappeared. Cleo changed the feed to infrared, but, almost as soon as the heat signatures became visible, moving through the trees, they vanished.

'Did we lose the feed?' asked Rayl.

'No,' said Cleo. 'They became shielded by something, probably more of that rock.'

'Were they PCP?' said Linda.

'It wasn't a uniform I've recorded seeing before,' said Cleo.

'That doesn't mean they weren't, though,' said Andy.

Linda looked back at the holo map. It was obvious that at least half the fleet had been enticed off on the red herring into the neighbouring system. The ships that remained had moved to encircle the planet at a set distance and started firing random laser bolts, both in towards the planet and outwards into empty space.

'What are they doing that for?' said Rayl. 'They can't hurt us with the shields up.'

'No,' said Andy. 'But if one of those bolts as much as grazes us, it'll cause our shields to flare.'

'We need to get out of here fast,' said Linda as she looked back at the image of Hunus below. 'They're going to have to manage without us for a little longer,' she said.

After giving Ed and Phil another hail with no response, she lay on her couch, wondering in which direction they should make their escape.

'I have an idea,' said Cleo.

'It'll be better than mine,' said Linda as she handed control of the starship over to her.

The ship powered out towards one of the PCP fleet.

'Whoa,' said Andy. 'Towards them?' he asked, raising his eyebrows.

'I think I know what she's doing,' said Rayl. 'There's no fire coming from underneath the big attack ships.'

'Correct,' said Cleo. 'They're like an aircraft carrier from Earth. They consist mostly of hangars, which are full of smaller ships for invasions and have very few armaments of their own.'

'And none on the underside,' said Linda, nodding while watching the Gabriel zip underneath one of them and stop dead.

'I've put us at five hundred metres,' said Cleo, 'just outside their shields and slaved into their helm so if they move we move with them.'

'That's pretty cool,' said Andy. 'Won't they detect that?'

'Hopefully not, but if it seems otherwise then you two can make use of your DOVIs and mess with their ship.'

'And their heads,' said Linda.

45

HUNUS GATE COLON – HUNUS, ANDROMEDA

EPOCH 128, SPAN 9371, JUNCTURE 192.5

Ed froze as ten armed PCP black guards joined the Mogul in the control room. He could see the soles of Phil's boots behind them in the rest room and hoped to hell he was unconscious and not anything worse. His eyes moved to his laser rifle he'd placed on the floor beside him.

'I wouldn't advise any movement towards that,' said the Mogul, noticing his glance. Several clicks and beeps sounded as weapons were activated, reinforcing the warning. One of the guards stepped forward and picked up his rifle.

'Who are you?' asked Ed, staying very still and keeping his hands in full view.

'How rude of me not to introduce myself,' said the Mogul. 'My name is Byelz Buyb and I'm the Commander of the PCP navy.'

'What's left of it,' said Ed, the recognition of his name sending chills down his back.

The Mogul's eyes widened in shock at being spoken to in such a disrespectful manner and the nearest guard kicked Ed's legs out from under him as he attempted to stand, sending him crashing back down.

'Your lack of reverence is disturbing, Mr Virr.'

'Well, that's a fine way to treat a fellow commander,' said Ed, pulling himself back into a seated position again.

'Oh no, little man. You're not a commander, you're not even a captain. You see, I've done a little research on the sad little Daxxal planet called Gaia. It seems one of my ancestors visited a few thousand years ago and reported finding the breeders most unresponsive. An insignificant backward race, still in the Stone Age. So, you see, Mr Virr, you're of little consequence to me. That Theo starship, however –' he pointed at the ceiling '– and all its galaxy-conquering technology is to be mine – and you're going to help me.'

'How did you know my name?' Ed asked.

A man, who'd remained hidden in the rest room, emerged smiling.

'I told him,' said Trkors.

'Trkors!' exclaimed Ed, momentarily taken aback. 'So, you were a traitor to your colony all along?'

'No, Edward. I've been a servant to my gods all

along,' he said, bowing to the Mogul, keeping his eyes averted.

'I think you're a little confused, Trkors,' said Ed. 'Your gods were wiped out by—'

The kick in the chest from Trkors caught him unawares and sent him backwards into the cabinet. The back of his head collided with the edge of the control panel, rendering him unconscious.

ANDY WAS POKING around the attack ship's systems with his DOVI, not looking for anything in particular – just being nosy to stave off the boredom of inactivity.

They were so close to the enemy ship, the holomap image only displayed a single vessel. Though the Gabriel was nearly five hundred metres in length, it was dwarfed by the leviathan above them.

Linda had made the observation lounge at the highest point of the ship, out of bounds for their guests from the Vlepon. The view was completely obscured by the ugly PCP vessel and she thought it would prove too traumatic for some of the survivors.

'Shit, they're here,' said Andy, suddenly disturbing the silence on the bridge, which caused both Linda and Rayl to jump.

'Who's where?' asked Linda, her heart rate racing.

'The remainder of the Vlepon crew.'

'What? On that ship?' she said, pointing up.

'Yep, in a detention cell on the forty-first level.'

'We have to get them away from there,' said Rayl.

Linda glanced over at Andy.

'They'll kill them,' Rayl reiterated, sitting up straight and glaring at them both.

'Cleo, do you have any idea how to get the surviving Vlepon crew off that ship?' asked Linda.

'Not without someone going aboard, no,' she replied.

'Shit,' said Andy. 'I knew you'd say that.'

'We've got movement at the colony,' said Rayl.

'Oh, no.'

'What d'you mean, "oh, no"?' said Linda.

'I think someone's being tied up like my father was.'

The holomap image changed to a distant view of the colony.

'Can't we get a closer image?' asked Andy.

'Too far away,' said Rayl. 'We need to be in orbit.'

'Get the camera image from the Cartella,' said Linda.

'Bollocks, I didn't think of that,' said Rayl.

Linda gave her a sideways glance.

'Where'd you learn that word?' she asked, moving her eyes over to Andy, the grin on his face disappearing and suddenly becoming very busy on his control panel.

The image zoomed in to show four figures near the colony entrance.

'That's Phil,' Andy gasped, watching three PCP guards tying his hands over his head and attaching them to the colony rock face.

'Oh, shit,' said Linda. 'Where's Ed?'

'Cleo, take the Cartella down to two hundred metres out from that ledge and arm the cannons,' shouted Andy.

'I can't fire at anyone,' she said.

'No, but you can scare the living shit out of them.'

ED HEARD a familiar voice calling his name. He was having trouble focusing on it as someone seemed to have used a nail gun on the back of his skull and his hands were stuck together for some reason.

He squinted as sudden daylight woke him from the semi-conscious clutter of his mind.

'Ed, for fuck's sake, wake up,' called Phil.

He realised now: he was being dragged out onto the raised deck at the entrance to the colony. His hands were tied with some sort of lockable cuffs and Phil was already there, with his hands similarly cuffed and attached to the rock wall high above his head.

'Hang out here often?' he asked as his three guards

raised his hands to attach him to a second metal ring alongside Phil.

Phil gazed across at him, his eyes wide with horror. 'How can you joke at a time like this? You do realise he's going to kill us?'

'Not quite yet, he's not. He wants the Gabriel and that's going to be his downfall.'

'You know about the self-destruct programming then?'

'Cleo has a self-destruct programme?' he asked, giving Phil a surprised look.

'Ed, can you hear me?' called Linda.

'I can.'

'Stand by – we're going to give them a wake up with the Cartella's cannons.'

'No, don't. We've got it all in hand. You show the Cartella's here, there'll be a hundred gunships down here in minutes and they'd soon find it.'

'You've got it all in hand, eh? Well, forgive me for being sceptical, but aren't you chained to a wall?'

The Mogul strode out the control room door and approached Ed. He looked up at the sky and smiled. He leant against the wall, placing himself in between Phil and Ed.

'Had a little chat with your friends, have you?' he asked, continuing to gaze upward. 'Pretty little ship, I'm told. Got a nice powerful beam weapon too, I'll bet. Shame they can't use it without hitting you too.'

The other four guards exited the control room, one carrying the NASA bag, which was now seemingly full. The Mogul sent him and a colleague down to prepare the shuttle.

'Thought I might take those and make copies,' said the Mogul. 'Just in case some other dumb traitor decides to steal them.'

'Leave now and you will remain alive,' said Ed, noticing Phil adopt an expression of astonishment. 'Well, until Huwlen Senn and the AOP fleet catch up to you.'

'Huwlen Senn,' laughed the Mogul. 'The other half of the fleet, under the command of the Sachem Mogul, have the fate of that sad little man and his ragtag fleet well in hand.'

'The offer still stands,' said Ed.

The Mogul elbowed Phil in the stomach, hard. Caught completely off guard, Phil shrieked and hung there crying in agony. Ed shut his eyes and gritted his teeth.

'Your starship will immediately uncloak and surrender to the nearest PCP vessel,' the Mogul continued.

He waited a few moments and, on hearing nothing from his ships above, pointed at one of the guards.

'Give me your weapon,' he said, snatching the laser rifle from the guard's outstretched hand. He removed the safety and pointed it at one of Phil's legs, looked at Ed, smiled and pulled the trigger.

Click. Nothing happened.

He smashed the rifle butt into the guard's head, crushing his skull. The guard crashed backwards, landing at the feet of one of his colleagues, and the Mogul threw the rifle on top of him.

'Have one of you idiots got one that works?' he bellowed.

Snatching another rifle off the next, very nervous, guard in line, he removed the safety, pointed it at Phil again and pulled the trigger.

Click. Again, nothing.

'One of your technology tricks, is it?' he growled, glaring at Ed. 'Try deactivating this,' he said and dropped the rifle. He pulled a gleaming eighteen-inch serrated blade from a scabbard across his back, which had been previously hidden by his tunic.

Phil's eyes opened wide as he saw the blade glinting in the sunlight. He turned his head to look at Ed. 'Help me,' he whispered, his face as white as a sheet.

The Mogul roared with laughter and stepped back in front of Phil.

'Bye bye, insignificant Theo child,' he said, raising the blade.

Three things happened in the next second: the powered locks on the cuffs clicked open, Phil dropped to the ground like a stone and Ed pushed himself off the wall and threw himself at the Mogul with every ounce of energy he could muster.

The blade sparked as it skimmed the stone wall where Phil had been. The Mogul staggered back from Ed's collision, snarling. But he soon recovered. He was seven foot tall and built like an ox. Ed wasn't.

The guards instantly moved forward to defend their charge, but the Mogul waved them back.

'No, he's mine,' he roared, turning his attention back to Ed. 'At least you've got a bit of fire in your belly, little Gaia human.'

Ed saw the blade coming up at him. He jumped back and tripped, landing on his back. Looking up, he noticed a sudden glint in the Mogul's eye, but something wasn't quite right. The sword dropped out of the Mogul's hand and clattered onto the deck.

Ed realised the glint wasn't in his eye. There was something metallic protruding out of it. It looked like an arrow head.

A look of shock replaced the snarl as the Mogul fell to his knees, then he tipped back, snapping the arrow shaft that had penetrated the back of his neck and he went still.

Ed stayed down as more arrows thudded into the

group of guards. Five went down screaming, leaving Trkors and the last two guards. They turned and sprinted through the control room door, shutting it behind them.

A group of hooded figures appeared over the parapet of the deck, warily encroaching on the scene. They quickly put two of the still-moving guards out of their misery.

'Are you injured, Ed?' a girl's voice asked at the same time as firing a second arrow through the heart of the Mogul.

'Not really,' he said. 'I think Phil's a bit shaken up, though.'

'We need to get you away from here. Follow us,' she said.

'Wait,' said Ed. 'Who are you?'

She slowly pulled back her hood.

'It's you!' exclaimed Ed. 'You're the girl we chased back into the colony and you were then presented to me by your father. What's your name?'

'Yes. My name is Fallow. I really think we should be getting back underground. We can be detected from orbit out here.'

'What happened to everyone else?'

'They took them away two days ago,' she said, pointing up.

'Then how did you escape?'

'It's standard procedure to hide us in the labyrinth when a ship is detected in orbit.'

'Why didn't Trkors let them know about you hiding in there?'

'Trkors was an outworlder and a newcomer. He wasn't trusted or told half of what goes on here.'

'Okay. We'd better get out of here.'

'Before you go, Ed,' said Cleo, 'can you lay the Mogul out straight so I can get the Cartella to scan him, then drag the bodies into the colony so they can't be detected?'

'What about the three that disappeared in there?' said Phil, pointing to the control room doorway. 'One of them was Trkors and he knows about the children now. They'll contact a PCP ship if they come out.'

Ed pulled his backpack out from under a dead guard and rummaged inside.

'Let's give them something to keep them occupied,' he said, pulling out the cylindrical grenade.

'I'll get the door,' said Phil as he reached up and found the handle in the recess.

Nothing moved.

'They've locked themselves in.'

Ed nodded and picked up his laser rifle.

'Stand aside, good sir, and I'll use the master key.'

He activated his weapon and blasted the lock into its component atoms and slid the door open.

His personal shield powered up in a millisecond as Ed was blown back across the deck. Trkors, who'd been sitting on the stairs with an activated weapon, swung it around towards Phil.

Phil saw it coming and dived through the open colony door as a section of the alloy frame vaporised.

Two arrows struck Trkors only a split second apart, the first of which lodged in his shoulder and twisted him to the right, which caused his final laser shot to go high. The second arrow hit him in the throat. He dropped the weapon and grabbed the arrow shaft. The look of shock was frozen on his face as he fell forward, headfirst out onto the deck, wriggling for a moment before going still.

'Are you okay, Ed?' shouted Phil, nervously peering out from the colony door.

'I've had better days,' Ed replied, dragging himself off the deck again and staggering back to the control room door, warily eyeing Trkors's body, which lay twitching face down at the foot of the stairs. He quickly primed and lobbed the grenade up the stairway. 'At least I had your shield device to protect me.'

'Yeah, but that was its first test and it was a laser weapon at point blank.'

'Fuck. Really?'

They all heard the *thunk* as the grenade detonated up in the control room. Ed slid the door closed as the muffled sound of shouting and laser weapon fire came from within.

'I don't think we need to worry about them anymore,' said Ed, slinging his backpack over his shoulder.

'We really do need to go – right now,' said Fallow, urging the group towards the pathway down the hill.

'There are two more guards down at their shuttle,' said Phil.

'Not anymore.'

'Oh, okay,' Phil mumbled.

Ed realised Phil really shouldn't have come down with him. Theos just weren't cut out for violence of any kind.

He thought that was a strange thing to think —only a few months ago, the most violence he'd ever witnessed was a punch-up in a student bar at the university. It worried him just how nonchalantly he was able to cope with such dangerous situations and hoped it wasn't going to come back and bite him one day.

As he joined in the column descending the hill, he promised himself a long holiday when they got back to Earth.

46

THE STARSHIP GABRIEL – HUNUS SYSTEM, ANDROMEDA

EPOCH 128, SPAN 9371, JUNCTURE 193.7

Andy, Linda and Rayl heaved a sigh of relief as they looked back on the demise of the Mogul and his henchmen. There had been no reaction from the fleet around them, which Andy thought was a bit surprising.

'You'd think one of their ships would have some sort of contact with the Mogul,' he said.

'Or one of those guards would have a panic button or some sort of contingency for the unexpected,' replied Linda.

'They really haven't been challenged for thousands of years, have they?' he said. 'All the technology they have, all the technology they've stolen, and they wouldn't know a research and development department if it kicked them in the nuts.'

They'd watched as the PCP had ceased the random

cannon fire to retrieve the two sections of the broken cruiser. The front section had become influenced by the planet's gravity and was dangerously close to dropping into the atmosphere.

'I've got an idea,' said Linda, suddenly sitting up. 'Cleo, did you get a voice record of the Mogul down on Hunus?'

'Yeah.'

'Could I transmit using his voice?'

'What, like you did with Quixia?'

'Yes.'

'Yeah, no problem.'

'Okay, do it and patch me through to the bridge on the ship above.'

'Are you sure they don't already know he's dead?' asked Andy.

'I would've thought there'd be some reaction,' said Rayl, 'but not one ship as much as blinked.'

Linda looked thoughtful for a moment.

'Perhaps they're not permitted to overlook a Mogul. After all, they're not even allowed eye contact.'

'I wouldn't want to,' said Andy. 'Ugly fuckers – just the thought's enough to put you off your tea.'

'Okay then, are we agreed that I at least give it a try?'

'Fine by me,' said Andy, glancing across at Rayl.

'Er, yes. Me too,' she said, looking surprised. 'I didn't think I had much of a say in operational matters.'

'Yeah, we're a democratic ship,' said Linda. 'Everyone on this bridge gets a say.'

'Doesn't mean we listen, though,' said Andy, giving her a wink.

'I'll have you for that,' growled Rayl.

'That's what I was counting on,' he said, grinning.

'Enough, you two,' said Linda. 'This is an innuendo-free zone until the operation is over. Is that clear?'

They both nodded and Linda swung her feet onto the deck. 'I think I need to be standing for this one. Cleo, can you turn the bridge lighting red when I'm online with the PCP?'

'No problem.'

'Okay, open the channel.'

The bridge lighting went a deep maroon and Linda clenched her fists.

'Captain, send the gatekeeper colonists back down here now, along with the Daxxal prisoners,' she said, using the exact voice pattern of the Mogul. Andy and Rayl stared at her, their eyes wide.

'Yes, my Mogul. We hadn't heard from you for some time. We were getting concerned,' came the reply. 'Are you sure you want them all?'

'Are you questioning my orders?' she shouted. 'Do I need to find a captain that knows his place?'

'No, my Mogul. My apologies. They will be sent down immediately.'

'Have them dropped next to my ship and get the shuttle back up to you as fast as possible. Is that clear?'

'Yes, my Mogul. They're on their way.'

Linda signalled to Cleo to cut the transmission.

'Wow,' said Andy. 'Scary Spice – that should be your new handle.'

Both Linda and Rayl looked at each other, neither having a clue what he was on about.

'We have movement,' said Cleo. 'I'll make sure their shuttle doesn't come too close to us.'

One of the attack ship's large hangar doors – on its starboard side – slid slowly open. They had to wait ten minutes before a large, overweight and ugly winged ship exited and headed directly for the planet.

'Shit,' said Andy. 'They didn't design that thing for its aesthetic value, did they?'

'Ed's just asked me to land the Cartella,' said Cleo.

'How's it doing on power?' asked Linda.

'A few hours left yet.'

ED RETRIEVED THE NASA BAG, which contained the data units from the PCP shuttle. The bodies of the two guards were nowhere to be seen.

He'd asked Cleo to bring the Cartella down and land it near the shuttle so he could load it easily. It was heavy so he didn't want to carry it too far.

'Ed, it's Linda. Can you remain hidden down there for a little longer?'

'Sure. What's going on?'

'There's a large transport ship on its way down with the colonists and the remaining Vlepon crew aboard.'

'How would you know that?'

'Because I told them to.'

'What?'

'I'll explain later, but they don't know the Mogul is dead, okay?'

'Okay.'

'Have you got the control room data units?'

'Absolutely.'

'Okay, just get back here with the Vlepon crew and we can go home.'

'How many soldiers are on that transport?'

'I don't know, but they've been instructed to drop them and get the ship back up here immediately.'

'Right, how long have we got?'

'About twenty minutes.'

Ed sprinted over to the tree line where Phil and the youngsters were hiding and told them about the transport.

'Where are the bodies of the two guards from the shuttle?' Ed asked Fallow.

'Hidden underground,' she said, pointing back into the forest.

'How far?'

'Two minutes.'

'Show me,' said Ed, beckoning Phil to follow.

She took them a few hundred metres into the trees where, at the foot of a stone cliff, hidden by a huge flowering shrub, was a small, narrow gap. They all slid through, although Ed found he had to take his backpack off to manage it.

He found himself in a wide passageway, which led away into blackness, heading downhill at quite a steep gradient.

The guards' bodies were just inside the entrance, along with the bodies of the two Vlepon crew.

'Strip the uniforms. That one's about your size, Phil,' said Ed, gesturing at the smaller of the two.

Phil looked at the body with horror.

'You want me to touch that?' he said, clenching and unclenching his fists.

'Just the uniform,' said Ed. 'That transport will be expecting someone on the ground to show the prisoners where to go.'

Phil glared at the body again, hesitating.

'I'll get it,' said Fallow as she started stripping the uniform from the guard and handing it to Phil.

Phil slowly put the outer garments on. The boots were a little large and the trousers slightly short, but apart from that, he looked the part.

Ed's fit so well they could have been made to measure. He grabbed an Exo stun gun from his backpack and put the guard's helmet on.

'Fuck me,' said Phil. 'I wouldn't have known it was you. Do I look as menacing?'

'Absolutely terrifying,' said Ed, slapping him on the back. 'Come on, we've a shuttle to convince.'

They trotted back through the trees to the clearing and Ed asked Cleo to open the Cartella's outer airlock. He hefted the NASA bag and his backpack inside and instructed Cleo to take the ship back up to five hundred metres.

'Make sure you avoid the transport coming down, Cleo. Some of their flying leaves a lot to be desired.'

'We've just witnessed some of that,' she said.

The airlock closed and the Cartella was invisible again. Just a low whining and a sudden squall of wind gradually fading above was the only evidence of its ascent.

'What if they recognise we're fake?' said Phil, looking down at his short trousers.

'You stay over by the tree line,' Ed said, indicating

the pathway up to the colony entrance. 'Your slight wardrobe indiscretion won't be seen from there. And keep facing forward. There's blood on the back of the jacket.'

'Ah, no. There isn't, is there?' said Phil, looking as if he might throw up.

A loud sonic boom from above made them glance skyward.

'Positions please, everyone,' said Ed, pushing Phil towards the pathway.

The transport ship must have slowed very quickly as it appeared above the clearing only a few moments later, vortices flowing off its winglets. It was much larger than Ed had envisioned and it reminded him of an oversized, pregnant Chinese ore carrier. He placed himself next to the smaller shuttle's airlock and watched as the pilot swung the heavy ship around and landed close by on eight quickly extending struts, which sank into the grass slightly.

As soon as the wind and flying debris settled, he strode confidently over to the front airlock, that opened almost immediately.

A soldier, noticing Ed's uniform, stood very stiffly in the doorway and saluted. Ed thought it best to repay the compliment and saluted back.

The first indication he knew he'd screwed up was the look of astonishment on the soldier's face; the second was that he grabbed for his holstered weapon. Ed flew up the now extended stairway, grabbed the arm, which was raising towards him, holding some sort of pistol and half-dragged, half-threw him off the stairs.

He landed hard, headfirst and remained stationary. Ed watched him for a moment. When he didn't move, he turned and stepped through the airlock to peek inside the ship. Three further soldiers stood guard over the main hold of the vessel. They seemed relaxed, probably because there were no windows on the ship and wouldn't have known about their colleague's dilemma. They all noticed him and saluted.

This time he just nodded.

The prisoners were all crammed together on the deck floor in double rows with their heads bowed, the men on one side, the women on the other.

One by one, he quickly did his DOVI trick on the soldiers' firearms, as he had earlier with the guard's laser rifles. He turned quickly as a shout from behind startled him.

The soldier outside had miraculously recovered and stood with a look of utter contempt on his face. He again started to raise his pistol, staggered a bit and pitched forward, collapsing face first on the ground. Two arrows protruded from his spine.

The other three soldiers pulled out their weapons

and pointed them straight at Ed. He smiled and extracted his Exo gun from under his tunic.

Two of the soldiers stopped suddenly and started fiddling with their pistols. He was only able to stun one of them before he was hit suddenly from behind.

The last thing he remembered thinking was why women were screaming, then blackness ensued.

47

THE STARSHIP GABRIEL – HUNUS SYSTEM, ANDROMEDA

EPOCH 128, SPAN 9371, JUNCTURE 195.2

'Ah shit,' exclaimed Andy. 'It's taking off again.'

'Ed's still on there,' said Linda.

'What do we do?' said Rayl.

The three of them sat frozen, staring at each other for a second.

'That transport comes from the ship above us,' said Cleo. 'It has to fly right by. I can tractor it into our empty hangar.'

'But that'll give our position away,' said Andy.

'Not necessarily. There'll be confusion at first and, while the slow chains of command are clanking, we move hastily across and hide under a different attack ship.'

They looked at each other again.

'Well?' said Cleo impatiently.

'Erm, it's better than anything I can think of,' said Andy.

'Me too,' said Rayl.

'Our ship's moving,' said Linda, 'closer to the planet.'

'So are two of the cruisers. Look,' said Rayl, pointing to the holomap.

As Cleo had slaved the Gabriel's helm into the bigger ship's systems, they moved with it. They watched as the three-ship convoy approached the planet and positioned itself in a stationary orbit above the continent where the colony was situated.

'Phil, get out of there now. I have a bad feeling about those cruisers,' called Linda.

As she spoke, five small targets began tracking away from one of the cruisers, heading into the atmosphere.

'Are those shuttles?' asked Rayl.

'No,' said Andy. 'They're missiles.'

'Phil,' Linda called again. 'For fuck's sake, get out of there.'

'Can you repeat that?' said an out-of-breath Phil.

'Incoming missiles,' shouted Linda. 'Get under cover.'

'It's okay, I've just got in the Cartella. I'm leaving now.'

'Don't go too fast on this side of the planet,' she

said. 'They could probably track you by the air displacement.'

'Or the boom trail,' said Andy.

'We've got more launches,' said Rayl. 'They're transports like the one Ed's on – six of them.'

'Well, I hope whoever Ed's friends were down there, they know how to hide,' said Andy. 'It's about to get very loud.'

'Ed's transport is five minutes out,' said Linda. 'Are you all ready, Cleo?'

'Absolutely.'

'What are you going to do about the PCP crew?'

'Annoy them with extreme belligerence.'

Linda looked across at Andy, who returned an expression of incomprehension.

'Do you want me down in the hangar, Cleo?' Andy asked. 'To help with your beliger— billiga— whatever that was?'

'No, I can deal with them. You three get us away from the crime scene and hide us under another one of these monsters.'

They all waited and watched as the transport ship slowly heaved its way back into space and approached its mother ship. Cleo disconnected them from the attack ship's helm and quickly positioned the Gabriel between the two, turning the ship so that the hangar was facing the transport and away from any keen-eyed observers on the bigger ship.

Timing it perfectly, she waited until the opportune moment, opened the hangar door, activated the tractor beam and dragged the transport ship inside.

'Got 'em,' she said. 'Linda, go now.'

Linda gunned the throttle and the Gabriel launched away from the attack ship and across towards the remainder of the fleet.

THE SHOUTING WAS what brought Ed back to consciousness. He'd been dreaming about the Mogul plunging his serrated dagger into his chest. He was quite happy the noise dragged him away from that.

Although, on opening his eyes, he found the situation was not an awful lot better. Realising that he'd been knocked unconscious for a second time that day explained why his head felt like it had been split in two.

His hands and feet were bound and a soldier was shouting and pointing a rather large rifle at him. Then, for some unfathomable reason, the soldier suddenly jumped back, smashed into the bulkhead wall and remained stuck there.

'You've been a very naughty boy,' said Cleo, appearing in all her royal splendour. She removed the weapon from the soldier and handcuffed him to a weightless handle.

A cheer rang around the ship as she similarly attached the other two soldiers, although one was already unconscious anyway.

Ed heard a rattle behind him and the room fell almost silent again, except for a few gasps. Turning his head, he came face to face with a pair of boots. Glancing up, he realised it was one of the pilots down from the cockpit. He stood in the doorway at the foot of the cockpit stairs, pointing a laser pistol at Cleo. He smiled; she smiled back; he pulled the trigger; nothing happened.

Another cheer resonated from the prisoners as he looked quizzically at the weapon.

'Oh dear, has your ray gun broken?' said Cleo, holding her hand out.

The pistol flew out of his hand and into hers. She pointed it over his shoulder and pulled the trigger. A laser bolt zipped past his face and buried itself in the stairway behind him with crack and a spray of sparks.

'Seems to be working now, doesn't it?' she said, raising her eyebrows.

He got the implicit message and raised his hands.

'And you too,' she called out. 'It's no good thinking you can ambush me at the top of the stairs. You may enrich us with your presence either the easy way or the hard way.'

Silence ensued.

'Suit yourself,' she said.

Ed heard a shout, then a thud, and another crewman dressed in what must be a pilot's uniform appeared upside down at the foot of the stairs, almost knocking his colleague over.

He slowly got up, wincing in pain and hobbling. After assessing his co-pilot's predicament, he raised his hands too.

Cleo secured them in a similar way to the others and turned to speak to the populace, who were sitting on the floor, smiling and staring at her with an air of reverence.

'Welcome to the Starship Gabriel,' she said. 'Those of you from the planet Hunus, we will be taking you home as soon as possible. Please make yourselves comfortable either in here or in the hangar. Refreshments have been provided.' A cheer sounded around the seated group again.

She raised her hand to silence the crowd.

'The remainder of the Vlepon crew, if you will follow the lit corridor through to the other hangar, your colleagues are awaiting your arrival.'

This brought another slightly lesser cheer as there were only eleven of them.

She knelt down beside Ed. 'I think you need a little lie down in the auto-nurse.'

Ed nodded and suddenly wished he hadn't as the pain was nauseating. He attempted to stand, felt even worse and slumped down again.

'I've got this,' said Cleo and picked him up as if he weighed nothing.

'Don't tell Andy about this,' he whispered as the airlock cycled open and she carried him down the steps, closely followed by some of the passengers.

'THEY'RE FIRING AGAIN,' shouted Andy. 'Hurry, Linda.'

The fleet in front of them began growing larger, and random laser fire began crisscrossing around them.

The Gabriel shuddered as their luck ran out. A laser bolt ricocheted off the shields, causing them to flare and every PCP laser gunner in the fleet had a nice illuminated target to aim at.

'Shit, shit, shit,' shouted Linda as she swung the ship around, trying to lose the now constant hammering against the shields. It was no use: the more they were hit the more the shields lit up.

'Shields at seventy-seven percent,' called Andy.

'How many of those GDA drones do we have left?' asked Rayl.

'Four, I think,' said Andy.

'Turn around and put that attack ship between them and us. It'll be so big behind us they'll start hitting it too.'

Linda nodded and swung around, putting the fleet behind them and the attack ship dead ahead. She jinked left and right and up and down, which caused several laser bolts to miss and hit the PCP ship in front of them. The firing lessened slightly…

…only for the two cruisers either side of the attack ship to open up instead.

'Now use two of those drones on the cruisers,' said Rayl, 'like you did before.'

'Oh, good girl,' said Andy. 'I haven't got time to reset the warheads this time, but I'll just target all the missiles at the same point in their engineering sections.'

Luckily, the cruisers remained stationary to give their gunners more chance, so Andy was quickly able to eject the two drones from the hangar and jump them behind the cruiser's shields.

At first, he didn't think it had worked as the missiles exploded on impact instead of boring their way inside. But, as he'd staggered the launch of each one by just a tenth of a second, they struck in a line and each one penetrated a few decks further.

They knew something had happened as the laser fire stopped, first on one, then closely followed by the second. Next, both cruisers started to sink out of their orbital tracks, the gas jets of their manoeuvring thrusters flashing like crazy, trying to compensate for the loss of their main drives.

It was a losing battle, though. The ships had been positioned in such a low orbit to be able to accurately target their missiles that the planet's gravity was now winning over the feeble thrust of the jets.

Dozens of lifeboats began ejecting as the captains had given the abandon ship order.

The laser fire from the fleet behind them stopped as they got close to the attack ship; its small bore laser fire grew in intensity but had little effect on the Gabriel's shields.

Cleo did her trick with the helm again as they shot underneath and stopped on a dime. Their shields were able to settle and recharge and the Gabriel became invisible again.

Linda, Andy and Rayl watched the firework display as two monstrous battle cruisers dropped ever lower into Hunus's atmosphere. The fiery trails multiplied over and over as the ships gradually broke up and disappeared to either burn up or impact the surface.

'I hope nobody's underneath those when they land,' said Andy.

'We should get out of here right now,' said Linda. 'It won't take them long to work out where we are.'

Almost just as she spoke, two powerful tractor beams reached out from the bow and the stern of the attack ship and enveloped the Gabriel's shields.

'Shit,' said Andy. 'Linda, full power – get us outta here.'

'I'm trying.'

'The rest of the fleet is coming this way,' said Rayl.

'Bollocks,' said Andy as he tried to activate the weapon systems. 'They're not fucking engaging.'

'That's because they're not activated,' said Rayl. 'Their beam is disrupting some of our systems.'

'Cleo,' shouted Linda. 'Activate the Palto.'

'That's one of the disrupted systems,' said Rayl, sounding worried.

'Cleo, we need you to organise a workaround – quickly.'

'Working on it.'

'The fleet is getting closer,' called Rayl. 'Can't you guys use your DOVIs to turn off the beam?'

'No,' said Cleo. 'They've developed a workaround within their shield contrariety.'

'Can we jump?' said Andy, starting to look concerned.

'No, all drives are offline,' said Linda.

The Gabriel shuddered quite severely.

'The fleet is engaging us,' said Rayl. 'And we can't avoid any of their fire this time.'

'Cleo, anytime now would be good,' called Andy, wincing as the ship shook again.

'Shields at sixty-seven percent,' said Rayl.

'Still trying,' said Cleo. 'Their beam is adaptive and counteracts every move I make.'

'Shields at forty-two percent.'

'The gate's opened,' said Andy. 'Something came through again.'

Whatever it was, took a direct hit from one of the mines like last time and was completely vaporised.

The ship lurched to one side as more fire was unleashed against its failing shields.

'What about the last of the drones?' asked Linda, glancing at Andy, a look of dread on her face.

'I can programme them but I can't launch them.'

'Shields at nineteen percent,' said Rayl, sounding very scared.

'Oh, shit,' said Andy, slapping himself in the face 'What the fuck is the answer to—'

'What the hell?' shouted Linda, pointing at the Holonav.

The Cartella had appeared inside the shields of the attack ship and, with its cannons, let rip at the giant ship's main arrays. The tractor beams failed immediately and all systems on the Gabriel came back online.

The Cartella quickly jumped away before any of the PCP gunners realised what had happened.

'Cleo, Palto up now,' called Linda, her face as white as a sheet.

'Palto activated.'

As the Holonav went blank, Linda engaged the main drive and shot straight up. Andy recognised a similar vibration from the last time they'd used this manoeuvre and knew the result wouldn't be good for the ship above them.

'Palto off please, Cleo. Cloak and full shields.'

'Shields at fifty-six percent and rising,' said Rayl.

She carried on up for two more seconds, jinked left away from the planet and watched as the Holonav came back online.

The scene, when it cleared, was of complete devastation. The attack ship, huge as it was, had almost been cleaved into two about one third of the way down its length.

It hung, spinning slowly, folded at ninety degrees and emitting debris and gasses in every direction. Just a few decks remained and the outer hull kept it from breaking completely in two. Smaller ships and escape pods began pouring from the doomed vessel as, this time, not even the manoeuvring jets attempted to keep the inevitable from happening.

Very slowly, the behemoth started to roll over

lengthways, gathering speed as gravity began to claim it, emitting the now familiar glow as the leading edges touched the upper atmosphere.

The remainder of the fleet had long since stopped firing; a lack of a target had probably been the reason for that. They slowed their approach, most likely in shock at seeing one of their most powerful vessels taken apart in such an appallingly clinical manner.

'Where did Phil go?' asked Andy.

'He embedded the jump,' answered Rayl, 'to make sure they couldn't follow him.'

'I didn't think he could fire at anyone,' said Linda.

'He only targeted their arrays, so he didn't break his inbred protocol,' said Andy. 'We all owe him our lives. I don't know about you two, but I'm going to hug the life out of him when he gets home.'

'Same here,' said Linda. 'I've never been so scared. That was way too close.'

'We need to set some SOPs,' said Rayl, 'especially for potential conflict situations.'

'SOPs?' said Andy, puzzled by the acronym.

'Standard Operating Procedures,' said Rayl. 'Rules of engagement, if you like. The GDA runs on them.'

Linda had run the Gabriel's Alma drive at the stops, aiming straight at the star. The remaining fleet had restarted the random laser fire again, but it seemed to lack the aggressive nature of before and appeared to be performing more of a defensive discipline.

'I'm going down to see if Ed's okay,' said Andy, getting up and walking towards the tube lift.

'The gate's opened again,' called Rayl, which caused Andy to spin round and stare at the Holonav.

Sudden multiple forks of lightning caused all five hundred of the mines guarding the gate entrance to explode as one, the huge flash prompting the three of them to shield their eyes.

'Bloody hell,' said Andy. 'Who the fuck has the power to do that?'

48

THE BRIDGE, KATADROMIKO 31 – HUNUS GATE, ANDROMEDA

EPOCH 128, SPAN 9371, JUNCTURE 197.8

'Fleet will disperse into echelon beta twelve,' Senior Captain Gade Kil'nur said into the transmitter, speaking to the fleet of eleven GDA Katadromiko Class Cruisers. 'Please confirm optimum firing designations and await further orders.'

He looked over his shoulder and received a nod from the two gentlemen who were sitting on raised seats to one side of the bridge officers.

Commander Bache Loftt and Ambassador James Dewey watched the holo map intently as the eleven cloaked, fourteen-kilometre battle cruisers quickly spread out to face the remaining PCP fleet.

The PCP's random laser fire had changed when the minefield exploded, and now concentrated on the area around the three moons.

'How certain are we that it was the Gabriel they

were attacking?' asked Dewey, glancing at Loftt. 'We only got a fleeting glimpse of the situation before the drones were destroyed.'

'They're searching for a cloaked target,' he replied. 'The Gabriel doesn't have our new absorbent shielding. Its shields would flare with just a glancing blow.'

'I thought Theo technology was generally ahead of the GDA.'

'Predominantly it is. It's rare for us to introduce new kit first, but not unheard of.'

'Is there any way of knowing where the Gabriel is?'

'No.'

'How are we going to ensure we don't hit them?'

'We can't be one hundred percent sure, but the beam gunners have been instructed to pulse fire.'

'What difference does that make?'

'After examining the wreck of the PCP ship the Gabriel defeated over Paradeisos a few months ago, we learnt that their shielding is slightly inferior to ours. It's very good at absorbing laser fire, but it quickly overloads when attacked with a wide band Asteri Beam.'

'So, we're using the beams on pulse to overload and penetrate their shields, then follow up with the big lasers to knock out their arrays and propulsion. Pulsing the beam stops it from punching a hole right through the ship, continuing out the other side and possibly hitting a friendly.'

'I thought the Asteri Beam was designed for planetary targets.'

'It is,' said Loftt. 'We're just having to adapt on the fly.'

Dewey sat back in his seat and watched the huge Holonav display in the centre of the bridge, where he could see the collection of PCP warships blindly firing around Hunus's three moons.

Once the tenth captain had confirmed his optimum position and had his allocated targets locked, Kil'nur again glanced at Commander Loftt. 'Let's be at 'em, Captain,' said Loftt. 'Shall we give them a little poke with a stick and test how aggressive these fuckers are?'

The captain raised his eyebrows at his commander's lapse in bridge etiquette and unusual turn of phrase, but nodded anyway and gave the uncloak order to the fleet.

The eleven monstrous vessels suddenly materialised amongst the PCP fleet. For a few moments, nothing happened. Then Dewey noticed the weapon systems on the PCP ships repositioning away from Hunus and pointing directly at the newcomers.

'Communications,' said Kil'nur. 'Open a universal channel please.'

'Channel open, Captain,' said an officer below and to his left.

'This is Senior Captain Kil'nur of the GDA intergalactic expeditionary task force. PCP fleet, please respond.'

'I don't converse with captains, senior or not,' replied a booming voice.

Kil'nur gave a rueful smile and glanced over at Loftt. One of the attack ships in the centre of the holo map began flashing red.

'Is that ship conversing with us?' asked Dewey.

'Yes,' said Loftt, standing up. He signalled Kil'nur to remain silent.

'Unintroduced PCP representative, this is Commander Loftt. Please run along and find someone of sufficient rank who has the authority to converse with perhaps a commander or indeed a captain, senior or not.'

Dewey chuckled to himself. He'd noticed how Loftt's sense of humour and sarcasm had come to the fore since spending time with Virr and Faux.

'I am a Mogul. I will communicate only with your President or King.'

'Sorry,' said Loftt. 'Fresh out of kings – but, in actual fact, I don't really want to converse anyway. I just want you to listen and do as you're told.'

'Your insolence will be your downfall, little insignificant Daxxal man. Perhaps it has escaped your notice but the last time I counted, you seemed to be a little outnumbered and it's about to get worse.'

The remainder of the PCP fleet that had previously jumped over to the neighbouring system, looking in vain for the Gabriel, began to jump back.

Kil'nur signalled for the extra vessels to be included into the targeting computations.

'Oh, I'm so impressed, my little overconfident friend,' said Loftt, glaring at Dewey, who'd snorted while trying to stifle a laugh. 'But I fear it makes no difference. Attention all captains of the PCP fleet, you have five minutes to surrender your vessels or face serious consequences for you and your crews.'

All eleven Katadromiko cruisers cloaked and vanished.

'How many are there?' called Loftt.

'Ninety-three,' said one of the bridge officers. 'But three of those seem badly damaged.' They began flashing in blue on the Holonav.

'I'm finding a lot of ship debris flying around,' said another voice. 'Especially in orbit of the planet.'

'I think they must have tried to bully the Gabriel,' said Loftt, giving Dewey a glance.

'How do we know the debris isn't the Gabriel?' said Dewey, a slightly nervous tone to his voice.

'Metal composition,' said the voice from below.

'Theo ships are semi-organic and there's none of that material present.'

Dewey hadn't noticed he'd stood up at the mention of ship debris. He looked back at the Holonav and sat back down again, the relief written all over his face.

'It's okay,' said Loftt, giving Dewey a reassuring smile. 'They'll be fine and hiding close by.'

'YOU HAVE A LITTLE LIE DOWN,' said Andy as he stood next to Ed who was lying prostrate in the auto-nurse.

'Bollocks.'

'Don't worry, we'll take on ninety enemy warships. We don't need you.'

'Bugger off. My brain hurts.'

'With the help of eleven Katadromiko cruisers.'

'Bolloc— WHAT?' said Ed, sitting up too quickly. He groaned, holding his head in his hands and lay back down again. There was a flashing red light and an alarm sounded on the auto-nurse control panel.

'The cavalry has just come over the hill.'

'Eleven Katadromikos?' Ed asked, his face a mixture of amazement and pain.

'Yeah.'

'How did they operate the gate?'

'They must have made a controller like yours.'

'Bloody hell. Have they engaged the PCP fleet?'

'Not yet. Loftt's giving them the opportunity to surrender.'

'Bache is here?'

'Yeah.'

'Yeah, right. Like they're going to surrender.'

'Nah, not a chance.'

'Bloody hell, how long have I got?' he said, pointing at the readout on the control panel.

'Twenty-two minutes.'

'How long's he given them?'

'About another three minutes.'

'Shit, I've gotta see this.'

Ed sat up, slowly this time. The alarm still sounded, but was ignored. He climbed out of the auto-nurse cocoon and stood. His head pounded as he cradled it in his hands.

'Not so good, eh?' said Andy.

'No.'

Cleo appeared, a hypodermic syringe in her hand. Ed shrank back at the sight of it.

'Have it,' she said, ignoring his hesitance and plunging the needle into his arm.

'Ow, shit. What's that?'

'Painkiller, doomsday strength. Now get upstairs. It's about to get interesting.'

They both ran for the tube lift, Ed still grimacing

and rubbing his arm.

'Two minute warning, ladies and gentlemen,' called Captain Kil'nur over his ship's tannoy. 'Secure all bulkhead doors and adopt combat decompression protocols.'

Everyone on the bridge who wasn't seated, did so immediately. Harnesses popped out from the sides of all the seating, into which everybody quickly fastened themselves.

Dewey glanced over at Loftt with raised eyebrows as he buckled his belts.

'In case of explosive decompression,' he said, in answer to the unspoken question. 'Stops you getting sucked out of the ship through a bulkhead failure or a puncture hole.'

'I don't think I want to even imagine either of those scenarios,' said Dewey, noticing hand holds also appearing out of the floor, walls and ceiling.

'In case of gravity failure,' said Loftt, following his gaze.

Dewey nodded, realising again just how long these guys had been doing this.

'Communications,' said Kil'nur, watching the countdown reach zero and then pointed at Loftt. 'Open a channel for the Commander.'

'Channel open, sir.'

Loftt nodded and cleared his throat.

'PCP fleet, I believe it's decision time. Those wishing to comply and save your ship, please shut down your weapon systems, jump to these co-ordinates and await further instructions.'

Eight ships jumped, but not to the indicated co-ordinates and not anywhere in the Hunus system.

'Let them go,' said Kil'nur to his GDA ships. 'Concentrate on the remaining fleet.'

The answer from them came only a split second later as a blizzard of laser fire reached out from all the remaining PCP vessels, some of which was so indiscriminate, it flared the shields of their own ships.

'Well, set my bunk alight,' said Kil'nur, his eyes wide with disbelief. 'These idiots are as disciplined as a drunk Yelloon cave rat.'

He looked at Loftt with a jaded expression and shrugged his shoulders.

'Go ahead, Captain,' said Loftt. 'You have no choice.'

Kil'nur turned back to the Holonav, nodded to his communications officer and spoke clearly to the other ten Katadromiko captains.

'Commence offensive measures against your designated targets in your own time.'

The words were hardly out of his mouth before all eleven Katadromiko cruisers opened up with their full complement of Asteri Beam weapons, all set on their widest aperture.

Each cruiser had six of these fearsome weapons and the sight of sixty-six of them ripping into the PCP fleets shields was quite spectacular. The bridge contingent was forced to cover their eyes as the targeted ships almost disappeared behind bright white flaring shields.

It also caused the random enemy fire to become much more concentrated as they followed the beam pulses back to their source. But the GDA's shields had been used in combat countless times before and had been perfected to such a degree that the PCP laser fire barely scratched them.

'Shields at eighty-nine percent, Captain,' called the officer, who was manning one of the defensive measures consoles.

Kil'nur acknowledged the lieutenant and turned back to the holomap again.

James Dewey sat in awe, watching the six huge fifty-metre diameter beams pulsing into their ship's two designated targets, one of which was the bigger carrier-type ship the Mogul had been talking from. Although it wasn't one of the heavier gunned ships, Loftt had designated it as probably the command ship and to be targeted in the first phase.

The two vessels began flashing orange on the holomap and Dewey was about to ask Loftt what that meant, when he spoke first.

'Their shields are at less than ten percent,' he said. 'Any minute now they'll turn green and the laser gunners can earn their ration of rum.'

Dewey chuckled as he realised Loftt had been reading up on old Earth naval customs. Sure enough, five seconds later the two vessels turned green and the fearsome ship-to-ship lasers kicked off.

He felt the vibration, as well as heard the harmonic echoes that were running around the massive ship, change as the beams ceased and the lasers cracked, whipping lumps of pure energy across the void at light speed.

Large pieces of the PCP ships disappeared, vaporised in the blink of an eye: targeting arrays, navigation arrays, propulsion nozzles, weapon nacelles and anything that looked important.

Within ten seconds, the two warships had become dead in the water, reduced to floating hulks.

'Select secondary targets and commence,' said Kil'nur.

'Four ships have jumped, Captain,' came the call. 'No, seven … eight … thirteen…'

'Have any jumped to our designated surrender co-ordinates?'

'Three, sir.'

'Katadromiko 21, jump to the surrender co-ordinates and attend to those three vessels. Remember your disciplines and don't let them sucker you into a trap.'

The Asteri beams had recommenced targeting two more of the remaining PCP fleet, as had the other nine remaining Katadromikos. Five more PCP ships jumped away.

'I'm noticing a trend, Captain,' said one of the officers.

'Go ahead,' said Kil'nur.

'The majority of the ships jumping away are the bigger carrier type.'

'Any conclusion as to the reason, Ensign?'

'They're the Mogul flagships. Target them first,' called Ed, butting in on the conversation, his voice booming around the bridge over the tannoy.

'Edward, you're alive. You're alive, indeed,' shouted Dewey, trying to stand, but was pulled back by the seat harnesses.

Everyone on the bridge turned to stare at him in amazement, except for Kil'nur, who jammed his hands on his hips and glared.

'Ambassador Dewey, are you here too?' said Ed.

'Yes, Edward. How are you guys doing?'

'Well, apart from a missing Cartella and a lump on my head the size of a grapefruit, we're fine.'

'Who's in the Cartella?'

'Phil.'

'It's okay, I'm here,' said Phil.

'Oh, cool,' said Ed. 'We're all together again.'

Kil'nur threw his hands up in the air and glowered at Dewey.

'With all due respect, Ambassador, we're in the middle of a war here, not a fucking family reunion,' he thundered.

Loftt put his hand on Dewey's shoulder and shook his head.

'Thank you,' said Kil'nur. 'And, Edward, whoever you are,' he shouted, as he turned back to stare at the holomap, 'I will want to know how you got onto my fucking bridge. But for now, piss off.'

'So sorry.'

'SO SORRY?' questioned Linda.

'Well, I couldn't think of anything better to say.'

'I could've,' said Andy, grinning from his couch.

'Of that, I have no doubt,' said Linda, standing up from hers and signalling for Ed to do the same.

As soon as he stood, she enveloped him in a bear hug.

'Don't you ever scare us like that again.'

Ed smiled and squeezed her close.

'I seem to remember someone else picking a fight with a Mogul not so long ago.'

'Yeah, well,' she said. 'Let's just call it quits – no more saving the universe.'

'Okay, from now on we leave it to the GDA.'

'Oh, yuk!' exclaimed Rayl, suddenly.

'We're allowed a cuddle,' said Linda.

'No, not you,' she said. 'A live body's just been ejected from an airlock on that attack ship.' She pointed at one of the defeated PCP ships in the middle of the battle.

'Magnify it,' said Ed.

As the image grew, it soon became obvious who it was.

'It's a Mogul,' said Rayl.

'Good riddance,' said Andy as they all watched the tall, red figure stop thrashing around and become still.

'That's Tyann Kky,' said Ed, looking closely.

'Who's he?' asked Linda.

'The commander of all their armed forces. Huwlen showed me pictures of their senior staff.'

'That's a good sign,' said Andy. 'I wonder how many of them are left now.'

'It's got to be less than half,' said Linda, returning to her couch.

'Permission to come aboard,' said a cheery sounding Phil.

'Ah, at last,' said Linda. 'The hero returns.'

Ed, along with everyone on the bridge, looked relieved to see an intact Cartella uncloak and settle in the starboard hangar.

'When it's safe to do so,' said Ed, 'I want to check the kids are safe down on Hunus. They were planning on returning to the caves before that missile strike. I need to make sure they're okay and thank them properly for saving mine and Phil's life.'

'They sent a contingent of ground troops down as well,' said Linda.

'Really?' said Ed. 'Then we need to help them asap.'

'I don't think we're going to be waiting very long,' said Andy, gesturing to the vastly depleted numbers of the PCP fleet.

'Get us over there,' said Ed, reclining on his control couch.

49

THE STARSHIP GABRIEL – HUNUS SYSTEM, ANDROMEDA

EPOCH 128, SPAN 9371, JUNCTURE 199.8

The holomap display of the colony on Hunus was not good. Several fires were still burning in the area, presumably from the missile bombardment.

As the Gabriel got closer, they could start to make out more detail.

'The troops seem to have landed further out than usual,' said Linda. 'Their ships are about two kilometres away from the colony.'

'I think the normal landing area is too cratered after the missile strike and the path up to the colony looks damaged,' said Rayl.

'The majority of the soldiers seem to be building things around the landing site,' said Andy.

'I'm hoping the kids are safe, hidden underground,' said Ed. 'The soldiers haven't found anyone to fight.

They've probably lost contact with their mother ship and decided to make camp.'

They all turned their attention to the second display, which showed the state of play above the planet. Of the original ninety-three PCP vessels, fifty-one were now stationary, toothless hulks, twenty-seven jumped away and fifteen had surrendered without firing a shot.

Senior Captain Kil'nur had sent four of his cruisers in pursuit of the fleeing vessels, although most had embedded their jump co-ordinates and had vanished without a trace. Only three had been caught and neutralised.

'Katadromiko 31, this is Captain Virr of the Starship Gabriel – do you copy?'

'Finally learnt some manners then, Mr Virr?' replied Kil'nur.

'Ah, yes – sorry about that, Captain. I got a little carried away in the thick of battle.'

'Perhaps you could explain how you punched straight through into my bridge tannoy system? Especially when my shields are supposed to be impenetrable.'

'I'd love to,' said Ed. 'But I don't understand some of the new Theo technology.'

'I'm sure I wouldn't, either. Perhaps you'd like to share the files with one of my technical officers?'

'Files on the way,' said Cleo.

This surprised Ed, although he didn't show it. It wasn't common for Theos to so quickly give away the secrets to new technology and he made a mental note to ask her about it later.

'Files received,' said Kil'nur, sounding surprised.

'Hello again, Edward,' said James Dewey. 'We're all very glad you're safe and well, but I do recall your mission being one of intelligence gathering and not declaring war on the entire Andromedan fleet.'

'Would you like me to explain face to face, Ambassador? I have the surviving crew from the Vlepon on board who are quite keen to go home.'

A slight pause followed before Kil'nur spoke again.

'Uncloak and approach on this vector.'

A course appeared on the holomap, Linda locked on to it and the Gabriel travelled uncloaked for the first time in the Andromedan Galaxy.

An hour later a troop shuttle from Katadromiko 31 picked up a very relieved Vlepon crew. Ed, Andy and Linda took the Cartella over to the monster vessel and settled the little ship down next to the captain's personal shuttle in a small hangar on the port side.

A ten-minute internal train journey took them up to the bridge and they were escorted through to the captain's private office on the far side of the huge room.

It was their first time inside a Katadromiko Class Cruiser and they'd all ogled at the scale of everything, especially the central atrium, with its river, trees and birds.

Ed spent the next half an hour explaining what exactly had taken place over the last few weeks.

'So, this Huwlen Senn character,' said Loftt. 'You believe he can be trusted?'

'I do,' said Ed, nodding.

'And you reckon, as he's the leader of the new administration, he would be willing to sign a cessation of hostilities?'

'Absolutely,' he said, realising Loftt's command of the English language had dramatically improved since their last meeting.

Loftt nodded and glanced across at Kil'nur.

'How do we contact him?' asked Kil'nur.

'Transmit this message,' said Ed, giving him a data unit. 'Only he can read it and he'll be along as soon as he can.'

Kil'nur disappeared out onto the main bridge, returning without the unit.

'Are you aware there's a contingent of PCP soldiers down on Hunus?' asked Ed.

'Yes, we are,' said Loftt. 'They've been trying to contact their ship for several hours. It's on the to-do list.'

'It's only that I have the civilian population from that colony sitting in one of my hangars. I know they'd really appreciate being able to go home.'

'Okay, I'll push it up the agenda,' said Kil'nur, typing a message into a keypad on his desk. 'How many of them are there?'

'Over four hundred.'

'I'll send a troop ship over to ferry them down as soon as the marooned soldiers have been neutralised.'

'I believe a celebration drink is next on the agenda,' said a smiling Commander Loftt. 'I would like to personally thank the other members of your crew. Shall we adjourn this assembly and reconvene at the bar on the Gabriel?'

'Can I second that proposal?' said Andy, putting his hand up a little too enthusiastically.

Dewey rolled his eyes and shook his head.

'I'm surprised you haven't built your own pub on that ship, Mr Faux,' he said.

'What a bloody good idea,' said Andy, glancing across expectantly at Ed.

Ed ignored the opportunity to comment and spoke to Captain Kil'nur instead. 'Would you like to join us, Captain?'

Kil'nur gave Loftt a quick glance. On receiving an almost imperceptible nod, he handed operations over to one of the other Katadromiko captains.

'I would very much like to try some of this genuine beer I've been hearing so much about,' said Kil'nur as he led them to the door and back through the bridge.

'I believe he means real ale,' said Andy. 'The best beer on Earth comes from England.'

'That's fighting talk,' said Linda. 'You can keep your brown stuff. I'd rather have something a little lighter from Missouri.'

THE FOLLOWING MORNING, Ed appeared on the Gabriel's bridge to find Linda and Rayl already busy, running the show.

They both looked up and grimaced at the sight of their very dishevelled captain.

'Oh, dear,' he said, noticing their pinched expressions. 'Do I really look as bad as I feel?'

'A corpse would look healthier than you,' said Linda. 'You look like an old black and white movie, all colourless and grainy.'

Rayl giggled and quickly averted her gaze as Ed turned and glowered at Linda.

'It's all the Faux's fault,' he said, slumping onto his control couch.

'I seem to recall it was you who first mentioned

margaritas, Mr Virr,' said Linda as she finished manoeuvring the ship. 'Not the best idea on top of that industrial painkiller Cleo gave you.'

'That reminds me,' he said, looking up. 'Cleo, any chance of another of those?'

'No,' boomed Cleo's voice, which caused him to wince. 'You can't. They're for extreme circumstances only. You can have some aspirin.'

'Bugger,' he said, suddenly realising Linda had been moving the ship. 'Are we in orbit around Hunus?'

'Yep.'

'What about the PCP troops down there?'

'Persuaded to surrender overnight by an Asteri Beam cutting through each of their troop carriers and a unit of GDA Syntagma Eleven, which I'm told is their equivalent of our Delta Force, or your SAS.'

'How many survivors?'

'About half of them. They refused to believe that the fleet had been destroyed.'

Ed sighed and studied the holomap.

'How are they doing with the rest of the fleet?'

Rayl touched a few icons and stared intently at the results. 'The PCP ships that surrendered all have GDA bridge crews and are to be handed over to Huwlen when he arrives. They're about halfway through boarding the damaged ships; some are surrendering, some not. They reckon another couple of days at least to subdue the final pockets of stubborn resistance.'

'Hmm.'

'What does, "hmm" mean?' asked Linda.

'It was better than saying "errgh",' he said, resting his head in his hands.

'Ah, right,' said Linda. 'If it's that bad, go back to bed.'

'Andy?' he asked with a questioning look.

'He's worse than you.'

'What about Dewey, Loftt and Kil'nur?'

'I don't know. They were gone this morning.'

'Cleo,' called Ed, looking up at the ceiling again. 'When did our guests leave?'

'At four fifty-six am.'

'Oh dear. Do I want to know the details?'

'Commander Loftt and Ambassador Dewey were singing American Air Force drinking songs.'

'And Captain Kil'nur?'

'Senior Captain Kil'nur was being supported by the other two and thought his shuttle's pilot needed to be force-fed a slice of pepperoni pizza.'

'Oh dear.'

'Stop saying, "Oh dear".'

'Sorry.'

'Go to bed.'

'Okay.'

'We'll call you when they come for the colonists.'

'Or when Huwlen arrives.'

'Go to bed.'

'Okay.'

50

THE STARSHIP GABRIEL – HUNUS SYSTEM, ANDROMEDA

EPOCH 129, SPAN 9371, JUNCTURE 040.4

The GDA troop carrier filled a large gap in the Gabriel's port hangar, but was still able to manoeuvre itself around for a gentle landing, facing the door.

A very relieved crowd of colonists watched on as the crew prepared the carrier for the coming insertion back to their homes on Hunus.

Ed, who looked a lot better after a little more sleep, Andy – who didn't and Phil and Linda all arrived to see them off.

Breex separated himself from the smiling crowd and approached Ed, grinning from ear to ear, and enveloped him in a giant bear hug.

'We can never repay you for this, Edward,' he said, sounding apologetic and nodding a greeting to Linda, Andy and Phil.

'Actually,' said Ed. 'Your kids already have.' He

proceeded to tell Breex how some of the older children had saved his and Phil's lives by killing the Mogul. Breex's jaw nearly hit the floor as he listened intently, clearly shocked.

'Our children did that?'

'Some of them aren't children anymore, Breex. Make sure you give them plenty of support. They've had to grow up far too early.'

'Which ones were they?' he asked.

'They wore scarves over their faces, so I never did find out,' said Ed, telling a little white lie.

Breex nodded, but didn't push the point.

'We had no idea about Trkors, by the way,' he said. 'He became my friend when he arrived and always expressed such hatred for the Moguls.'

'I think that was a spur of the moment "save my arse" decision,' said Ed. 'I don't believe he'd been a spy all along.'

'Nor me,' said Breex.

'I hope the kids are okay and the bombardment didn't damage too much down there,' said Andy as he also received a hug from Breex.

'Our lump of rock is quite robust, Andrew. I'm sure the colony will be fine.'

'To make sure, the GDA will provide you with a freighter-load of supplies, just in case,' said Ed.

Andy looked at Ed with raised eyebrows.

'Was this your doing?' he asked.

'I might have mentioned something to Loftt last night.'

They all turned as a shout from the troop carrier crew signalled them to begin loading. It was a sizeable ship, but would still prove a bit of a squeeze.

'Good luck, Breex,' said Ed. 'Let us know the kids are okay.'

'Of course. Make sure you come back and visit us too,' he said, turning to go. 'We may seem quite primitive, but we party well.'

'It's a date,' Ed called as he watched Breex join the back of the line and finally disappear inside the carrier.

A few moments later the antigravity drives spooled up, and the ship lifted, moved slowly across the hangar and slipped through the invisible shield barrier. They watched the carrier power away and, as they turned to head for the door, Rayl's voice boomed over the tannoy.

'I need you up here, guys.'

'On our way,' said Linda.

They almost fell out of the tube lift as it appeared through the floor of the Gabriel's bridge. It proved quite snug with four passengers.

'Who had their hand on my arse?' said Andy, looking at Linda accusingly.

'Guilty, your lordship,' said Linda. 'Too good an opportunity to miss.'

'You know I normally charge for that.'

Ed noticed Rayl staring at Andy, who suddenly shut up and sat on his couch. Linda caught Ed's eye and grinned, nodding at him knowingly.

Once they were all settled on their control couches, Rayl spoke and pointed at the holomap.

'Huwlen's here,' she said as the unmistakable image of a Hercules Class Cruiser grew larger on the display, entering the system fast but under conventional drive.

'Are we completely sure that's the Retribution?' said Linda.

Almost before she'd finished speaking, four Katadromiko cruisers uncloaked and surrounded the huge vessel.

Ed quickly opened a wide band communication channel as the ships turned to face each other, all activating their weapon systems.

'Everyone, hold your fire.'

There was silence for a few moments before a familiar voice filled the bridge.

'Uncle Eddie, is that you?' said Huwlen.

'What kept you?' said Ed.

'It was uphill all the way and it's a heavy ship to pedal, although it seems you've done okay without me.'

'We've experienced a little skirmish, yes.'

'Little skirmish? It looks to me like half the PCP

fleet is in ruins. You could've left a few more for me to commandeer.'

'Minor damage – quick cut and polish. They'll be as good as new.'

'There are still a few undamaged ships for me, though, I hope?'

'There are. Where's the rest of your fleet?'

'I left them in a system a few light years away. Seventy-two ships suddenly jumping unannounced into a war zone would not have ended well.'

'No, you're right there. Okay, if you approach this location with weapons deactivated and shields down, I'll personally introduce you to the GDA commander and organise an official recognition of the AOP and cessation of hostilities.'

'Couldn't have put it better myself. Make sure you've some of that beer waiting for me.'

Andy chuckled as Ed put his head in his hands with a pained expression.

FIVE HOURS LATER, the official declarations were signed and the GDA recognised the AOP as the ruling council of the region. Both organisations had agreed to having associate membership of the other and ambassadors would be exchanged in due course.

The surviving ships were handed over and the crews of the damaged ships rescued. All ex-PCP crews were given a choice of signing allegiance to the new administration and resuming their careers or spending a considerable length of time on a penal colony.

Unsurprisingly, the result was that over ninety-nine percent chose the first option.

Huwlen brought the rest of his fleet across and each ship was allocated a damaged vessel to tractor back to Locy'fer Station, which had now been renamed Senn Station. Apparently, if you tractored the damaged ship in close enough, you could incorporate them inside your fold envelope.

Commander Loftt organised a huge celebration banquet onboard his cruiser. All the senior officers from both organisations were invited, including of course the crew of the Gabriel.

Ed, Andy, Linda, Phil and Rayl were all awarded the Fellowship of the Ancients, a new award, commissioned by Huwlen Senn to recognise altruistic acts of extreme heroism, which were beneficial to the new order.

In return, Commander Loftt presented both Huwlen Senn and Cort Erebus with the Chrysos Aspida Politis (Gold Shield Citizen) or C.A.P, the highest award the GDA can bestow, acknowledging their bravery and leadership in overthrowing the inhumane, barbaric Mogul regime.

Further research undertaken in the secret history cache, deep underground on Arus'Gan, discovered that the Moguls had indeed massacred the old council of Ancients, gradually seeding the notion that they were descendants of the order. After more than ten millennia, the truth had been buried and no one had known any different.

Quite where the Moguls had originally come from was still something of an enigma. It could have been anywhere in the farthest regions of Andromeda or, indeed, from any of the five hundred plus galaxies programmed into the gateway.

The Sachem Mogul, Dakk Reeph, had been foolishly headstrong and rash. Instead of disappearing and seeking a new base of operations thousands of light years away, he went against all advice and turned his small protection fleet around to confront Huwlen Senn and the newly-formed AOP head on.

He was a lifelong bureaucrat, completely naive in battle tactics and had stupidly not been listening to Kky regarding Senn's fleet possibly obtaining cloaking technology.

The resulting confrontation had lasted less than seven minutes.

Reeph's small twelve-strong fleet had come under heavy fire from seventy-two warships, which had instantaneously appeared all around them.

In moments, his fleet had been adrift and defenceless. To his horror, the surviving crew members were being bombarded with evidence regarding the Mogul's true origins and he very quickly found himself, along with the surviving members of the council, being dragged towards the nearest airlocks.

The twenty-seven PCP attack ships that jumped away from Hunus were not pursued. They were designated militant renegades and, if found, to be aggressively engaged without warning.

Out of the six hundred and sixty-six Moguls, five hundred and seventy-nine were officially recorded as deceased, at least twenty-seven escaped on the attack ships and seven were found hiding on Arus'Gan, which left fifty-three unknowns. Huwlen organised an extremely generous bounty for the capture or death of the surviving Moguls, which instigated a plethora of bounty hunters disappearing off in all directions, some never to return.

The AOP council couldn't reach a majority decision over the Moguls' offspring. Killing several hundred boys and young men was deemed too barbaric, even if they were Moguls. So, for the time being, they were kept in a secure establishment at a secret, remote location until a definitive decision could be made.

Ed received a message from Breex on Hunus that the children were all safe and had not been outside during the bombardment. The colony had received only superficial damage to the very top level and the gate control room was completely intact. He thanked them again for the large consignment of supplies, even if some of the food items were a little peculiar.

The surviving crew of the Vrachos, who'd been marooned on the newly-named planet Pyli in Sector 497 had been picked up before Loftt had brought the Katadromiko fleet through the gateway and dispatched back home on a GDA fleet support vessel.

First Officer G'ann was severely reprimanded for his unwarranted treatment of the Gabriel's crew.

Rayl, much to everyone's relief, especially Andy's, had decided to stay on the Gabriel after Ed offered her a permanent crew position. As an only child, she had no close family to return to and going back to her home planet of Trigono III would have been too traumatic without either of her parents. Because of her age, Ed agreed to be her official guardian, although this would be a temporary arrangement as she would turn eighteen in three months.

Finally, after much deliberation, Huwlen decided to award Cort the prestigious position of the AOP's Ambassador to the GDA. Cort was thrilled and left his inherited business interests to be run by his late father's board of directors. He knew his age and lack of experience was against him, but the faith Huwlen had demonstrated humbled him and made him doubly determined to succeed.

He gave the crew of his newly-inherited super yacht the choice of coming with him to Daxxal or being assigned new positions within the Erebus Corporation.

They unanimously elected to remain. Partly because of the prestige of being the ambassador's crew and, moreover, the healthy pay rise offered with the elevated position.

It was around the middle of the following day that both the Gabriel and the Erebus V, along with an escort of four of the Katadromiko cruisers, set a course between the three moons above Hunus and left Andromeda to begin the week-long journey back to GDA space.

EPILOGUE

BUTTERMILK SKI AREA – ASPEN, COLORADO, EARTH

24TH FEBRUARY, 2051, 12:19PM

Ed stood, waiting at the bottom of the Sterner Catwalk beginners' run, adjacent to the newly updated Summit Super Express Gondola.

He'd just ripped down the Spruce Face black run and guessed he'd probably have at least a fifteen-minute wait for the other four who were traversing the junior run. With a last glance up the hill, he clipped out of his skis and clumped over to an outside bar servery, ordered a mulled wine and dropped into one of the deckchairs that overlooked the nursery slopes.

A few snowflakes fell lazily from snow clouds on the approach. He watched as one landed in his hot, spiced wine and instantly melted. The sun became slowly obscured by the leading cloud and the sudden temperature drop made him shiver. He quickly pulled on and zipped his ski jacket right up under his neck.

He sat there, thinking about what had happened over the last year and smiled. The discovery he'd made only fifteen months ago had completely changed not only his life, but the lives of every human being on the planet. Now, travelling to the stars really was a reality – even to another galaxy – thanks to the hospitality of Huwlen and the AOP.

The GDA scientists were already testing the other gateway destinations. The possibility of travelling to another five hundred plus galaxies was mind-blowing and, for obvious reasons, had to be checked out thoroughly, one at a time.

After Cort had been formally inducted as the Andromedan Ambassador for the GDA on Dasos, the council had gone into a scheduled recession and the Gabriel had travelled straight back to Earth.

The first meeting had been with Ed's old friend and the Gabriel Corporation's lawyer, Ian McMichael. He'd been busy while they were away, setting up and recruiting for the new company's various departments, which were to deal with the licensing of all the new Theo technology.

The accounting department was one of the biggest. It had to deal with the staggering sums of currency flooding in from almost every nation on Earth. Already, the company had liquid assets of over two trillion dollars and they'd seen on the news that the first customers had already taken possession of the first generation of Earth-designed jump ships.

James Dewey had been true to his word, regarding the promised use of his ski lodge. The following February, the crew of the Gabriel had gathered at the six-bedroomed chalet in Aspen, Colorado.

Cort had joined them too. He was fascinated with the concept of sliding down a mountain on planks and was an enthusiastic beginner. Rayl was also a first-timer and keen to learn, especially as Andy proved to be a surprisingly patient instructor.

Both learners had spent the last two weeks on the nursery slopes with Linda and Andy, gradually progressing from snowplough to paralleling. And today was the day Ed had promised to take them across to Aspen Mountain for some more serious slopes.

Ed watched the resort instructors leading their nervous, wobbly beginners left and right down the slight gradient. He remembered back to his first attempts, fifteen years ago in Whistler, and the euphoria he'd felt the first time he'd skied non-stop from the very top of Blackcomb Mountain, back down to the bars and restaurants surrounding the ski lifts at the base of the slopes.

They'd all recently discovered that skiing was good for their privacy, considering their new celebrity status. They could have a relatively hassle-free holiday hidden underneath all the ski wear. Everyone looked the same under hats and goggles.

A chef and housekeeper had been sourced to run the lodge for them after signing a non-disclosure agreement, which further helped to secure their anonymity.

Ed was suddenly knocked out of his daydream as a figure stopped in his peripheral vision and spoke.

'Good afternoon, Mr Virr.'

Shocked at being recognised underneath his fur hat and goggles, he turned slowly to find Jim Rucker grinning at him.

'Fucking hell, Jim. I nearly soiled my salopettes.'

'Want another one of those?' said Jim, gesturing to Ed's almost empty glass.

'Yes, but firstly, how did you find me?'

'You're the only one sitting all wrapped and goggled up. You stand out like a strawberry in a bowl of peas.'

'Shit, really?'

Ed looked around nervously. If the media discovered where they were, it would very quickly turn into a circus.

'Hey, Jim,' called Andy as he demonstrated the perfect parallel stop right beside the table and looked back up the hill. Ed and Jim followed his gaze to see Cort and Rayl, escorted by Linda, only fifty metres away and skiing quite confidently.

'Looks like the past couple of weeks have gone

well,' said Jim, watching the three sweep up to the table and make perfect stops. All except for Cort, that is, who, right at the last minute and much to everyone's amusement, caught an edge and face-planted right in front of the whole bar.

'I've been practising that manoeuvre,' he said, grinning from ear to ear and then blowing snow out of his nose.

'Olympic standard, by the look of it,' said Jim. 'But I shouldn't take the piss; I'm crap at anything requiring balance.'

'You can balance on a bar stool for hours,' said Andy, slapping him on the back. 'Even after twelve Stellas.'

'Well, apart from—' He stopped abruptly as a short, stocky man with a head-mounted camera pushed into the group.

'Mr Virr, d'you have any comment about Xavier Lake?'

There was a momentary pause as everyone just stared at the journalist.

'Ah, crap,' said Jim, grimacing.

'Xavier Lake?' said Ed. 'Why would I have any comment about him?'

'Haven't you heard?' said the journalist, looking around at everyone to ensure he had video of all their faces. 'He escaped in one of your ships this morning.'

'What?' said Ed, looking at Jim and raising his eyebrows.

Andy clipped out of his skis, grabbed the journalist by the shoulders, spun him round and pushed him away through the tables and chairs.

'Are you not going after him in your super ship?' he shouted over his shoulder as Andy manhandled him out of the bar area.

Everyone turned to look at Jim.

'That's why you're here, isn't it?' said Ed.

'Yeah,' he said dejectedly. 'The American government asked me to ask you—'

'If we'd like to find him for you?' interrupted Ed.

Jim nodded.

'Can't they ask the GDA to pick him up?' said Linda.

'They have bigger things to worry about than an escaped Earth prisoner.'

'Who's Xavier Lake?' asked Cort, glancing around the group.

'A royal pain in the arse,' said Andy as he returned to the group. 'Did he escape on his own?'

'No, his personal thug Floyd Herez and Columbian drug lord Nicolas Aranjuez disappeared with him too.'

'Oh, great. It gets better,' said Ed.

'They were supposed to be in maximum security,' said Linda.

'Coming to a cinema near you: *Arseholes, the Sequel*,' said Andy.

'And there's one other thing,' said Jim, looking apologetic. 'They're going to provide a professional investigator to work with you.'

'We don't need one,' said Ed.

'I'm told it's non-negotiable.'

'Who is he?' asked Linda, quickly, before Ed could object.

'A retired FBI investigator called Anthony Vaux.'

'You are bloody joking,' said Andy, sounding genuinely shocked.

They all turned to look at him.

'Why, have you heard of him?' asked Jim.

'Heard of him!' he raged, glaring. 'He's my fucking dad.'

THE END

FROM THE AUTHOR

Dear Reader,

First of all, I wanted to say a huge thank you for choosing to read *The Andromedan Fold*. I sincerely hope you enjoyed Ed and his crew's second adventure into space. The idea for these stories came to me a few years ago – it just took me a while to realise I should write them down.

If you did enjoy *The Andromedan Fold*, it'd be fantastic if you could write a review. It doesn't have to be long, just a few words, but it is the best way for me to help new readers discover my writing for the first time.

If you'd like to stay up to date with my new releases, as well as exclusive competitions and giveaways, you're welcome to join my Reader Group at my website, www.nickadamsbooks.com. I will never share your email address, and you can unsubscribe at any time.

You can also contact me via Facebook, Twitter, or by email. I love hearing from readers – I read every message and will try to personally reply to everyone.

Thanks again for your support.

Best wishes,
   Nick Adams

CPSIA information can be obtained
at www.ICGtesting.com
Printed in the USA
LVHW111307280221
680177LV00026B/217